The people of Hannik had had warning of her coming. As dusk fell, a flight of demonic harbingers had come winging from the south, and as they hovered over the town a huge, shapeless, membranous face had taken form in their midst and announced the imminent arrival of the Margravine of Mortal Dominions. Minutes later a horde of tiny elementals with shrill voices, needlelike claws and barbed tails that delivered an agonizing sting had swarmed in mass invasion through every building and driven the townsfolk out onto the streets to welcome Ygorla.

The Margrave of Han had been foolish enough to rally his militia into a show of resistance. His house had been the first to be set alight and now the huge blaze, fed by the shrieking fire elementals, hurled an unholy glow into the sky on the eastern edge of the town, like a gory artificial sunrise.

It had taken less than five minutes for Ygorla's host to shatter the militia's brief, brave but futile stand; now, black beasts with razor teeth slavered and snarled over the warriors' remains.

Ask your bookseller for the Bantam Spectra fantasy titles you may have missed:

BLACK TRILLIUM by Marion Zimmer Bradley, Julian May, and Andre Norton
CHRONICLES OF THE KING'S TRAMP, BOOK 1: WALKER OF WORLDS by Tom DeHaven
EIGHT SKILLED GENTLEMEN by Barry Hughart
CLOVEN HOOVES by Megan Lindholm
KING OF MORNING, QUEEN OF DAY by Ian McDonald
THE DAGGER AND THE CROSS by Judith Tarr
BRING ME THE HEAD OF PRINCE CHARMING by Roger Zelazny and Robert Sheckley

From Raymond Feist
MAGICIAN: APPRENTICE
MAGICIAN: MASTER
SILVERTHORN
DARKNESS AT SETHANON
PRINCE OF THE BLOOD
DAUGHTER OF THE EMPIRE (with Janny Wurts)
SERVANT OF THE EMPIRE (with Janny Wurts)

From Casey Flynn
THE GODS OF IRELAND, BOOK 1: MOST ANCIENT SONG
THE GODS OF IRELAND, BOOK 2: THE ENCHANTED ISLE

From Katharine Kerr
THE BRISTLING WOOD
THE DRAGON REVENANT

From Elizabeth Ann Scarborough
THE SONGKILLER SAGA, VOLUME #1: PHANTOM BANJO
THE SONGKILLER SAGA, VOLUME #2: PICKING THE BALLAD'S BONES

From Margaret Weis and Tracy Hickman
THE DARKSWORD TRILOGY: FORGING THE DARKSWORD
THE DARKSWORD TRILOGY: DOOM OF THE DARKSWORD
THE DARKSWORD TRILOGY: TRIUMPH OF THE DARKSWORD
DARKSWORD ADVENTURES
ROSE OF THE PROPHET: WILL OF THE WANDERER
ROSE OF THE PROPHET: PALADIN OF NIGHT
ROSE OF THE PROPHET: THE PROPHET OF AHKRAN
THE DEATH GATE CYCLE, VOLUME 1: DRAGON WING
THE DEATH GATE CYCLE, VOLUME 2: ELVEN STAR
THE DEATH GATE CYCLE, VOLUME 3: FIRE SEA

The Chaos Gate Trilogy
Book III

THE AVENGER

Louise Cooper

SPECTRA ™

BANTAM BOOKS

NEW YORK · TORONTO · LONDON · SYDNEY · AUCKLAND

THE AVENGER

A Bantam Spectra Book / February 1992

ISBN 0-553-29111-4

Bantam Books are published by Bantam Books, a division of Bantam
Doubleday Dell Publishing Group, Inc. Its trademark, consisting of the
words "Bantam Books" and the portrayal of a rooster, is Registered in
U.S. Patent and Trademark Office and in other countries. Marca
Registrada. Bantam Books, 666 Fifth Avenue, New York, New York
10103.

PRINTED IN THE UNITED STATES OF AMERICA

OPM   0 9 8 7 6 5 4 3 2 1

THE AVENGER

1

The hour was late, but the twenty or so people still in the dining hall weren't overly anxious to leave. The fire blazing in the vast grate had been replenished yet again, the curtains were closed against the bitter winter weather, and it was more pleasant simply to sit passing the time in good company and with a few flagons of wine than to brave the castle's chilly and dimly lit corridors to retire to bed.

Most of those present were senior Circle adepts, among them the High Initiate Tirand Lin, but two noninitiates had joined the group as they gravitated to a wide semicircle of chairs around the hearth at a respectful distance from the fire's enormous heat. Shaill Falada, Matriarch of the Sisterhood, had lapsed into a comfortable semidoze. The fire's light softened the worry lines in her face, and her skin, its southern tan in sharp contrast to the paler complexions of the castle dwellers, had taken on a warm, ruddy glow. Opposite the Matriarch, at the High Initiate's side, sat a tall man with a stern, serious face, considerably younger than his long white hair might imply at first glance. To all intents and purposes he was nothing more than a sailor shipwrecked on the Star Peninsula during a gale and now recuperating at the castle; only three among this company knew his true identity, and they had vowed to obey his command not to reveal the truth to their colleagues. Ailind, lord of Order and brother to Aeoris, had his own reasons for wishing to keep his presence in the mortal world a secret, and although he had cultivated the adepts' friendship, he had

1

also taken care not to exert his influence—at least not publicly.

Servants had cleared away the remains of the evening meal, and the company's conversation had been drifting between a number of idle topics. In recent days there had been little time and less inclination for leisure, and these evening gatherings had become a small and precious oasis of relative peace. It wasn't that the crisis that hung over the world could be forgotten or ignored even for this short period; far from it, for there was little doubt now that Ygorla, the usurper and self-styled empress, had a hold on the land that no mortal power could break. But the castle of the Star Peninsula was the one bastion that Ygorla and her demon father couldn't breach at will. Here the Circle and those who had taken refuge with them were secure, and until now their task had been to maintain that security and keep the key players in the fight against Ygorla safe from her depradations. The enforced inactivity didn't sit well on most of the adepts' shoulders; the more hotheaded would have preferred to join battle, physical or occult, with the sorceress, while even the most prudent fretted at the fact that thus far their strategy seemed to consist of little more than an exchange of carefully worded letters between the Circle and the usurper. Only during these brief interludes, like the calm eye at the heart of a storm, did they make an effort to shake off their frustrations and their doubts and pretend for a while that life had returned to normal.

However, the hiatus couldn't last. Even at these gatherings there was always someone who, deliberately or not, introduced the sour note, the sudden reminder that cold reality was only a chance word away. This time the culprit was Sen Briaray Olvit, a senior adept with a reputation for speaking first and thinking later and one of the only three present who was party to Ailind's secret. They'd been discussing wine, debating the relative merits of the Han and Prospect vineyards, when, with a grimace, Sen said, "We're assuming, of course, that the question of our preferences isn't going to become purely academic before the next harvest. By the time this business is over, neither Han nor Prospect nor anywhere else may have a vineyard left, for all we know."

Tirand eyed Sen sourly. He'd known that the reminder of their predicament must come but had hoped that, for tonight at least, they might have had a longer respite. He thought of trying to steer the conversation back onto a happier subject, but before he could speak, someone else picked up Sen's thread.

"You've a point there, Sen, and it has far greater ramifications. Wine's a luxury that we could easily survive without; but what about our more fundamental needs—the basic foodstuffs? Has anyone yet calculated how long we can continue without fresh supplies?"

Everyone looked at Tirand. The High Initiate sighed inwardly. He didn't want to turn his mind back to such unhappy matters, but duty must come first. And the question was a valid one that should have been tackled before now.

"So much depends on how long this crisis is to continue," he said. "Thankfully, all the tithe caravans from the provinces arrived before we were effectively besieged here, so our winter stores are up to their usual level. Now, normally of course we receive fresh tithes in the spring, as soon as the weather improves enough for the mountain passes to be negotiable again. But this year . . . as you say, we can't be sure of anything. There may be no caravans; there may be no provisions for the provinces, let alone for us. You're right; it's something that we haven't previously taken into account, and it's a serious oversight."

An elderly woman spoke up. "Do you think we should ration, Tirand?"

"Until we know precisely the state of our stores, I can't say for certain. But I think we'd be well advised to at least consider the possibility."

On the far side of the hearth the Matriarch set down her wine cup. "My women and I can help you there, Tirand," she said. "When I was in Wishet, years ago, we had a season of disastrous floods—you'll be too young to remember that—and there was rationing in the province for nearly half a year afterward. What I learned then may be useful now, and it'll be some small recompense for having encumbered you with extra mouths to feed."

Tirand smiled at her. "You haven't encumbered us, Shaill, and I trust you know that as well as I do!"

"You're very chivalrous, my dear, but you won't silence my conscience, nor the nightmares I suffer about having fled here to sanctuary while Sister Fiora and the other Seniors stayed in Southern Chaun. If you'll entrust me with cataloguing the castle's supplies and drawing up a contingency, I'll feel that I'm at least contributing something practical and useful." She paused a moment, considering, then added, "I might enlist Calvi's help. It would benefit him, I think, if he had something positive to do, however mundane the task might be."

"That reminds me," Sen said, "Where is our young High Margrave tonight? I didn't see him at dinner, and it's not like him to miss a meal."

Tirand glanced around the hall. Sen was right: Calvi Alacar, brother and reluctant successor to the murdered Blis, wasn't among the gathering; in fact Tirand couldn't remember having seen him since earlier this afternoon.

"I hope he hasn't gone down with this winter rheum that's scourging the castle," the Matriarch said. "I thought he looked a little sickly this morning. I meant to mention it to Sanquar, but it—"

She stopped in midsentence as, so suddenly that they all started, the doors at the far end of the hall crashed open. Tirand turned in his chair, his eyes shocked and angry. "What in the name of—"

He, too, got no farther as he saw the two figures who had entered the hall. One he knew all too well; his own sister, Karuth Piadar, with whom at present he was barely on speaking terms. The other . . . the High Initiate's eyes focused on the tall, black-haired man at Karuth's side, and an ice-cold shock went through him. He couldn't explain it—the man was a total stranger; he had no reason for alarm—but there was something about him, something in that cool, aquiline face, something in

4

the intensity of the feline green eyes, that struck fear into Tirand's heart. And Karuth: There was high color in her normally pallid cheeks; she looked defiant, almost *triumphant. . . .*

Then, from behind him, Ailind of Order uttered a sharp and swiftly suppressed oath.

The black-haired man smiled. "Ah. So you recognize me, old friend, even after all these years?" He spoke quietly, but his voice carried across the hall. Then, moving with the grace of a cat, he walked toward them. Tirand saw Ailind's face flush with fury. Bewildered, he looked to the lord of Order in mute appeal, but Ailind ignored him, his gaze fixed on the approaching figure. Confused and suddenly unsure of himself, Tirand rose slowly to his feet. The stranger stopped three paces from him, inclined his head, and said, "Good evening, High Initiate. My compliments to you and to the Circle." The quick green eyes focused on the Matriarch, and he made a more courteous bow. "Madam."

"Sir . . ." The Matriarch's own eyes were alight with curiosity. "I'm afraid you have the advantage of me. Do I know you?"

He smiled thinly. "I believe you know *of* me, lady, though we've not met before."

If Tirand had been watching Ailind, he would have seen that the god was motionless, rigid, his expression twisted and ugly. But Tirand was too caught up by the twin reactions that were rising in his own mind. He felt afraid of this stranger—and at the same time he felt that in some subtle way the man was mocking him.

His voice rang sharply out before Shaill could speak again. "Who are you?" His tone was aggressive. "What is your business here?"

Again that chilly smile—a smile, Tirand saw, of utter confidence. The black-haired man made a careless gesture toward Ailind.

"Ask your friend and mentor who hides behind you like a serpent behind a bush," he replied crisply. "He knows me very well."

Tirand's face purpled. *"Do you know who—"* Then,

5

suddenly realizing what he had been about to say, he bit the furious words back. But the stranger finished the sentence for him.

"Do I know who this creature is? Yes, High Initiate, I do. Which is more than can be said for the great majority of your companions, isn't it?"

Tirand's hectic color deepened. "Damn your insolence! Who are you to enter this hall uninvited, to—"

The stranger's eyes changed. Only Tirand saw the full impact of the change, for the green gaze was locked on his own, and it silenced him as he realized that, whatever this being might be, he was not human.

"I am Tarod," the black-haired one said softly. "Brother to Yandros of Chaos. And I do not require the invitation of one of Order's puppets to enter the hall that our own servants built an aeon ago."

There was a flurry of sound from the company; shocked exclamations, gasps, hissing intakes of breath. Sen and two others were on their feet; the Matriarch gripped the arms of her chair until her knuckles turned white. Tirand began to tremble.

"That . . . ." he said in a strained voice, "is impossible. . . ."

Tarod's look grew malevolent. "Impossible, High Initiate?"

"You are . . . you're a fraud, a trickster!"

Tarod sighed. "As you wish." He snapped his fingers toward the far end of the hall, and all down its length, one by one, the torches in their wall brackets dimmed and went out. Only the firelight remained, and by its red glow Tarod scanned the half-circle of stunned faces around him.

"Just a trickster's small magic, High Initiate," he said sardonically. "I assume it's nothing that a first-rank novice couldn't achieve at the blink of an eye?" Tirand didn't reply, and Tarod snapped his fingers again, this time toward the hearth. The fire went out, plunging the hall into darkness save for a thin bar of illumination shining under the doors from the passage beyond. Someone stifled a scream, and there was a clatter as a chair was knocked over. Then Tarod looked up at the shadowed rafters of the great hall, and as he did so, the roof seemed to melt away and the hall was open to the sky.

This time the scream was in earnest, and another voice shrieked out in terror. "Gods, no, *NO!*" The Warp, which Tarod had summoned and brought sweeping down out of the north, was howling directly overhead. Shielded by the warm, bright security of the hall, by its thick walls and closed curtains, the adepts had been utterly unaware of the storm's approach, and as the sight and sound of it smashed down on them, they were thrown into panic. The Warp's awesome voice, like the crying of a thousand tortured souls, beat against their senses; the high, thin hurricane-shriek that rode with and above the storm set the castle's foundations quaking in response. Crimson and emerald and silver lightning shattered across the sky, its brilliance hurling the hall and its scrambling, cowering occupants into a mayhem of savage tableaux. And over it all, far up in the tormented heavens, the great, dim bands of dark color wheeled slowly, inexorably across the world.

Suddenly from somewhere near the empty fireplace a voice roared, *"Stop this!"*

Ailind was on his feet, his eyes burning gold and fired with loathing. Tarod looked back at him across a dozen huddled forms, and his own eyes narrowed. Then he glanced up—and the Warp flicked out of existence. The lightning and the dim wheel of color vanished; the howling voices shattered into nothing. Stars glared coldly down from a clear sky, and at the eastern end of the hall the faint glow of the rising first moon stained the top of the roofless wall.

Slowly the prayers and the moaning died away as one by one the company realized that the supernatural storm had gone. The fire flared into life once more, and then the torches—and when Tirand and a few others dared to raise their heads, they saw that the hall roof was whole once more and the scene had returned to normal.

Very slowly Tirand got to his feet. He looked once at Tarod, a look of shock and fear and hatred, then turned to assist the Matriarch, whose voluminous robe was hampering her efforts to rise. The rest, too, were recovering their composure; Sen and two helpers were restoring the tipped and scattered chairs, while others, finding that their legs were unwilling as yet to support them, sat shakily and mutely and tried to regain some semblance of dignity.

Behind Tarod another figure moved, and Karuth rose from where she'd been crouching, face hidden in her hands, by one of the long tables. She'd anticipated something like this, though the suddenness and violence of the Chaos lord's show of power had taken her unawares. Tarod glanced at her and smiled. She hesitated a bare moment, then returned the smile, shaking her long, dark hair back from her eyes and blinking rapidly in the renewed light. Tirand was too preoccupied to notice the look that passed between her and Tarod—but Ailind was not. Understanding dawned on the lord of Order's face and, pushing aside an adept who had inadvertently blocked his way, he took a step toward her. *"You—"* he began. Tirand, hearing him, turned sharply; but before Ailind could say any more, Tarod stepped into his path.

"High Initiate." His eyes were as cold as the sea's depths as he turned his back on Ailind, effectively shifting the focus of attention from him to Tirand. "I trust I have proved myself to your satisfaction?"

The Matriarch, who was now reseated, made a strangled sound that might have been a sob or a near-hysterical snort of laughter. *"Proved . . ."* she said. "Gods, I—*gods!*"

Tarod looked past Tirand to where she sat, and his manner changed. "Madam," he said, "I must ask your pardon for making my point so emphatically. I have no ill-will toward any mortal here"—he put the faintest of emphases on the word *mortal*—"but it is essential that none of you should be in any doubt as to my true nature. I'm only sorry that I distressed you."

Shaill swallowed. "I—accept your apology, my lord," she replied with careful but unsteady formality. "And I trust that in return you will . . . understand why at this moment I do not rise and bow to you as protocol might otherwise dictate."

Tarod smiled. He had already taken a liking to Shaill, and admired her refusal to be intimidated. "I need no show of respect, lady. Courtesy and honesty"—he flicked a pointed glance in Tirand's direction—"are quite enough." He raised his head, surveying them all. "Now that your doubts about me have been assuaged, perhaps we might turn to the matter of someone else's honesty— or lack of it." Abruptly he swung around, and as his green gaze clashed with Ailind's, his voice grew venomously challenging. "It's time for your charade to stop. Either you tell our mortal friends the truth about yourself and your purpose here, or I will. The choice is entirely yours."

Ailind stared back at him. Tirand, watching them both, opened his mouth to speak, then thought better of it. His face was white. Quietly Sen Briaray Olvit moved to stand beside him and laid a hand on his shoulder, but he, too, said nothing.

"Well?" Tarod prompted acidly. "We are all waiting."

A shudder ran through Ailind, and those who were closest to him felt the psychic shock wave of his fury. Though they were nonplussed by the Chaos lord's sudden and seemingly groundless challenge to the white-haired mariner, the sudden change was a warning, a first hint that Ailind might not be all he seemed, and one adept, groping at something akin to the truth, gasped, choked the sound back, and gripped the arm of his nearest neighbor. Tarod and Ailind continued to face each other, and there was a sudden move backward among the company as everyone felt the charge of raw power that was building between the two motionless figures. Suffocating, savage, lethal, that power was so alien, so unhuman, that it didn't so much as acknowledge their existence. The minds of the two adversaries had shifted out of the mortal world into another, unimaginable dimension, and any mortal fool enough to get in the way would be swept aside and trampled to dust.

How long the silent challenge continued no one could later begin to calculate. To some it seemed only a matter of moments; to others it was as if a mortal lifetime had crawled by while the two adversaries stood face-to-face in wordless, moveless, yet appalling conflict. Though the fire and the torches were undimmed, their light seemed to have no strength; vast shadows loomed through the hall, taking on shapes redolent of the most abysmal nightmares, and fevered imaginations caught the grisly echoes of unhuman laughter and monstrous whisperings. Once a vicious wind soughed through the hall, stirring the tangle of Tarod's black hair and the smooth shimmer of Ailind's white, chilling human flesh to the marrow before it faded into nothing. Silence gripped the hall like a steel hand. Then, so gradually that at first it seemed to the human watchers like a dream, a light began to flare into life above Tarod's heart. Cold, white, dazzling, it grew to a glare and coalesced into seven rays of blinding brilliance that began to pulse with a slow but perfect rhythm. Ailind smiled. It was the first change of expression to show on his face, and it seemed to be composed of contempt and pride and resignation all at once. Then a second light began to glow above his heart. Steady and utterly symmetrical, it shone like the unbearable gold of an alien sun and formed the outline of a lightning flash, frozen and still and eternal—the age-old symbol of Order incarnate. Without knowing that he did it, without even knowing that his hand had moved, Tirand touched the badge at his shoulder, the ancient badge once worn by his long-dead predecessor, Keridil Toln, in the days when Order had ruled the mortal world without opposition, and his throat contracted until he could barely breathe.

Then suddenly it was over. The borderline of the moment was blurred, but in the space of three human heartbeats the psychic battle had ended and the return to normality was complete. A log shifted in the fire, crackling loudly and sending up a shimmer of bright sparks; it broke the hiatus, and the watchers shook their heads like people emerging from a drugged sleep. The torches blazed along the hall's length, their brilliance restored; no monstrous shadows crawled across the walls now. And Tarod and Ailind looked for all the world like nothing more than two mortal men facing each other with the firelight dancing on their rigid figures.

Tarod was the first to breach the silence. He bowed curtly to Ailind and said, in a careless tone that didn't quite mask the underlying anger, "I salute you, cousin. It seems we are evenly matched."

Naked dislike glinted in Ailind's golden-brown eyes. "As you say, Chaos. Perhaps it's no more than either of us should have expected."

No one else dared utter a word. Tirand was breathing hard; Sen, still at his side, was whey-faced. The Matriarch's head was bowed seemingly in prayer, and, alone and away from the gathering by the fire, Karuth could only stare mutely at the scene, her face expressionless.

"So," Tarod said, "If they haven't already worked it out for themselves, as seems likely, I think it's time for one of us to tell our mortal friends a few cold facts. Will they come from your lips or from mine?"

Ailind shrugged, affecting disinterest, and the Chaos lord looked at the strained faces of the castle dwellers. His gaze lit lastly on Tirand and held there.

"Or maybe the High Initiate would prefer to tell the tale in his own words?" he said softly. "You understand my meaning, don't you, Tirand? You and two others present in this hall know what manner of being you harbor within your walls. Not some poor shipwrecked mariner rescued from a winter storm, but a lord of Order, a brother to Aeoris, who swore you to secrecy on pain of his displeasure and seduced you with his promises of a return to the old ways for which your heart privately yearns. Isn't that so?"

Tirand colored hotly. "You twist the truth—"

"No; I *tell* the truth. It's an unpleasant habit, but one which we of Chaos often choose to indulge against all mortal expectations. That's our nature, High Initiate, as you would know if you'd learned your catechisms a little less one-sidedly. Now, I ask you again, as I also ask the

11

lady Matriarch and the adept who stands at your side and lends you his moral support: Do you acknowledge that I'm right in what I say?"

The eyes of the entire company were on Tirand, and he felt suddenly like a young student brought before his teaching master to answer for some shameful deed. Then, hard on the heels of that feeling, came anger—righteous anger, not only on his own behalf but on that of the whole Circle. He was the High Initiate! He had renounced any loyalty he might once have professed to Chaos, and in that renunciation he had been supported by the Council of Adepts and by the other two members of the ruling triumvirate. Now a lord of Chaos stood before him and accused him of deceiving his fellow adepts—but by what right? He'd done his duty to the Circle and to his own conscience. His fealty was to Ailind and the lords of Order. *They* were his gods, his only gods.

Ailind spoke, quietly but with emphasis. "You've nothing to fear from Chaos, Tirand. Whatever Tarod might wish you to believe, he has no power over you. You are under *my* protection." He gestured carelessly, almost contemptuously toward the watching adepts. "Answer his question. It's of no moment to me."

The lord of Order was smiling, and Tirand met Tarod's chilly gaze with a sudden surge of confidence that wasn't entirely of his own creation.

"Yes," he said clearly. "It's the truth. And it changes nothing."

There was a harsh susurration as his listeners heard him. Then the elderly woman adept rose abruptly from her chair. Her face was ashen.

"Tirand—are you telling us that . . . that all this time, a lord of Order has been in our midst, and yet you kept his presence a *secret*?"

Tarod glanced at her. "That is precisely what the High Initiate is telling you, madam. On the order of this being in whom the Circle has been foolish enough to put its trust, he—and a few others—have deceived you."

A heavyset, dark-haired man spoke up. He looked from the High Initiate to Tarod and finally to Ailind and, with an effort, addressed the lord of Order directly. "Is it true, sir? Are you . . ." He swallowed. "Are you one of our seven gods?"

Ailind's expression was unreadable as he inclined his head. "I am."

"Gods!" Then, realizing what he'd said, the adept's face colored. "Forgive me, I meant no disrespect, I didn't—"

Tarod interrupted his flustering with a wry smile. "Save your embarrassment, adept. Your oath is a compliment."

The man collected himself and nodded. Then, his composure still uncertain, he turned back to the High Initiate. "Why did you keep this a secret, Tirand? Why didn't you tell us? All this time, unknowing—"

From a short way off a new voice said, "He had no choice. None of us did."

They'd forgotten Karuth. She came forward into the firelight, and Tirand's posture abruptly stiffened as he saw the steely glint in her eyes. Karuth ignored him and looked directly at the disconcerted adept. "I can't deny my own involvement," she said. "I, too, kept the secret." She flicked a glance in Ailind's direction, which might have contained a measure of contempt, though the unsteady light made it impossible to be certain. "My brother is no more to blame than any of us. As I said, we had no choice in the matter."

The elderly woman spoke again. "How many others were there, Karuth? Who else knows?"

Karuth hesitated, and Tarod spoke for her. "There are four others, madam. The Matriarch, though I regret to say it. Your High Margrave. This good adept here," he indicated Sen, who couldn't meet his gaze, "and one other senior member of your council who isn't present at this gathering. For reasons best known to himself your god chose to withhold the knowledge of his presence here from the rest of his worshippers." His feline eyes narrowed abruptly. "You must thank physician-adept Karuth Piadar for the fact that he has been unmasked. She alone had the courage to defy the strictures that were laid upon you all, and call on Chaos to . . . shall we say, redress the balance."

Tirand's jaw clenched, and he stared at Tarod. For a moment his eyes were blank, as though with shock. Then, as though neither the Chaos lord nor Ailind nor any of the watching adepts existed, he turned slowly to face his sister. His voice shook with fury and he said, "From this moment you are no longer an adept! I pronounce anathema on you. I cast you from the Circle— and I only wish that present circumstances didn't prevent me from banishing you from this castle to rot in obscurity!"

Karuth's cheeks flamed as Tirand's words brought all the grudges, the resentments, and the bitterness of the old quarrel between them flaring back to the surface. She couldn't control her tongue and she didn't even try, but retaliated with a venom that matched his. "You may be Ailind's puppet, but Ailind no longer has a free hand here!" she retorted savagely. "And I'd remind you that the Circle doesn't consist only of its High Initiate. Your word is not immutable law, brother, and your anathema doesn't impress me!"

"Don't *dare* to call me brother!" Tirand exploded. "I have no sister! Do you understand me? The lying whore who stands before me now is no kin of mine!"

There was a momentary, ugly silence. Like two warring cats, Tirand and Karuth faced each other, oblivious of their shocked audience. No one else spoke, no one made the smallest attempt to intervene. This had suddenly focused into a vicious personal quarrel, and though the entire Circle might be well aware of the rift between the High Initiate and his sister, to see it flaunted before them in such an embarrassing public display was quite another matter. Then with a violent gesture Karuth put one hand to her own shoulder. There was the sound of fabric ripping as she tore the gold adept's badge from her dress. She clenched it in one fist, and her voice cut through the tense atmosphere like vitriol.

"We understand each other, Tirand Lin. I spit on the

Circle—and I spit on the fawning coward who calls himself its leader!"

She hurled the badge at Tirand. It struck him above the right eye; Tirand clapped a hand to his face with a shout of outrage, and at the same moment Tarod and Ailind both started forward—

"Karuth! Tirand!" The Matriarch's chair scraped back, and Shaill was on her feet. She strode forward, ignoring the two lords, and interposed herself between brother and sister.

"This is *disgraceful*!" Shaill so rarely showed real anger that her fury now was all the more startling, and it stopped them all in their tracks. The Matriarch treated Karuth and Tirand to a searing look. "I'd expect more civilized behavior from two mewling infants! It's not to be tolerated!"

There was a long pause. At last Tirand looked away and muttered something that might have been an apology. Karuth tried to hold Shaill's gaze but failed, and stared down at her own feet. Shaill continued to watch them intently until she was satisfied that neither was about to launch into a fresh assault, then she allowed her rigid posture to relax a fraction.

"I think we have all had quite enough to contend with for one night." Her voice wasn't entirely steady, but her stare was still sharp as she scanned the gathering, challenging her colleagues to disagree. No one did. "I *strongly* suggest, with respect to you both, my lords," she bowed stiffly first to Ailind, then to Tarod, "that our most prudent course would be to withdraw, with what little grace is still left to us, before matters become completely out of hand." She sucked in breath between clenched teeth. "We will say nothing more about this unfortunate display but will excuse both physician-adept Karuth and the High Initiate and trust that a sound night's sleep will give them both cause to feel rightly ashamed." Another pause, then: "Indeed, we would *all* benefit from a sound night's sleep. Very grave matters have come to light this evening. We will be better equipped to face them, as regrettably it seems we must, with clear and cool heads."

She gave them all one last look, only flinching a little as she met the gazes of Tarod and Ailind, then turned and, with great dignity, began to walk toward the doors. Halfway she stopped and looked back.

"If in the midst of this deadly crisis we can do no more than sink to the level of squabblings and tantrums," she said, "then whatever our loyalties, I fear there's little hope for any of us."

2

Any adept with psychic sensitivity would have backed hastily out of Tirand's path as though fleeing a Warp as the High Initiate strode toward his bedchamber on the castle's upper floor. Outwardly his face was stonily immobile, but his emotions blazed in his eyes and raged in his vitals to the point where he felt that his only hope of relief would be to physically explode.

He didn't want relief, though. He wanted revenge. Revenge on Karuth for her blatant defiance of himself and Ailind; revenge for goading him into losing his temper and forcing him to suffer the subsequent humiliation of Shaill's tongue-lashing. And above all, revenge on Chaos, the architects of this whole miserable mess. A few minutes ago, as the gathering broke up and, in an atmosphere of extreme tension, everyone went their separate ways, he had tried to speak to Ailind. The god, however, was unwilling to listen; he had been watching the creature from Chaos like a cat watching a snake and had dismissed Tirand with only a curt "In the morning, High Initiate," before stalking away. Tirand had never been easily moved to hatred, but at this moment he hated Chaos with every grain of feeling his soul could dredge up from its depths. And his own sister, his faithless, treacherous, underhanded, lying *bitch* of a sister, consorting with them, plotting with them, setting out to wreck *everything*—

The part of him that still clung to a thread of rationality knew that he was overreacting, but Tirand didn't care. In all his life he had never been so angry that he had

17

felt an urge to kill, but at this moment he believed he could have slain Karuth without a qualm.

His bedchamber lay along the next corridor. He was approaching the turning, careless of whether the noise of his footsteps disturbed anyone, when a door leading off the passage behind him opened with a squeak of hinges. Tirand would have ignored it—in his present mood he didn't trust himself to speak civilly to anyone—but a voice, urgent and not entirely steady, called his name.

"Tirand!" It was Calvi Alacar, the High Margrave. Tirand halted, fought down a black urge to snap out an angry response, and turned.

Calvi stood in the doorway of his room. He was fully dressed still, but had taken a blanket from his bed and wrapped it about himself. His youthful face was an unhealthy color, his fair hair damp with sweat, and he seemed to be shivering.

"Tirand . . ." Calvi glanced swiftly along the corridor to reassure himself that there was no one else about, then hastened toward the High Initiate, almost tripping over the blanket's trailing edge. "Tirand, I've got to talk to you! It's about Karuth—she—oh, gods, I don't know where to begin. I was so *frightened,* I didn't dare come down; I've been in my room trying to think, trying to—"

Tirand's voice cut him sharply off in midflow. "Karuth? What about her?"

"She . . . it was in the Marble Hall, I know I shouldn't have gone in there, but I just *knew* something was amiss, and so . . ." Then the words trailed off as he saw the High Initiate's expression.

Tirand said harshly, "You *know* what she's done?"

Calvi's face turned paler still. "Then the emissary from Chaos—"

"Is in the castle now and has made himself known to me, yes." He frowned. "How did you find out about it?"

The young man shut his eyes momentarily, as though trying to blot out an unpleasant memory. "I was there. I tried to stop her but she wouldn't heed me. I saw her perform the ritual; I saw him appear. . . ." He put a clenched fist up to his mouth. "Gods, Tirand, I've never been so frightened in my life!"

Tirand's well of reason had almost run dry, but enough rationality remained and struggled to the surface to stem his impulse to curse Calvi for a fool and a weakling. He couldn't have stopped Karuth from carrying out her intentions. Knowing his sister, Tirand doubted if anyone could have stopped her, short of resorting to brute force, and Calvi had neither the temperament nor the physical stature for that. He could imagine what Calvi's approach must have been: an appeal to sweet reason. And he could imagine Karuth's response to it.

Calvi said quaveringly, "What are we going to do?"

"Do?" Tirand's curt, humorless laugh made a nearby wall torch flicker briefly. "It appears there's nothing we *can* do. Neither the High Initiate nor the High Margrave nor the Matriarch nor the combined might of the Circle can influence the situation one whit."

"Surely lord Ailind—"

"Even lord Ailind has no control over Chaos in this world. Yandros's brother is here, and no one can send him back where he came from. He *claims,*" Tirand's mouth twisted savagely, "that Karuth had as much right to call on him as I and the Council of Adepts had to call on the lords of Order."

"I don't believe that!" Calvi said fiercely.

"Of course not; it's a blatant breach of all Circle law. But as Karuth Piadar apparently now considers herself exempt from her oath of obedience, she has disregarded that law, and Chaos is of course only too happy to abet her." He shivered. "I dread to think what havoc their emissary means to wreak. There's no doubt that he'll be set on sabotaging lord Ailind's plans to combat the usurper and instigating some evil scheme of Chaos's own devising. And we haven't the power to prevent him from doing anything he pleases."

Calvi shook his head. "I can hardly credit that Karuth could commit such an act of betrayal! To disobey the Circle is one matter, but to dare to defy lord Ailind—"

"I don't pretend to comprehend her motives," Tirand interrupted grimly, "and they're no longer of any interest to me. As far as I'm concerned, Karuth is no longer a Circle adept and no longer my sister."

Calvi's eyes widened in shock. "You've expelled her?" he asked, appalled.

Tirand didn't want to discuss that; his feelings about their public quarrel were too ruffled still and too ambiguous to be comfortable. "Her future here is a matter for the Council of Adepts," he said stiffly, evading the need for a direct answer.

Calvi studied his face for a moment, then thought better of what he had been about to say. He dropped his gaze. "Gods," he said unhappily, "what an abysmal mess."

Tirand eyed him sourly. "I doubt if you've ever spoken a truer word, my friend. But like it or not, the deed's done and we must live with it as best we can." He paused, then: "I intend to call a full meeting of the council tomorrow morning. Whatever else happens, it's vital now that we present a united front in loyalty to lord Ailind and against Chaos's machinations, and I'll need the support of the triumvirate. Can I count on you, Calvi?"

The young man flushed. "Of course!"

"Even if Karuth and I are opposed in every respect? I mean no offense, but I know that you've always admired her and I don't want you to find yourself in an invidious position."

"No." Calvi's flush deepened and spread to his neck. "No, Tirand, there's no question of any ambiguity." He met the High Initiate's gaze again, though with some effort. "I can't stop myself from liking Karuth; affection can't simply be extinguished like blowing out a candle. But admiration and respect . . . well, that's a different matter, isn't it? You'll have my support." He grimaced. "For what little it might be worth."

"It's worth a great deal," Tirand told him.

"As to that . . ." Calvi tried to force a laugh, but the attempt wasn't a success. "Well, we'll see, won't we?"

He hunched his shoulders under the blanket. "I'd best let you get some sleep."

Tirand nodded. "I'll see you at breakfast." He wouldn't want breakfast, he knew, but appearances must be maintained.

"I . . . ah . . . I think perhaps I may not . . ." Calvi tried to express what he meant with a gesture, then looked at Tirand with a mixture of guilt and shame. "I think I'd prefer to stay in my room until it's time for the meeting."

Grimly Tirand wondered what Calvi had been subjected to in the Marble Hall to have sapped his courage to this extent. But he made no comment, only said, "As you please. I'll say good night, then."

"Yes. Or if it's not a good night, I pray that at least it'll be a quiet one."

It occurred to Tirand, as he walked away along the corridor, to wonder at the flush that had come to Calvi's face when the question of his loyalties had been raised. Calvi and Karuth? No, impossible. He'd have known if there was anything between them; there'd have been some rumor, however slight. Besides, Calvi was more than ten years Karuth's junior and surely she, even *she,* wouldn't be such a fool as to get involved.

Calvi, though . . . the High Initiate frowned. The dividing line between admiration and infatuation could be precariously thin, and Calvi had always been impressionable. If he harbored hopes, unfulfilled wishes, it could add an extra complication to the picture, and that was something Tirand could well do without.

He stopped and looked back along the corridor. Calvi had disappeared, and his door was closed. Suddenly Tirand's anger, which had abated a little while they talked, came surging back. This time, though, he had enough self-possession to force it down to a manageable level and to dismiss the idea of going back to Calvi's room and tackling him. He had more than enough to contend with already. More than enough.

The slamming of a door a minute later was the only

outward clue to the High Initiate's feelings as he gained the sanctuary of his bedchamber.

With only the dull glow of the fire to illuminate it the dining hall felt vast and hollow and faintly hostile. The temperature was dropping rapidly as the fire sank, and Karuth shivered, pulling her shawl more closely about her shoulders as she waited respectfully for Tarod to precede her out into the corridor.

The Chaos lord seemed in no hurry to leave. He stood near the hearth, looking about him at the tall windows, the paneling, the long lines of tables and benches, the curtained gallery above the hearth. She couldn't see his expression, but he had the air of one who, returning home after a long absence, was taking time to absorb and enjoy familiar surroundings again. Karuth knew that, a hundred years ago, Tarod had taken human incarnation and had grown up in the castle as a Circle initiate. The story was enshrined in history now of how the young adept had finally revealed his true nature and had used his awesome powers to bring Chaos back from exile and establish the new age of Equilibrium, and it gave Karuth a strange frisson to think that that figure from the distant past and the god whom she had called upon tonight were one and the same. She tried to imagine Tarod in those far-off days, as a child, as an adolescent, as a young man, forming friendships and rivalries, excelling at some subjects yet poor at others; living, in fact, a life that had close parallels with her own youthful experience. But imagination failed her, and she thrust the thoughts aside with an inward shiver.

He still seemed to be lost in his reverie, unaware of her. She wondered if she was intruding, but though prudence counseled that she should leave, another and stronger urge made her stay. Paradoxically she felt more secure in his presence than she would have done alone, despite all that had happened. Or perhaps, she thought, being honest with herself, *because* of all that had happened; for whatever else might follow tonight's events, she knew that she would effectively be a pariah in the eyes of the Circle and therefore in the eyes of all the castle's residents. She had expected nothing less; indeed, before performing the rite that had opened the Chaos Gate, a part of her had taken perverse delight in the prospect. But while the proud and dramatic anticipation of being cast in such a role had had its appeal, the harsh reality was proving to be a very different matter. She hadn't reckoned on the sense of terrible loss and insecurity engendered by suddenly finding herself cast out from the only society she had ever known. Nor had she reckoned on the fear that came hard on isolation's heels. Not a logical fear—not, for example, the dread of a knife blade in an unlit corridor one night or poison in a cup of wine; this was a civilized age—but the formless yet devastating fear of knowing that she was utterly friendless.

Or almost friendless. Tarod had once known the bitter sting of being an outcast, and she dared to believe that memories of his own experience had prompted him to feel sympathy and affinity for her in her plight. But that, even if it was true, guaranteed nothing. Dared she put it to the test? It was another part of her reason for lingering in the hall, though it was tangled inextricably with other motives and with the simple need not to be alone. But she wasn't sure now if she had the courage to broach the subject to Tarod.

She was so preoccupied with her thoughts that she didn't know he was watching her, so when he suddenly spoke her name, she started violently.

"Karuth." His green eyes were like a cat's gaze in the half-light. "I thought you had left with the others."

She blinked rapidly, striving to regain her composure. "No, my lord. I—" A worm of self-pity squirmed. "I suspect my company would have been unwelcome to them."

Tarod made no comment, but she sensed that he was neither impressed nor moved by her small show of bitterness. He walked toward her and laid the back of one hand against her cheek.

"You're cold."

"No; truly, I'm well enough." She drew away, gratified by the contact yet at the same time wary of him. "Thank you . . ." She swallowed, feeling that something was trying to stick in her throat.

"All the same, you should go to bed. There's nothing more to be done tonight."

Karuth nodded reluctantly, then looked up at him. "What of you, my lord? We've prepared no rooms for you—if you'll tell me what you require, I—"

He silenced her with a shake of the head. "There's no need. I'll make my own arrangements." A faintly malevolent smile. "I'm not Ailind: I won't require splendid lodgings and a dozen servants running after me to remind everyone that I'm here." He took her arm in a formal but companionable way and led her toward the double doors. "Go to bed, Karuth, and try to sleep. You may not think it likely now, but daylight will put a different perspective on your doubts."

She started to say, "I have no doubts," then stopped, aware that he'd judged her feelings better than she could judge them herself. She knew she was being gently dismissed and wasn't about to argue with him, but she also knew that sleep wouldn't come easily tonight, if at all. And there was the other thing, still unresolved. . . .

They reached the doors. Tarod opened them, then stopped and uttered a soft, amused laugh.

Outside the hall, silent on the floor, waiting, were cats. There must have been fifteen or twenty of them of every color and size and age, and each one was gazing alertly, almost raptly, up at the Chaos lord's face. One, the gray animal that had often in the past attached itself to Karuth, opened its mouth and mewed what sounded like a welcome.

"Well, now," Tarod said, and there was genuine pleasure in his voice. "I'd forgotten that Chaos has these good friends among the castle's inhabitants."

The cats approached, purring, rubbing against his legs and against Karuth's skirt. Tarod crouched to stroke them one by one, then glanced, smiling, at Karuth. "I once had good reason to be grateful to one of their ancestors," he told her. "A creature very like this little gray beast, in fact."

Karuth could feel, though dimly, an aura of warmth and pleasure emanating from the cats' telepathic minds. Their mood gave her confidence, as did their unexpected effect on Tarod, for with this show of affection he suddenly seemed more approachable.

She said, before her courage could fail, "My lord, there is something I wanted to ask."

The green eyes quickened with easygoing interest. "Ah, I thought so. What's troubling you?"

She felt foolish; again he'd anticipated her, and she should have expected no less. She drew breath, clasping her hands tightly together.

"It's Strann, my lord."

"Strann?" Tarod's tone and expression didn't give the smallest hint of his inward reaction. "What about him?"

"I'm . . ." And she thought, *Don't dissemble; tell the truth.* "I'm afraid for him." She ran her tongue over lips that were suddenly uncomfortably dry. "I know he made a mistake, and in that sense he failed in the task that Yan—your br—that lord Yandros set him; but I believe he *is* a true ally, and without Chaos's protection he may be at risk if the High Initiate or—or anyone should . . ." Realizing that she was babbling, making a fool of herself, she subsided into silence with the sentence unfinished.

Tarod gave the gray cat a last gentle stroke with one fingertip and stood up. "You think that Ailind may take out on Strann what he can no longer take out on you?"

He voiced her feelings with such accuracy that her cheeks flamed. "Yes," she said.

"Where's Strann now?"

"In a room in the main wing. He's still a prisoner, whatever appearances might suggest. And there's another matter. . . ."

Tarod looked at her queryingly, and without having originally intended to say more, Karuth found herself telling him the story of Strann's ruined right hand— Ygorla's personal joke to ensure that her messenger remained loyal.

"Without his music he has nothing," she finished unhappily. "And she has told him that only she can undo her sorcery and restore the hand again."

Tarod gazed at her with an odd expression. "You're a highly qualified physician, Karuth. What do you say to that?"

She stared at the floor. "No human skill could repair the damage she did, my lord. It's . . . monstrous."

He was silent for so long that she began to feel uneasy, and when she ventured to look up again, she saw that his face was grim and his eyes had a brooding and dangerous light in them. Unsure of her ground, she tried to find some way of easing out of the hiatus, but he forestalled her.

"Show me where Strann's room is," he said.

The tone was abrupt and brooked no questions. Karuth made a small bow, not daring to speak, not yet daring to believe that he was ready to look favorably on her plea. She glanced along the length of the broad corridor, saw no one about, and without a word turned to lead the way toward the main stairs. Behind them, like flowing water or a low-lying trail of smoke, the cats followed in silent procession.

In the hours since Karuth had left his room, finding any form of distraction hadn't been easy for Strann. He had been fed, which at least was something to be thankful for, and he'd tried to occupy himself by making the meal last as long as possible; but finally, with only half of the food eaten and the rest stone-cold and unpalatable even if he'd had an appetite in the first place, he gave up the pretense.

In one way, he reflected, his lack of appetite was probably a blessing, for it made the role that Karuth had asked him to play that much more convincing: a man recovering from fever, out of danger now but still conva-

lescent and weak. He and she both knew that the brief
sickness he'd suffered had been no natural attack but a
ploy on Chaos's part, a way of reaching Karuth through
him, but it was vital that no one else should suspect anything untoward. To that end Strann had silently and pa-
tiently suffered a thorough examination by Sanquar, the
castle's second physician and Karuth's assistant, and
had, he hoped, made a convincing play of it; certainly a
good enough show to avoid being forced to answer any
potentially dangerous questions. Sanquar had finally
gone, and shortly afterward he'd heard his two guards
also walking away along the passage outside, presumably
judging him safe to be left alone for the night. He'd tried
the door as soon as they were out of earshot, but of
course it was locked. Now, with nothing else to hold his
attention, he was prey to all the thoughts and worries
that he'd been trying to keep at bay.

He knew that Karuth had a mission to carry out,
and he suspected that it was a task set her by Yandros,
the greatest lord of Chaos, though Karuth had refused to
confirm that. Safer for him to know nothing, she had
said, and though that might be true, nevertheless Strann
didn't like it, and liked it still less when his mind dwelt
on the little she *had* told him. An emissary of Order in
the castle . . . and Order's gods knew of his own purpose here and knew the details of the message he had
brought. Seven Hells, Strann thought bitterly, but he'd
walked whistling into that trap. To reveal the nature of
Yandros's predicament and blithely announce the fact
that a Chaos god's soul-gem had been stolen, while one of
Order's own lords sat not three paces from him listening
to every word . . . a half-brained dog couldn't have
hoped to do better. Now, in an eleventh-hour bid to unravel the damage he'd managed to wreak, Karuth was
putting herself in mortal danger. She'd tried to play it
down, but he wasn't a fool, he knew the nature of the risk
she was taking, even if he could only guess at the details.
And if anything happened to her because of his stupidity . . .

27

Savagely Strann threw the bedclothes back, got up, and paced across the room like a cat in a cage. Damn pretending to be stricken to his bed; if he lay there inert for one moment longer, he'd start tearing down the bed-hangings or snatching up the pots and potions that damned physician had left on the table and throwing them around the room, or shouting fit to bring the guards racing back from whatever comfortable cranny they'd found for themselves. He went to the window, pulled back the curtains, and looked out. Nothing to see; the courtyard was empty, silver and black with snow and the contours of the ancient stone walls. This was a chillingly oppressive place, he thought. Hard to imagine anyone with any warmth in their soul looking on it as home, let alone a woman like Karuth. Then thought of Karuth brought the sick fear surging to the surface again, and he let the curtain fall and turned tensely back to the room.

Two candles had been left burning in sconces fixed to the wall. They gave just enough light to see by, and with his good hand Strann felt in the capacious pockets of his smallcoat, bringing out the odds and ends he found there. A handful of coins. Two broken pen nibs. A scrap of parchment; something written on it, but the ink had run and made the script illegible. A quartz pebble, rough-edged, a good-luck charm of some sort, though it had brought him little luck lately. Two spare strings for his manzon . . . he put them away again quickly, forcing down the anguish they conjured. Some old, dog-eared gambling cards, and a die with one edge so worn that it would no longer fall true. He tossed the die in his hands, then discarded it in favor of the cards. The pack wasn't complete, but he could play one of the simpler games with it—Harvester's Hazard, for instance, wagering against himself and taking an additional bet on which side would win. Anything, *anything* to make the hours pass and keep him from dwelling on any but the most trivial of matters.

He sat down cross-legged on the floor, divided his

small store of coins into two heaps, and awkwardly, one-handed, began to shuffle and deal the cards.

By the time he started on his third round, he was finding it nearly impossible to concentrate on the game. Despite his efforts to ignore it, fear was getting the better of him. He was afraid for himself and his own precarious future; but the greater fear—and, having few illusions about himself, he was honest enough to admit that it came as a surprise—was for Karuth. Where was she now? What was she doing? Above all, was she safe? Not knowing was the worst of it; not knowing, and being powerless to do anything to help her, especially because if it hadn't been for him, this whole ugly mess wouldn't have come about in the first place. If only he could get out of this room. If only he could—

The latch of his door clicked, and Strann's mind froze. His heart missed painfully, and he looked up in time to see the door open. Someone, barely more than a silhouette between the candlelight and the equally faint illumination from the passage, appeared on the threshold. A familiar voice said, "Strann?"

"Karuth!" Dropping the cards, Strann started to his feet. "Is all well? What have you—" Then he bit the rest of the sentence back as he saw the tall figure who had entered the room behind her.

In this low light Tarod wasn't clearly visible, but instinct sounded a warning in Strann's psyche, and he stood motionless, his hazel eyes narrowed and wary. The Chaos lord didn't speak but gestured slightly toward the wall sconces, and the dozen or so unlit candles fixed there flared into life. The room brightened, and Strann saw his face for the first time.

"*Uhh . . .*" He didn't need to look at Karuth for confirmation; the resemblance to Yandros was enough to tell him the truth, and unsteadily Strann took a pace backward. "My . . ." he could barely make his tongue obey him. "My lord . . ."

"Sit down, Strann." Tarod closed the door. "And don't run away with the fear that I'm here to punish your stupidity. Your link with my brother provided us with a means of reaching Karuth, so in the event you were of some use. Let's say, shall we, that the one deed cancels out the other and that you can consider yourself absolved."

Staring at him as though hypnotized, Strann groped his way to the bed and sagged onto it. He tried to ask a question, but coherence was beyond him. "What—that is, I don't understand how—"

Karuth said quietly, "I performed a rite, Strann, that opened the way between our world and the realm of Chaos. That was the task lord Yandros asked me to undertake when he spoke to me through you." She paused. "It seemed wiser not to tell you until it was done."

Cold sweat broke out on Strann's face as he had a small inkling of the risk she must have taken. Just for a moment he wondered if he was hallucinating again, but then dismissed the idea. This was no fever dream; this was as real as his encounter with Yandros on Summer Isle.

He was still trying to get his mind and his voice under control when Karuth crossed the room to him and caught hold of his hand.

"Strann, there have been great changes in the castle tonight. My brother knows that lord Tarod is here, and he also knows that I was the one who opened the gateway to Chaos."

Tarod interjected. "More to the point, Ailind of Order is also well aware of it. He can't take revenge on Karuth, for she's under my protection and he has no power whatever over me. But you might be another matter."

Strann forgot his diffidence and looked at the Chaos lord in shock. "As a target for his anger? But surely—"

"Don't ever make the mistake of underestimating a creature like Ailind," Tarod said sharply. "No mortal could hope to match the lords of Order for pettiness and spite, and if Ailind thinks he might strike back at Karuth by turning on you, he'll do so. I think, therefore, that it

will serve us all best if I extend a measure of protection to
you as well as to her."

Strann's skin prickled as the sweat's chill was suddenly replaced by a rush of hot relief. Karuth still had
hold of his hand; she squeezed his fingers, and he returned the grip with all his strength.

"Thank you, my lord," he managed to say at last.
"I'm more grateful than I can express."

"It's not a matter for gratitude, Strann. It simply
wouldn't be in Chaos's best interest to jeopardize one of
the few allies we have. If you consider yourself indebted
to anyone, let it be to Karuth for pleading your case."
Then he looked at Karuth. "The hour's late. You'd best
take Strann away from this room and find him another
lodging for what's left of the night."

She nodded, too thankful to speak. Strann rose from
the bed, wondering whether his legs were going to support him or whether they'd collapse, but as Karuth
started to lead him toward the door, Tarod suddenly
said, "Wait—just one moment."

They stopped. Tarod walked across the room, and
Karuth stepped deferentially aside as he reached Strann
and stood facing him.

"Your hand." Tarod looked down at the gauntlet
that covered Strann's ruined stump, and suddenly his
voice was strangely gentle. "Take off the glove, Strann.
Let me see it."

Strann tensed, and his gaze searched the Chaos
lord's face as though he was half convinced that this was
the prelude to some unpleasantness. Tarod's green eyes
held his steadily, and after a moment he dropped his gaze
and very slowly pulled the glove free. Even now he had to
force himself not to flinch at what was revealed.

Tarod touched the blackened and twisted stump
with a long forefinger. His look became introverted again,
as it had done a few minutes before in the hall, and he felt
a quick flash of anger. Strann's hand evoked old memories of his own tribulations in this world, and a time when
he had suffered a similar torment. It was meaningless
now, but if he chose to conjure them to mind, he could

still recall the agony of shattering bones, and the rage and bewilderment of a monstrous betrayal.

He suppressed his thoughts and said, his tone giving nothing away, "The sorceress did this to you?"

Strann nodded, not trusting his voice.

"As a safeguard to ensure your good behavior?"

Strann wetted his lips. "That was what she said."

"I see." Tarod's fingers spread, covering the stump. Strann felt something—not quite pain but akin to it, heat and cold and something else he couldn't name—flare in nerves that should have been dead. Then Tarod withdrew his fingers.

Strann looked down—and shock hit him with a dizzying punch, as though the room, the castle, the stack, the entire world, had turned on its head around him.

His hand was whole again.

Tarod smiled kindly, almost sadly she thought, at Karuth. "I'll wish you both a good night," he said, and left the room.

Stunned and silent, Karuth stared at the door swinging to behind him. She couldn't articulate what she felt, couldn't find words, couldn't even gather her flailing thoughts. Then suddenly the paralysis broke; she turned toward Strann, her face radiant—and stopped.

Strann had covered his eyes with his hand, the restored hand, and the tangles of his light-brown hair hid the rest of his face from her view. He made no sound, but his shoulders were shaking, and Karuth turned away again, realizing that he didn't want her to see even if she couldn't help but know.

She wasn't used to this, she told herself, and pushed a thumb and forefinger against the corners of her own eyes, blinking rapidly. Tirand, yes; many times when he was a little boy, and then of course in later years, when their father died . . . but that had been different. He was her brother and younger than she was, so there had been no embarrassment and she'd known what to do for the best. Now, though, she felt out of her depth. Strange; in her years as a physician she'd witnessed births and deaths by the score, dealt with pain and fear and grief;

seen almost every aspect of the mortal condition that could be imagined, from the kindest to the cruelest. But in all those years she didn't think she had ever felt as helpless as she felt at this moment, or as moved by such a simple sight as that of a man crying.

3

Strann spent the remainder of that night in Karuth's room. Firmly ignoring the small inner voice that accused her of a modicum of self-deception, Karuth told herself that it was simply the most logical solution to the immediate problem of finding him new and safer quarters, and Strann, though he made a show of diffidence, took little persuading.

No reference had been made to Strann's reaction to the healing of his hand. The breakdown had been short-lived, but when Strann recovered his composure, they both took care to behave as though nothing untoward had happened. However, the incident did serve to dispel some of their wariness, and the shared though unspoken memory of it drew them together in a way that might otherwise have been impossible. With Karuth's door closed and bolted behind them, and with candles blazing and the fire rekindled and warming the room, they began to lose their constraints and settle into cautious but warm companionship. Karuth set a jug of wine and spices to mull on the hearth trivet, and when the brew was ready, she poured it, and they sat together on a rug, warming hands and feet at the blaze.

They both felt the need to talk, but somehow it seemed that conversation was impossible. To speak of trivial matters in the wake of tonight's events and all that they portended would have been grossly incongruous, yet those events were too close and too momentous; they needed a respite, a chance to let the strains of recent days ebb a little and allow them a breathing space. But they could find no topic that fell between those two extremes, and so, as they drank their wine and watched the flames, they were silent. The silence continued and became uncomfortable after a while; despite the wine, tension had begun to grow up between them once more, and neither knew how to stem it. For his part Strann was in a dilemma. He didn't know Karuth well enough to be sure whether her suggestion that he stay with her tonight had been prompted by simple expediency or by something more, and he was anxious not to give offense by making any presumptions. He'd never encountered such a problem before, for among the kind of women with whom he'd associated throughout his carefree, itinerant life the question simply didn't arise. But he could no more compare Karuth to such old flames as the tavern harlot Yya, or even eager and reckless Kiszi, daughter of a rich Shu-Nhadek merchant, than he could fancy himself qualified to be High Initiate. Karuth was in another sphere entirely; not merely well born, but a *lady* in the true sense of the word. His personal feelings toward her were something else entirely; for the moment he dared not consider them, and he didn't quite know what to do or what to say.

It was Karuth who finally broke the hiatus when she set down her wine cup, rose to her feet, and crossed to where her manzon lay near the bed. She took the instrument from its case and looked thoughtfully at it for a few moments. Then she came back to the hearth and held the manzon out.

"Play for me, Strann," she said gently.

He looked at the instrument, then up at her. For the first time since his arrival at the castle she saw a glimmer of the old Strann's smile, and she knew that the instinct that had prompted her had been a sound one. Strann wouldn't have dreamed to ask if he might so much as touch the prized instrument of another musician, but the chance to play again was what he wanted more than anything in the world. It was the bridge they had both been seeking, the common ground that would cement their tentative and as yet precarious relationship. He knew it too. The knowledge was reflected in his smile, and he was grateful.

Strann said, "I'll play for you gladly, lady. But on one condition—that you'll also play for me."

She laughed, and there was a slight break in her voice. "No. I wouldn't dare."

He took the manzon from her and settled it across his knees. "I seem to remember," he said, deliberately keeping his voice light, almost careless, "a certain time on Summer Isle, in happier days, when someone—I mention no names—took you to task for your reticence. The approach was sheer impertinence, but it had the desired effect. I *had* hoped that you might have remembered the lesson." And he played a short, complex phrase on the instrument.

As the sound died away, Karuth's gaze slid to his face. "Hand-Speech . . ." she said. "Strann, if I were a mistrustful woman, I'd suspect you of trying to shame me into capitulating."

Strann grinned. The notes he'd played had been phrased in the code of the Guild of Master Musicians. Hand-Speech, as it was called, was a sophisticated musical language, but Strann's message had been simple and to the point. *Will you deny me the pleasure that you ask me to grant you?* he had said.

Abruptly Karuth laughed. "Very well, then," she conceded. "I'll not deny you. Though I'll tell you now that I'll have far more pleasure from your playing than you can hope to have from mine!"

"That's a matter of opinion. And taste."

She looked back at him levelly. "Don't try to inveigle me with flattery; I'm not impressed. And tune the fifth string, it's flat." Then the last vestiges of tension collapsed, and she sank down onto the rug beside him. "Oh . . . Strann, you fool. Just play for me."

Strann's hands stroked the polished wood, curled over the strings. He said no more, but began quietly to play a slow, old air. The firelight shone on him, creating warm lights in his hair, shadowing the planes and angles of his face as, eyes closed, he forgot all else and lost

himself in his playing. Karuth listened, rapt, and in the
candlelit room the spell of music began to steal over them
both, to bind them in warmth and intimacy and peace.

They did sleep for the last few hours before dawn.
Strann made himself a makeshift bed by the fireside, from
rugs and from blankets that Karuth brought him from
her linen chest, and they wished each other good night
with a clasp of hands and a kiss that was chaste, almost
childlike. Strann was oddly touched by that, and a little
surprised by his own reticence, which certainly didn't fit
with his usual nature. He found himself deeply anxious
not to risk offending Karuth by making any assumptions;
whatever his desires, her goodwill—her *friendship,* in a
true sense—was too important to him, he realized, to be
risked. And despite everything, he was strangely and privately happy. Perhaps, he thought, with a flicker of the
ironic humor that had been forced into dormancy during
his recent trials, as the years advanced, he was becoming
more of a romantic than he would have imagined possible.

In the bed, shielded by the heavy hangings, Karuth
watched the fire's fading glow reflecting on the wall opposite. From where she lay she couldn't quite see Strann's
recumbent form, but she had heard his breathing slow to
a shallow, steady rhythm and guessed that he had fallen
asleep.

Karuth, too, was tired, but she had a suspicion that
sleep wouldn't come to her quite so easily. Effectively
alone now, and with no need to maintain a public mask,
she was beset with an overwhelming urge to laugh at her
behavior with Strann tonight. What a child she'd been.
What a silly, prudish—yes, that was the word, *prudish*—
child. Whatever had become of her much-vaunted experience and independence? She'd behaved more like a nervous virgin of sixteen than a worldly woman in her
thirties, torn between hope and fear, eagerness and trepidation, desire and . . .

Well, she asked herself, and what? Not the opposite
of desire, that was for certain. Unlikely paramour though
he might seem, with his scarecrow appearance and wry

wit that he was as likely to turn on himself as on any other target, she *did* find Strann attractive; more so, in fact, than she wanted to admit even to herself. And she was sensible enough to her own qualities to know that Strann, in his turn, was attracted to her. Yet tonight neither of them had been prepared to make the first crucial move toward breaking down that last barrier, and Karuth didn't quite know why. There would have been no shame in it, no later cause for recrimination; they were both old enough to judge and choose their own pleasures, and the mores of their time didn't frown upon such liaisons. But somehow the logical thing, the expected thing, hadn't happened. In fact, she thought, it was as if they'd both set out to avert it.

She turned over, pulling the bedclothes more closely around herself, and stifled a sudden urge to giggle in a way she'd not done since she was an adolescent. She and Strann behaving like children in an adult game, cautious and demure and never once daring to overstep the bounds of propriety. *Virginal.* It was ludicrous. Yet she was strangely glad that tonight had ended as it had. Pleasure notwithstanding, she wouldn't have wished it any other way, at least not yet. She didn't think of Strann as a lover but as something more; far more than could be expressed or fulfilled by simple physical gratification. And she was complimented by the knowledge that he seemed to share and reciprocate her feelings. It gave her a sense of reassurance . . . and that, Karuth thought as sleep claimed her at last, was worth more than gold, for it set the seal on a true and lasting friendship.

The Council of Adepts assembled an hour after sunrise the following morning. Circumstances compelled Tirand to open the meeting to the entire Circle whether council members or not, and the castle grapevine had clearly been working at full pitch overnight, for by the time the triumvirate, flanked by the senior councillors, took their seats on the high dais, the hall was packed to capacity.

Ailind, it seemed, had accepted that his identity could no longer be kept a secret, and he took the central chair that had been reserved for him between Tirand and the High Margrave. He had cast off the trappings of his assumed role and was dressed now entirely in white garments edged with gold, with a white cloak cast over his shoulders and a thin gold circlet holding back his long white hair. His eyes, as he scanned the hall, glittered like topaz.

Tarod, perhaps deliberately, arrived late. There was a stirring when the double doors opened to admit him, but he took no notice of the sea of nervous faces that turned to watch him as he walked down the central aisle toward the dais. In sharp contrast to Ailind he wore unadorned black, though his cloak, perhaps mockingly, was the green that denoted a seventh-rank Circle adept—the rank he had held during his own mortal incarnation. With no trappings, and no circlet to tame the tangle of his black hair, he looked unkempt and dangerous, and even Tirand's determination faltered when he met the contemptuous green stare as the Chaos lord acknowledged him briefly before taking a seat at the end of the dais table, at a pointed distance from the high adepts.

From where she sat near the back of the hall, Karuth felt the atmosphere grow sour with tension. The news of the Chaos emissary's arrival had taken only a few hours to spread, but even in that short time she was well aware that enough rumor had been attached to the facts to embroider the story thickly with half-truth and exaggeration. The adepts knew what Tarod had done to prove his identity, and already that tale had been turned into a saga of terror and mayhem. They also knew who among their own number had been responsible for performing the rite that had allowed Chaos to enter the castle and disrupt the High Initiate's plans—and if Karuth had felt outcast in the wake of her brother's tirade last night, it was nothing compared with the atmosphere that greeted her in the chill light of morning. Cold looks, a turning of backs, a wall of implacable hostility. Today she was a pariah; and it brought home to her the enormity of what she had done.

She tried to catch Tarod's eye as he walked past, but he paid her no heed. When the shifting and the murmuring finally died down, Tirand rose to his feet.

"My friends." His voice was strained, its tone unnatural. Karuth looked at his face and knew that he hadn't slept. "I have called this meeting for reasons that I think are already known to the great majority of those present in the hall." He glanced at Ailind. "Last night I and a number of my colleagues were . . . obliged . . ." He faltered. "Obliged to . . ."

The Matriarch reached out, and her fingers closed over his arm in a gesture that was intended to convey support and reassurance. Tirand cleared his throat and began again.

"Last night circumstances arose that we had not foreseen and that have presented us with a problem . . . a new problem . . ."

"High Initiate." Tarod's voice cut crisply across Tirand's floundering, and the Chaos lord leaned forward. "I suggest that we dispense with these pleasantries and come to the point without any tedious dissembling. I don't doubt that the great majority of the adepts in this hall are already aware of my identity and that of our white-haired friend who sits beside you. But for those who don't yet know, or don't yet believe what they have heard, allow me to clarify the matter once and for all." His vivid emerald stare swept the gathering. "I am Tarod of Chaos, brother to Yandros; and this erstwhile mariner, who until now has been so reluctant to reveal his real identity, is Ailind, brother to Aeoris and emissary of Order." He looked at Tirand again, and his eyes grew malevolent. "And that, High Initiate, is the crux of the problem you seem so reluctant to explain."

The hall was silent. Tirand looked miserably from Tarod to Ailind, then stared down at the table. "Yes," he said at last in a barely audible voice. "Yes. That is the crux of the problem."

"High Initiate, you will allow me to speak." Ailind

rose, laying a hand on Tirand's shoulder and gently but decisively forcing him to sit down. He glanced contemptuously at Tarod, who looked back at him with ironic interest, then turned to face the gathering.

"Adepts of the Circle, I am, as you have already heard, Ailind, brother of Aeoris—and therefore I speak to you with the full sanction of the powers of Order." He paused to allow the significance of this statement to take effect, then continued. "Not long ago, at the behest not only of your High Initiate but of all your rulers, you revoked your former fealty to Chaos and placed yourselves solely in the hands of those who for centuries past, until the sham of Equilibrium was imposed on this world, were your only true gods. You called on us for help in your time of crisis; we answered you. Yet now one of your own adepts has defied the Circle to which she owes duty and has called upon the demons of Chaos to involve themselves in mortal affairs. Whatever tales or rumors are now circulating, the truth is simple: An emissary of Chaos has come among you without invitation and in direct contradiction of your rulers' and your gods' will. Yandros has broken the pact that he himself made with your ancestors, and in doing so has betrayed you all."

Tarod laughed. The sound was so unexpected that it silenced Ailind, and every gaze in the hall turned to the tall, black-haired figure at the end of the table.

"Ailind, you and your kind don't change." Tarod stood up, and the green cloak swung vividly around him. "You strut and you bluster and you deliver your sermons, but amid all these fine words you overlook the one point that is central to this affair. I was called. I am here. And you haven't the power to remove me."

Ailind's eyes flashed. "You were *called*?" he retorted contemptuously. "By whose sanction? The Circle has pronounced anathema on you and your demon brothers, and your presence in this world flouts the law of Equilibrium!"

Tarod smiled malevolently. "Chaos doesn't need the sanction of the Circle, my friend. The will of a high adept is enough to satisfy the law *we* made."

The slight emphasis wasn't lost on Ailind, but he returned the smile with a chilly twisting of his lips. "A traitress and a blasphemer? Karuth Piadar is no longer a high adept of this Circle, and she will live to regret the day that she defied her rightful lords!"

For one moment Tarod stood motionless—then, so fast that mortal eyes and minds couldn't assimilate it, his left hand snaked out and, with a gargantuan flash of light, a double-edged broadsword of crimson fire, twice the length of a man, came smashing down along the table's length. There was the sound of wood splitting and splintering; a woman councillor screamed shrilly, and Calvi Alacar jerked backward, almost pulling his neighbor with him.

Tarod stood motionless, his eyes locked with Ailind's and his expression lethal. The sword pulsed in his hand, spilling blood-red radiance over his wrist. The blade's entire length was buried in the table, and where it had struck, the wood was beginning to char and smolder.

"I will warn you once, Ailind of Order." The Chaos lord spoke with venomous softness, but every ear in the hall heard his words. "I tolerate no threats toward my servants, and I will brook no attempts at retribution. If you have a spark of wisdom, you'll learn and accept before it's too late that you are not master here!"

Ailind's eyes turned to molten gold. He raised his own right hand, the fingers clenching; but before he could retaliate, a voice cried out,

"My lords! My lords, please have some pity on us!"

Shaill Falada had risen to her feet. Her face was as white as her Sisterhood robe, but she didn't flinch as she looked from one to the other of the two antagonists.

"My lords, it seems I must again plead for a spark of sanity amid mayhem!" she said. "Your quarrels are surely not ours, and I had been led to believe that the purpose of this meeting was to find a solution to our differences, not to deepen them." She glanced at Calvi, who had been helped back onto his chair but was shaking violently. "The High Margrave is greatly distressed, and I have to confess that I'm in little better straits. *Please,* can we be calm?"

With a faint, wry smile on his face, Ailind lowered his hand. Tarod looked for a moment at the broadsword, then relaxed his grip on it. The sword faded and vanished, and the Chaos lord bowed in the Matriarch's direction.

"For the second time, madam, I apologize to you. You're quite right; we'll find no solutions on this road." He straightened, and his emerald gaze flicked to Ailind. "If nothing else, I think my cousin of Order will concede that we share one common purpose between us, the purpose that brought us both here in the first place. Although"—and abruptly his voice grew savage—"it would have been better for all concerned if the meddling servants of Order had kept to their business and left Chaos to deal with its own problem in its own way."

Ailind's eyes flickered dangerously again, and Shaill said in desperate appeal, "My *lords* . . ."

Tarod raised both hands palms outward in an acquiescent gesture. "Again, lady Matriarch, I ask your pardon." He smiled wryly at her. "And I thank you for your intervention."

Shaill's answering smile was reserved. "I hope, sir, that you will assume nothing from it. I'm by no means Chaos's champion, and I like this situation no better than anyone else. However, it's quite obvious that nothing can be done to change it now. It's clear to me that you and lord Ailind are evenly matched—that shouldn't surprise us, for, after all, it's surely the whole basis of Equilibrium? And as you say, if nothing else, you at least have one common aim: to destroy the usurper who threatens us all." Her eyes narrowed with sudden, angry pain. "I share that aim, too, my lords. My predecessor, Ria Morys, was also my dear friend, and if the evil-hearted little monster who murdered her can be brought to justice, I'm not about to quibble over whether the power of Chaos or Order is better equipped to achieve it. All I ask . . ." She hesitated, stared down at her tightly clasped hands for a moment, then looked up once more.

"All I ask, sirs, is that you tell us how it's to be done. For it seems to me that so far we've heard not one single word from anyone about that."

There was silence as the Matriarch sat down. Tarod and Ailind exchanged a long look, and it was Tarod who spoke first.

"Well, my friend, the lady Matriarch has put us both in our places, I think."

Ailind gave Shaill a look that suggested her temerity wouldn't be forgotten. "Perhaps, then, you would care to answer her question and enlighten us all as to your intentions? I think we must know the truth, Chaos." His amber eyes took on a cynical glint. *"All* of it."

There'd be no point in prevaricating, Tarod thought. The lords of Order were well aware of Chaos's predicament now, and even if he tried to avoid the issue, Ailind would ensure that the Circle would not be kept in ignorance for much longer. And he'd use the knowledge. He'd use it in any way he could.

The Chaos lord's green eyes scanned the hall quickly, then lit on Karuth's face. Strann wasn't with her. Not surprising, and perhaps at this moment just as well for the bard. He turned his head again to regard Ailind, and his tone was carefully indifferent as he said, "Of course. All of it."

It was a silent, pensive crowd that finally left the great chamber some two hours later. As she moved with the tide flowing slowly toward the double doors, Karuth was reminded incongruously of some of the Higher Rites she'd witnessed since rising to the Circle's senior ranks; there was the same air of solemnity, the same sense of awesome occasion mingled with a tinge of anticlimax now that the event was over, and a subconscious reluctance to return to the mundanities of everyday life.

Not, she reminded herself, that life in the castle was likely to be mundane from now on. The two beings who were even now watching their audience's departure from the dais had put an end to any hopes she or anyone else in the hall might have nurtured that a swift and simple solution to their problems would be found. That revelation had been a hard blow to Karuth's confidence, for she had anticipated—no, more than that; she had firmly *believed*—that Chaos would have the means to defeat the sorceress Ygorla and her demon father where other powers had failed. Tarod's words to the assembly, however, had shattered that fond illusion.

The Chaos lord had been quite brutally frank with his silent audience. To the surprise and chagrin of Ailind and Tirand, he had made no attempt to disguise the truth of his own and his brother lords' dilemma, nor to minimize its significance. He had told them of the plot that the demon Narid-na-Gost had made to steal the soul-stone of a Chaos lord, and of how he had fled with the stone in his possession to join his daughter in the mortal realm, where together they had embarked on their plan to usurp the High Margrave's throne on Summer Isle and from there to rule the world. And, simply and bluntly, Tarod had told the assembly that there was nothing Chaos could do to stop them.

There had been uproar at that. When at last the furor ceased, Tarod had explained the full nature of Narid-na-Gost's trickery. Chaos was effectively under ransom. With the soul-stone of his brother in the usurper's hands, Yandros was powerless to make any move against Ygorla and her father, for if he did, they would destroy the stone and his brother with it. Although that would see the end of their ambitions, Yandros would not pay such a price for their downfall.

Ailind had listened to this in silence, occasionally affecting a yawn in order to hide a small smile. However, the smile had faded when Tarod went on to say that Order, in its turn, was as powerless as Chaos to make any move against their common enemy. Narid-na-Gost, he said, was a being of pure Chaos, and Ygorla, though half human, shared that heritage. Order had no power over Chaos's denizens; that, Tarod ironically reminded his audience, had already been proved here in the castle. Whatever Ailind might wish his followers to believe, neither he nor his great brother Aeoris could influence or even touch the usurpers in any way. And they could all be sure that Ygorla and Narid-na-Gost knew it.

There was, Tarod said, no clear-cut or immediate solution to the stalemate in which they all found themselves. But now that Chaos had been called upon and had taken its place upon the stage of this drama, there would be changes. He was aware that Order had already made the first move in a strategy of its own, by issuing an invitation to the usurper to visit the castle. Chaos had no power to prevent that, nor any wish to do so; but Tarod intended to make his own plans to welcome Ygorla. Chaos and Order did indeed share a common goal, as the Matriarch had already pointed out. But their means of achieving that goal would differ, and it was for each adept to look to his or her own conscience and choose a path accordingly.

When she finally gained the doors and the press of bodies thinned as the crowd dispersed into the corridor, Karuth surreptitiously scanned the faces around her. However, it was impossible to infer much from what she saw. As yet the adepts were too shocked to react coherently to what they had heard, and until the numbness that had followed on shock's heels wore off, there would be a hiatus. But once the hiatus was over, what then? How *would* they respond? And where would she find herself placed once her peers' loyalties had been declared?

She looked back over her shoulder but from this angle could no longer see whether anyone still remained on the dais at the far end of the council hall. The triumvirate were leaving; she glimpsed Tirand's curly hair and the white of the Matriarch's robe near the doors, but neither Tarod nor Ailind had yet emerged. For a moment Karuth felt an impulse to speak to Shaill, but then thought better of it. She had her work to attend to, and for the moment it was better that she concentrate on that rather than torment herself with ifs and might-bes.

Someone jostled her, started to apologize, then saw who she was and walked quickly away with the apology unfinished. Karuth stared after the departing back for a few seconds, then sighed and turned toward her infirmary.

The last stragglers reached the doors and filed out, and Tarod, who had been idly thumbing a stain on the table-top, rose to his feet. As he stepped down from the dais and started to walk away, Ailind's voice rapped out sharply.

"Chaos."

Tarod stopped, turned. Ailind was standing beside the High Initiate's empty chair. They were alone in the hall now, yet their presences seemed to crowd the room's cavernous space.

"Before we go our separate ways," Ailind said coldly, "I wish to warn you of one thing. If you harbor any visions of taking command here, I would strongly advise you to forget them. I've no intention of sitting passively by while you corrupt the Circle to your cause, nor have I any intention of allowing you to interfere in any way with our strategies. I may not be able to undo the treachery that brought you here, but inasmuch as I have no power over you, you have none over me. Do I make myself clear?"

Tarod smiled. "Quite clear. And I acknowledge and accept that while we're both in the mortal world, our strengths are evenly matched, so there's little point in our wasting time and effort in vying with each other for precedence." He paused, and the smile became a shade more unpleasant. "However, I'm also well aware that you and Aeoris would like nothing better than to see my brother's soul-stone destroyed and the balance of Equilibrium tilted in your favor, and I assure you that I'll use any means at my disposal to see that your wish does not come true."

Ailind looked thoughtfully at him. "Very well," he said at last, "I think we understand each other."

Tarod's eyes glinted malevolently. "Oh yes, my friend. I believe we always have."

He walked toward the doors, leaving the lord of Order gazing after him with a face as inscrutable as the sacred statues in the Marble Hall.

4

Tarod knew that he was the focus of a good deal of attention, both open and covert, as he emerged from the main doors and walked down the steps and across the snowy courtyard toward the library. The day was so gloomy that lights already shone in a good many of the castle's windows, and the Chaos lord's preternaturally sharp eyes didn't miss the telltale shadows of figures watching from a number of the embrasures. A few people were in the courtyard itself, mostly servants about their business or students braving the cold to stretch their legs; they paused as he passed by, their gazes following him silently though they didn't otherwise acknowledge him. Tarod ignored the scrutiny, but he wasn't entirely indifferent to it. In fact it amused him in more than the obvious way, for it brought back more old memories of another time— another age, by this world's standards—when once before he'd been the center of attention in the castle. There were parallels, too, in the motive behind the curiosity. Once again Chaos was feared and mistrusted by the Circle, as it had been in the days before Equilibrium, when the gods of Order had ruled unopposed for centuries. Once again he was Chaos's only avatar in the mortal realm, and once again he and the High Initiate were at loggerheads. Ironic how history was repeated; though Tarod reminded himself that any comparisons between Tirand and Chaos's old adversary, Keridil Toln, were invidious. About the only similarity between them, he thought, was that they both had an uncompromisingly stubborn streak. Keridil, however, would have tempered his stubbornness with a larding of wisdom, or at least pragmatism, and he had also been secure enough in himself to know and admit that his judgment wasn't infallible; a quality that Tirand certainly didn't seem to share.

Well, Tarod, thought, so be it. This time there were no old ties of friendship such as he had formed with Keridil to complicate matters, so he could ignore any considerations of Tirand Lin's safety or future. If the High Initiate had chosen to set himself against Chaos, Chaos would react accordingly, and Tirand could expect no quarter if and when matters came to a head. Yandros had often dryly teased Tarod that his taste of mortal life a century ago had hampered him with an understanding of and compassion for the human condition. True or not—and Tarod didn't believe for a moment that it was—he wasn't about to let any such considerations get in his way now.

He reached the small door that led down to the library vaults and began to descend the narrow spiral stairs. Every stone of the castle was familiar to him, and each tiny detail served to sharpen the memories further: one treacherously worn and chipped stair that even after a hundred years still hadn't been repaired; a section of wall where damp always seeped through and gave off a musty smell; another place (his fingers traced the outline as he passed) where a long-dead student had once defiantly carved his own initials. Small mundanities, echoes of old lives, past times . . . a quick, wry smile flicked across Tarod's lips as he realized that he was in danger of falling prey to sentiment. Yandros would have been amused. Then the smile faded abruptly as he neared the foot of the staircase and the library door came into view ahead. Memories were a luxury to be indulged at another time; he had a more immediate task to attend to.

In his blunt speech to the adepts assembled in the council hall, Tarod had deliberately omitted one salient fact. He'd told the Circle of the plans the usurper and her sire had hatched for dominion over their world, but Chaos knew that Narid-na-Gost wouldn't be satisfied with control merely of the mortal realm. He had higher ambitions; and the most powerful key to those ambitions lay here in the castle's foundations.

Tarod and his brothers were well aware that a great many of the castle's peculiar properties were a closed book to the men and women of the Circle. Some, like the Maze, had fallen into disuse only during recent years, though even so, the lapse had been long enough for them already to have been debased or forgotten. Others, though, had lain inert for far, far longer; since an age long before the formation of Circle or Sisterhood or Margravates, when Chaos had reigned unchecked in the mortal world and another race of sorcerers, with powers beyond the Circle's imagining, had made the Star Peninsula their stronghold. Those ancient adepts were long dead, and their brand of sorcery had been stamped out with the return of Order's followers to the world; their knowledge and skill had been wiped from the annals of history, and many of the castle's secrets had been buried with them. But yesterday, for the first time in centuries, one of the greatest of those lost secrets had been woken from its long dormancy. The Chaos Gate was functioning again—and that was the ultimate weapon that Narid-na-Gost yearned to control.

Tarod had no doubt that the demon knew of the Gate and its properties. Narid-na-Gost was one of Chaos's own, and though the Gate had been closed for untold ages, its existence and its function were far from forgotten in the gods' realm. Its powers were a great deal more complex and far-reaching than Tarod had intimated to Karuth, and if control of those powers should fall into Narid-na-Gost's hands it would spell disaster not only for the mortal world but also for the lords of Chaos themselves. Now, though, Narid-na-Gost wasn't the only potential threat. Though the Gate's primary purpose was to provide a portal between the world of Chaos and the world of men, it could also be used to open the way to other realms, and now that it was functioning once more after centuries of dormancy, there was a good chance that the Circle, with Ailind's active connivance, might try to use it for their own purposes. Tarod intended to ensure that they did no such thing.

The library was empty, as he'd known it would be. The torches in their wall sconces were dead and the vaulted room pitch-dark, but Tarod needed no light and made his way to the low door, partly concealed by shelves, that led to the Marble Hall. Again the sense of old familiarity overtook him as he began to walk along the narrow, downward-sloping passage, and at last the soft, gray-silver glow from the hall's own door began to filter through the corridor. But then abruptly something else impinged, cutting across his reverie and alerting him.

Someone else had arrived at the hall before him. Not Ailind; he'd have sensed the lord of Order's presence long before this. But someone . . . Approaching the silver door, Tarod slowed his steps and focused his consciousness, then recognized the intruder. He smiled. Of course; it was logical. He could even believe that the High Initiate might have acted on his own volition and not at his master's bidding. . . .

The door opened soundlessly before Tarod, and he stepped into the Marble Hall. Even through the shifting, pastel-colored mists he saw Tirand immediately. The High Initiate was standing at the edge of the black circle in the center of the mosaic floor and staring down at it as though striving to fathom its secrets. His figure, hunched and tense, was a study in grim and almost desperate concentration, and for a moment Tarod came close to pitying him, for if nothing else he couldn't fault Tirand's diligence and devotion to what he saw as his duty. However, the feeling fled as swiftly as it had come, and the Chaos lord allowed his footsteps to become audible as he walked across the mosaic toward the young man.

Tirand's head came up sharply, and he swung around. His mouth opened to deliver a reprimand to whoever had had the temerity to disturb him; then he saw who the intruder was.

Tarod inclined his head. "High Initiate. I see you don't believe in wasting time."

Fear, resentment, and uncertainty mingled in

Tirand's expression, but leavening them all was a measure of defiance.

"I think, lord Tarod, that I'd be unworthy of my station if I took any other course," he replied with stiff formality. His gaze flicked briefly toward the door; Tarod knew what he was thinking, and made a careless gesture.

"Leave or stay, as you please, Tirand. You've a perfect right to be here, and your presence makes no difference to my own business." He, too, moved to stand at the edge of the black circle, and his eyes took on a glint of malevolent humor. "Though I must confess that I fail to see what you hope to learn from merely staring at the Gate. Or did you have something else in mind?"

Tirand flushed and didn't answer. Tarod paced slowly around the circle's perimeter.

"If you and Ailind harbor any thoughts of using the Gate to Order's advantage, I'd strongly advise you to abandon them," he said. "I imagine I don't need to remind you that this is a powerful force, and to meddle without understanding its properties could have unfortunate consequences."

The High Initiate's color deepened. "The Circle has no need of any of Chaos's artifacts," he said defensively.

"I'm gratified to hear it." Tarod's tone was sarcastic. "And I assume that your distaste for us will deter you from any further indulgences of your curiosity in the future." He paused. "I have no personal animosity toward you, Tirand, whatever your masters may wish you to think. To be frank, I'm indifferent to you, and that's probably just as well. But I warn you, in your own interests, don't try to best me and don't try to impose your will and your prejudices on those who may not share your distorted view of Chaos."

Tirand stared back at him. "I'll do what I consider to be my duty, lord Tarod. Nothing more and nothing less."

That stubborn streak again, Tarod thought. Aloud, he said, "I'm sure you will. Just take care that you know the extent of your jurisdiction. And don't forget that, in one respect at least, we're fighting on the same side whether you like it or not. I believe you're intelligent enough to bear that fact in mind in the days to come. Don't prove me wrong."

For some seconds Tirand continued to look at him. Then he made an abrupt formal bow, turned on his heel, and walked out of the hall.

Tarod watched until the silver door had closed silently behind the High Initiate's departing back, then sighed and turned back to the black circle. Comparisons were invidious, but again he couldn't help drawing parallels between Tirand and Keridil Toln and finding Tirand sadly wanting. Keridil himself had never been a friend to Chaos, but when Equilibrium was established, he had pledged to uphold the right of his fellows to choose their own loyalties as conscience dictated. He'd kept that pledge for sixty years, and his successor, Chiro Piadar Lin, had been faithful to his example. Tirand, though . . . was it foolishness, Tarod wondered, or blind arrogance that had made him go against the precedents set by better men and try to turn the world on its head? Tirand wasn't an idealist in the classical mold. He had no vision, no shining goal, no burning spark of the true reformer; indeed, if he'd had such qualities, Chaos would have been a good deal better disposed toward him. He was simply a biased man, and recent events had fueled his bias to the point where he'd been duped into believing that his was the only wisdom and that that wisdom must be imposed on the world, whether the world willed it or no.

And behind Tirand's prejudices lay the bloodless, stultifying hand of Aeoris of Order. . . .

Tarod felt a wave of scathing contempt sear through him, and for a moment a black aura flickered into life about his frame before he brought it under control.

Aeoris, always Aeoris. He'd never accepted Order's defeat during the turbulent times of a century past, and since the day of the great battle between the gods he'd been waiting like a dormant but watchful snake for an opportunity to strike at Chaos and snatch back his old ascendancy over the mortal realm. Aeoris wanted all or nothing; for him there could be no half-measures, and in his eyes the war wasn't over by any means and wouldn't be over until one side or the other was utterly crushed. With Chaos compromised by the treachery of one of its own creations, he had grasped his opportunity to influence the Circle through its weak and inexperienced leader and to sow the seeds of a strategy aimed at upsetting the balance of Equilibrium beyond recall. Tirand wasn't truly to blame. His only real faults were his gullibility and the lack of confidence that made him too ready to capitulate to a greater power. If the High Initiate knew the truth, Tarod thought venomously, his views might change. The lords of Order were uninterested in the havoc that Ygorla and her sire might wreak on the mortal world; they wanted only to use the situation against their ancient enemy, Chaos. But to try to convince Tirand of that would be futile. Ailind, and through him Aeoris, had already laid an unshakable claim to the High Initiate's trust, and within the strictures of Chaos's own pact there was nothing Tarod could do to change matters.

He glanced again toward the silver door, and his mind registered the fact that Tirand had left the library and was on his way back to his own chambers. Returning his attention to the circle, he focused his will and raised his left hand, palm outward. The hall's pale mists shivered. A column of darkness materialized above the circle, and within the darkness, dimly visible, the spectral outline of a great black gate appeared. The portal stood open, as it had done since Karuth had performed the Speaking of the Way that brought it from dormancy, and beyond its dark bulk unnameable colors shifted and unnameable shapes moved in the void between dimensions. Again Tarod gestured with his left hand, describing an arc through the air. A chill, green-tinged aura began to glow around the gate, tiny, sparking pinpoints of light glittering about it like flecks of mica in rock. There was a warping of perspective, as though an image in still water had been suddenly disturbed, and the air in the dark column's vicinity shuddered briefly, suggesting that something had sounded a note far below the audible spectrum. As the shuddering ceased, perspective stabilized once more; and within the column the black gate had closed.

Slowly the image faded until both it and the acid-pale aura were no longer visible. Satisfied, Tarod lowered his hand, and the column of darkness also vanished, leaving only the circle, inactive now in the mosaic of the surrounding floor. In truth, Tarod knew, closing the Chaos Gate had little practical value as a precaution, for anyone who wanted to probe the Gate's secrets would need only to repeat Karuth's ritual of the previous day to bring it to life again. However, despite Tirand's foray to the hall, Tarod believed that no serious attempt would be made to use the Gate, and the link he'd now formed with it would ensure that he was alerted instantly to any speculative tampering. For the time being, at least until the arrival of the usurper and her sire, that would be enough.

He took a long, thoughtful look around the hall, seeing more in its dimensions than any mortal eye could have discerned. Then he turned his back on the black mosaic circle and on the seven statues of the gods looming in the pale, drifting mists and walked away toward the silver door.

———————⇒ ⊂———————

"I'm sorry, Karuth." Sanquar, her assistant and the castle's second physician, saw Karuth's rigidly controlled expression, and his tone was despairing. "I wish I hadn't had to tell you. But what else could I do?" He bit his lower lip in a mingling of embarrassment and sympathy. "It was only some of them. Not all. Not all, by any means."

Karuth knew that he was probably lying or at least exaggerating in an attempt to leaven the news, and she shook her head. "It's all right, Sanquar, there's no need to try to break it gently or pretend that it's only an isolated few. I'd have found out the hard way soon enough; better that I hear it from you rather than make a fool of myself." She set her medical bag carefully down on the table, resisting the impulse to damn self-control and fling it across the room. "It wouldn't be good protocol, would it, to ask who were the main objectors?"

Sanquar's cheeks colored, and he couldn't meet her eyes. To spare him, Karuth changed tack. "I'm only sorry that it means more work for you."

"I'll cope." Sanquar forced a pallid smile. "There's a senior healer in the Matriarch's party, Sister Alyssi. I'm sure I can enlist her help if the need arises."

"Yes. Yes, do, if you need to." She looked around the infirmary. "I don't doubt I'll find more than enough to occupy me here, and if anyone should suddenly decide that their need of a physician is more pressing than their distaste for me, I'll be available."

Sanquar winced faintly at the savagery in her tone. "It isn't that bad, Karuth."

"Isn't it?" Karuth looked down at her shawl and realized to her surprise and chagrin that she'd been unconsciously shredding the fringe; fine threads were scattered on the floor by her feet. "No," she added tightly. "Well, perhaps it is and perhaps it isn't. I don't know, and anyway I've only got myself to blame, haven't I?"

Sanquar hadn't been present in the council hall this morning, but the details of the meeting were now common knowledge, and he was aware of what had transpired. He said, "I don't agree. Knowing you, I've no doubt that you did what you did for a good reason. Besides . . ." He hesitated, then an edge crept into his voice. "When the first shock passes and people have time to think more clearly, you might find there's more sympathy with your views than you expect."

She frowned. "What do you mean?"

Sanquar looked defensive. "I'm not a Circle adept, so it isn't my place to predict or presume anything. But *some* individuals might feel less than happy about the secrecy that seems to have surrounded everything lord Ailind has done since he arrived here, including the fact that he wasn't even willing to reveal his identity to any but a chosen few."

Karuth was surprised. Sanquar rarely voiced a vehement opinion, let alone a controversial one, and to hear him speak in such a way took her aback. He saw her expression, and a slight smile creased his face.

"Don't look so startled, Karuth. You may accuse me of being biased, and I couldn't argue if you did; but I still don't think you'll find I'm entirely alone in my opinion."

"I . . ." She hesitated. "I wasn't aware that you *were* biased, Sanquar. I didn't know that you felt an affinity with Chaos."

"With Chaos?" Now it was Sanquar's turn to be surprised; then his smile returned, this time with a hint of self-mockery. "That isn't what I meant. I've never had any particular affinities where the gods are concerned, never really thought about it at all. My bias is in *your* favor. But then, you've known that for a very long time." He dropped his gaze, turned to take hold of his medical bag, and added, in a light and matter-of-fact tone, "I'd best start my round or I won't be finished before dark. I'll see you later in the day."

He left, and Karuth set about tidying the infirmary. She felt touched by Sanquar's last remark, yet also a little guilty, for, as he'd intimated, she had known for many years that he loved her. He had always suppressed his feelings, aware that they'd never be reciprocated, but they and the loyalty they engendered were as strong as ever. Karuth's conscience had never been entirely easy on the subject of Sanquar's unrequited love, but she reminded herself, as she'd done many times before, that she must not allow herself to feel responsible for his problems —and especially so now when, to add to the conflicts that already beset her, she had a new complication to contend with in the form of Strann.

In the cold light of the new day, and with the prospect of the council meeting looming before her, she'd had no time to consider the possible implications of Strann's reappearance in her life. She'd left him still sleeping in his makeshift bed on the floor of her room, and more urgent events had eclipsed all thoughts of the hours they'd spent together and of what their growing friendship might become. Now, though, the thoughts crept up on her, and she realized that—perhaps unwittingly, perhaps not; she didn't know him well enough to be sure—Strann had taken her by surprise and snared a place in her affections. At the late High Margrave's wedding, which seemed a lifetime ago now, although it was still less than two years, Strann had flagrantly broken all the rules of protocol to introduce himself to her and persuade her to play a duet with him, and despite her brother's disapproval she'd taken an immediate liking to him. He might have been a blatant opportunist, he might have been using her as a means to gain the ear of a wealthy potential patron, but his machinations had been to her pleasure and benefit as well as his own, and he'd had the honesty not to disguise his motives with flattery or obsequiousness as some others might have done. At the time, Karuth had suspected that they might have a little more in common than the music that had brought them together. Now, after a few quiet hours to get to know each other a little better, she was sure of it, and that was what had taken her unawares.

It had been several years since Karuth had allowed herself to enter into anything but the most casual of affairs. After the sudden and unexpected death of their father she had felt that her first priority must be to help Tirand shoulder the burden of his responsibilities, and even though Tirand no longer needed or wanted her support, she'd grown into the habit of avoiding any serious involvements. Now, though, she had a suspicion that her feelings might be changing. What Strann thought or felt about her she didn't know, and nothing would have induced her to ask him. But what had begun as a sense of comradeship in the face of adversity, and a wish to help an old friend at a time of need, was now becoming, at least on her part, something stronger.

Her mind turned the unquiet thoughts over and over as her hands worked mechanically to rearrange a few supplies that weren't in the places where she liked them to be kept. When someone knocked lightly on the door, it was a moment or two before she could gather her wits and turn, pushing back her hair, to call, "Enter."

The door opened, and Strann came in. Karuth felt her cheeks coloring, for an instant irrationally convinced that her inner thoughts were written in letters of fire on her face for him to read. The moment passed quickly enough, but she must have seemed wary, for Strann hesitated.

"I'm sorry, I didn't mean to disturb you."

"No. No, that's all right." She forced herself to relax. "Come in, please. In truth, I'm glad to see you. Glad to see someone who's willing to speak to me."

He closed the door behind him, and his hazel eyes, narrowing in a brief, assessing glance, told him a good deal more than Karuth would have wished. "What's wrong?" he asked quietly.

"Oh . . ." She shook her head, trying to appear careless. "Nothing. Or nothing that matters or was any more than I might have expected." She indicated the empty infirmary with one expressive gesture. "It appears that my patients, or anyway the great majority of them, would prefer to be tended by my assistant from now on, rather than have any dealings with the Circle's pariah."

"Ah." Strann walked slowly toward the fireplace. "I see. Then the meeting didn't go well for you?" He saw the answer in her face and nodded. "I can't say I'm surprised." A pause, then: "Do you want to tell me about it?"

To her own chagrin, Karuth realized that she *did* want to talk and that Strann was possibly the only living soul she knew to whom she'd be willing to confide her unhappiness and her fear. Still, she felt a constraint, a sense that to unburden herself to him would be to test a relationship that was as yet too uncertain. Torn, she hesitated, until Strann said, "Don't forget that I already owe you more than one debt. I promise you this won't go very far toward repaying it."

She looked at him, saw mischief in his eyes, and realized that he knew exactly what she was thinking and was teasing her for it. Abruptly her shoulders relaxed, and she gave a little laugh that sounded far more like her old, natural self.

"Strann, you should have become a Circle adept, not a bard. You'd show the Sisterhood seers a thing or two!"

"I'm not psychic. Observant, perhaps—and anyway I like to think that I'm coming to know you better than you think." He found a chair that wasn't cluttered with the spoils of her unfinished reorganization and sat down. "So. Tell your good friend Strann all about it."

Reassured and cheered by his attitude, Karuth did, unconsciously lapsing into the bardic manner of storytelling instilled by the Guild Academy of Musicians, which had taught her to combine clarity and accuracy with economy of words. Strann listened without interrupting as she told him all the salient details of the morning's meeting in the council hall and of its aftermath, and when she finished, he leaned against the chair back and let a long, slow, whistling breath escape between his teeth.

"By all the fourteen gods," he said, "I honestly didn't think the High Initiate was quite such a fool." Then, seeing her expression; "I'm sorry, Karuth; I know he's your brother and you may not like my saying it, but I'm not going to lie, even for your sake. He *is* a fool. Doesn't he want to see Ygorla defeated? Because if he does, then by siding so stubbornly with Ailind and refusing to listen to anything Chaos has to say, he's playing straight into her hands!"

"Tirand doesn't see it that way," Karuth said.

"No, he doesn't, because Ailind and his own prejudice have blinded him to the truth. You know that, but you're unwilling to accept the situation, or you wouldn't have taken such risks to champion Chaos's cause when all the odds were against you. Admit it, Karuth. If you don't believe that your brother has let bias get the better of sense, why didn't you simply agree with him and bow your head to Order's will?"

"All right," Karuth said, "I'll admit it. But it doesn't make any difference, Strann, does it? Tirand won't listen to me, and with the High Margrave and the Matriarch both in agreement with him, I've no hope of swaying the Council of Adepts."

"For now perhaps not. But once people have had time to reflect on what's happening and, more to the point, what *could* happen, that might start to change."

Karuth frowned as she recalled Sanquar's acid remark about secrecy and mistrust and uncertain loyalties. Before she could speak, though, Strann continued.

"Karuth, you feel a natural affinity toward Chaos— as I do, though I'm only now starting to fully realize it— and I can't believe that you're the only adept in the entire Circle who has such feelings. Logically it's impossible, or the entire structure of Equilibrium would have collapsed years ago and our only gods would be the gods of Order. Recent events have shaken people's faith in Chaos, but lord Tarod's arrival here is certain to change that. People will realize, if they haven't begun to already, that the Chaos lords *are* united with us in their desire to see Ygorla destroyed. They'll *have* to believe it; the evidence is indisputable. And when they do, they might just begin to ask themselves what really lies behind Order's machinations and what they really seek to achieve."

He heard Karuth's quick, involuntary intake of breath, and suddenly her gray eyes grew as wary as a wild animal's. Carefully she said, "You . . . believe that they have . . . a greater plan?"

"I don't simply believe it, I know it. Yandros stood as close to me as I am to you now and he told me the truth. Oh, yes, the lords of Order want to see Ygorla die —but more even than that they want to gain possession of the stolen soul-gem. And if they succeed, then you and I and everyone else in this benighted world may brace ourselves for the shattering of Equilibrium and all that that implies."

Karuth remembered what Tarod had told her: a return to the old ways that had blighted the world before the time of Change; Order ruling supreme and unchallenged; Chaos crippled, banished, its influence gone from the world. . . .

Strann said quietly, "I've never been a religious man, Karuth, but as a bard I learned the old stories, and perhaps because of my calling I've delved deeper into our history than most. Can you imagine what it would be like to live under a regime that forbade you to speak Chaos's name without committing blasphemy? Can you imagine yourself in the place of the innocents who were stoned to death at public executions because it was thought—only *thought,* mark you—that the color of their hair marked them as puppets of Yandros? Can you think, can you even *conceive,* of what it must have been like to live in a world where the only laws were the laws made by Ailind and his brothers?" He hunched his shoulders. "I can't. Or rather I think I can, but I don't want to."

Karuth had studied enough of the world's recent history to recognize and understand Strann's meaning, but she shook her head. "Strann, it wasn't like that! Only in the last days, before the battle between the gods—"

"When Order reigned supreme but feared that their supremacy was about to be challenged. Yes, I know. But if the balance is upset now, do you think for one moment that Aeoris will repeat the mistake he made a century ago? He won't. He'll crush anyone who even *thinks* to oppose him and consign their souls to the Seven Hells!" Strann's voice took on a hard edge. "It's already begun, Karuth. You told me so yourself. Ailind's edicts, Ailind's orders; what he did to you when you tried to defy him, and the warning he gave you. Remember that, and imagine what would have befallen you by now if you'd failed in your bid to call on Chaos."

He was right. Since the opening of the Chaos Gate and Tarod's arrival in the castle, Karuth had been protected from Ailind's influence, and it had been all too easy to forget the nature of the risk she had run. Others, though, might not be so lucky.

She said, "But will people realize what's happening, Strann? Will they see the danger—and even if they do, will they be ready to champion Chaos against Ailind and against the triumvirate? Because that's what it will mean."

There was silence. Somewhere in the castle's depths Karuth could hear running footfalls: a servant on some urgent errand perhaps, or a student late for a lecture.

Normality impinging, despite everything that had happened since last night. Even the presence of the gods in their midst hadn't entirely disrupted the mundanities of life. At least, not yet. . . .

Strann said quietly, "I can't answer that question, Karuth. I don't think anyone could. But—and I speak only for myself—if there's anything I can do, any way I can influence events in however small a manner, I mean to try." He reached out and took hold of her fingers, and she looked down to see that he was grasping them with his right hand, the hand Tarod had healed. "As I've already said, I've never been a religious man. But the thought of living in a world ruled solely by the gods of Order sends a shiver through me. It's not like my fear of Ygorla; that's something else entirely, something a thousand times worse, and I couldn't even begin to describe it to you. But it *is* fear. I believe in Equilibrium and I desperately don't want to lose it." He released her and studied his restored hand for a moment, then added with a flicker of faintly grim humor, "Besides, I owe Chaos a very great debt, and it probably wouldn't be wise to overlook that. So if it must come to this, if it must be a choice between Order and Chaos, then my loyalties are sure." Abruptly his smile faded, and something close to dread glinted in his hazel eyes. "When I consider the alternative, Karuth, I know in my bones that it's the only sane option."

The windows of Ailind's apartments in the castle's east wing looked out on the courtyard, a striking vista of stark black and white following a further overnight snowfall. Since his return from the council hall the lord of Order had been idly watching the comings and goings of the castle's inhabitants, but now he stepped back a pace, and his eyes refocused on the window glass rather than on the view beyond.

Quietly, respectfully, Ailind said, "My brother . . ."

The window turned to opaque gold. Light flooded from it, then the surface rippled and a figure with flowing hair as white as Ailind's own, and pupilless eyes like golden spheres in his aristocratic face, appeared in the arched aperture. Aeoris, greatest lord of Order, gazed out from his own dimension, and his light, mellifluous voice created whispering echoes in the room.

"Ah, Ailind. Do you have further news for me?"

"Nothing of any immediate significance, my brother." Ailind smiled reservedly. "Our cousin from Chaos has been unwise enough to tell the Circle the truth about Yandros's dilemma, but I rather think that he'll find less sympathy for his cause than he hopes."

Aeoris nodded. "That's much as I'd expected. And how do our own plans progress?"

This time Ailind's smile was broader. "The High Initiate has had no response from Summer Isle as yet, but I've little doubt that the usurper will accept his invitation. When she arrives, I think I've found the ideal morsel with which to bait our trap. One that her conceit won't be able to resist."

Aeoris's eyes narrowed fractionally as he read what was in his brother's mind. Then he uttered a soft, short laugh. "I *see*. That's a very astute ploy, and I approve it wholeheartedly. You'd do well, I think, to provoke your quarry a little before the usurper reaches the castle, to ensure that the ground is prepared and fertile."

"Even if it means running the risk of alienating others?"

"There's no danger of that," Aeoris assured him. "Where would they turn? To Chaos? I hardly think so! No; you can achieve your aim without jeopardizing the adepts' faith in us. Their mistrust of Chaos goes too deep now, and even if some have misgivings, they won't be enough for Tarod to play on."

Ailind nodded. "Speaking again of Tarod—he is taking steps to protect the gateway in the Marble Hall."

Aeoris shrugged. "Let him, if it amuses him and keeps him from trying to meddle in our affairs. We have no interest in the Chaos Gate at present; our concerns are more immediate. Which brings me to one last matter, Ailind: the High Initiate. After this morning's revelations do you think he'll still command the personal support of the adepts?"

"I believe he will, or in any event the great majority of them. There may be a few who resent the fact that he told them nothing of my presence here until Chaos forced his hand, but that won't count for anything against other considerations." Ailind's lip curled. "Karuth Piadar's perfidy has engendered a good deal of sympathy for Tirand that he might not otherwise have had. If anyone else turns against him and throws in their lot with Chaos, it'll likely as not only serve to deepen that sympathy as a matter of principle. And I've no doubts about Tirand himself. He's loyal, and he'll stay loyal."

Aeoris looked pleased. "Then Karuth may inadvertently have performed a service for us after all. How amusingly ironic. . . . well, I'm very satisfied thus far. Report to me again as soon as there are any further developments, Ailind. I shall continue to watch for any sign of activity in the Chaos realm, and we'll see what's to be seen when the usurper arrives at the castle."

Ailind bowed reverently. "My brother."

Aeoris inclined his head. His image vanished from the window, and the golden glow faded to leave only the cold, mean winter daylight filtering into the room.

5

"Everything's ready." Hair as black as pitch, with a steel-blue glint to it, swung and fell about the young woman's perfect figure as she paced across the dais, surveying the empty audience hall with satisfaction. Pent-up energy radiated from her like a psychic wave, and she turned to snatch up her favorite silver-gray fur cloak from where she'd carelessly cast it across the seat of the great throne. "Just four days. Think of it: just four days and I shall be *there!*"

From the position he had taken in the shadow of a marble pillar, Narid-na-Gost watched his daughter with unquiet crimson eyes. It was rare for him to venture into the Summer Isle palace's public rooms; he preferred to avoid all contact with Ygorla's court and stay closeted in the eyrie he'd created for himself in the highest of the towers. But with their departure imminent he had finally, if grudgingly, left his sanctuary to prepare for the long journey ahead.

Ygorla cast the cloak around her shoulders. Immediately two huge, sleek black forms, half cat and half hound, sprang to their feet from the shadows behind the throne, uttering throatily eager sounds. She waved a graceful hand at them. "No, my pets, not you. You are to stay here and see to it that no ideas of rebellion are entertained in my absence!" As the monsters subsided, she turned on her heel, and the blue eyes in her exquisite, heart-shaped faced focused piercingly on her sire's hunched form. "You're very quiet, Father. Haven't you anything to say?"

The demon shrugged. "What is there to say that you

haven't already iterated a dozen times over?" His voice was peevish. "You're excited enough to satisfy us both. Why should I exert myself?"

She knew the reason for his sullenness, and laughed. "Still harboring doubts, dear Father? You'll see matters very differently when we arrive at the Star Peninsula, I assure you. Besides"—she stepped down from the dais and sauntered toward him—"you seem to forget that you have as much to gain as I have from this venture of ours. More, if anything."

Not for the first time Narid-na-Gost's ear caught a hint of resentment in her tone. No, more than a hint; these days she was taking fewer pains to disguise her attitude toward him, and he was well aware that his old ascendancy over her was rapidly slipping. For seven years he'd been her teacher and her only mentor. She had looked up to him, admired him, she had been in awe of his power and obedient to his every word. Even in the early days of her reign on Summer Isle she had paid him the reverence that was his due and, more to the point, had been ready to listen and defer to him. But as she savored the power she had gained and began to feast on it, her confidence was rapidly outgrowing any notions of deference. The demon had expected nothing less; she was after all the child of his own creation, and to have her always subordinate to his will would not have suited his plans for them both. However, as her deference toward him had begun to fade, so also had her respect. Confidence had grown into arrogance, and now that she had power of her own, she was no longer afraid of Narid-na-Gost's censure, or even of openly opposing him. They had quarreled long and bitterly over her plan for a triumphal progress northward through the land to the Star Peninsula, and in the end it had been Narid-na-Gost who had backed down. To his chagrin the demon had realized at last that he had no choice but to capitulate, for Ygorla's attitude had been straightforward; she would go with him or without him, but either way she *would* go. And he had no power to stop her.

So, despite Narid-na-Gost's misgivings, all was now

ready, and Ygorla's black ship with its crew of animated corpses would sail on the morning tide. The demon wasn't looking forward to the prospect, although nothing would have induced him to stay behind, for whatever he might say to Ygorla, the lure of the Circle's stronghold and the means it offered him of reaching the coveted Chaos Gate was too strong. But there had been a further contretemps between father and daughter over the manner of their progress northward through the provinces. Narid-na-Gost favored a sly, swift, and secretive journey to cover the distance to the Star Peninsula in the shortest time possible, but Ygorla would have none of it. What was the point, she had demanded caustically, of being empress of the entire world if she could not flaunt her rulership in the world's face? She wanted her subjects to *see* her; moreover, she wanted them to grovel before her, worship her, feel and understand the terror of the power she wielded. Nothing less than full panoply would do. At sunset tonight they would land in Shu-Nhadek, capital town of Shu Province, and from there they would be borne across the land by a means of her devising, which she had refused to reveal to him, amid a procession of elemental and mortal slaves. From Shu to West High Land the people would learn to know their empress, Ygorla said gleefully, and they would learn the *real* meaning of fear.

Narid-na-Gost knew that nothing he could say or do would sway his daughter. Wise or foolish, she had the upper hand now, and the demon was beginning to realize that he might have made a grave mistake. He watched her as she skipped down from the dais, the silver cloak swirling around her and her houndcats purring their approval as they watched from beside the throne. At Ygorla's throat something glittered, something that was almost hidden by the folds of the fur but that showed just a hint of deep and intense blue light. The soul-stone of a Chaos lord, the gem that Narid-na-Gost had risked his own existence to steal and that was the talisman of their safety and the cornerstone of their power. Ygorla had taken it from its protective casket and now wore it on a golden chain about her neck, a blatant display of her contempt for any power that sought to oppose her. He had counseled fiercely against such a brazen challenge, arguing that, though the first battle might have been won, the war was still unresolved, and to underestimate Yandros could be a lethal error. Ygorla had laughed in his face and called him a coward and a fool, and that had been the end of the matter, for again he had not the power to argue with her. And there, he thought, lay the nub of it. It had gone too far; she was beyond his ability to control, and with the stolen gem in her sole possession she held the key both to his ambitions and to his safety. For seven years she had needed him far more than he needed her. Now, though, the positions were reversed, and Narid-na-Gost knew that his future was in her hands. He wondered how long it would be before she, too, realized that truth.

He said nothing as she swept past him toward the double doors at the end of the hall. At her approach the doors opened—the demon guards were thoroughly attuned to their mistress's will—and she stepped out into the passage beyond.

"My litter is ready," she said crisply, looking back over her shoulder at her sire. "I shall go on to the harbor to ensure that my orders for our departure have been properly carried out. We sail in an hour, Father. Don't be late aboard." Then she turned again, hair and cloak swinging, and the guards fell deferentially into step behind her as she swept away toward the palace's main doors.

From the beginning Narid-na-Gost's lack of enthusiasm for this venture had been a great irritant to Ygorla. She had expected him to share her avid delight in the prospect, to relish it, to make the most of it, but instead she'd been forced to listen to him carping and complaining and arguing that she was attempting too much too soon. Last night, during yet another clash between them, she'd finally lost her temper altogether and had stormed down from the tower to the audience hall to vent her rage on the hapless and unsuspecting court. Eleven of

her human slaves had died violent and ugly deaths before
her fury abated to a level of simmering but marginally
less deadly unpredictability, and finally she had screamed
at the rest of her cowering minions to get out, out, *out,*
and had sat watching her supernatural houndcats devour
the corpses they left behind while she planned revenge on
her sire.

Revenge, however, hadn't materialized. Instead, in
typically mercurial fashion, Ygorla had suddenly decided
to ignore Narid-na-Gost's cowardly carpings and behave
as though the latest quarrel, along with all the others,
hadn't taken place. Her temper had been assuaged by her
display of savagery and her sense of humor restored by
the terrified reactions of her court, and she had seen no
reason why she should allow her father's sourness to
spoil the pleasure she felt at the prospect of her journey
to the Star Peninsula and its aftermath.

She had therefore risen to greet the day of her departure in a good mood, and now as she approached the
great, pillared entrance, she dismissed all thoughts of
Narid-na-Gost and his complaints and focused her attention avidly on what lay ahead. One disappointment
clouded her horizon, but it was a small detail and not
enough to do more than mildly vex her. She had hoped to
conjure a Warp storm to accompany her on her journey.
It would have been the perfect final touch to have ridden
in her chariot with the howling choir of sound echoing
about her like the damned souls of unhuman creatures
and the great bands of color marching across the sky
above her head to herald her arrival to a cowed populace.
But her efforts to conjure a Warp had met with failure,
and after destroying any number of elementals in her
search for the secret she had finally conceded that it
couldn't be done. Or at least not yet. With time, she
thought. With time, and control of the Chaos Gate, and
mastery of other realms than this, it would be a very
different matter indeed.

She emerged into the fresh morning, into sunlight
made brazen and unnatural by a gloomy radiance that
shone down from above the palace. More of her demon

servants were lined up along the terrace, forming a guard
of honor; behind them, ranks of minions fawned and
bowed and waited, as they had been bidden, to cheer her
on her way. Her ornate litter, supported on the backs of
four hideous white mutant horses, was ready, its sapphire
velvet curtains drawn back for her. Ygorla drew a deep
breath, drinking in the atmosphere and not caring one
whit that its gaiety was a sham and bred of terror rather
than joy. She looked up to where the huge seven-rayed
star, the emblem of Chaos with which she had mocked
and deceived the world, hung above the palace towers
like a grimly pulsing omen. *Four days,* she thought. *Just
four more days. And then, Tirand Lin, we will see whether
you and your Circle are men of sinew or men of straw!*

When Tarod entered the dining hall, there was a general
scraping of benches and scrabbling of feet as people rose
hastily from their places at the long tables. The Chaos
lord glanced briefly over the faces of the adepts gathered
for the evening meal, then strode along the main aisle
toward the fireplace, where Tirand sat with the Matriarch and Sen Briaray Olvit.

Tirand stood up when he realized that he was the
target of Tarod's attention. His face looked drawn and
bone-tired, and his eyes were warily hostile. The Matriarch had insisted on heaping his plate with food, but
most of it lay cold and untouched; only his wine cup had
been refilled and emptied several times. Tarod saw the
uneaten meal and the flagon beside it and, a little to his
own surprise, felt a faint flicker of sympathy. Then it was
eclipsed by more urgent considerations, and he nodded
with brief courtesy to Sen and Shaill before addressing
Tirand directly.

"High Initiate, I think it would be as well for you to
know that the usurper has left Summer Isle and is making her way north."

Tirand's knuckles whitened where he was gripping
the table edge. "North . . . on her way *here*?"

"Yes. Don't bother to ask how I know or whether I'm certain; take it as a fact."

Tirand started to say, *"Gods—"* but checked himself quickly; no one used the old oath now, provided they remembered in time. He licked his lips and met Tarod's gaze with an effort. "Do you know how long it might be before she arrives?"

"I'd surmise four days or thereabouts. She could travel more quickly if she chose to, but she seems eager to make the most of her first sortie to the mainland."

Tirand frowned. "But we've received no message, no declaration . . ."

"That's no more than I would have anticipated. For want of a less complimentary word, she's mercurial. You'll probably find that a messenger of some form will come on the eve of her arrival."

"Yes." Tirand nodded. His eyes lost their focus, and for a moment he seemed mentally and physically paralyzed. Then, abruptly, he jerked stiffly upright. "I must tell lord Ailind!"

Tarod's lip curled cynically. "I think you'll find that he already knows, High Initiate, but hasn't considered it worth informing you." He paused, then, after a few moments when Tirand didn't speak again, added, "I shall leave you to do as you think fit. Oh, and if you find Ailind unwilling to keep you better informed from now on, your sister will more likely than not know where I can be found."

Tirand's head came up sharply at that parting shot, but Tarod was already walking away. The High Initiate picked up his cup and drained it, then bowed quickly to the Matriarch.

"Please excuse my hasty departure, Shaill. I must find lord Ailind immediately—I'm sure you understand."

Shaill gave him a look that, had he been less preoccupied, might have surprised him. "Go of course, Tirand, if you want to. But is there a great deal of point?"

"Point?" Tirand looked blank, and Shaill and Sen, who had been twirling a fork thoughtfully between thumb and finger, exchanged a glance. Sen shook his head almost imperceptibly, and the Matriarch, understanding, said, "No, it doesn't matter. Go, yes. I'll be interested to hear what lord Ailind has to say to you."

The High Initiate hurried away, and when he was out of earshot, Shaill sighed heavily.

"He's young and inexperienced, Matriarch," Sen said quietly.

She nodded. "I know, I know. But it isn't just that, is it?"

"Let him be for a while yet. He must come to terms with this in his own way, as must we all."

A glimmer of humor showed in Shaill's expression as she looked shrewdly at him. "What's this? The hothead Sen Briaray Olvit counseling caution? You must be getting old, my friend!"

"Perhaps. Or maybe I'm learning a few lessons I should have discovered in my lost youth," Sen rejoined. "Either way I don't think it would be wise to stir up dissent."

The Matriarch raised her eyes to survey the scene. Tirand had already gone out through the great doors, but Tarod, she saw, was still in the hall. The diners were watching him as he threaded his way between the tables, and when Shaill read the mix of expressions in their faces, they confirmed her suspicions and her fears. Then she realized where Tarod was going. She hadn't noticed the small group by the window, and the presence of one individual in particular surprised her. So, she thought, the crosscurrents were already starting to flow, and more strongly than she'd expected. . . .

She rose. "Sen, will you forgive me if I desert you for a few minutes? There's someone I would like to speak to."

Sen smiled. "Certainly. Provided, of course, that you're not just looking for an excuse to escape my company!" She didn't respond to the jest, and he frowned. "Shaill?" Then abruptly he guessed what was in her mind. "Shaill, take my advice and leave well enough alone."

Shaill gazed soberly back at him. "I would very

much like to do that, Sen, but I don't think I can. All is *not* well enough, you see. And I don't think I dare leave it alone any longer."

"Strann. I'm surprised to see you here."

Strann looked up as his name was spoken, and blanched.

"My lord . . ." He scrambled to his feet and knocked a flagon flying. Wine poured across the table in a wave and flooded over the edge, soaking Karuth's skirt before she could evade the flood. Tarod looked at the four stricken faces and, ignoring the gathering puddle on the floor, sat down at one end of the bench. Immediately Strann's and Karuth's two companions—a woman whose brown cloak marked her as a third-rank adept and a man some years younger—began to back away from the table. Their eyes, Tarod saw, reflected awe and fear, but underlying those emotions was a third: reverence. The Chaos lord smiled at them and said, "Don't leave on my account. As Karuth already knows, I have little time for formality."

The man swallowed, and spoke. "Thank you, my lord, but we've no wish to intrude. We were simply passing an idle hour. We'll take our leave and wish you all good night." He looked at Strann and Karuth. "Thank you for your company."

He took the woman's arm, and they moved away. Tarod stared after them for a few moments, then his dark eyebrows lifted faintly. "It's a pleasant change to encounter someone with a degree of self-possession," he said. "Who is he?"

"His name is Neryon Vargo," Karuth told him. "He qualified as a teaching master a few years ago and has stayed on as a tutor here."

"And if he doesn't take a little better care of himself," Strann put in suddenly, "he may well be the *late* Neryon Vargo before many more days have passed!"

Karuth hissed, *"Strann!"* and Tarod turned his unquiet green gaze to the musician. Strann was drunk, he saw immediately, drunk enough to have lost a good few of his inhibitions and therefore to speak his mind even in the presence of a god.

He said, "What do you mean by that, Strann the Storymaker?"

The deliberate use of his old if unofficial title brought Strann up short. He met Tarod's eyes, then abruptly sat down.

"Forgive me." He controlled his voice, though with some difficulty. "I spoke out of turn."

"That's nothing new, from what I hear of you. Tell me what you meant, Strann."

Strann leaned on the table, then realized that he'd placed his forearms squarely in the spilled wine. He swore softly, but the blunder helped to dispel the alcoholic haze, and by the time he'd squeezed wine out of his sleeves and met Tarod's eyes, his expression and his mind were clearer.

"I'm probably exaggerating the threat, my lord, but I have an unpleasant feeling that there's going to be trouble in the castle before too long," he said.

"I see." Tarod's face remained neutral. "And what form do you think it will take?"

Strann looked unhappy. "It's hard to know how best to put it, but . . . well, Neryon Vargo and his adept friend might have been the first to approach us, but they're not the only ones. I'm experiencing it, and so is Karuth. Friendly overtures toward us. They want me to play songs for them or tell stories, and they want to ask Karuth a lot of questions. Nothing unsubtle, of course, and at this stage they're still very cautious; after all, it's been only three days since . . . well, since . . ."

"Since my arrival here gave them the freedom to choose their loyalties?"

"That, yes . . . but there's more to it. Now that people have had a little time to think clearly, a growing number are coming to feel that they were deceived by Ailind and to resent it. They don't trust him, and—I've said this before in front of Karuth, so I'll say it again—

they don't trust his supporters, including the High Initiate. They believe that Chaos has acted more honorably than Order, and they're ready to say so."

Two young men passed their table at that moment. By the look of them they'd both drunk too much wine, and one was leaning heavily on his companion's shoulder as they swayed and staggered toward the doors. They were too preoccupied with the problem of staying on their feet even to notice Tarod's presence. Karuth watched them stumble by, then leaned forward, keeping her voice low-pitched but speaking urgently. "There have been quarrels among the students, lord Tarod. Factions are forming, and one or two of the clashes have already been enough to need disciplinary measures. So far it's only been hard words and the occasional fist, but if feelings start to run higher, it could soon come to worse than that."

Tarod nodded. Karuth and Strann had only confirmed the signs he had already gleaned for himself over the past day or two. The majority of the Circle still supported Tirand, and the more conservative adepts would continue to do so; if nothing else, they would feel dutybound to take their High Initiate's part and uphold his decisions as a matter of principle. But the voices of dissent were growing both in number and in volume, and as people came to realize that the powers of Order and Chaos were at a stalemate within the castle and neither had the advantage, hostilities on both sides were beginning to show more publicly. Tarod had heard arguments between servants, students, and adepts alike, had felt the atmosphere within the castle's walls growing grimmer and more tense almost by the hour, and he sighed inwardly at the stupidity of mortals. Wasn't the threat posed by the usurper enough for them? Must they also look for reasons to bicker and fight among themselves, rather than try to resolve their differences or at least learn to accept and live with them?

"Strann predicted this," Karuth said. "But I don't think either of us realized how quickly it would happen or how entrenched people's attitudes would become."

"Tension's at the root of it," Strann added darkly. "Waiting for some word from the south or for news from any of the provinces is fraying everyone's nerves. It's like a dangerous gas building up in a mine; if there's no outlet through which it can escape, then before long it'll only take one spark to trigger off an explosion."

"You put it accurately and succinctly, Strann," Tarod said. "It's a pity that you can't use your eloquence to convince a few of the unconverted."

Strann looked wryly at him across the table. "I'm pressing my luck even to dare show my face in this hall, my lord. It's only the knowledge that I'm under your protection that allows me this degree of public freedom; if I tried to take any further liberties, I'd get very short shrift indeed." He frowned. "That's what makes me so *angry*. People must *surely* realize that this squabbling is distracting them from the real threat, and they must realize the risk they're running by allowing it to continue!"

"Don't be too sure," Tarod told him. "Remember, to them Ygorla is as yet little more than a name. They may have been on the receiving end of a few small and unpleasant demonstrations of her power, but they've yet to experience it at first hand. That, Strann, is where you have the advantage—or perhaps I should say disadvantage—over them."

Strann was surprised to see both understanding and sympathy in Tarod's green eyes, and his face colored slightly. "Well, yes . . . I suppose that's true . . . though even if I *could* persuade these people to listen to me, I doubt if an account of my own experiences would sway them. As you say, to them Ygorla is too remote as yet."

Karuth started to say, "If only—" but she was interrupted by a sudden noise from outside the hall, audible even over the general hum of talk and clatter of plates: a crash, as though something or someone had fallen heavily, followed by raised but indistinguishable voices. Her physician's instinct for trouble assailed her, and she was already rising to her feet when a shout that mingled righteous anger with despair carried from beyond the hall's half-open doors.

"Stop that! Wilden, put it down and stop being a bloody fool!"

"Oh, no . . ." Karuth edged out from behind the table, ignoring Strann when he tried to call her back. Others in the hall were alerted too; several men were making toward the doors, and the Matriarch, halfway to the table where Tarod and his companions sat, stopped in her tracks.

Suddenly from outside there was a shriek of pain, and a face, wild-eyed, appeared around the doors' edge.

"For the gods' sakes, where's the High Initiate? And a physician—quickly, *quickly!*"

Strann shouted in alarm, "Karuth!" but she only called back, "Wait there!" and began to run down the hall. Shaill saw her and hurried to join her, and together they ran outside in the wake of the three men.

Emerging from the hall, Karuth halted with a horrified oath. On the floor of the broad passage outside, a young man knelt hunched over and coughing, both hands clasped to his stomach and blood pumping in a bright, gory torrent between his fingers. A crimson stain was spreading rapidly across the floor almost to the feet of another youth, his mouth hanging open and his chest heaving, who brandished a knife with a fearsomely long blade in one hand. A small crowd had already gathered, including two of the castle stewards. One made a tentative move toward him, but he slashed out wildly, forcing the steward to jump back.

"No!" Rage and alcohol slurred the youth's speech. "Let him *die,* let him bleed his filthy *life* away!" He staggered, and another wild sweep of the blade narrowly missed two unwary adepts. "He's scum; he's a liar, a traitor!" He sneered drunkenly at the crowd around him. "Just like the rest of you—all groveling and sniveling to that filth who calls himself lord of Order. I'll show you all! I'll show you." He made an effort to grab the knife hilt in both hands, missed, and tottered several paces across the floor before he could regain his balance. Sway-

ing, he raised the blade high above his head. "Chaos! Yandros of Chaos!"

Shaill clutched Karuth's arm. "Sweet gods, Karuth, he's so drunk he's out of his mind!" She looked quickly over her shoulder, raising her voice. "Someone, run for the High Initiate! *Hurry!*"

Even if they found Tirand in time, Karuth thought, it was unlikely that he could do anything. She'd placed the drunken young knife wielder now, as one of the two who had staggered past her table a few minutes ago. Wilden Kens, that was it; a second-year student and an arrogant, hotheaded idealist who was far too young to have learned how to hold his liquor. She couldn't imagine how in all the Seven Hells he'd been permitted to carry that knife, but though he had no skill, he was a deadly opponent in his present state; even the castle's most experienced swordsmen could be killed if they tried to tackle him. And his victim had to be pulled out of the melee quickly, or he'd bleed to death.

Karuth shook off Shaill's arm, shouldered between an adept and a steward who were both too startled to react in time to stop her, and stepped into the arena formed by the watchers.

"Wilden Kens!"

The young man blinked, swayed again, then recognized her. His face broke into a huge, proud, and inane grin. "L-lady Karuth . . ." He hiccuped on the second syllable of her name. "See what I did? He said we were demons. All Chaos's followers are demons, and Karuth Piadar's a whore, he said, and—and—there, you see, I defended you, defended your honor!" He waved the knife, forcing her to shrink back. "Yandros! *Yandros!*"

"Put that blade down, Wilden." Karuth's voice was even, but black fury simmered just beneath the surface. "Put it down, *now.*"

He shook his head mulishly. "N-n-no. He's got to *die.* Got to."

"*Wilden.* I won't tell you again." Slowly Karuth started to walk toward him, her eyes warily on the hand that held the knife and one arm reaching out. "Obey me,

Wilden. You've brought enough trouble on yourself; don't wade in deeper."

There was by now a considerable crowd in the doorway as more and more people emerged from the dining hall to investigate the fracas. Strann had fought his way through the crush with judicious use of elbows and heels, and when he saw Karuth moving toward Wilden, alone and unguarded, what had begun as unease spilled suddenly over into panic.

"Karuth!" he shouted. "Karuth, don't try to tackle him!" He started to push in earnest, struggling to get through the remaining press of bodies and reach her, but before he could make any headway, someone else came from behind him. The crowd were swept aside like cornstalks before a reaper's scythe, and Tarod stalked into the arena with eyes like death and a black aura burning around him. He made a single gesture, and the knife in Wilden's hand turned first red- then white-hot, before disintegrating in a shower of molten fragments. As Wilden screamed, clutching his scorched fingers, Tarod's left arm swung to deliver a powerful but entirely physical backhanded blow that sent him spinning backward and crashing to the floor.

"You stupid, mindless, ignorant *child*!" The Chaos lord's voice rang through the corridor with such venom that his listeners cringed back. "Haven't you any more intelligence than a *worm*?"

Wilden Kens started to cry; then his stomach heaved, and he vomited the results of an evening's drinking onto the flagstones. Tarod stared at him for another moment as the black aura faded, then with a gesture of withering contempt he turned away.

And came face-to-face with Ailind, Tirand, and Sanquar.

By sheer coincidence they had all arrived together. In the first throes of the emergency few people had realized that Karuth was in the dining hall, so the cry for a physician had sent a messenger flying to the infirmary, where by good luck Sanquar had been seeing a late-night patient. Tirand had been found in Ailind's apartments in the east wing, and the lord of Order had accompanied the High Initiate as he hastened to the hall. They were confronted with a crowd frozen into a tableau by Tarod's violent intervention, and for Tirand and Sanquar at least the scene had an immediate and significant impact, for Strann had by now reached Karuth's side and was holding her in a tight embrace, to which relief added an extra dimension. Sanquar looked at Strann with bitter understanding, Tirand with hatred. Then the High Initiate snapped,

"What in the name of every demon ever created has been going on here?"

The barked question broke the stalemate, and Karuth left Strann's side and ran to where the wounded student had collapsed facedown on the floor.

"Sanquar!" She supported the youth's body with one hand while the other slipped under his torso. "It's a knife wound to the stomach; he's bleeding to death! Bring your bag—"

Her words cut off. There was no wound. Blood still pooled in a slick on the floor, but her exploring fingers found only the undamaged cloth of the young man's shirt and no trace of even the smallest cut. Stunned and confused, she looked up. Tarod smiled at her and lifted his narrow shoulders in a shrug.

"He's an innocent victim. Why should he suffer for this fool's stupidity? He'll sleep for a few hours now, and he'll be no worse for his experience tomorrow."

A babble of voices began to break out as various witnesses tried to make their versions of the incident heard above the rest. Under Sanquar's direction the sleeping youth was carried away to be put to bed, and a steward and two adepts took charge of Wilden Kens, who, suffering under a combination of his drunkenness and Tarod's assault, was by this time barely conscious. As servants set about cleaning the floor, Tirand shouted for silence and, when the noise subsided, surveyed the crowd and asked again to hear the full tale.

The truth was very much as Karuth and Strann had suspected. Wilden Kens, leaving the hall after an evening's drinking and bolstered by it into a state of aggressive bravado, had picked a quarrel with a fellow student he met in the corridor and whom he knew to be a supporter of Order. What began as a slanging match quickly turned into physical violence, and Wilden had drawn the knife and stabbed his opponent, fully intending, as three separate witnesses confirmed, to kill him. Tarod and Ailind both stood aloof from the hubbub, and Tirand was hard-pressed to keep order as everyone tried to chime in with details, observations, and opinions. It quickly became clear that although everyone condemned Wilden Kens's behavior, some had a good deal of sympathy with his attitude, and as the talk began to grow heated, Karuth felt a hand close on her arm. She turned and saw Strann at her side.

"Come away," Strann said quietly. "There's nothing more either of us can do, and I for one don't want to get embroiled in another quarrel."

Karuth knew he was right. Adding her own voice to the many already striving for precedence would only complicate matters further. She let Strann lead her away back into the dining hall. Tarod saw them go, but made no comment and no attempt to stop them.

In the hall, which was empty now, they returned to their table, and Strann poured them both another cup of wine. Karuth listened for a few moments to the babble of voices beyond the doors, then her gray eyes met his, sharp and narrow with pain. "Can't they see, Strann? Don't they realize that in effect they're only carrying on where Wilden left off?"

Strann didn't want to go over it all again, and besides, he only had to look at her face to know that her question didn't need an answer. He picked up his cup.

"I'm going to get drunk," he said flatly. "And I'd strongly suggest that you do the same."

Karuth hesitated, then nodded. "Yes," she replied. "Yes, I think you're right, Strann. At the moment, it's the only option that seems to make any sense."

6

There had been another snowfall before midnight, but three hours later the sky had cleared again and the second moon hung low and sullen in the sky. The castle was silent, lamps and torches extinguished and all the human inhabitants if not yet asleep then at least in their beds. As he emerged from the door of the northernmost of the four towering spires, where he had chosen to make his quarters, Tarod paused for a moment to test the atmosphere underlying the apparently peaceful scene. As he had expected, tension was like a physical presence in the air, stifling, dark, and ominous. If human dreams and desires could be transmuted into physical form, the Chaos lord thought, then tonight the castle would be inhabited by a host of demons to match anything that his own realm had ever created.

A few minutes earlier, alone in one of the chill and long-disused rooms at the spire's summit, he had focused his will and his power to speak across dimensions to Yandros. He didn't need his brother's sanction for what he intended to do, but felt it as well to keep Yandros informed of what was afoot. In fact Yandros was already well aware of how matters stood in the castle; but he in turn had had news to impart to Tarod concerning Ygorla.

"She's already cut a swathe through Prospect Province, and it amused her to make a detour into Southern Chaun," the greatest Chaos lord had told him.

Tarod's eyes narrowed. "The Matriarch's cot?"

"Yes. She didn't do a great deal of damage considering her hatred of her old home, but she inflicted a few exemplary punishments and she's now carrying several hostages with her." Yandros's eyes changed color from silver to black. "I'll leave it to your discretion as to whether you tell Shaill Falada."

Tarod nodded. "And now?"

"She's in Chaun Province but moving east toward Han. Clearly she means to make the most of her royal progress." A pause. "If you carry out your plan, I'd suggest the province capital, Hannik, as a possibility. It's heavily populated; I imagine that Ygorla will be unable to resist the temptation to put on an impressive display there."

"Yes." Tarod nodded again, his own green eyes thoughtful. "Yes, I think you're right. Thank you, my brother."

He was oblivious of the night's bitter cold now as he crossed the courtyard and entered the castle by the main doors. The latch and the hinges creaked abominably, stirring yet more old memories, and as if from nowhere a cat materialized, running to him and purring loudly as it rubbed against his legs. Tarod smiled and touched a finger to his lips as though engaging the cat in a private and secret conspiracy. At a gentle mental command the creature scampered away back to the dark and its arcane prowlings, and Tarod's footsteps echoed as he walked through the vast, deserted entrance hall toward the gracious staircase with its carved banisters. There were a great many ghosts in this ancient place, he thought. Easy to imagine long-dead faces taking shape in the shadows, or to hear the voices of past inhabitants granted a brief, whispering return to life as they merged with the natural night sounds of an ancient building that was never entirely silent. Cold air wafting under a door might be taken for a sigh or the soft rustle of a skirt or cloak. A draft in the corridor, rattling an extinguished torch in its sconce, might imitate the small noise of cups on a tray or the scuff of a careless boot heel on stone. Smiling at his own fancies, Tarod started to climb the stairs; then, halfway to the top, paused and looked up.

Ailind stood on the long landing above him. With no

human witnesses to see, he'd cast off the small disguises that he used to keep a semblance of mortality. A faint, pale aura pulsed about his lean frame, and his eyes, without iris or pupil, shone like molten gold in the darkness.

He said, "I've been expecting you."

Tarod inclined his head and allowed himself the ghost of a smile. "I thought you might have been. Where shall we talk? The dining hall seems as good a place as anywhere."

"As you like." Ailind moved to the head of the stairs, and together they descended and crossed the flagged floor. In the hall the fire was out, and the ranks of tables and benches made hard, angular shadows in the gloom. They approached the hearth, and at a gesture from Tarod a bright blaze sprang to life in the grate. Ailind stared at it for a few moments, then turned to look his counterpart and adversary directly in the face.

"It doubtless galls both of us to acknowledge it," he said, "but in this, if in nothing else, I think we have a common cause that obliges us to put aside our differences."

Tarod swung a bench around toward the fire and sat down. "Your thoughts echo mine, Ailind." His emerald gaze flicked shrewdly to the lord of Order. "Something must be done. And after what I saw tonight, I'm convinced that none of our human friends can muster the authority to impose any control over this trouble. We must take matters into our own hands."

Ailind nodded. "It disgusts me to say it of Order's own servants, but they're rapidly proving themselves as foolish as the followers of Chaos." Tarod ignored the jibe, and the lord of Order steepled his fingers. "I'll be blunt with you. This infantile behavior among the castle's inhabitants must *not* be allowed to continue, for two reasons. Firstly it's clearly quite ridiculous for the adepts to be quarreling among themselves at a time when they should at least make a show of unity in the face of the usurper's threat. The more divided they appear, the weaker she will take them to be; and that's not in either their interests or ours."

Tarod nodded acknowledgment but said nothing.

"Secondly," Ailind continued, "I'm sure that it suits your purpose no better than it suits mine to be constantly distracted by these squabbling factions. We both have more urgent matters to concern us than the pacifying or chastising of blindly stupid mortals, and unless something is done to resolve the situation, then the only victors in this conflict will be the usurper and her demon sire. We don't want that to happen any more than you do. We, too, want to see Ygorla destroyed, for in the long term her survival is no more in our interests than it is in yours. But these contemptible rivalries are threatening to jeopardize us both." He looked up. "They need a lesson. A short, sharp, but effective lesson to teach them the proper priorities."

Tarod's face registered no change of expression, but Ailind's words confirmed the suspicions that he and Yandros had shared for some time now. It was no surprise to find that Ailind was entertaining similar thoughts to his own, but the fact that he had chosen to act on them could only mean one thing: Order *did* have a strategy in mind. Doubtless Ailind wouldn't admit it even now, but it was obvious; for nothing would have persuaded him to swallow his pride and propose an alliance unless he had a precise and urgent motive.

He smiled, though with a degree of irony. "I've underestimated you, Ailind," he said. "It seems that for once you're prepared to put common sense before your beloved principle. I wonder what could have prompted such a change of heart?"

Ailind didn't rise to the bait, but the corners of his mouth flickered. "Neither of us can afford to pay too much attention to principle under the present circumstances. Like it or not, we have to adopt a purely pragmatic stance for the time being, and pragmatism creates its own necessities. The lesson must be brought home to your followers and mine alike; if one faction were to be involved without the other, that would serve only to deepen the divisions and make matters worse. Neither of us can influence the other's servants, so, however regrettable it might be, we have no choice but to work together."

And work, Tarod thought, *toward whatever devious scheme you and Aeoris have formulated to achieve your own ends. . . .* But he kept the thought to himself. Ailind was no fool; he must realize that Tarod was well aware of an ulterior motive, so there was no point in elaborating the fact aloud. This move was to Chaos's benefit as well as to Order's; for if the trouble among the adepts wasn't nipped in the bud, there would soon be more bloodshed, and that would serve no one.

He met Ailind's unhuman golden stare and said, almost carelessly, "Very well. It seems we're agreed—and I have a proposal." Ailind looked surprised, and he smiled. "Let's stop pretending that we hadn't both anticipated this meeting, Ailind. I've been considering the problem for as long as you have, and I believe I have a fitting solution. I think the most effective way to bring our mortal friends to their senses would be to show them at first hand the manner of adversary they'll soon be forced to confront. And the best and simplest way to do that is by using the Maze."

The Maze was only one among many of the castle's devices that Yandros cynically called "the Circle's lost playthings." It lay outside the gates, on the stretch of sward clothing the granite stack on which the castle was built. To all appearances it was nothing more than a rectangle of unusually bright and lush grass; in fact it had properties that the adepts, in the peaceful years since Keridil Toln's young days, had forgotten how to utilize. Though the Maze was a creation of Chaos the lords of Order knew it well, and Ailind looked amused.

"Ah, yes," he said. "It was the cause of a good deal of speculation and effort a while ago, wasn't it? I seem to recall that some of the adepts tried to resurrect its secrets."

"They did, and they failed." Tarod's eyes glinted. "Less than a hundred years have passed since it was in regular use, but in that time they've not only lost the skill to operate it, they've even lost all records of its function."

"Perhaps they'll learn two lessons for the price of one," Ailind observed. "Very well, I agree with your suggestion, and I'd recommend that we choose a small party composed of our most senior followers to take part. If they can be made to realize the real nature of the danger, they should be able to muster enough influence between them to put a stop to this destructive, petty bickering."

Tarod nodded, then smiled with dark humor. "This is a rare day, Ailind. Chaos and Order in cooperation."

Ailind shrugged. "As I've already pointed out, pragmatism creates its own necessities. In the longer term, of course, it changes nothing."

"Of course. If it did, we wouldn't be what we are."

They exchanged a look in which untold centuries of a rivalry that no mortal mind could ever hope to comprehend were momentarily and devastatingly encapsulated Then abruptly Tarod rose to his feet.

"We'll summon them to gather here. I suggest tomorrow night, two hours before second moonset. The rest of the inhabitants will be asleep, so we won't be troubled by any intrusions."

Ailind made a mental calculation. "By then the usurper should be making her way through Hannik . . . yes, that's a sound choice. Very well." He, too, stood up, and glanced at the fire, which flickered once and died. "Until tomorrow, then. And let us both hope that this will produce the desired effect."

Tarod preceded him out of the hall, and for several minutes Ailind stood beside the dead fire, contemplating the results of the encounter. His face was inscrutable, but in truth he was pleased. He didn't believe for one moment that Tarod had underestimated his reasons for suggesting their unlikely alliance; but he was satisfied that the Chaos lord hadn't divined his third, unvoiced reason for wanting to put a stop to the adepts' private warfare.

It would not suit Order's strategy to have strongly differing factions within the castle, for differing factions meant a wider choice of options for any individual who should become disaffected with Order's cause. One such individual was to be the bait in the trap that Ailind and

Aeoris planned to lay for Ygorla—and Ailind wasn't willing to risk driving the bait into the welcoming embrace of Chaos's adherents. This development, he thought, when combined with enough suitable goads, would serve their plan very well indeed. . . .

The two lords had their own methods of reaching the minds of their human servants, and so in the dead of the following night seven bleary-eyed people were surprised to feel themselves compelled to leave their beds and make their way down to the dining hall. The choice of seven was coincidental, though it had a certain aptness. Tarod and Ailind had agreed that all three members of the triumvirate should be included as a matter of course, but they also agreed that the Matriarch, with her common-sense approach and her increasingly determined refusal to side with one faction or the other, was in effect neutral. Order's supporters were represented by Tirand, Calvi Alacar, and Gant Faran Trynn, a senior member of the Council of Adepts and a teaching master with a fearsomely strict reputation among his students. Tarod's choice comprised Karuth, Strann, and—to Ailind's surprise—Sen Briaray Olvit. Sen certainly wasn't known as a follower of Chaos, but he was the kind of man to accept the truth when it confronted him and to acknowledge his own errors; and that, Tarod said loftily, was likely to serve Chaos's purpose far better than blind loyalty.

It had not been a good day for the assembled company. The fight of the previous night had had repercussions that Tirand was fast coming to realize were beyond his ability to control. No one, it seemed, could even agree on a suitable punishment for Wilden Kens, and the clashing opinions that had led to further arguments in the wake of the incident were growing more sharply divided. A younger and sillier element had been inspired by Wilden's assault to indulge in private vendettas of their own, and though none of the skirmishes were serious, Karuth had been kept busy attending to bruises, grazes, black eyes, and even a broken arm after one of the castle's children had pushed another down a flight of stairs. The other members of the party had tried in their various ways to bring some influence to bear, but appeals to reason had little effect, and direct orders were increasingly ignored. So it was a tired and dispirited group that answered the summons and found the two gods waiting for them.

In as few words as possible Ailind told them what he and Tarod intended to do. They were to see at first hand the depredations that Ygorla was wreaking on the world as she traveled toward the Star Peninsula, by visiting Han Province through the medium of the Maze.

Tarod didn't know whether to be disgusted or amused by the mixture of astonishment and chagrin on the adepts' faces, and with only the faintest hint of irony in his voice he explained to them the lost secret that they had tried in vain to unravel. The Maze, he said, was a portal; not, like the Chaos Gate, a gateway between worlds but a means of making small adjustments to time and space. In the past it had been used to place the castle fractionally out of kilter with the world's normal dimensions, so that it became inaccessible to anyone who didn't know how to traverse the Maze's intricacies. By entering the Maze under his own and Ailind's aegis they would be able to witness what was happening at this moment in the town of Hannik. And the sights they saw and the news they brought back to their fellows would, so the two lords fervently and sternly hoped, put an end once and for all to the petty madnesses that were presently infecting the castle.

The seven mortals listened to the order in bemused silence. They had all been harboring private hopes that one or other of the gods would step in to end the growing troubles, but none had anticipated anything like this—and certainly they hadn't expected to find Tarod and Ailind united in their intentions.

Calvi, his eyes heavy from lack of sleep, ventured one question. He addressed it to Ailind, taking great care to avoid the gaze of Tarod.

"Forgive me, my lord, but I must ask . . . will there be any danger to us in this?"

Ailind's pale eyebrows lifted, and his expression grew cold. "Are you a coward, High Margrave?"

Calvi flushed, and the Matriarch said a little sharply, "The High Margrave only voices what we all wonder, lord Ailind, but unlike the rest of us he's not ashamed to admit the truth. That, in my opinion, is the opposite of cowardice."

"And to answer your question, Calvi; no, there's no danger." Tarod's emerald eyes focused on the young man, who found himself obliged, though very reluctantly, to return the look. "As I've explained, by using the Maze we will set ourselves slightly apart from the reality of Hannik. It will feel to you as though we are there, but we'll be shielded and therefore safe."

Calvi nodded, then stared down at his feet. He looked miserable, as though he were trapped between two equally unpleasant opponents, and Strann frowned, wondering at Ailind's supercilious and contemptuous attitude toward one who was, after all, one of his staunchest servants. No one else had anything to say, so Tarod suggested that without any further delay the seven should change into more practical clothing and meet again in the courtyard. Strann now had his own room, a small but pleasant enough chamber along the corridor from Karuth's apartments, and as they left the dining hall together, he took her arm and whispered close to her ear, "Did you detect something amiss in Ailind's behavior toward the High Margrave?"

"Amiss?" Karuth glanced at him. "No. It's nothing more than I might have expected from him. The lords of Order are cold fish, Strann, and they've little regard for human frailties."

"All the same, don't you think it seemed a little . . . excessive?"

She shrugged. "Not by Ailind's standards. Poor Calvi . . . I'm glad Shaill spoke up for him. I would have liked to say something, but I don't think he'd have appreciated it from me."

"Quite." A pause. "He's terrified of Tarod, isn't he?"

"He has reason to be, Strann." Karuth remembered Calvi's first encounter with Tarod, in the Marble Hall on the night when she had performed the ritual that brought Chaos to the human world. Calvi had tried to intervene, tried to protest Tarod's presence, and Tarod had finally lost patience with him. Karuth would never know the nature of the vision he'd conjured in Calvi's mind, but it had triggered the High Margrave's fear and his hatred in equal measure.

Strann, who didn't know the details of that incident, said, "Perhaps he has; I don't know. All the same, it seems to me that Ailind is bent on alienating him. Under the circumstances that doesn't make much sense."

They were nearly at the top of the stairs, and Karuth stopped, turning to look at him with a searching gaze. "What do you mean, Strann?" she asked, her voice suddenly alert. "What plot are you hatching that you haven't told me about?"

"I'm hatching nothing," Strann said. His voice, Karuth realized, was odd; there was tension in his tone that hadn't been there a few moments ago. "But I'm beginning to wonder . . . and it's just an instinct, nothing more concrete than that . . . if someone else might be."

Snow and frost and the low-hanging second moon had turned the night to silver. Karuth wasn't alone in drawing an involuntary, awed breath as their party stepped outside the castle's gigantic gates and the whole glittering vista of the stack and the peninsula beyond spread out before them. Far below, the ever-present sound of the tide surging against the great headlands was crystal clear in the stillness, but the sea itself was a vast, dark, and shining mirror under moonlight and starlight, while the sky overhead formed a deep, velvet-black backdrop.

Karuth felt one of Strann's gloved hands close tightly on hers and his other arm slip around her shoulders to keep her warm, but they were both too enraptured by the night vista to notice Tirand's quick, angry glare, Calvi's resentful glance, or Tarod's slight smile as they drew close together. Ailind had already walked on ahead. Like his counterpart from Chaos, he was careless of the bitter weather and wore only the lightest of clothing, and now he waited for them at the place where in the crackling, frosted grass a darker rectangle showed clearly on the sward.

Approaching the Maze, Karuth smiled wryly. "When I think of the hours that Arcoro Raeklen Vir and I spent searching among the old records for clues to this," she said, "I feel ashamed to call myself a sorceress."

Strann raised a querying eyebrow. "Arcoro who?"

She was surprised to catch herself feeling pleased by the thought that he might be jealous. "A senior adept who happened to hit upon the idea at the same time as I did." Then her face clouded. "He was one of those who went south to try to help the Margraves in their stand against Ygorla. We've heard no word from any of them since they left."

Strann squeezed her fingers. "Yandros grant they'll soon be safe home again."

He hadn't realized that Tarod was within earshot, and started when the Chaos lord's voice carried softly to him from a few paces away. "Yandros would, Strann, if it were possible for him to do so." He came to stand beside them and laid a hand lightly on Karuth's arm. "We're ready. This won't be a pleasant experience, and some may find themselves less prepared than they thought. Do what you can to help them."

He walked away to join Ailind, and Karuth stared after him. Her arm tingled where his fingers had touched it, and she felt a peculiar lurch of emotion within herself, something between fear and pleasure, together with the shocked knowledge that the Chaos lord had paid her a great compliment. Who, she wondered, would be the weak links? Calvi, certainly, and perhaps Shaill too; for all her worldly strength and wisdom the Matriarch had a rare compassion that might make her vulnerable. And Tirand? She looked at him now, standing stiffly and a little defiantly at Ailind's side, as though determined to display his unshakable loyalty to the world. Yes, Tirand was vulnerable. Far more so than he would have anyone believe; more, perhaps, than he knew himself. What she could do to help him Karuth didn't know. But forewarned was forearmed; at least she must try if the need arose.

Ailind stepped aside as Tarod approached the Maze. The Chaos lord made no show of it but simply spoke one word in a tongue that had been lost to the mortal world a millennium ago and stepped into the dark, grassy rectangle. Tirand glanced at Ailind as though for sanction; the lord of Order nodded, and the High Initiate followed in Tarod's wake.

They both vanished. Someone—Karuth suspected it was Calvi, though she couldn't be sure—uttered a small, shocked sound, quickly suppressed. Sen, with a characteristic shrug and a wry glance over his shoulder, followed, and Gant Faran Trynn stepped after him as calmly as if he were entering his own schoolroom. The others, Karuth and Strann and Shaill and Calvi, moved forward after them, and without pausing to think, without daring to consider for one moment what might lie in wait for them, they entered the rectangle together, with Ailind only a pace behind them.

Even Strann's bardic skills couldn't have described the sensation that swamped them all as they entered the Maze. Karuth felt as if she were moving in seven different directions at once, not all of them physical; the faces of her companions seemed to dart and swim at random around her, their astonished expressions almost comical. Brilliant light, black darkness, noise, and silence, and something that was neither and yet both all assailed her together, and she felt aware, *alive,* in a way she'd never experienced before. From a long, long way off it seemed that Tirand's voice was calling, *"Keep together! Keep together!"* but the words were meaningless and only made her want to laugh. Then suddenly came a sensation as of rushing through a huge yet claustrophobic vortex. Her surroundings inverted, everted—and the world returned to normal.

But it was not the world of the castle stack; not the clear, still, frosty, and peaceful beauty of the Star Peninsula. The first thing that brought Karuth's reeling senses tottering back to reality was a smell of smoke, acrid and vile, tainting the night air. Then she heard the noise. It had two major components. The first was an eerie, alien, and horribly rhythmic sound, like the slow crack of displaced air as many gargantuan wings beat the night in awful concord. And the second was the shrill, desperate din of a great crowd, cheering and praising and shouting as though their very souls depended on it.

Karuth felt the unmistakable, physical grip of hands holding her and pulling her upright as she almost lost her balance and fell. Strann's hair brushed against her face and his gasp hissed in her ear, and then with one final lurch the transition was complete, and she found herself standing huddled among her companions on the solid pavement of a broad town square. Fine rain was falling, but it wasn't enough to extinguish the flames of the torches that formed a great, blazing avenue that turned the darkness to a terrible parody of day. Nor could it touch the other lights, the flaring, twisting mayhem of wild colors that danced and whirled and seared and burned in the air above the procession heading toward the square along Hannik town's broad main thoroughfare.

Karuth saw the ten warped monstrosities, harnessed in pairs, that flew slowly and with dire grace along the street. She saw the vast, black open carriage sailing in their wake, wheelless, five feet above the ground and surrounded by an insane host of impossible shapes and forms, and she heard their ululating cries rising like the howls of the damned over the crowd's cheering. Rocking and lurching in the carriage's wake were two wagons, heavily curtained in black and pushed by more creatures that rightly belonged in a nightmare. And lining the square and the broad road beyond she saw people, countless numbers of people, soaked by the rain, shivering, shuddering, horrified, falling to their knees and raising their arms in hysterical supplication as they paid the homage of stark and helpless terror to the supernatural power that had enslaved them all.

Then, as though her senses had been suddenly and stunningly enhanced, comprehension had suddenly taken hold of her, and Karuth's eyes focused with awesome clarity. Twenty-one years rolled back as though they had never existed, and with the complete and appalling certainty of recognition her wild-eyed stare locked onto the beautiful, deadly, laughing face of the child she had helped to bring into the world: the daughter of Chaos and the deadly empress, Ygorla.

7

The people of Hannik had had warning of her coming. As dusk fell, a flight of demonic harbingers had come winging from the south, and as they hovered over the town, a huge, shapeless, membranous face had taken form in their midst and announced the imminent arrival of the Margravine of Mortal Dominions. Minutes later a horde of tiny elementals with shrill voices, needlelike claws, and barbed tails that delivered an agonizing sting had swarmed in mass invasion through every building and driven the townsfolk out onto the streets to welcome Ygorla.

The Margrave of Han had been foolish enough to rally his militia into a show of resistance. His house had been the first to be set alight, and now the huge blaze, fed by shrieking fire elementals, hurled an unholy glow into the sky on the eastern edge of the town, like a gory artificial sunrise. It had taken less than five minutes for Ygorla's host to shatter the militia's brief, brave, but futile stand. Now black beasts with razor teeth, gigantic cousins to the "pets" that prowled the Summer Isle palace, slavered and snarled over the warriors' remains, while the Margrave, bound in spiked chains, was paraded through the streets atop a hump-backed, eight-legged, giggling horror to demonstrate to the townsfolk the price of folly. Behind him stumbled his entire household; the Margravine, her three daughters and a son no more than five or six years old, and all their servants. Some cried out in misery, others were stonily silent. All had had their eyes put out.

After these pitiful victims, milling along under the

shadow of the flying beasts' wings like chicks under the guard of some monstrous hen, came more of the townspeople. They seemed to have been snatched from the crowd to swell Ygorla's retinue, and as the procession moved on, Karuth saw unhuman silhouettes darting here and there among the onlookers, picking men, women, and children seemingly at random and forcing them to join the grotesque parade. As they moved down the main street like a slow, deadly tidal wave, someone gripped her arm, and she looked up, her face stark, to meet Tarod's gaze.

"Move back," he said in a low voice. "Climb the steps of the building behind you. The vantage will be better."

It was impossible to tell whether the Chaos lord was moved by what he saw or indifferent to it. Ailind's expression was equally inscrutable as he ushered his own followers up the broad steps of an imposing house that fronted onto the square, probably the home of one of Hannik's many wealthy vintners. Beneath the house's portico they were sheltered from the drizzle, and the steps' height set them apart from the melee on the pavement below. With her view no longer obscured by bobbing heads and waving flamboys, the hideous enormity of the scene came home to Karuth like a physical blow. Her companions were also reacting; she could hear Sen Briaray Olvit swearing savagely, repetitively under his breath, while Calvi had covered his eyes and the Matriarch was whispering over and over again, *"Oh, the poor souls . . . the poor, helpless souls. . . ."* When Karuth glanced sidelong at Strann, his face looked like something carved from bleached wood; only his eyes, focused with terrible intensity on the street, were animated, burning with suppressed emotion.

Suddenly Tirand swung around. His face was deathly pale and his voice quivered as he hissed desperately, "We must do something! We can't stand by and let this continue!"

Tarod shook his head, and Ailind reached out to restrain the High Initiate as he seemed about to break away from the party and plunge into the crowd. "No, Tirand!" the lord of Order said sharply. "We can do nothing. Stay here."

Tarod glanced at Tirand with a hint of sympathy. "For once I agree with my cousin, High Initiate. Any heroic gestures would be utterly futile. Besides, these people aren't even aware of our presence; remember, our reality is fractionally out of kilter with theirs. We're here to observe, nothing more."

Tirand stared at them both in turn, his face stricken. For a few moments he looked as though he would ignore their warnings and follow his instinct, but abruptly the rebellious impulse subsided as he realized they were right. Karuth couldn't help but feel for him. She, too, was racked by the goads of frustration and rage and the extra spice of guilt at her own passive role. But she, like the others, said nothing, and they all continued to watched as Ygorla and her entourage drew unstoppably nearer.

The cheering of the crowd grew frantic as the procession entered the square. Everyone seemed to be trying to outvie his neighbor in shouting praises to the empress, and even children too young to understand what was happening were exhorted by their parents to add their voices to the din. Ygorla herself was clearly visible now, a small, solitary, but imposing figure in the carriage's high-backed seat, swathed in silver fur and with enough jewels to buy half a province glittering at her neck, on her fingers, and in the circlet that crowned her steely-black hair. Her eyes shone almost as brightly as the gems, but with an avid greed and ferocity that was demonic in itself, and her full lips were parted in a smile of fearsome triumph. Strann felt his stomach turn over as he looked at her, and he had to fight an instinct to cower back into the portico's deepest shadows. Even a glimpse of this creature who had been his personal tormentor and whose sadistic cruelty he had witnessed so often was enough to smash what little courage he possessed, and the fact that he was out of her reach, with two gods to protect him, made not a whit of difference. He hated Ygorla with all his soul, but he also dreaded her, and the hatred wasn't enough to overcome that primal reaction.

Tarod was aware of Strann's discomfiture but for the moment the Chaos lord had other preoccupations. He wasn't entirely surprised to see that Narid-na-Gost wasn't with Ygorla in her carriage, but he wondered where among this gaudy, ghastly spectacle the demon was hiding. Possibly he lurked in one of the black wagons, among his daughter's baggage, appropriate enough if what he had gleaned about Ygorla was true. There was no doubt that he was here—Tarod could sense his presence as a cat might sense the proximity of a mouse—but amid the mayhem it was impossible to locate him. Something else, though, *could* be traced with pinpoint accuracy, and Tarod's green eyes smoldered fiercely as they lit again on Ygorla. What he sought was invisible to the eye, hidden beneath the folds of her enveloping fur cloak, but he knew it was there. The stolen jewel of Chaos, his brother's soul-stone. He felt its presence, felt his own being respond to it, and experienced a surge of tight, bitter fury at the knowledge that it was beyond his ability to reach.

The convoy moved on until the first of the flying horrors drew level with the doorway where the castle party stood. Then Ygorla snapped her fingers. The carriage stopped smoothly and instantaneously, and she rose to her feet. All around her the throng fell silent, and as their noise died, a sense of suffocating tension pervaded the atmosphere. Somewhere, hidden behind the tall bulk of the Hall of Justice that dominated the square, the crackle of flames from another burning building became audible in the quiet. From another direction, and farther away, a human voice was wailing in the mindless monotone of utter despair.

Ygorla's head flicked around, and her nostrils flared as she heard it. Her fingers snapped again, and something greenish white and with no visible head detached itself from where it had been clinging to the underside of the carriage and flowed away in the direction of the distant, wailing dirge. Moments later the sound was cut off.

Ygorla nodded, satisfied, then turned to face the main body of the crowd.

"My people!" No human present, save for Strann, had ever heard her voice before. It was as exquisite as her face, Karuth thought, like liquid silver; yet with a cloying sweetness that made her shudder with intuitive revulsion. "My dear, good people! I am pleased with the welcome you have given me! You have proved yourselves to be loyal and obedient servants, and I deem you worthy of my rule!"

The tension relaxed a fraction, though still no one dared to make a sound. Then Ygorla smiled. The smile was pure, savage venom. "However, in one matter and one alone I am *not* pleased. Tonight as I entered this town to bring you the blessing of my presence, there were some—few, perhaps, but enough to arouse my anger—who in arrogance and foolishness sought to deny their rightful empress. Most have already suffered the punishment that befalls all who refuse me my proper homage. But that is not enough."

"Sweet worlds around us," Sen whispered hoarsely, "what sort of a monster *is* this?"

Strann could have answered him, but didn't, only huddled deeper into his coat and tightened his grip on Karuth's hand. Ygorla continued speaking.

"I want more than fitting punishment for the guilty. I want assurance, indeed I want *proof,* that no man or woman, no child or crone, not even the lowliest crawling *insect* in Hannik town, will ever harbor for one moment a single disloyal thought against their suzeraine!" She allowed a few moments for this warning to strike home, then went on. "But how will I know that this will be done? How am I to be *sure*? It must be proved to me. It must be proved beyond all shadow of doubt that the good and upstanding people of Hannik will keep the promises of fealty that they make at my feet tonight!"

A rising babble began to fill the square as the more courageous or more cowardly of the citizens—Karuth couldn't decide in her own mind which they were—protested their undying loyalty. Others soon joined in, and

Ygorla tilted her head like a bird, making a great show of listening and weighing up what she heard. At length she raised one arm in a commanding gesture. The cries and exhortations faded and died, and when silence had fallen again, Ygorla shook her head with slow, deliberate emphasis.

"Dear subjects, you touch my heart. But I am afraid it is not enough. Not *nearly* enough." She leaned a little over the side of the carriage and addressed someone or something in the shadows below. "Bring the transgressors."

There was a brief, scuffling movement behind the carriage, then the Margrave of Han, still chained and mounted on the eight-legged, humpbacked abortion of a beast, was led forward by a crew of chittering, cackling creatures, which bore a faint though twisted resemblance to misshapen rats. After him came his wife, children, and servants, kicked and prodded by more of the small horrors; they were herded together in the square where the crowd could see them clearly.

"This shamed and sorry man," Ygorla said in tones like syrup that made a parody of pity, "was the ringleader of those who thought to deny me, and with him stand the creatures of his household, who through their fealty to him must also be held guilty of his crime. And yet is it not true that *all* of you have in the past given fealty to this miserable traitor? Was he not your Margrave, and did you not all bow your heads to him?"

The throng shuffled uneasily. Ygorla smiled again. "Yes, of course you did. So you are also guilty. Is that not true? Is that not *just*? Indeed yes, it is. But I am a merciful empress, and I am minded not to bear grudges but to forgive. I forgive you all, my good and honest people. And as a token of my bounty and my leniency I shall allow *you* to be the instruments by which this sorry group of traitors meet their fitting end!"

Next to Tirand, the Matriarch cried out involuntarily, *"By all that's sacred, she can't mean to—"*

Tirand gripped her upper arms, hugging her to his

side. "Don't, Shaill. Don't say it; don't even think it!" He looked at Ailind. "My lord, surely she won't do this?"

Ailind shrugged, and Tarod said softly, "You don't know her, High Initiate. By her standards this is a harmless game."

The crowd had also begun to comprehend Ygorla's ploy, and those who didn't rapidly reached understanding when gaunt shadow shapes moved among them, handing out armfuls of stones. In the not too distant past, stoning had been the established method of execution throughout the provinces. Condemned as barbaric by the more enlightened Margraves as well as by the Circle and Sisterhood, it had fallen into disuse for all but the most dire crimes, but it wasn't entirely extinct, and every town of fair size still had its stoning post, stained with the gruesome evidence of former punishments. Now Ygorla's vivid blue eyes scanned the ocean of shocked faces around the square, and her voice rang out once more.

"Do your work well, and for each of these treasonous worms who falls to the stoning I shall choose but five more from your numbers to accompany them to the Seven Hells! But if you fail to please me, if you fail to convince me of your love and loyalty, then for each of these damned souls *fifty* more will feed my pets tonight! *Do you understand?*"

They did, and as, slowly at first but with increasing eagerness as desperation overcame conscience and humanity, the citizens of Hannik began to close in on their hapless Margrave and his family, Tirand turned in frantic appeal to Ailind.

"She can't mean it! She can't *do* it! The people—they can't, surely they won't—"

Ailind's face was grim. "Fifty of the townsfolk for each member of the Margrave's family, Tirand. Only five if the stoning pleases her. There's no third choice. What would you do if you were among their number?"

"But the Margrave—I know him; we all know him, he's our *friend*! And his wife's the sister of one of our adepts; she was born in the castle!"

Tarod looked over his shoulder. "And neither you

nor we nor anyone can do anything to save her! Don't you understand, Tirand? At long last you're seeing the real nature of Ygorla and the threat she poses!"

As though he'd been in a trance and someone had suddenly and violently slapped his face, the reality of their predicament came fully home to Tirand for the first time. Whether because of the old bond between her and her brother or because Tarod's harsh words had had the same effect on them all, Karuth, too, felt the realization hit her like cold water. She'd believed that she was fully aware of the situation; but in fact until this moment she had been one step removed from true understanding, shielded from it by her own ignorance. Now, though, she learned her lesson. The Margrave and his family . . . not faceless strangers, not mere numbers on a grim message from far away but real people, friends, helpless and about to die . . .

Her eyes were blinded by tears, and she didn't see the first stone fly from the crowd closing in on Ygorla's prisoners. But she heard the dull thump as it found its target and heard the anguished scream of the Margrave's youngest daughter as, blinded though she was, she tried to fight free of her captors and struggle to her father's side. A huge, suffocating pain flared up in Karuth's chest, driving the breath from her lungs and making it impossible to draw another. She clung frantically to the unraveling threads of her self-control, struggling not to cry out, not to scream as the Margrave's daughter had screamed, and she hated herself for her own selfish grief when it was *they* who were in agony, *they* who were lost, *they* who were dying—

Like an ugly and deadly hailstorm then, the stones began to fly. In the crowd women were sobbing, but even as they sobbed, they raised their arms and they hurled the missiles and they reached out to the black shadow shapes who brought them more. The Margrave was bound to his hideous mount and could not fall under the onslaught; instead he was buffeted like a rag doll, jerking this way and that, blood coursing down his face, down his arms, down his torso as the rocks found their mark.

Beneath him the eight-legged thing giggled hysterically, unmoved by the stones that rebounded from its hairless hide. Then the first of the women fell. Then the little boy. . . .

"No!" Calvi's voice shrieked out with no warning, and shock went through Karuth like a knife. She spun around and saw the young High Margrave clutching at Tirand's cloak, with tears streaming down his cheeks.

"No, *no!*" Calvi babbled. "I can't, I can't I *can't!* Stop it, Tirand—in the name of the gods, stop it, *please!* Get us away—if there's any mercy left in the world, *get us away!*"

Tarod and Ailind exchanged a glance, and Tarod nodded curtly. He spoke one word, the alien tongue again, and Karuth felt as if a huge fist had punched up from the stone beneath her feet and hurled her skyward. She tried to cry out, but her voice took wing and flew away, and then she was tumbling, tumbling, back through the vortex that took her apart and slammed her back together again, back through noise and silence, color and darkness, a titanic voice laughing—

The ice-cold north wind stung her face as she stood breathless and shuddering on the snow-covered sward of the castle stack.

Eight silhouettes stood beside her, etched against a sea that glared silver under the setting moon. For a moment they were all motionless, then suddenly Calvi's voice broke the hiatus as it had done only moments before in Hannik.

"It can't be true! Tell me, someone tell me—it isn't *true!*"

The Matriarch moved to comfort the sobbing High Margrave, but Calvi turned away from her. In the gloom his eyes scanned frantically for Karuth, and he ran to her, reaching out.

"Karuth! Oh, Karuth, what are we to *do?*"

His arms went around her and he clung to her. Karuth was appalled; she hadn't expected this, hadn't expected the breaking of Calvi's control to drive him to seek her embrace, and with a secondary shock she glimpsed the unconscious emotion that lay behind it.

"Calvi!" She couldn't cope with this now. She didn't want it at any time, but *now* . . . it was crazed, pathetic —it was a terrible presumption and imposition, and it made her bitterly angry.

"Leave me alone!" With all the strength she could muster she threw him off and pushed him away. Calvi stared at her, his face registering a bewilderment that only made Karuth more hostile. Like a cornered animal, she looked from one of the faces around her to another and another, and suddenly she felt that she was going to break apart. A small moan escaped her, and she turned from them all, broke from them all, and ran over the sward toward the castle gates.

Strann caught up with her in the courtyard. He was a fast runner, and the others were still some way behind him when he caught hold of Karuth's arm and pulled them both to a perilous halt on the icy and treacherous flagstones. He turned her around so that she was facing him, but he didn't say anything. For some seconds Karuth held his gaze, searching his face, trying to interpret what she saw in his eyes. Then she burst into tears.

"It's all right. It's all right." Strann held her as he might have held a child, her face pressed against his coat, his arms tight around her and one hand patting her back.

"Oh, Strann . . ." Karuth's voice was muffled by the coat and ugly with crying. "I can't face them!"

"You don't have to. They're a long way behind, they're not running after us. Come on." Gently he disentangled one arm and led her toward the main doors. "I'm going to take you to your room and make up the fire and get you a big flagon of wine."

"I don't want any wine. . . ."

"Yes you do. Come on," he said again, cajolingly now and with a tenderness that Karuth in a more observant state would have wondered at. "I'll look after you, Karuth. I'll look after you."

———————⊃ ⊂——————

The rest of the party entered the courtyard in time to see Strann and Karuth disappearing through the doors. Tirand and Shaill had taken charge of Calvi, now silent and subdued in the aftermath of his outburst, and they both drew their own conclusions. Tirand's face, already set and stony as he battled against his own tide of emotion, grew grimmer and unhappier than ever, and Shaill felt little surprise. She hadn't failed to notice the cautious but swift development of the relationship between Strann and the High Initiate's sister, but though she had strong reservations about its wisdom, she didn't consider it her business to interfere. Besides, they all had far graver matters to concern them now. After tonight, she thought desolately, all else was so trivial as to be meaningless.

Sen Briaray Olvit was the last of the human party, following the stooped figure of Gant Faran Trynn. He was aware that Tarod and Ailind were walking just behind him and he wanted to speak to them, but he wasn't yet sure if he could trust himself to say what was in his mind without his voice breaking, and Sen was proud enough to want to keep his composure. At last, though, as they began to climb the steps, he stopped and turned around.

Tarod and Ailind were two steps below him, and thus their eyes were almost on a level with his own. Sen cleared his throat.

"My lords . . . one question."

"Ask." Tarod smiled at him, though reservedly.

Sen nodded. "I like to think that I speak without prejudice. I believe, lord Tarod, that that's why you chose me to be among your party, although you know I have a loyalty to Order."

Tarod smiled again but said nothing.

"It's just that . . ." Sen hesitated, then suddenly the words came out in a rush, and with them the bile and the rage and the sense of unbearable helplessness that had been building up like a cancer inside him from the moment they returned through the Maze. "My lords, what *is* it that drives this monstrous woman? You tell us she's half human, but *surely* no human soul can have sunk to such depths as she has plumbed tonight?"

The two gods looked at each other. Neither needed any special insight to know what the other was thinking, and Tarod was aware that Ailind could, had he chosen to, have taunted him by alluding to Ygorla's Chaotic heritage. But as yet the truce between them still held, and Ailind focused his peculiar tawny eyes back across the empty courtyard.

"It grieves me to say it, adept Sen, but you touch on the crux of this whole dismal affair," he said gravely. "It's precisely the usurper's humanity that gives her the capacity for such barbarism." His glance flickered briefly to Tarod's face. "My counterpart of Chaos knows full well that whatever our differences, his essence and mine are pure, and untainted by the corruption that afflicts mortals. You must, I'm afraid, look to your own heritage if you're to understand what motivates a creature like Ygorla."

Sen looked stricken, and Tarod took pity on him. "Don't be too dispirited by my cousin's harsh judgment, Sen. I'll tell you now that we of Chaos—and the lords of Order, too, even if they're reluctant to admit it—have the capacity to do far worse than Ygorla could ever dream of, and the fact that we're not hampered by such grubby little ambitions as she harbors should make that statement all the more frightening to your kind. But as Ailind says, we are the *unadulterated* embodiments of Chaos and Order, and that means unadulterated by human greed and human vanity. In your present mood that may not be much comfort to you, but I hope that when you've had a little time to dwell on it, you might take heart from the knowledge that we have no more love for the usurper than you have."

Sen stared at them both. He couldn't speak, he didn't know what to say. But they had shocked him.

"Yes . . ." he managed at last. "Yes, my lords. I—believe that I'm beginning to understand you." He swallowed, then made a formal bow to each in turn. "I thank you for your frankness. And though the sentiment's hardly appropriate under the circumstances, I wish you both a good night."

"I'm sorry." Karuth drained her cup and smiled pallidly up at Strann, who stood beside the hearth rug with the flagon in his hand. "I've behaved abominably tonight and I should have had more self-possession. Will you forgive me?"

Strann smiled. "Have some more wine."

"No." She covered the cup as he made to refill it. "No, I don't want to get drunk. I've done that too often lately. It's a sign of weakness."

"Are you afraid of being weak?"

She considered this. "No-o. To be honest, I don't think I am. But tonight it seems . . . I don't know, I feel as if it would be an insult to . . . to them. . . ." Her voice cracked, and she put her knuckles against her mouth.

Strann set the flagon aside and knelt down beside her. The firelight shone warmly on his face, softening its lines. Trapped gases sizzled suddenly from one of the new logs, making a homely crackle.

"Don't be afraid to shed tears for them," he said softly. "A time has to come when you let the mask down, Karuth. You can't be a constant tower of strength to the world."

Karuth smiled, a quick, painful moue. "Am I so transparent?"

"Not to the world. But to me . . ."

"Don't." She put a hand out to cover his, trying to silence him. But he wouldn't be silenced.

"Don't tell the truth? Why shouldn't I? Especially to you."

"Strann . . ." But the words she'd meant to say

110

wouldn't come. Despite her protestations she'd already allowed him to persuade her to drink three cups of wine, and although she wasn't drunk by any means, she was mellowed, and the hard and terrible edges of memory and emotion had been softened. She tried to pull her hand away, but he grasped her fingers and held on.

"I'm not going to leave you tonight, Karuth. I'll sleep on the floor at the foot of your bed, like a jongleur to his patron or a dog to his mistress, to protect you from those bad dreams lurking in your mind."

Karuth looked up quickly. "Patrons and mistresses? Do you really have such a low opinion of yourself?"

A faint grin. "Yes."

"Then you shouldn't. You shouldn't. You're . . ." The words wouldn't come. She shook her head helplessly. "You're *Strann,* and I think that should be enough to be proud of. I think . . ."

"You think what?"

She knew, but she couldn't bring herself to say it. It wasn't that the habit had died in recent years; she'd never learned it because it had never been really true before. Now that it was, she couldn't find the courage to give it credence by giving it voice.

I think I love you. Crazy; insane. What was love— what did it mean? Not this, she thought, out of her depth. Surely not the certainty that this fool, this flighty, mercurial, untrustworthy jongleur—his word, *jongleur*—that this bard, this genius, this private and special man, was the *only* man she had ever met whom she could truly love?

She put her hand to her mouth again and laughed. Almost, she thought, *almost* she sounded like her old self.

"Strann, you fool," she said. "Stay with me. Please stay with me. And if you say one more word about . . . about sleeping on the floor, about being my dog . . . I'll . . ."—another wave of laughter; she quelled it— "I'll never, *ever* allow you to play my manzon for as long as you remain within these walls!"

She didn't want to have to explain any further. And when Strann reached out to take the wine cup from her, and his hands, light and gentle yet more sensual than anything she'd ever known, touched first her shoulders, then her arms, then her breasts, and his fingers closed and cupped in a way that sent a shudder of sheer, shattering joy through her, she knew that there was no more need for words. She turned her face up to his, met his seeking lips with her own, returned his kiss with a passion she hadn't known she could possess. For now, just for now, the horrors of Hannik and the monstrous threat of Ygorla slid away into an abyss and were gone, lost, forgotten. This was now; this was real. Strann was real. And something was happening between them that could heal the wounds and drive away the doubts, and give them both, even if only for a few short hours, something close to fulfillment and peace.

There was one moment, one tiny interlude in the sweetness, when she remembered what he was and what she was, and the pragmatism that had ruled both their lives for so long. She said, "I'm no virgin, Strann. And I'm not one of the pretty girls of Shu or Wishet or Southern Chaun who take life and love as they find them. . . ."

"No." Strann kissed her eyelids, and his fingers gently caressed her mouth, making her want to laugh without knowing why. "You're Karuth. *My* Karuth. Always, love. Always . . ."

8

The story that the seven humans brought back to the castle was enough to silence the quarreling factions. An hour after the cold, watery dawn had broken over the Star Peninsula, the High Initiate called a meeting of all the inhabitants, adepts, laity, and servants alike, and in the vastness of the dining hall, which was packed to capacity, the grim saga of the seven's experience in Hannik was told. Tirand, who hadn't slept since their return, had progressed past the point of exhaustion to a state of feverish, almost hypnotic energy. It wouldn't last, but while it did, he was desperate to ensure that no one would be left in any doubt of the enormity and urgency of Ygorla's threat. Quarrels, vendettas, animosities, he said with a bitter passion that shocked his listeners, were a base mockery when held against the reality of what they must steel themselves to face, and anyone with the arrogance to believe that their personal concerns had any meaning now deserved no kinder a fate than that suffered by the Margrave of Han.

"Seven of us have seen with our own eyes the madness that the usurper has unleashed on the world," he concluded as his hollow, haunted eyes scanned the gathering. "I entreat you, *all* of you, to take heed of the lesson that we've learned, because if matters go on as they are, if the quarreling and the disunity continue, then it won't be long before this castle falls as Hannik fell last night. And if that happens, you'll need no tales told at second hand to bring home to you the horrors of suffering under Ygorla's yoke."

Tirand's words, endorsed by brief but profoundly

113

effective speeches from Shaill, Sen, and Calvi, had an immediate and sobering effect. As the castle dwellers made their way out of the hall, Tarod and Ailind watched them, reading faces and the mood of the minds behind them and psychically testing the new atmosphere. Tension was still the overriding emotion, but the nature of the tension had changed. Already quarrels were being forgotten and grudges eased as individual personal concerns evaporated before this new and shocking awareness of the castle's common enemy. Tarod knew it would take time for the full impact of the revelation to take hold, and the change of attitude wouldn't be achieved entirely without setbacks. But he believed—no, he amended; knowing what he did of human nature, he *hoped*—that in two days' time, when by his calculations Ygorla and her entourage would reach the Star Peninsula, the castle would be united and thus prepared.

He caught Ailind's eye across the width of the hall, then looked away again. The brief alliance between them was a thing of the past now. Created out of necessity, it had achieved its purpose and become redundant, and relations between the two lords had returned to their customary state of aloof and contemptuous distrust. Briefly Tarod had come close to feeling mild regret at that, for there could be no doubt that the combined strengths of Chaos and Order were formidable, and while they were at a constant state of siege, a great deal of potential was wasted. That was doubly ironic when he considered the nature of the problem that had forced them into cooperation, but the small impulse of fellow-feeling toward Ailind didn't last. Ailind, Tarod reminded himself, was subject to the will of his great brother Aeoris, and Aeoris's aim was to smash the restrictions forced on him by Equilibrium and regain his old ascendancy over Chaos.

That led Tarod to speculate on what Ailind's next move would be. He had no illusions that the events of the previous night would have shaken Tirand Lin's loyalty to his masters of Order, and the High Initiate was likely to be a willing if not entirely witting conspirator in Order's bid to wrest the Chaos stone from Ygorla and use it for their own ends. Tirand would have to be watched, Tarod thought. A pity that he and Karuth were still barely on speaking terms, for her influence on her brother would have been useful. Still, there were other means and other methods. And one idea in particular, which had occurred to him last night as he saw Karuth and Strann entering the castle together, might be prove to be very valuable. . . .

Although the events of recent hours had ended the threat of open warfare among the castle dwellers, it couldn't obliterate the deep underlying divisions between the supporters of Chaos and Order. As the day wore on, it became clear that though differences had been set aside in the face of the common enemy, there was to be little agreement between the two sides over the question of how they might combat the threat that Ygorla posed. And for the seven who had accompanied the gods on their sojourn into Han Province, there were other and more personal difficulties to contend with.

The worst affected among them all was Calvi. Still several months short of his twenty-third birthday, he was, as the Matriarch said privately to Tirand, too young and too inexperienced for the role that had been forced on him since his brother's murder. Calvi's was a sensitive soul, easily moved and easily hurt, and though he had an innately cheerful nature, that simply wasn't enough to overcome the effect on his spirit of all that he had been through. Shaill decided it wouldn't be tactful to add that Calvi's miseries had been complicated further by the small incident with Karuth on their return through the Maze. She knew well enough that Calvi was infatuated with Karuth and had been for years. She doubted if he'd ever considered the thought that they might become lovers, for it wasn't that kind of a devotion, but he had long harbored a possessiveness toward her that went deeper than mere friendship. Karuth's loyalty to Chaos—and in particular to Tarod, whom Calvi seemed for some unknown reason to loathe intensely—had already ousted the young High Margrave from what he saw as his privileged place in her sphere; now he was faced with another and far greater rival for her affections, in the form of Strann. And Calvi was jealous.

Shaill suspected that Tirand was also aware of Calvi's misplaced sentiment, but she took care to avoid airing the subject. The High Initiate made no secret of the fact that he despised Strann, and he was clearly furious at his sister's attachment. However, there was nothing he could do. Having disowned her, both as her brother and as her High Initiate, he couldn't hope to influence her now, and he wasn't foolish enough to try.

Karuth knew that she was the object of a good deal of scrutiny and speculation, but for the time being she refused to let herself dwell on it. The sudden change in her relationship with Strann had left her breathless, bemused, even a little shocked, and she needed a chance to assimilate her own feelings as well as to gain confidence in his. Strann had told her that he loved her, and she believed him. But even now, even after the joy of their first night together, even after he had moved from his room into her apartments and they were living as one, she still felt unsure of him and unsure of herself. She couldn't help but wonder if perhaps they were both too worldly, and the pattern of their individual lives too set, for this newfound happiness to last. But whatever the truth of it, whatever the future might hold, she wanted to cling to this, and keep it, while she could.

That evening Ailind summoned the triumvirate to his quarters. It was high time, he said, to make the final arrangements for the welcome that the Circle would prepare for the usurper, and he had certain instructions that he wished the three leaders to pass on to their subordinates.

Tirand still wasn't entirely happy with the lord of Order's insistence that Ygorla should be welcomed to the castle with apparently open arms, and what he had seen in Hannik had deepened his doubts further. He feared that the supposed trap, the nature of which Ailind still hadn't revealed, could all too easily rebound on them and the tables be turned to Ygorla's advantage. If that should happen, then the Circle would in effect have surrendered the world's last bastion against her power without even token resistance. The High Initiate wasn't alone in his feelings; many senior adepts, including Sen, shared his fears, and even Calvi had voiced a view that the plan involved too great a risk. But Ailind was uninterested in their opinions. He had given instructions, he said, and he expected them to be obeyed. Did the Circle have faith in their gods, or did they not?

Tirand was alarmed by the ominous question and hastened to assure Ailind that his own faith was both unshaken and unshakable. As High Initiate his word was still law here, and he would see to it that the god's instructions were obeyed to the letter. Now, sitting uncomfortably on the edge of an uncushioned chair in Ailind's room, with Shaill and Calvi beside him, he listened as the lord of Order set out the course of action that was to be followed.

Ygorla, as Tarod had said and Ailind's own scrying had now confirmed, would reach the Star Peninsula within two days. When she arrived, Ailind told them, he wanted all three members of the triumvirate to welcome her with all the ceremony appropriate to the rank she claimed for herself—in other words, as though she were truly the High Margravine.

At this Calvi turned his head sharply away and uttered a soft profanity under his breath. Ailind's golden eyes focused sharply on him. "You have something to say, Calvi?"

Hunched on his chair, with elbows resting on his knees, Calvi looked hunted, miserable, and angry. "She murdered my brother, who was the rightful High Margrave, and she stole his place on the Summer Isle throne, and now you say I must bow the knee to her as though she were his true heir?" His voice was low-pitched and harsh.

"Yes, that is what I say."

Calvi shook his head. "I won't do it, my lord. I *can't!*"

Ailind frowned at him. "Are you stupid, then, as well as weak?" Calvi's head came up, but before he could protest, the god continued, "I have no time for fools, Calvi Alacar, nor for arrogant children who think to question the wisdom of their betters! You are here because circumstances have placed you in a position of responsibility, but those circumstances do not please me any more than they please you! You've already shown yourself to be more of a liability than an asset: don't try my patience further by believing for one moment that your entirely notional rank entitles you to an authority that you're not fit to wield!"

Shaill's jaw dropped at the sheer, harsh injustice of this statement, and even Tirand was visibly shaken. Calvi stared at the lord of Order for a few seconds, his face frozen. Then, with a convulsive movement that sent his chair skidding back across the uncarpeted floor, he stood up. Two high spots of color burned on his cheeks, as if the flesh had been scorched, but he didn't speak. Words had failed him, and even had he been able to articulate his feelings, he wouldn't have dared utter them to Ailind's face. Only his eyes showed something of his fury and his humiliation—then he turned, walked blindly, unsteadily to the door, and left the room. Shaill started to her feet as though to follow him, but Ailind intervened curtly.

"Sit down, Matriarch."

She turned, her face shocked and angry. "My lord—"

"Madam, sit *down*. You won't benefit the boy or yourself by running after him to mop his tears, and our purpose will be achieved more swiftly and more efficiently without him to hamper us."

The Matriarch looked in appeal to Tirand, but Tirand refused to meet her gaze. A shade more gently, Ailind added, "Calvi has a great many lessons to learn, and one of them is the lesson of his own limitations. We can't afford to have a weak link in our chain, Matriarch."

Their eyes met; the god smiled faintly. "Mother him later if your conscience still urges it, but for now we've more important matters to attend to."

Shaill couldn't argue; she wouldn't have known where to begin. Slowly she subsided back onto her chair, and watching her, Ailind felt a sense of satisfaction. Doubtless when this meeting was over, Shaill would seek Calvi out, and doubtless the remarks he himself had just made would reach the young man's ears. Well and good. It seemed that the seeds he had sown were beginning to germinate and take root. . . .

Calvi didn't stop until he reached the north wing. Then, in a deserted corridor lit only by two torches, which guttered in their sconces from a stray draft, he slowed to a halt, turned to the wall, and pressed his face against the cold stone. His pulse was pounding, and the rage was a bitter, seething gall in his chest.

Why had lord Ailind treated him in such a way? This wasn't the first time he'd felt the sharp edge of the god's tongue—indeed, he recalled now that Ailind's patience had been growing shorter and shorter in recent days—but never, *never* had Calvi imagined that it would develop into this.

What had he done to warrant such withering contempt? Resentment flared like ignited phosphorus as Calvi answered his own question. He'd done *nothing.* He'd been a faithful servant of Order, he'd supported Tirand and Shaill, and if his strength had been less than theirs and his experience lacking, gods, hadn't he *tried*? What more could anyone ask from him than his best?

Or was that it? he wondered savagely. Was he simply a child in Ailind's eyes and therefore useless, worthless, and best discarded? But if that was so, then why the charade of including him in the first place? Why hadn't the all-wise and all-knowing god simply patted his head, given him toys to play with, and sent him to the schoolroom to sit with the other children?

He was shaking now as reaction combined with the fury and made him feel physically sick. Aware that by this behavior he was only fueling the fire that Ailind had already set alight, he pushed himself away from the wall, jerked viciously at his crumpled woollen tunic, and pushed his hair back from his eyes.

And saw the cats.

They were sitting on the floor not three paces away, staring at him with that unnerving intensity that their alien eyes could express so uniquely. Two of them, one gray and one jet black with white paws. Calvi was disconcerted, for he'd always found the castle cats largely indifferent to him, and apart from an occasional and casual show of affection, he tended to ignore them. Now, though, there could be no doubt that he and he alone was the object of their acute interest. He hadn't the psychic talent to communicate in a crude way with them as some people did, but he could almost believe that these two felt sympathy for him and were trying to tell him so.

Calvi sniffed, wiped his cheeks with the back of one hand, and dropped to a crouch, holding out his fingers.

"Cats-cats . . ." he cajoled. "Come, then. Come and talk to me. The gods know I could do with a friend at the moment."

The black cat blinked, while the gray shook its head as though something had irritated it. Then abruptly both turned their heads as something new caught their attention. Calvi looked up and saw someone coming along the corridor toward him. For a moment he didn't recognize the newcomer, but then the long, fairish hair, the sharp face with its prominent nose, and the fact that he was carrying Karuth's manzon, all registered at once.

Calvi straightened, feeling something turn to stone inside him. Strann stopped.

"High Margrave?" He looked puzzled. Calvi chose not to acknowledge the fact that he also looked concerned. "Are you all right?"

"I—" Calvi's voice caught and he silently cursed himself. Recovering, he said coldly, "Yes, thank you. Why should I not be?"

A slight frown appeared on Strann's face, but he didn't argue the point. He nodded, made a small bow, and turned into a side passage that led toward the main staircase. As he disappeared, the two cats rose to their feet and padded silently in his wake. Calvi stared after them for a few moments. Then very softly he said something harsh and savage, which did nothing to relieve the emotions churning inside him, and walked away in the opposite direction.

When the sun rose on the day of Ygorla's anticipated arrival, the castle was ready to receive her.

Ailind's instructions had been carried out to the last detail. Ceremonial banners and tapestries, some unused for centuries, had been brought from the storerooms to decorate the great entrance hall, and more were hung from windows on the upper level, making a bright display in the courtyard. A suite of rooms had been prepared for the usurper's use and furnished with the best of everything, and in the great dining hall preparations were being made for a celebration ball to welcome the castle's guest.

There had been a good deal of indignation when this last move was announced. Even Shaill, who normally could be counted on to support Tirand in public even if she harbored private doubts, had spoken out vociferously against the idea.

"It's a crowning insult!" she had said. "It will be hard enough for us to keep up a congenial pretense in the first place, but to be expected to celebrate in *this* manner, with dancing and music and frivolity . . . it's little short of obscene!"

Other voices joined hers in the protest, but in the end Tirand, or more accurately Ailind, had his way, and the preparations began. Food from the castle's siege-depleted stores was made ready, the dining hall was decked out with yet more banners, and in the long gallery that ran the hall's width, above the vast hearth, the portraits of past High Initiates, High Margraves, and Matriarchs were judiciously removed. A good number of people resented this last gesture in particular, but again Ailind was adamant. Ygorla, he said, must be given the impression that the Circle was ready to capitulate. The presence of the portraits would be too challenging; they must come down.

Tirand supervised the removal personally and experienced a small frisson when he saw the paintings of his own father, Chiro, and of Chiro's predecessor, Keridil Toln, before they were reverently wrapped in oiled cloth and carried away. He couldn't help but wonder what Keridil in particular would have said had he been alive now to witness what was afoot in his old domain. It was comfortable to think that he would have supported the cause of Order as diligently as Tirand himself was doing, but somewhere in the back of Tirand's mind lurked a small shadow of doubt. He'd been only nine years old when Keridil died, but he remembered the old High Initiate well; such a powerful personality and influence couldn't help but make its mark even on the mind of a child. And he harbored a feeling that Keridil would have been far from happy with Ailind's continuing refusal to explain the full details of his strategy.

In truth Tirand himself was far from happy with the lord of Order's secrecy, and doubly so because he was aware that dissatisfaction was growing among the adepts and spreading even to members of the council. They hadn't yet reached the point of positive opposition, and he doubted if it would ever come to that, at least among those loyal to Order. But if they wouldn't dream to question the wisdom of their god, their High Initiate was another matter. His own position was in danger of becoming precarious, and whereas Keridil Toln would doubtless have known how to cope with such a situation, Tirand did not.

One factor, though, was clear in his mind. Whatever it meant, whatever personal sacrifices he might be obliged to make in terms of his standing among the adepts, he couldn't falter now. He had pledged himself to Order, and that pledge would stand. Anything else was unthinkable to him. He trusted Ailind, he was certain that his trust was justified, and it was his duty to communicate that to his fellows in any and every way he could.

The last paintings were wrapped now, and a file of servants, students, and younger adepts carried their last burdens away toward the storerooms. Tirand stared after them for a few moments. Then, sparing only a brief glance over the balustrade at the preparations progressing quietly and efficiently in the hall below, he turned and left the gallery.

The gray cat intercepted Karuth and Strann as they were leaving the dining hall after breakfast. It ran to Karuth, pushed its hard little head against her legs through her skirt, then with a chirrup turned its attention to Strann, weaving between his feet and purring loudly.

Strann looked quickly at Karuth. "It wants us to follow it."

Her eyes widened. "You can feel its mind?"

"No. Not that. I just know it." He hesitated a bare moment, then added, "I think lord Tarod wants to see us. And he doesn't want anyone else to know of it."

The cat made a peculiar yowling noise that with a little imagination could have been taken for emphatic agreement. Then it trotted a few paces away from them and sat down facing the main staircase. Briefly it stared toward the upper floor, then it stretched out a hind leg and began industriously to wash itself.

Suspicion became certainty in Strann's mind. "Our room," he said and, catching hold of Karuth's hand, led her toward the stairs.

She smiled, noticing his use of the word *our,* and went with him.

Tarod was sitting on the unmade bed when they entered Karuth's apartments. They both bowed to him, and Karuth started to apologize for the chamber's untidy state, but he dismissed her apologies with a gesture and a smile.

"Karuth, do I have to keep reiterating the fact that I'm not Ailind? Sit down, both of you." They did, and he continued, "It's important that no one else should know of this meeting, for I have something to ask of you that must by its nature be known only to the three of us.

"As you're aware, the usurper should arrive at the Star Peninsula sometime before sunset today. When she does, I have work for you both—and it's a task that you won't find easy."

Karuth said, "Ask it, my lord. I feel I've done little enough in recent days; if I can be of use now—"

Tarod's emerald eyes focused on her with a sudden intensity that silenced her. "Don't be too rash, Karuth. You've yet to hear what I want from you. As for Strann . . ." He turned to the bard. "Strann, you won't like this, but if you're ready to do it, then it will be a great service to Chaos. I want you, when the usurper arrives at the castle, to take up your old role as her pet."

Strann's face grew very still. "Her pet . . ."

"Yes. The reason's straightforward. I need a source close to Ygorla, someone whom she trusts—at least to a point—and yet who is loyal to Chaos and will pass to me any information he learns that might be of use. You are the only mortal who can fulfill that criterion."

Strann stared down at the floor. "Oh, no . . ." he said, in a choked, ugly voice. "Oh, no . . ."

Karuth gripped his hand, but before she could speak, Tarod intervened. "I think you know our ways well enough by now to be aware that I won't force you into this. I *could*"—for an instant the green eyes became lethal—"but it isn't in Chaos's nature to coerce its servants; that's something we leave to Aeoris and his brothers. However, I would remind you that—in your own words—you owe us a debt. I am calling in that debt now."

Strann looked up and met the Chaos lord's cool stare. And he wondered how in all the realms of creation he could have deluded himself for one moment that he or

Karuth or anyone else had ever been anything more than a pawn in the eyes of such a being as Tarod. He'd seen the truth back on Summer Isle when Yandros had answered his inept but desperate call, and now it was brought home to him afresh by the unhuman steel he saw in the eyes of Yandros's brother.

He could refuse. Just as he could have refused Yandros in the first place. He was a free man; he could ignore the debt and turn his back and say, "No, I'll have no part of it." But if he did, what then? He'd earn the gods' contempt, but that shouldn't be something to trouble an unreligious man. Chaos wouldn't take retribution against him. But . . .

He couldn't bring himself to look at Karuth. He didn't yet know her well enough to know what she was thinking, but what she thought mattered to him. He loved her. It was an indescribably strange feeling, and it clashed horribly with all the free-and-easy ways that had become his watchword over the years, but it was true, and it had trapped him. He wanted to be worthy of her. But what would be the greater worth in her eyes—to do what Chaos asked of him or to refuse for her sake?

He looked at Tarod again. Those emerald eyes; so cool, so knowing. Unconsciously Strann's right hand flexed, and he recalled his own words to Karuth only a day or two ago. Though owing him nothing, Chaos had wiped out Ygorla's cruelty and given him back the purpose of his life, and for that alone he was beholden to them. Fool that he was, dupe that he was, he couldn't shrug his shoulders in the face of such an obligation. Chaos's form of justice might be harsh, but it *was* justice in its fashion. And that was vastly preferable to the alternatives that faced him now.

He cleared his throat. Against the background of silence the sound was rough and intrusive. Tarod smiled faintly, and Strann returned the smile, though with an effort.

"I don't think I need to say it, my lord, do I? I must have a better-developed conscience that I'd ever imagined . . . but yes, I'll do as you ask." He grimaced. "Or

125

rather, I'll try. Though the gods alone know if I'll succeed."

Tarod laughed wryly. "If the gods knew, Strann, then I wouldn't need to ask this of you. But I thank you. Albeit as one pragmatist to another."

Tentatively, experimentally, Strann squeezed Karuth's hand, but there was no answering response. She was gazing at Tarod and she looked bereft, but she didn't speak. At last, when he couldn't stand the silence any longer, Strann said, "It makes sense, Karuth. You must see that." Still Karuth said nothing, and he added, "I won't be in any real danger if I keep my wits about me, and I'm a good enough performer to do that."

She shook her head violently. "It isn't that. It's the thought of . . . of what it will *mean* for you to have to play such a role again. After all she's already done to you. . . ." her voice broke off.

Strann forced a pallid grin. "There'll be one great difference this time. I'll be actively working against her. Believe me, that will give me a great deal of comfort."

"But . . ." then Karuth shook her head again. What she really wanted to say was that she couldn't bear the thought of losing him so soon. They'd had so little time together since their affair had begun, and now circumstances were to force them apart again. But she couldn't utter the words in Tarod's presence. She didn't want to parade her deepest feelings before the Chaos lord; they were too private.

Tarod, however, needed no words to tell him what was in her mind, and his expression suddenly softened.

"I understand your feelings, Karuth," he said, "And I sympathize, though you may find that hard to credit. Remember, I once knew what it was to be human."

She flushed. "I didn't mean to imply—"

"I know you didn't. But bear it in mind. And although you might not be entirely happy with the prospect, there's a way in which your difficulties may help our cause."

"I don't quite understand you, my lord."

Tarod raised his dark eyebrows. "I'm sure I don't

need to tell you that your attachment to Strann hasn't gone unnoticed in the castle. When he appears to change his allegiance, it will seem to those around you that he's abandoned you for the benefits of a return to the usurper's service and that his affection was nothing more than a sham to keep him amused until his true mistress's arrival. There will, I think, be a great deal of sympathy for you."

Karuth looked back at him, her eyes narrowing as though with sudden pain. "You mean that with sympathy might come a reinstatement in my brother's affections . . . and also in his confidence?"

"Exactly."

"Then you also mean that"—she hesitated as her voice almost broke, then pulled herself together with a fierce effort—"that I can't confide the truth to anyone?"

Tarod's eyes were sympathetic, but he shook his head. "No. Even the Matriarch, though she's a fine and honorable woman and I know that you and she are close, can't be trusted in this. It's vital that no one else should know, Karuth; the smallest hint of any deception could put Strann at risk."

He was right; she knew he was right and couldn't argue. But to be so isolated with her secret, so *alone.* . . . Karuth blinked back tears that, unbidden and unwanted, were trying to well in her eyes—then the brief flush of self-pity turned suddenly to anger. She had no call to lament over her predicament! It was Strann who was to have by far the worst of it, Strann who must sacrifice all honor, all dignity, all esteem . . . and Strann whose life would be in constant peril. Disgusted with herself, she blinked again, rapidly, and her back straightened.

"I understand you, my lord." Her voice had the stiffness of enforced self-control. "I'll play my part. If Strann's willing to do what you ask, then in all conscience I can't do any less."

Tarod smiled gently. "Thank you."

There was silence for a few seconds. Then Strann cleared his throat.

"My lord, in the light of what you've just said . . ." His hazel eyes conveyed an apology to Karuth for bringing the discussion back to a prosaic level at such a moment. "If it's vital that everyone here should believe my defection is genuine, then we're faced with a problem. Lord Ailind knows the truth; in fact when I first came here, he was the one who convinced the High Initiate that my story wasn't a fabrication concocted by Ygorla to deceive the Circle. When I appear to return willingly to her side, he'll know there's something amiss."

"Ah, yes . . ." Tarod didn't seem troubled. "I see your point; but in all honesty I don't think we need worry about it. Ailind may have read your heart deeply enough to know that your basic sympathies lie with us and that you're no real friend to the usurper, but he also believes that above all else you're looking to preserve your own skin at any price. When he sees your apparent change of heart, he'll think you've come to the conclusion that you're more likely to stay alive under Ygorla's protection than under mine."

Strann looked dubious. "Will he, my lord? If he can see into my mind—"

"He can't, Strann, be assured of it. As Karuth already knows, Ailind isn't quite the all-seeing divinity that he likes mortals to assume, and he can't read your individual thoughts any more than I can or than Yandros could when you met him on Summer Isle." He smiled with sudden dark humor. "If we and our cousins of Order were capable of doing anything more than gauge the fundamental leanings of our human followers, then, I assure you, life would be extremely dull for us and extremely hazardous for you!"

Strann swallowed, not managing to smile back, and the Chaos lord continued. "As I said, Ailind will think that you've decided to join the faction that seems most likely to win this battle. The High Initiate will think the same, and I'll make sure they're encouraged in their view. You'll be ignored—and I don't doubt that Ailind will find an extra spice in my obvious chagrin at your defection."

"I see." Strann nodded, relieved. "Then I'd best

make sure that I'm careful to avoid your gaze from now on, hadn't I, my lord?"

Tarod chuckled. "Indeed you had, Strann." He rose to his feet. "I think for the time being there's nothing more to be said. We'll need to plan the finer details of this, but we have a little grace. I'll leave you now—I don't doubt that you'd appreciate a few private hours—and we'll speak again later in the day." He started to move toward the door, then paused and looked back at them. From the levity of a few moments ago his mood had abruptly sobered, and his expression was serious and a little sad as he said, "I regret the necessity for this, and I take no more pleasure in it than either of you. But it may be Chaos's only hope."

Karuth looked away, but Strann met the Chaos lord's eyes steadily.

"I'm not in a position to judge that, lord Tarod," he said. "But I've enough scores of my own to settle with Ygorla. I don't pretend to be courageous, or motivated by anything other than selfish concerns, but if I can do *anything* that might help to see her destroyed, then that'll be compensation in plenty for any humiliation she may inflict on me!"

9

An hour before dusk, as the sun was westering over the spectacular coastline of West High Land, the warning that everyone had been waiting for sounded from the castle keep. The horn's brassy tones reverberating through the courtyard brought an instantaneous change in the atmosphere as the high tension of suspense broke, and fear and alarm were sublimated in a fever of activity. Under other circumstances many of the castle dwellers might have prayed to the gods at such a moment, but with the gods already in their midst there was no such solace to be had.

From his eyrie at the top of the spire Tarod saw Ygorla's cavalcade emerge from the mountain pass and onto the dizzying headland. The sky was clear and the sun hurled spears of blood-red light at the mountains' high ramparts, turning the great rock faces to walls of roseate fire. The ten winged monsters with the black chariot in their wake sailed slowly out from between the peaks, and around them like a dark snowstorm whirled a horde of shrieking, gibbering elementals.

The spectacular procession made its way over the sward toward the narrow rock bridge that spanned the gulf between the mainland and the castle stack. Glittering shapes were detaching themselves from the elemental swarm now, fanning out into a formation, and as Ygorla's harbingers soared toward the castle, Tarod smiled a faint and very private smile and turned from the window.

They would be waiting for him in the entrance hall. Ailind hadn't liked it, but there was nothing he could do to prevent his adversary from joining the welcoming party. The lord of Order had originally thought to hide his presence from Ygorla, but Tarod had dismissed that idea contemptuously. What manner of creature, he asked, did Ailind think he was dealing with? Ygorla was half demon; to believe that she wouldn't detect him as easily as a dog sniffing out a fresh trail was both cavalier and foolish. Ailind had been forced to back down, albeit resentfully, and now both he and Tarod were to accompany the triumvirate when they went out to greet the usurper.

As Tarod moved toward the door and the spiral staircase beyond, there was a stirring among the clutter on the far side of the room, and three small shapes rose from where they'd been sleeping on an old and battered couch. One of the cats mewed as it made to jump down after him, but Tarod held up a warning finger.

"No. Stay here, little ones. The usurper has no love for you and your kind. Better that you wait."

The creatures subsided again, and he left the chamber. As the door tapped to behind him, he made a slight gesture with one hand, and the dark stairwell seemed momentarily to invert before he was standing at the spire's foot with the outer door open before him. As he stepped outside, Ygorla's harbingers appeared above the high black outer wall. Light showered down on the courtyard, rivaling the last of the sunset, and a sweet, singing note filled the air. Tarod smiled cynically at the usurper's blatant display, and turned toward the main doors.

The mechanism that operated the castle's great gates shifted into action with a deep grinding and rumbling that vibrated through every stone. As the gates began to grate back, crimson light flooded the courtyard to highlight the figures who stood waiting beyond the keep, and the horn that had announced Ygorla's coming now sounded again to herald the emergence of her hosts.

Tirand was dressed in the full ceremonial garb of the High Initiate, with a gold circlet on his head and a high-collared golden cloak flowing over his shoulders to his feet. Walking beside him, her arm stiffly and formally laid over his, the Matriarch was magnificent in pristine white, her face and the expression on it hidden behind a silver veil. Tarod and Ailind followed, their plain and almost careless garb in severe contrast to the pair's splendor, while in the courtyard behind them a phalanx of chosen adepts and sisters took their places on the steps to form a guard of honor. Calvi, however, was absent from the party. Tarod had noted this and had his suspicions as to the reason, but a casual query to Shaill had produced an evasive answer, and the Chaos lord wasn't inclined to press the subject.

The gates were fully open now. Under the arch the two gods halted and waited, watching, as Tirand and Shaill walked solemnly out onto the sward of the stack. As the pair emerged, the singing of Ygorla's whirling elemental heralds rose in pitch and excitement, and at the same moment the usurper and her followers reached the bridge.

The cavalcade stopped, and briefly the entire tableau was frozen as though captured in a single, timeless instant. Then the small, solitary figure in the floating carriage turned and raised one white arm in an imperious gesture.

Her entourage, from the misshapen things that cavorted about the carriage to the swirling, singing flitterers above the castle walls, vanished. The Matriarch started violently, prompting Tirand to reach out to her and steady her, and even across the distance that separated them the castle party could hear Ygorla's bright, brittle laughter. Then the remains of the procession began to move again. The black carriage advanced over the bridge, and behind it, rocking precariously on the narrow span, came the two curtained wagons that had followed the usurper in her grim progress through Hannik.

They crossed the bridge, and the carriage came to a halt. Less than thirty yards separated the two parties now, and Tirand and the Matriarch began to advance across the sward. The ten winged monsters settled on the ground, lurching and then folding their wings like giant bats, and the carriage hovered for a few moments before drifting gently to the grass in its turn.

From the castle keep came the renewed sound of horns as a fanfare rang out. Taking his prearranged cue, Tirand released the Matriarch's arm and walked on alone toward the carriage. The grounded horrors grinned at him, showing forests of yellow teeth; doing his best to ignore them, Tirand halted and made a sweeping formal bow.

"Lady." He had learned the art of projection, and his voice carried clearly and authoritatively as he spoke the words in which Ailind had carefully schooled him. "You do us inexpressible honor by condescending to grace us with your presence here. As High Initiate of the Circle it is both my duty and my delight to welcome you to the Star Peninsula and to lay at your feet all that our hospitality can offer."

Gazing from her chariot at Tirand's solitary figure, Ygorla felt a thrill of dizzying excitement. This was the moment for which her journey and all its triumphs had been a mere and now irrelevant rehearsal. Here was the High Initiate in the flesh, abasing himself before her as he threw open the gates of his stronghold. And behind him, not daring to come closer, the Matriarch of the Sisterhood in the full ceremonial regalia that Ygorla remembered so well from her own childhood at Southern Chaun. And the castle itself, decorated as though for a great festival and all in her honor. *Yes,* she thought, *oh, yes. My pet rat has done his work well. If they've let him live, he shall be rewarded for this. . . .*

But where was the third member of the triumvirate? She knew that Blis Hanmen Alacar's brother was at the castle and doubtless still whining over his family's demise. Likely as not he hadn't the courage to show his face in her presence, and that, too, pleased her.

Tirand was waiting for her to respond to his greeting. She paused a few moments longer, just enough, she judged, to make him uncomfortable and uneasy. Then with a graceful movement she rose to her feet, sweeping her fur cloak dramatically around her frame.

"My dear High Initiate!" She spoke as though to a much-loved but inferior friend, and in the sweetest of tones. "I am quite *overwhelmed* by your welcome. And the Matriarch, in person . . . I'm doubly flattered!" A moment's hesitation. "But surely there's someone missing? Where is my predecessor's young brother, Calvi Alacar?"

Tirand's face became wooden. "Calvi is—ah—indisposed, lady. He regrets deeply that he is unable to join us in greeting you."

Ygorla smiled agreeably. "I'm sure he does. A pity. I'd greatly looked forward to meeting him. Ah well, it seems I must endure my disappointment and curb my eagerness a while longer."

And from the arch of the castle gates a new voice said, "Perhaps, madam, we can compensate in some measure for the High Margrave's absence?"

Ygorla's head came up sharply, and she froze. Tarod had emerged from the shadows of the arch and was walking calmly and unhurriedly across the sward. At the same instant the usurper felt a violent psychic jolt as from within one of the curtained wagons Narid-na-Gost sensed the Chaos lord's presence.

Tarod smiled. "Greetings, Empress."

She didn't miss the venomous undercurrent in his tone, and a slight smile appeared on her face.

"Sir," she said sweetly. "I don't believe I have had the pleasure of your acquaintance."

She knew what he was, but his name was as yet unknown to her. Tarod returned the smile, his eyes coolly assessing her. "I am Tarod, brother to Yandros," he said.

"Ah . . . *that* one. But—your pardon if I'm mistaken, but I thought you said 'we' . . . ?"

"Indeed." The Chaos lord gestured toward the castle. "May I present my cousin and counterpart, Ailind of Order."

Ailind emerged from the gateway. He didn't speak, didn't acknowledge Tarod, but only raked the scene before him with a look of undisguised disgust. For a few seconds Ygorla stared at him with something like wonderment; then her smile broadened to a grin and she gave vent to a peal of delighted laughter.

"Oh, but this is splendid! Not content with sending the High Initiate and the Matriarch do me homage, even the gods themselves have come to pay their compliments! I am *enchanted*!" She tossed her hair back, and the laughter broke out afresh. She hadn't expected this, but in the wake of the initial momentary shock she saw suddenly what this new development meant. The lords of Order and Chaos had shown their hands, for the bare fact of their presence in the castle revealed the degree of anxiety and apprehension that she had created in the higher realms. With a rush of heady elation she realized that the gods feared her, while she in turn had nothing to fear from them. That pale, anemic creature of Order had no power to touch her, and Tarod, though he might have the power, wouldn't dare to use it for fear of jeopardizing his brother's soul-stone. She was invulnerable, and the knowledge amused her hugely, for it opened up an entire new spectrum of possibilities. Chaos and Order—she could play them off one against the other, tease them, mock them, and enjoy the spectacle of watching them dance to whatever music she chose to play. Oh, but this would be entertainment of a new and rare kind!

Her laughter had subsided, but the predatory smile still remained on her lips as with a regal air she rose from her seat and, deliberately ignoring Tarod and Ailind, extended a slim, velvet-clad arm toward the High Initiate.

"Tirand—I may call you Tirand? I thank you for your welcome, and I am very gratified to return at last to the place of my birth." Her ungloved hand curled, beckoning, and the priceless gems in her bracelets and rings glittered in the sunset light. "I shall now be pleased to allow you to escort me into the castle."

Tirand glanced at Ailind as though for a prompt, and the lord of Order nodded just perceptibly. The High

Initiate stepped forward, then hesitated as he realized
that the ten winged horrors still blocked his way. One of
them opened its jaws in a lazy yawn, and its eyes seemed
to laugh at him.

"Lady," Tirand said, trying not to back away again,
"we have no suitable stabling for your . . . for
the . . ."

Ygorla lifted her perfect eyebrows. "Oh, these?" she
said carelessly. "They are nothing. I shall dismiss them."
She snapped her fingers.

The ten demonic creatures dissolved. It was like
watching parchment consumed by fire; they simply shriveled, wasted, twisted out of shape, and crumbled to small
heaps of ash, which then merged into the grass and vanished. A smell like badly rotted meat whisked past the
High Initiate's nostrils briefly before fading. Ygorla
smiled daintily.

"There. They are gone and you may forget them."
She gestured back over her shoulder at the two wagons,
still and silent behind the carriage. "My requirements, as
you see, are quite modest, and I have only these two
small vehicles to be housed within your walls. One contains the few personal effects that I might need, and the
other . . . well, dear Tirand, I confess that I have
brought a small gift for you. I *do* hope that you'll accept
it, as a token of my esteem and goodwill!"

Tirand was thrown. The usurper's careless destruction of the winged beasts had already disconcerted him,
and he suspected some ulterior motive behind this new
gesture. Again he looked back, a silent appeal for help in
his eyes, but Tarod ignored him, and Ailind only pursed
his lips in a faint moue that implied he wanted no say in
the matter.

Feeling that he had no other option, Tirand inclined
his head. "Madam, you are too gracious." There was no
putting off the moment now, and though he flinched inwardly at the thought of so much as touching this woman's skin, he stepped forward. Ygorla caught hold of his
upraised hand in firm, cool fingers and stepped lightly,
almost negligently down from the carriage. As she

alighted beside him, Tirand was surprised by how small she was; the crown of her head barely topped his shoulder, and he wasn't a tall man. She looked up at him and her blue eyes seemed utterly guileless.

"Tell me, High Initiate," she said in a conversational tone that carried clearly to the others, "Do you always look to your masters of Order before making even the *smallest* move?"

Tirand flushed angrily, and she laughed. "And I was under the impression that you were your own man," she added before he could collect himself sufficiently to speak. "Ah, well. We shall see, shan't we?" She inclined her head with gracious condescension firstly to the Matriarch and then to Tarod and Ailind, then still holding Tirand's arm possessively, she walked across the grass toward the castle gates.

Karuth hadn't yet taken her place among those who waited on the steps of the main entrance. To her dismay Tarod had insisted that she should take part in the travesty of the welcoming rituals; the Chaos lord wanted her observations to add to his own, so she was obliged to go. But with the knowledge that they must soon be separated gnawing at her thoughts like a hungry predator, she was desperate not to leave Strann's side until the last possible moment, so they stood together at her window, looking out at the bedecked courtyard and waiting tensely for the usurper to appear.

They hadn't spoken for some while, for neither could find anything to say that wouldn't have been both trivial and futile. As soon as Karuth had gone, Strann was to change his clothes for the loathed flamboyant garments in which he'd arrived at the castle and to wait for the summons that he was sure wouldn't be long in coming. If nothing else, Ygorla would be curious to know what had become of him, and he had devised an approach that would, he believed, deceive both her and the castle dwellers into believing that he was still loyal to her.

For now, though, he didn't want to think about that. He wanted only to feel the warmth of the woman beside him and the touch of her dark hair against his cheek. And he wanted, if only for a few moments more, to shut his eyes and believe that this interlude wasn't about to come to an end.

Karuth had cried earlier, but now the tears were gone, although her eyes still bore traces of red at their rims. They had said so many things to each other during these last hours, foolish and loving and inconsequential things, which now she could hardly even remember, and she wanted to say more, but the words wouldn't come. Suddenly Strann's grip on her hand tightened, and she saw that the people below them were stirring, looking toward the gates.

"They're on their way." Knowing that she must take control before her resolve snapped, Karuth forced herself to step back from the window, breaking the contact with Strann. Her eyes expressed everything she wasn't capable of saying. "I must go. . . ."

Strann nodded. For perhaps five seconds they looked at each other, then Karuth flung her arms around his neck. *"Oh, Strann . . ."*

He kissed her one last time with an intensity and passion that almost shattered her resolve, and then, unable to meet his eyes again, she turned and ran to the door. Strann stood motionless, listening to the sound of her footsteps diminishing down the corridor. Then, when he could no longer hear them, he turned and, with a face as blank and expressionless as that of a corpse, began to strip off his clothes.

Sen Briaray Olvit moved aside to make room for Karuth, and she slipped into line between him and Sister Alyssi from the Southern Chaun cot. Striving not to think about Strann, Karuth looked about her and thought grimly that the white robes of the sisters mingling with the many rank-colors of the Circle adepts' ceremonial cloaks would have made a splendid spectacle under any other circumstances. Now, though, they were a mockery. And when a new fanfare from the keep announced the entrance of Ygorla, she felt her stomach contract with a surge of bitter loathing.

Tirand's face was stern and taut as he entered the courtyard with the slight but dazzling figure of the usurper on his arm. In slow and stately procession he led her across the black flagstones while Shaill, Tarod, and Ailind followed a few paces behind. As they drew level with the central fountain, the High Initiate nodded in a prearranged signal to one of the senior adepts. The sound of a boot stamping on stone broke the silence, and taking the cue which they'd rehearsed under Ailind's meticulous eye, the adepts stepped forward like a rank of well-drilled militia.

"Ygorla! Ygorla! Ygorla!" With each shout they punched the air with upraised fists in the age-old salute. Ygorla's face broke into a smile of delight, and as the salute's last echoes died away, a small, dumpy sister stepped out alone, bowed stiffly, then turned to face the line of white-robed women.

The Sisterhood choirs had long been renowned for the beauty of their singing, and Sister Amobrel Iva of West High Land was acknowledged as the finest choirmistress in four provinces. She had worked a small miracle with the hotchpotch of voices at her disposal, but even her skills and Ailind's forceful encouragement couldn't disguise a tense and bitter edge to the anthem that the sisters sang in honor of Ygorla. Alerted by her own musical training to nuances of pitch and phrasing, Karuth could well imagine the atmosphere in which this makeshift choir must have practiced their set piece. However, any failing was quite lost on Ygorla. She stood smiling, almost visibly preening as she savored the words of adulation, and when the song came to an end, she raised her hands and clapped theatrically.

"Good women, I *thank* you!" Turning, she addressed the Matriarch. "And I compliment *you*, Matriarch. I didn't realize that my lamented great-aunt had so worthy a successor."

Shaill went white about the lips, and for one ugly moment Tirand thought that she might spit in the usurper's face, but then with a great effort she collected herself and merely inclined her head.

"Now." Ygorla broke away from Tirand and moved lightly but deliberately across the courtyard. She was clearly enjoying herself enormously, and when she turned, her eyes sparkled. "High Initiate, I mustn't keep you in suspense any longer. If you will kindly lend the services of a few of your strong and manly adepts, I shall present you with my modest gift."

With no visible means of propulsion, the two curtained carriages had trundled into the courtyard in the wake of the small procession and now stood in the shadows near the gateway. Tarod had already sensed the presence of Narid-na-Gost in one of the closed compartments, but for the moment he was more interested in the second carriage, to which Ygorla was now directing four adepts.

Tirand watched with some trepidation as the four reached the wagon. He couldn't begin to imagine what form Ygorla's "gift" might take, and he wasn't sure that he wanted to find out. It seemed Shaill shared his doubts, for she moved closer to him and whispered, "Tirand, if this is some trick—"

"Pray it isn't," Tirand replied softly. "We'll soon—" but the words cut off in midsentence.

The four adepts had reached the wagon. There seemed to be a large crate of some sort under the black curtains, and as they prepared to lift it down, one of the men pulled the folds of fabric aside. The silence that crashed in on the scene was as devastating as any screaming or shouting would have been, as Tirand, Shaill, and the four men stared at what the curtain had revealed.

It wasn't a crate inside the wagon but a crude cage. Crushed against the bars and looking out at them was a face. Once it might have been the face of a man, but some hideous force had warped and torn and battered it beyond any semblance of humanity and turned it to a gargoyle from the blackest depths of nightmare. Its skin—if indeed there was skin beneath the mass of warts and growths and scales that covered it—pulsed with a sick, colorless radiance, while a few random clumps of dead-white hair that writhed with a life of their own sprouted from the otherwise naked skull. The creature's lower jaw had been split in half, and two mouths worked and drooled, their tongues caked crimson with the same blood that stained the smashed teeth, flickering, lapping, licking as though trying to speak. In one shattering instant Tirand's brain registered the other forms that crowded the cage's suffocating confines; the broken visages, the twisted limbs, the bodies squirming mindlessly and hopelessly as they strove to find space to breathe.

Then he saw the thing's eyes. Brown eyes, human eyes, filled with intelligence and understanding, agony and despair. Their terrible gaze locked on his face, and even as the High Initiate's mouth opened with a horror that he couldn't express, the travesty spoke his name.

"Ti . . . rand . . ." It was a piteous plea and also an acknowledgment of recognition. And though the two distorted mouths could barely form the single word, Tirand knew the voice.

"Arcoro. . . ?" He didn't believe it, he *couldn't* believe it. Not this, not this thing, this crawling, hideous, unhuman changeling. . . . "Oh, gods . . ." the High Initiate whispered, and began to back away. "Oh, gods, no, *no, NO* !!"

Shrill, zestful laughter rang through the courtyard and echoed from the high black walls. Tirand spun around and saw Ygorla standing behind him. Her hands were clasped raptly, and her blue eyes shone with unholy delight.

"There, my *dearest* High Initiate! My little gift for you and for the Circle! Are you not as pleased to receive this offering as I am to bestow it?"

He could recognize others now. Not just his old friend Arcoro Raeklen Vir, but the rest of them, the adepts and the sisters and the trained swordsmen who had gone south in the first days after the usurper's coming; the ones who had risked themselves to lend the Circle's strength to the fight against her. How she had found them Tirand didn't know, but she had, and she had used her power to torture them beyond endurance by warping their bodies, melting their flesh, turning them from human beings into monsters from the Seven Hells. Only their minds had she left untouched, and that was the vilest torture of all, for they knew what they had become, and that knowledge was the worst of all their sufferings.

Blindly the High Initiate stared at Ygorla. He couldn't reason, couldn't come close to sanity; all he had to hold on to was a white-hot wall of rage and hatred that bore down on his mind like a tidal wave.

"You—" He started forward, his hand clawing at his side, reaching for a sword that wasn't there. "You—"

Ygorla skipped back, and her voice, suddenly ferocious, cut through the white heat like a fist punching through fragile glass.

"Touch me once, Tirand Lin, and you shall be as they are!" Light flashed before her and fused into a vertical bar of searing brilliance. Stunned, Tirand stumbled back, turning his head away, and Ygorla reached out to pluck the incandescent spear and hold it negligently in her hand.

"One caress, High Initiate, is all it will take to twist your body beyond redemption. Do you wish to test my power?"

Tirand couldn't. Even in the extremity of his fury he knew that it was fruitless, and suddenly he covered his face with his hands, and a sound like a sob choked from his throat.

Ygorla looked at Tarod and Ailind. Neither had moved; both watched her warily, and she knew that they could have intervened had they chosen to. The fact that they had not chosen to gave her great satisfaction. She lowered the blinding spear, then her hand twisted carelessly and it vanished.

"I find you a little ungracious, High Initiate," she said with the honey of utter triumph. "You see, I have brought them *all* back to you. All your spies, all your envoys, all the men and women whom you sent to the provinces to lend support to the Margraves—and a few others cast in among them for good measure. I thought you would be glad to welcome them home. I thought they would be glad to *be* home. But"—she pursed her mouth expressively, then shrugged—"it seems I have misjudged you. Ah, well, that's the way of things, I suppose."

The Matriarch was weeping now, quietly, anguishedly. Ygorla glanced at her with distaste. "I am bored with this. I shall enter the castle, I think, and see what entertainments you have devised for my enjoyment. And you, dear Tirand, will accompany me."

The last words were delivered with a venom that Tirand felt in his marrow, and as the usurper turned toward the steps and the doors beyond, he could only stare after her, paralyzed. Ailind moved to his side.

"We must all continue to play our appointed roles, Tirand," the lord of Order said quietly. "Go with her."

"But . . . but they . . ." Tirand tried to gesture toward the cage but couldn't; he was helpless.

"I will do whatever can be done for them," Ailind told him. "Go now. Don't fail me, or you'll make her triumph all the greater."

There was some confusion now among the welcoming party. They'd witnessed the brief confrontation but weren't close enough to the cage to see its grisly contents and realize what had triggered the High Initiate's fury. But as Ygorla waited and Tirand struggled to regain his self-control, some adepts started to move tentatively down the steps and came close enough to see the horror for themselves. There were cries, screams—Tirand heard them as though through the dense mists of a fever-dream —and then someone, in a breaking voice, called for Karuth. She came, pushing through the growing press of people, and stopped dead at the sight of the gruesome offering.

"Yandros!" She didn't even try to stem the oath, and choked down bile that threatened to lurch up from her

stomach. Like Tirand, she felt rage overcome her, but unlike her brother she couldn't control it. She turned about, and her eyes, blazing, met Ygorla's cool, blue stare.

"You evil *whore!*" Her voice shook with a passion she couldn't even name. In all her life she had never known such grief or such wrath, and no words were adequate to express her emotions. "You spawn of the Seven Hells, may your soul rot forever in *agony* for what you have done!"

For one instant Ygorla's expression changed. Her first instinct was to kill this upstart woman instantly, but even as the impulse rose in her, she sensed that Chaos was protecting her. She could have dealt easily enough with that: One sight of the soul-stone and Tarod would have had no choice but to remove the shield he had placed around her. But what did it matter? This creature, whoever she might be, was of no significance. She'd have more value as entertainment if she was allowed to live.

She raised one slender arm and touched Karuth's cheek. Karuth flinched as though expecting her skin to burst into flames, and satisfied that she had made her point, Ygorla stepped back.

"I will remember you," she said, and, taking firm hold of Tirand's arm, led him away toward the doors.

10

"Fetch Sanquar! For the gods' sakes, don't just stand there; *fetch my assistant!*"

Karuth's screech snapped the paralysis that had frozen them all, and three people ran for the castle doors through which Ygorla and the High Initiate had now disappeared. Their movement was enough to trigger an immediate and violent reaction in their fellows, and a number of adepts rushed to the cage. They hauled it down, hacking and ripping at the bars until they came free from their wooden housing, and Karuth ran to join them, lending her own strength to their efforts.

At last they were able to bring the captives out. It was then that the Matriarch fainted, collapsing suddenly and silently and only just caught by a quick-thinking adept before she hit the ground. Looking at the human wreckage that was being gently maneuvered from the cage and lowered onto cloaks hastily spread on the flagstones, Karuth came close to fainting herself, and only the arrival of Sanquar with her medical bag, and the knowledge that her skills were needed now as never before, kept her upright.

Arcoro Raeklen Vir was the first of the victims she knelt to tend. She knew it was Arcoro, for his eyes and the terrible way he struggled to utter her name betrayed the truth to her as it had to Tirand. But everything else about him, *everything* else, was so foully changed that she could barely force herself to believe that this had ever been Arcoro's body, or the body of any human man, and her lungs heaved with her desperate efforts to maintain control as she tried to examine him. Sweet gods, where were his *limbs*? Where *were* they? And that torso, black and gray and purple with the ulcerous lesions that had erupted from within him, and so wasted, so *shriveled,* like the corpse of some starved reptile. . . .

A few feet from her another of the victims was screaming under Sanquar's ministering hands. With no tongue to form it the sound was hideous, and it was a woman's voice. Karuth started to raise her head, then looked quickly away again, terrified that she might see the tortured face of another friend staring back at her. But she glimpsed the swollen, bloated body, the stumps of arms thrashing like leprous white tentacles, and then Sanquar's voice, high-pitched with shock and strain, said desperately, "Gods, Karuth, oh gods, it's Sister Corelm from Southern Chaun—"

Corelm—one of her own friends. Corelm—who had been Ygorla's childhood teacher and among Ria Morys's closest colleagues. Karuth covered her face with both hands as suddenly all the horror of it crashed in on her, and her voice wailed up, *"No . . . oh no, oh no, oh no. . . ."*

"K . . . Karuthhh . . ." It was Arcoro. He had no arms to reach out to her, no hands to touch her, but his voice was still his own, as was the mind beneath his warped skull. With a fearsome effort Karuth made herself look down at him.

"You c-can't . . ." the twin distorted mouths made an awful mockery of his speech. *"There is nothing . . . to do . . . f-for usss now . . ."* Ropes of saliva ran down his split jaw. *"Hl . . . Hlee . . ."* He was trying, she realized with pity and revulsion, to say *please,* but could no longer form the sound rightly. More saliva flowed, tinged with pink. *"Hlee . . . let uss go. L-let uss go. . . ."*

A shadow blocked the gory sunset light that still flooded across the courtyard, and Tarod knelt at Karuth's side. She turned a stricken and tragic face up to him, her eyes beseeching.

"I can't mend what she's done to him! I can't do anything for any of them. It's beyond my skill, it's be-

146

yond *any* mortal skill! Please, lord Tarod, please help them!"

Tarod shut his eyes. He was as sickened as Karuth, though his reasons weren't entirely akin to hers. It wasn't the nature of the tortures Ygorla had inflicted with her sorcery. The bodies warped into freaks and monstrosities, the limbs shrunken and atrophied or conjured out of existence—these were hideous in their own right, but they were nothing that might not be encountered among the lower denizens of the Chaos realm, where physical form knew few limitations. But the nature of the mind that had dreamed up such torments and inflicted them without rhyme or reason but simply for the pleasure of bringing agony: That was another matter entirely. That was not and had never been and never could be Chaos's way. That was the evil contrivance of a *mortal* mind.

He sensed Ailind's presence and looked up to see that the lord of Order had approached and was looking at the tableau of Karuth and the tortured Arcoro. Emerald eyes and tawny eyes met; Tarod knew what Ailind was thinking, and for the second time they found themselves in accord.

The Chaos lord said softly, "I can't help them either, Karuth. There's only one thing I can do for them, and that is release them from their living hell."

She was horrified. "No! You have the power. You healed Strann, you made his hand whole again! You are *Chaos*!"

"But I'm not omnipotent." He laid a hand on her arm, knowing that he could never make her understand fully. "I healed Strann, yes. But these poor creatures have come too close to death for my power to restore them to what they once were. I might make their bodies whole again, but their minds have crossed the border that separates the will to live from the will to die. They yearn for death, Karuth; it's their only hope of peace. Though I may be a lord of Chaos, I don't possess the power over death that would allow me to erase that yearning. I can't take away from them the memories of what they have suffered."

Karuth's lower lip was trembling. "Is there . . ." Her voice cracked; she strove to get it under control. "Is there any power that could do it . . . ?"

"Only Yandros. And he will not do it, Karuth. For our brother's sake, he won't take the risk of intervening even in this."

She understood, and knew she must accept. Ailind, who until this moment had taken no part, spoke then.

"Like Tarod, I would heal them if I could, Physician Karuth." He seemed to have forgotten or at least set aside his animosity toward her, and the compassion in his voice made her look up at him, bemused. "But this is the usurper's work, and so it's beyond Order's jurisdiction. All I can do—all *we* can do—is grant their souls safe passage to our realms."

Tarod stared blindly at the flagstones. "We both have faithful worshippers here, Ailind."

"Yes." The lord of Order nodded. "Then let them go as their loyalties ordain." He paused, staring again at Arcoro, who seemed to have lost consciousness. "This is a sorry day for us both."

Tarod rose to his feet. He drew Karuth with him, steadying her arm in a courteous yet oddly intimate way. "You may stay if you wish, Karuth. But perhaps it might be better if you made your farewells now."

Tears trickled down Karuth's cheeks; she felt them like the sting of acid. "I have no farewells to make, my lord," she replied, her voice pitched so low that it was barely audible. "I would rather remember them as . . . as . . ."

"I understand. Go, then. Take the others with you and mourn in your own way."

The two gods watched as the group of adepts, two carrying the still-unconscious Shaill, moved slowly off toward the main doors and entered the castle. The second black wagon still stood untouched beside the first; briefly and savagely Tarod's gaze flicked toward it, but what he sensed within produced nothing more than a flash of utter contempt. Ygorla's victims were silent now, as though they knew what awaited them, and the courtyard was filled with an incongruous and cruelly ironic air of peace. The Chaos lord looked at his counterpart from the realm of Order, and he said, "I think we need no light for this."

Ailind nodded. Slowly, almost gently, the great black gates closed, shutting out the glory of the sunset, and gray gloom descended like a funeral pall. Tarod held out his left hand, Ailind his right. Their fingers touched, linked, and a dark aura flared about Tarod's frame while a tawny-gold radiance illuminated Ailind's tall figure.

The power began to rise. . . .

Ygorla's triumphal entrance into the dining hall was completed in total silence.

None of the ranked adepts who awaited her knew anything of what had happened in the courtyard, but enough had picked up the psychic current of the High Initiate's shock and misery for their planned and rehearsed welcome to be stillborn. The usurper, her arm still linked with Tirand's, paused on the threshold and looked around her at the decorations, the blazing candles, the rows of still, uneasy faces. Then she smiled.

"Well!" Her silver voice carried like the sound of a waterfall on a still summer day. "Compliment heaped upon compliment! Your Circle is clearly so awed by my presence that their voices have failed them!"

Tirand's eyes were like hellish embers burning in a face utterly devoid of expression. By a miracle of willpower he had clawed back his self-control but he was an automaton, a stuffed doll, unable to react with any but the most basic reflexes for fear of losing his slender grip on himself. He was rescued, however, by a senior council member and fifth-rank adept who stood among the silent crowd. She didn't know and couldn't begin to guess the reason for the High Initiate's paralysis, but with great presence of mind she looked up to the gallery above the hearth and signaled urgently at the group of musicians assembled there and waiting for their cue. Seconds later a grand and solemn melody echoed through the hall and, giving the lead to her colleagues, the councillor stepped forward and bowed gravely and formally to the usurper.

With the part of his mind that was still functioning rationally, Tirand knew that he would be in the councillor's debt for the rest of his life. He had heard the dangerous edge underlying Ygorla's words, for all their apparent sweetness, and though he knew now what she was capable of doing should she choose to take offense, he had been powerless to intervene. Now, as the music surged around him, he was capable of leading the usurper forward and at last, at long last, freeing himself from her touch to leave her standing alone in the center of the hall, receiving and reveling in the homage that was paid to her. Ygorla's eyes glowed like gemstones as one by one the adepts made their obeisances; she threw compliments like petals, touching a hand here, a face there, radiant in her supremacy while the men and women of the Circle mouthed their prepared speeches of welcome and praise.

But at last the parade was finished and there were no more words to be said. The music faded and ceased; silence fell once more. Then Ygorla looked about the hall, and suddenly her gaze became as shrewd and avaricious as a carrion bird's.

"There is one familiar face that I expected to see here, yet that is strangely absent," she said, turning to address Tirand directly. "Dear High Initiate, what have you done with my envoy, Strann the Storymaker? I would be *very* sorry to hear that he, like the High Margrave, is indisposed."

Tirand was taken aback and couldn't think how to answer her. Strann, he knew, was under Tarod's protection now, and even Ailind was convinced that the bard was no more a friend to the usurper than any of them. Though he disliked and mistrusted Strann, the High Initiate's antipathy didn't extend to the point where he was willing to betray him outright; Tirand simply wasn't that sort of a man. But what to say?

Ygorla was waiting, her perfect eyebrows raised in query and challenge. Wishing fervently that Ailind was here to help him, Tirand found his voice at last.

"Strann is—ah, our guest here, lady, of course." *Seven Hells,* he thought, *what about Karuth? If this creature discovers the affair between them, what will she do?* "At present, I think, he is . . . that is, I think he might be found. . . ."

From the direction of the doors came a familiar voice.

"My sweet Empress!"

Ygorla turned, and Tirand's head whipped around sharply.

Quietly, unnoticed by anyone, Strann had slipped into the hall. In astonishment and chagrin Tirand registered the fact that he was wearing the vulgar and garish garments in which he had arrived at the castle, together with a broad-brimmed and feather-decked hat, which brought back sharp memories of their first encounter at the High Margrave's wedding. And his expression . . . smug, self-satisfied—the look of a triumphant schemer.

Strann took three paces toward them, then swept off his hat with one hand and made an elaborate bow that brought him to one knee before Ygorla.

"Madam," he said, "I have awaited this moment with an impatience beyond even my powers to express! Welcome—a thousand times welcome!" And he clasped Ygorla's hand and kissed it lavishly.

For a few moments Ygorla stared down at him. Then she laughed. It was a peal of unrestrained merriment that echoed to the rafters, and as it subsided, she reached out and patted Strann's bared head.

"My rat, I truly believe that nothing will ever change you! How has your sojourn been? Have they treated you as befits the envoy of their Empress?"

Strann tilted his head to one side. He was striving to ignore the shocked faces around him and to force down the memories of other times when he'd performed in this way at the Summer Isle court. This was like those grim days repeated over again: the looks of horror and disgust and betrayal, the knowledge that he was earning the hatred and contempt of those who should have been his friends and allies. Karuth's face rose before his inner vision. He thrust it away and said, "I have few complaints, lady; though this cold northern climate doesn't altogether suit me."

She chuckled. "Then you shall have sweetmeats to warm you and a fire to sit by while you entertain me with stories of your trials. I shall see to it." Her gaze snapped sharply to Tirand. "I *hope*, High Initiate, that during the telling of those tales I shall hear nothing to displease me."

Tirand stared back, white-faced. Strann's behavior had utterly confounded him, and he was bereft of words. Fortunately for him, though, Ygorla was losing interest in this public scene, and before the High Initiate could find anything to say, she turned away from him again, tapping one foot as she surveyed the hall.

"I am tired," she announced haughtily. "I shall see the preparations that have been made to house me, and then I shall rest. My rat"—she snapped a finger at Strann, then her voice changed and became honey-sweet —"you will come with me, and we shall explore the High Initiate's hospitality together. Would you like that?"

"Lady," Strann said ingratiatingly, feeling as though his heart were turning to ashes inside him, "nothing would give me greater joy."

Tarod's face was devoid of expression as he left the courtyard and entered the castle by the main doors. Outside, Ailind still stood where only minutes before the bodies of Ygorla's victims had lain. There was nothing to be seen of them now, but it was Order's way to keep vigil in such circumstances, and he would be there for some while yet.

As he mounted the steps, Tarod had felt the passing rush of something that skimmed across the courtyard, invisible under cover of the gathering darkness, and scurried like a hunted animal to the vicinity of the southernmost spire. Narid-na-Gost, Ygorla's demon father, had no wish to be the target of his one-time overlord's attention and had snatched the first opportunity that came his way to find a bolt hole as far as possible from Tarod's presence. Fury seethed in Tarod, but he forced down the desire to pluck the demon from his hiding place and smash both his body and his essence into a thousand pieces. Whatever the provocation, whatever the justification, he *must* keep control of that urge, or the cause would be lost. In time, he told himself, there would be a reckoning. And when it came, Narid-na-Gost would rue the day of his creation. . . .

Ygorla and the entourage she had obliged to accompany her had by now made a grand progress to the suite of rooms that had been made ready for her, and the entrance hall was deserted. Tarod paused for a few moments, then turned in the direction of Karuth's infirmary. Four cats were sitting outside the door, but the bunch of twigs that indicated the physician's presence had been removed. Nonetheless Tarod opened the door and walked in.

Karuth was there as he'd known she would be, sitting hunched in a chair drawn close to the small fire and shivering. She didn't look up; she sensed instinctively who her visitor was, but she couldn't bring herself to look directly at him. In a small, flat voice she said, "I pray they've found peace. . . ."

"They have. If nothing else, I can promise you that." Tarod crossed the room and took another chair. Then he said, "I understand how hard this is for you, Karuth. We must work together now, to see it done and over as quickly as possible."

This time she did look up, and quickly, as she realized that he wasn't referring to her grief over the mutilated victims but to something else. Her cheeks were tearstained, and a hint of guilt crept into her eyes as their gazes met.

"I shouldn't be thinking of myself," she said, unhappily defensive. "But—"

"But you're human, and it's only natural for you to

be touched more deeply by matters that are closer to your heart."

Karuth nodded. "I . . . saw them leave the dining hall. Strann was . . . Strann was with her, and she—she was leading him, like a pet. . . ." Her hands, clasped tightly in her lap, started to tremble. "Tirand looked at me. It was just one glance, but I know what he was thinking." A long pause. "I don't know if I have the strength for this, lord Tarod. When I saw Strann like that, I wanted—I wanted to *kill* her, to take a knife and rip her heart out and dance on her corpse! I wanted to see her soul in hell if I had to carry it there myself!"

He hadn't misjudged her, Tarod thought; even in the depths of her misery the rage was there, and that alone would be enough to sustain her. He reached out, and his fingers closed over hers. "Hold on to that, Karuth. Don't show it—don't ever show it to anyone but me—but whatever else you may do, keep that flame alive. It's worth far more than you know."

Karuth uttered a small, broken laugh. It felt strange, so very strange, to be sitting in her own infirmary with her hand clasped firmly in the hand of a god. She couldn't imagine Ailind ever deigning to touch one of his followers, let alone show them this strange and disconcerting blend of sympathy and affection, and she felt an answering response within herself, a strange and almost mystical sense of warm comradeship that melted barriers. She said, "I don't think I could quench it, my lord, even if I wanted to. And I don't want to. I *don't.*"

Tarod rose. "Then I'll leave you now. You'll have others around you soon enough. Compose yourself as best you can, and be ready to meet them. But if you need me, speak my name. I'll hear you, and I'll answer."

She nodded gratefully. "Thank you, my lord." Then, as he moved toward the door. "Lord Tarod . . ."

"Yes?"

"Strann looked so . . . so *abject.* Do you think he'll be safe?"

Tarod considered for a moment, then smiled. "Yes, I

think he will. And knowing him, I'd say that the more
abject he looks, the safer he's likely to be. That's worth
remembering."

She managed a pallid answering smile of her own.
"Yes . . . yes; knowing him, I believe you're right. I *will*
remember that."

———————————

As Tarod left Karuth's infirmary to return to the north
spire, Strann was treading a tightrope that he knew might
at any moment pitch him into an abyss. He sat cross-
legged on a velvet cushion at the foot of the great four-
poster bed in Ygorla's suite of rooms and watched the
usurper in trepidation as she paced across the carpet toward the window.

"So," Ygorla said in tones like slivered glass, "you
let that creature who parades himself as lord of Chaos
restore your hand to you without one murmur of protest.
You allowed him to undo *my* work, and you went against
my will. I am not pleased, rat. I am not pleased *at all!*"

Behind her back Strann flexed the mended hand and
tried not to think about what he would do if, as seemed
horribly likely at this moment, she chose to undo Tarod's
work and at the same time ruin the other hand for good
measure. He'd been a fool not to anticipate this; he
thought he'd covered every eventuality in the tale he'd
spun to her of his sojourn here, but he had missed that
one obvious detail. Now he had to think, and think very
fast.

Ygorla had reached the window now and was staring out into the dark courtyard. "This is a miserable
place," she observed scornfully. "Little wonder that the
men of the Circle are so bloodless and their women so
devoid of spirit." She beckoned carelessly with one hand,
and a dish of small delicacies rose from an ornamental
table and drifted across the room into her reach. Not
troubling to look at what she selected, she took one and
chewed it. "Even their food tastes like something better

left to rot on the seabed. I shall find the cook who prepared this and have his skin as extra covering on my bed tonight." Then she turned on her heel. "Well? You haven't answered my question."

Strann had hoped that her momentary distraction might grant him a reprise, but he'd forgotten both her tenacity and her memory. However, the few seconds' respite had given him time to find the answer he was seeking. It was in truth an appalling ploy, and it sickened him. But knowing Ygorla as he did, he suspected that it might just work. That, and that alone, must be his criterion now.

He affected his most ingratiating expression and looked hungrily into her blue eyes. "Madam, I know I have done wrong. I knew it then; I know it now. But . . ." *Timing, Strann; timing.* He hung his head. "The temptation was too great. And I am, after all, only a mortal man."

That caught Ygorla's attention, as he had prayed it would. She put her head to one side and looked hard at him. "Explain."

Strann sighed. He had perfected that sigh over many years; it held just the right blend of resignation and sorrow to soften a hard heart without alerting its owner to any ulterior motive. "Sweet Empress," he said sorrowfully, "I have two loves in my life, as I am bold enough to believe that you know. My first is . . . well; I dare not say it aloud." He looked at her again, directly, frankly, lying with his eyes. "I shall leave my desires unspoken, as I know I always must. But the second is something I *can* express. I love my music, lady. For through my music I dare to believe that I might in some small way touch your heart. That was what the Chaos lord offered me. The chance to play my music, and so to make my time without you bearable by preparing for the day when I might play for you again."

Reflexively Ygorla took another sweetmeat and ate it, though it might have been a handful of grass for all the attention she paid it. Her face had taken on an extraordi-

nary expression, smug and yet suspicious together, and
with a frown that hinted at an unaccustomed depth of
thought.

At last she spoke. "You are very glib, rat. I'm not
sure if I entirely trust you."

Strann looked horrified. "Madam—"

"Be silent!" She crossed the floor and took his chin
in one small, pale hand, jerking his head up painfully.
"No . . . no; there's something more, isn't there? Something you haven't told me." She studied him carefully for
a few seconds, then the smallest hint of a smile played
about her face. "Rat, what are you hiding? What have
you done?"

Strann sent a silent but fervent prayer of thanks to
Yandros. It had worked—gods preserve his soul, but it
had *worked*. Now must come the hardest part of all.

"Ah, lady," he said, and the first signs of a grin
began to take form on his face. "I can't outwit you."

"I'd hope for your sake that you would never try."
Her fingers increased their pressure on his chin, but she,
too, was exhibiting a tentative ghost of a smile. "Tell me
the truth."

"Sweet Empress, what else can I do?" Suddenly
Strann was at his most impish. "The High Initiate, you
see, has a sister. . . ."

"Ah. I begin to *see*. Go on, rat. I think this might
amuse me."

Feeling sick to the pit of his stomach, Strann made a
pretense of careless dissembling. "In truth, my queen, she
has little to commend her, for she's of my own age and by
no means any beauty. Besides, once any man has looked
upon *your* face—"

She stopped that with a wave of one hand, but he
could see she was pleased. "Get on with your tale before I
lose my patience."

"Well . . . though she's drab and has chosen to follow the dull profession of a physician, the High Initiate's
sister likes to think of herself as a musician. And she
owns a very fine manzon; an instrument that, in my hum-

ble judgment, is worthy of better uses than the mere gratification of an amateur's pleasures. I admired that
instrument, lady. It shames me to say it, but I *coveted* it;
for I yearned to play *your* music on it."

Ygorla's smile blossomed into a huge, avid grin that
more than matched his own. "So you used your wiles to
charm yourself into this unsuspecting woman's good
graces?"

"My Empress, you phrase the matter more deli-
cately than I could have hoped to do!"

Ygorla's shriek of laughter was audible far along the
corridor beyond her apartments, shocking the two adepts
who, at her order, had been set outside to wait at her
beck and call. She released Strann with a playful push
that almost sent him sprawling, and skipped back to the
window, hugging herself in delight.

"Oh, this *is* diverting! To think of you, my draggled
and comical little rat, twisting the High Initiate's sister
around your little finger as though she were some cheap
tavern whore! I shall reward you for this, my pet, for
you've given me more entertainment with your story
than I've had in all my progress from Summer Isle!"
Then suddenly she grew still. "Wait . . ."

Strann tensed. She was so mercurial, so unpredict-
able, that for a moment he feared the worst. But when
she turned around again, her expression was one of glee.

"You say this creature is a physician?"

"Yes, sweet madam."

"Describe her to me. Is she dark or fair? Fat or
thin?"

Strann's heart thumped, but he didn't dare to evade
the question. "Dark, madam, with her hair in a braid.
Tall, and with little delicacy; not as a woman should be.
A pleasant enough face of its kind, I suppose, though by
no means—"

"I know her." Ygorla interrupted him as the recol-
lection of the brazen, dark-haired creature she'd encountered in the courtyard slipped suddenly into place. Of
course; of *course*. Karuth Piadar, that was her name.

She'd heard it on Summer Isle. Tirand Lin's only sister; the castle's senior physician and a spinster long past hope of redemption. So Strann had beguiled *her*. . . . Oh, she thought, but this was *funny*. Was the fool in love with her rat? Likely she was, or at least thought herself to be; after all, at her age she'd probably grasp at any chance that came her way, however second-rate and unlikely it might seem. And Strann had played on her loneliness and gullibility, all for the sake of a musical instrument.

Ygorla was suddenly glad that she hadn't given way to the impulse to destroy Karuth for the insult she had paid her. How much better it would be, how much more entertaining, to have her alive and suffering the indignity of rejection. How very, very *amusing*!

She flicked at the skirt of her dress so that it swirled about her frame, and danced back to where Strann knelt on his cushion.

"Call the servants, rat," she ordered him. "I have a message for the High Initiate's sister, and I want it to be conveyed to her at once!"

The two adepts came at Strann's call. He avoided their gazes, not wanting to see the repugnance that he knew would be in their eyes, and Ygorla addressed them sweetly.

"Take word to Karuth Piadar. I want her manzon so that my pet may play for me tonight. Bring it to me without any delay—and at the same time you may proffer my thanks for keeping my little musician safe for me until my arrival. I'm *sure* she will understand my meaning."

The two departed, and as the door closed behind them, Ygorla sprawled on the bed, stretching her slender limbs like a cat basking in sunlight.

"Strann, all the world shall hear your music before long. I shall see to it. But tonight I mean to grant you the privilege of playing for me and me alone." Suddenly she sat up and smiled a predatory, almost conspiratorial smile. "You have done all that I asked of you and more. I am pleased with you, my little pet. And now that I have you back in your rightful place at my feet, I mean to keep you there and never send you from me again. Does that gladden your heart, rat?"

Strann thought of Karuth; imagined her face when the two adepts brought their message, imagined what she might say, how she might feel. . . .

"Beloved Empress," he said, his voice muffled as he lowered his head in seeming reverence, "the truth of it is beyond my ability to express."

11

The ball in honor of Ygorla was to be held on the following night, and in the twenty-four hours between her arrival and the beginning of the feigned celebration the
castle dwellers were forced to come to terms as best they
could with the harsh reality of her presence among them.

Ygorla was a demanding guest. She had brought no
human retinue from Summer Isle, so she insisted on being provided with a legion of servants to wait at her beck
and call at any and every hour. She also insisted that
those servants should be high-ranking adepts, and found
it eminently amusing to set them to the most menial tasks
her imagination could devise. For the time being she
seemed bent on ignoring both the High Initiate and the
two gods, perhaps, as Ailind remarked to Tirand, in the
belief that they would take her indifference as a calculated insult. Tirand was deeply thankful not to be the
subject of her attentions; he had spent the night in private
vigil, mourning for the mutilated adepts and sisters
whose misery was now ended, and without some time to
recover he didn't think that he could have maintained his
composure if he'd been forced to come face-to-face with
the usurper again.

In fact Ygorla's apparent readiness to stay in her
apartments and ignore everyone and everything not con-
nected with her own indulgence was a source of some
puzzlement to the Circle. Knowing her reason for coming to the castle, the adepts had anticipated an immediate
and violent confrontation, but instead the usurper behaved as though her only intention was to enjoy her new
surroundings and revel in the atmosphere she had cre-

ated. Beyond a few short-lived and relatively innocuous displays of temper, she didn't trouble to flaunt her powers, and many senior adepts suspected that she was waiting for her hosts to make the first move. But if this was a waiting game, her hosts had yet to discover the rules.

Ailind was adamant that there should be no change in Order's strategy. The Circle must continue to treat Ygorla solely as an honored guest. No challenges were to be issued, no mention made of her claims or her ambitions. They would simply bide their time until the usurper grew tired of her diversions and made her intentions clear. Those who disliked this edict—and there were a good few—might have appealed to Tarod for an alternative, but since the ugly affair of the prisoners Tarod had returned to the north spire and wasn't seen about the castle. Ailind had his own view on the reason behind the black-haired lord's abrupt withdrawal and was amused by the thought that the defection of Strann, whose loyalty Chaos had so blithely taken for granted, had put a spoke in the wheel of their plans. As Ailind remarked scathingly to the High Initiate, even Tarod might have anticipated that Strann had only one loyalty: to himself, and his own survival and advancement. But that was well and good; from Order's point of view it simply removed one more potential nuisance from the field of play.

On the morning of the planned celebration the bustle of activity in and around the dining hall couldn't disguise the atmosphere of acute tension that pervaded every level of the ancient stronghold. Ygorla hadn't deigned to make an appearance, but screams of alternate rage and laughter were heard from her apartments, and her adept-servants went about their errands with bleached faces and tight-pressed lips.

Shortly after a sparse and subdued breakfast, the triumvirate met in Tirand's study. Shaill had had to use all her persuasive powers to coax Calvi to the meeting. Since the debacle with Ailind two days before Ygorla's arrival, the High Margrave had hardly left his room. Shaill knew that Ailind had paid him a further snub by deliberately excluding him from the formal welcoming party on the previous day, and she was at a loss to understand the god's reasons. Calvi needed help and encouragement now, not this cold, belittling disdain, but Ailind had crushed any attempt she made to debate the matter, and the Matriarch knew that, whatever his private feelings, she could expect no support from Tirand. But it worried her to see the degree to which the spirit seemed to have gone out of Calvi, and she hoped that she might be able to persuade him into a more confident state of mind.

There was little to be said at their meeting; it was merely a formality that allowed the High Initiate to convey Ailind's final instructions for the evening's ordeal. But when the business was over and Calvi was already making to leave, Shaill said, "Tirand—what's to be done about Karuth?"

"Karuth?" The High Initiate looked at her warily. "I don't quite understand. . . ."

This, Shaill thought, had gone far enough. She sat down again in the chair she'd just vacated, and her voice became firm.

"I think you *do* understand, Tirand, but you don't want to talk about it. Well, I think you must. This feud between you and Karuth has gone on for too long. Isn't it time to bridge the gulf between you; and wouldn't now be the most generous time to do it, for compassion's sake?"

Calvi had almost reached the door, but he stopped and looked back, suddenly watchful.

Tirand stared down at his desk. "You mean Strann. . . ." He seemed to have to make an effort to speak the name aloud.

Shaill, though, had no such scruples. "Yes, I mean Strann." She shook her head. "I hadn't *dreamed* that this would happen. That evil-hearted guttersnipe . . . he duped me into believing that the tale he spun us all was genuine, and now *this*. . . ."

"He duped us all, Shaill. I believed his story, too, though it didn't make me dislike him any the less." He grimaced. "Even lord Ailind took the view that he was Chaos's pawn, until events proved otherwise."

"Indeed; and now it seems that your instinctive dislike of the creature proved sounder judgment than anyone's logic. But, Tirand, if we feel betrayed, what must poor Karuth be going through now? And for pity's sake, don't say that she's asked for this and therefore deserves it, because I won't believe you mean a word. However deep your quarrels run, she's still your sister."

Calvi spoke up. "I'd like to help her, Shaill, if I can."

"I know you would, Calvi, but I still think that Tirand should also try."

Tirand looked up at last. His eyes were unhappy. "Of course I feel sorry for Karuth. I wouldn't be human if I didn't. But"—he made a helpless gesture—"I don't know. How can I behave as if the rift between us had never happened? After some of the things that were said, I can't simply walk up to her and offer the open hand of friendship. It isn't that easy, and she wouldn't trust it."

"Don't be too sure of that," the Matriarch told him. "It takes more than words, however harsh, to erase thirty years of fellowship. Bear that in mind while you think over what I've said. And remember that at this moment Karuth is in dire need of a friend."

Tirand did think over Shaill's words when she was gone, and his fundamental honesty made him admit that he wanted to take her advice. Not just for Karuth's sake, though that was more of an incentive than he had expected it to be, but also for his own, for he knew in his heart that he hadn't been truly happy since their feud began. He *wanted* to heal the wounds. He wanted the old friendship, the old companionship again. And as time went by, he was beginning to feel that perhaps his judgment of his sister had been a little too hard.

But how to make the first move? That was the stumbling block. He was so afraid that Karuth would see any attempt at reconciliation as either motivated solely by pity or, worse, a ploy to snare her when she was at her weakest; and Tirand knew that if that should happen, he wouldn't be able to explain it to her. He'd never been good at expressing his feelings in words; he didn't have that enviable easy facility that some men possessed—men like Strann, he thought, and a black desire to find the bard and kill him rose suffocatingly in his heart. *He* was at the root of all this, he and Yandros of Chaos, who had tempted Karuth into defying the Circle in the first place.

"Damn, damn, *damn!*" Tirand tried unsuccessfully to vent his feelings in the mild expletives and thumped a clenched fist down on his desk. It was no use. He *couldn't* do what Shaill wanted, for however much he might wish to, there was the old stumbling block again, the feelings of resentment and betrayal that even his compassion for Karuth in her present straits couldn't overcome. If he made any move toward her, those feelings would be there, lurking in wait and ready to trip him. He dared not take the risk, or he could end up by making matters infinitely worse than they already were.

He sat down in his chair, his shoulders sagging. Unbidden, words came to his lips, and he whispered them into the quiet and private isolation of his room.

"Oh, Father . . . what am I to do? What am I to *do*?"

———————

"I still say you're a fool."

The voice, sharp and querulous, grated on Ygorla's temper as she rummaged through trunks of clothes, throwing aside one gown after another, and she swung around to face her father's hunched and twisted figure.

"*You* say, *you* say. I'm sick of hearing what you say! And if you think for one moment that I'm going to permit my pleasures to be spoiled by listening to you, then you can think again!"

Narid-na-Gost glared at her with hooded eyes, and a cynical smile cracked his sharp, unhuman face. "This so-called celebration, then, is so pleasurable that it gives you a temper like a shrew and a demeanour to match? I *am* impressed."

Ygorla's eyes flashed dangerously, and she opened her mouth to utter a venomous and powerful curse, but the demon raised a crooked finger in warning. "Don't try your powers on me, daughter! You're not my equal yet, whatever you may like to believe!"

She subsided, though unwillingly, and he shifted his position so that he could observe the courtyard through the window. "You are in danger of overstepping yourself, Ygorla," he said severely. "That is the nature of my concern, as you should know full well by now. I have only your future—*our* futures—at heart."

Ygorla had pulled another dress out of the trunk, a gorgeous confection of shimmering crimson and black silk overlaced with gold thread. She held it up, stared at it for a moment, then with a petulant gesture ripped it in half and threw it across the room. But she hadn't missed the faint placatory note underlying the demon's words, and when she looked at him again, her expression, though still angry, was calmer.

"Your concern for our future is no greater than mine, Father," she snapped. "But *I* am perfectly capable of bearing that in mind while still enjoying myself, and enjoy myself I shall!" She made a dismissive gesture that took in the entire room. "What have I to fear from anyone here? They're nothing. They haven't even the power to raise an elemental without resorting to lengthy rituals that take half a day to complete! And they are *terrified* of me. Even their precious High Initiate is like a quaking jellyfish when he stands before me!"

"Perhaps." Narid-na-Gost was still staring out of the window, as though, she thought, he were looking for something. "But there's more than the castle's human inhabitants to consider."

"Tarod and Ailind?" Ygorla laughed shrilly. "They are the *least* of my worries! The strutting fool from the realm of Order has no power whatever to touch me, while our good friend of Chaos . . . well, Father, what will he do? What *dare* he do, but keep seething silence?" Her hand went to her neck, and she twirled the chain on which hung the glowing blue soul-stone. "I need only show him this and smile at him sweetly and he is putty in my hands because he has no other choice! And he hates it. Oh, how he *hates* it!"

Narid-na-Gost hunched still further into the window seat, looking more than ever like some mutated bird of prey. "You may crow over your ascendancy, daughter, but remember the tale of the hunter who teased his starving hounds once too often. Tarod is dangerous. He still has more power than you and I together and multiplied tenfold, and if you make one mistake or give him the smallest opportunity, he'll destroy you."

"And destroy his brother's soul into the bargain? I think not." A glimmer of amusement was creeping into Ygorla's eyes as she surmised what truly lay behind her sire's carping, and she added in a honeyed tone that didn't deceive him for a moment, "But then perhaps that's the difference between us, dear Father—that you are afraid of him and I'm not."

Furious resentment flared in the demon's eyes. "I am not afraid of him! But neither am I so foolish as to constantly taunt and test him and flaunt my strength in his face!"

"Why not? It makes for good entertainment, and there's absolutely nothing he or any of them can do to retaliate." A corner of satin in the trunk caught her eye suddenly, and she pounced on it. "Ah! *This,* I think! Gold, with sapphire blue to show my eyes at their best and also highlight my little trinket. That will suit the occasion very well."

Realizing that as usual his arguments and warnings were falling on deaf ears, Narid-na-Gost turned to the window again. "Our purpose in coming to the Star Peninsula was not to indulge you in your endless pleasure seeking, but to find and gain control of the Chaos Gate," he said sulkily. "The door to my final goal lies within the walls of this castle, yet you waste time in meaningless frippery when there is work to do!"

Ygorla paused to eye him sidelong. She'd noted the fact that he had said *my* final goal and not *our* final goal, but she didn't comment. Seeing that she wasn't about to condescend to answer him, the demon continued with increasing rancor.

"I have spent more than enough time in this petty mortal world! By now we should have presented our ultimatum to Yandros. By now his capitulation should be complete, and I should be making ready to return to the realm of Chaos as its new overlord. The Gate is here, the way is prepared, and we have the trump card in our hands, but still you do *nothing*! I grow bored with waiting, Ygorla. I grow bored with waiting for our demands to be made—and I grow bored with waiting for you to tire of your pleasures!"

"Then join me in them," Ygorla suggested carelessly. She had the gown out now and was smoothing it, enjoying the sensation of the fine fabric under her fingers. "Why should you not? Music and feasting and dancing—well, perhaps not dancing"—she glanced over her shoulder, and her eyes raked his twisted, dwarflike frame with its clawed feet and prominent hunch—"but I'm sure you could find other diversions. There are some pretty enough women here, and they should be honored by your attentions."

"I have no interest in worthless human frolics!" the demon snapped savagely. Ygorla turned her head away again, hiding a smile of triumph. Her jibe had found its mark. She knew that above all else her sire resented his own grotesque appearance, which the Chaos lords had bestowed carelessly on him and which, as a low demon, he hadn't the power to alter. Given that power, Narid-na-Gost would have transformed himself into a form that no mortal woman could resist, and Ygorla didn't know which amused her the more, the thought of what he would have done with such an opportunity or the thought of his roiling and helpless frustration that the opportunity was denied him.

Aloud, and quite blithely, she said, "Then the loss is yours, dear Father, for it's a poor life that doesn't enjoy a frolic once in a while. And I for one mean to make the utmost of tonight's celebration." She paused and looked at him once more, smiling. "Won't you reconsider? After all, no one here even knows of your presence in the castle yet—apart from Tarod and Ailind, of course."

That, too, went home, and she saw the slight shudder before he could control it. He *was* afraid. Not of Ailind; even Narid-na-Gost accepted that he had nothing to fear from the powers of Order. But Tarod was quite another matter. Strange and fascinating, she thought, how even the boldest of dogs could never entirely lose the instinct to grovel to its one-time master. . . .

She couldn't see Narid-na-Gost's expression now, but his voice when he spoke was cold and hostile.

"You may play your childish games, but I will keep myself to myself until such time as *I* deem it expedient to do otherwise."

She shrugged. This was growing tiresome, and she was bored with taunting him. "Very well, then," she said. "Go and skulk away in that spire you're so fond of, and I wish you joy of it. I, however, intend to have fun!"

The demon rose to his feet. "As you please, daughter. But I'd strongly advise you to remember my warning!"

He gave her one last look that conveyed a good deal more than any further words would have done. Then the window bay contained only the curtain shifting, as though in a sudden draft, and the demon had vanished.

For a few moments Ygorla stared at the spot where he had been standing. Then she shrugged, gave the gold-and-sapphire dress another shake, and yelled for one of the adepts posted outside to send her three serving girls and a dressing maid this instant, if they valued the eyes in their skulls.

When Karuth heard that she had no choice but to attend the ball, she crushed an instinct to run to the stables, saddle the fastest horse she could find, and ride out of the castle, across the causeway, and away into the mountains. It was a crazed and short-lived impulse, but the thought of being forced to take part in this parody with a calm face, and even pretend to enjoy the festivities, was more than she thought she could bear. Since the usurper's coming, she had spent most of her time in the infirmary, but her efforts to carry out her work and pretend that nothing untoward had happened were a great strain, for as well as the constant burden of Sanquar's silent compassion she had had to endure the commiseration, sometimes wordless, sometimes volubly expressed, of her patients. Tarod had been right when he'd predicted that there would be a great deal of sympathy for her in the wake of Strann's apparent heartless perfidy, and even the most sanctimonious of her former critics had tried clumsily to condole with her. Their kindness moved her to private tears on several occasions, but so far she had managed to keep a calm public face. This, though, would be a far greater trial, and she wasn't sure that she was ready for it.

But, ready or not, the thing had to be faced. Ygorla had insisted that every initiate of the Circle, from highest to lowest, must attend on her tonight, and no one dared gainsay her. So with dread and misery in her heart Karuth closed up the infirmary shortly after sunset and went to her bedchamber to prepare. Two cats followed her, slipping into the room between her feet as she entered. Karuth moved to shoo the animals out but then relented. They'd do no harm, and she was touched by their persistence. In varying numbers they'd been following her about all day, and she knew that in their cryptic way they were trying to express their own form of understanding and support.

She changed her clothes and dressed her hair with the methodical yet mechanical attention of one keeping a rigidly tight rein on her emotions. Subconsciously determined to strike a sharp contrast with the mood Ygorla would impose on the evening, she chose a close-fitting and almost severe wine-red gown with long sleeves and a high neckline and adorned it only with a chatelaine's belt of wrought silver links and the Guild badge that proclaimed her as a Mistress of the Musical Arts. A matching silver-link band to hold back her hair, and the seven-rayed-star ring given to her years ago by her old teacher, Carnon Imbro, and she was ready. Or, she thought as she gazed at her reflection in the polished glass, as ready as she could hope to be.

Distantly, from the dining hall, she could hear the strains of music. Involuntarily her gaze moved for a moment to the empty space by the wall where her manzon case usually rested, and one corner of her mouth twitched in a smile totally devoid of humor. Then, as she took a deep breath and prepared to leave, someone knocked softly on her door.

"Who's there?" For an irrational instant Karuth felt certain that her visitor was either Strann—impossible, she reminded herself, *impossible*—or Tirand. Then the door opened.

"Karuth?" It was the Matriarch. "May I come in?"

Karuth's shoulders slumped. "Shaill . . . yes, come in, please." Her expression relaxed a little as she realized that perhaps of all the inhabitants of the castle, Shaill was the one whose company she needed most at this moment. "I'm so glad to see you."

The Matriarch smiled sympathetically. "I hoped you might be, my dear. It's time to go down to the hall, and I thought you'd be glad of someone to walk in with you."

"Yes." Karuth bit her lip hard as emotion welled, then blinked rapidly. "Yes. Thank you."

Shaill glanced sideways at herself in Karuth's mirror and grimaced. "I should lose some weight. This is what comes of too much administration and not enough practical work." She twitched the full skirt of her white silk gown, which she wore tonight in preference to the Matriarch's traditional robe—perhaps, Karuth suspected, as her own form of snub to the usurper. "Well, then. If we're both as ready as we'll ever be, shall we go?"

The cats followed on silent paws as the two women left the room and walked toward the main staircase. They converged on several other groups, all of whom bowed to the Matriarch, but no words were exchanged. For all the edicts that this was to be treated as a celebration, tension was a palpable presence in the air.

They descended the stairs. When they reached the ground floor, the cats glided away; nothing, it seemed, would induce them to approach Ygorla's vicinity. Karuth hung back, allowing the other adepts to go on ahead of them, and when the Matriarch looked at her, her face was still and pale.

"We must go on, my dear." Shaill laid a hand over hers and squeezed gently. "I know how hard this is for you, but it has to be faced and overcome."

"I know." Karuth whispered. She took several deep, quick breaths. "Do you know where . . . if . . . whether lord Tarod is here?"

Shaill shook her head. "I couldn't say. But even if he is here, I don't think you should rely on him. He's likely to have other matters to concern him tonight."

There was a pause while Karuth steeled herself. Inwardly she had a sudden wild desire to confide in Shaill and tell her the truth about Strann. She'd seen the sympathy in the Matriarch's eyes, though she hadn't expressed it directly, and she wanted Shaill to know that Strann's seeming betrayal wasn't real. He would be in the hall tonight, she knew it as surely as she knew her own name, and in the eyes of all the castle dwellers he would be seen as the liar and the turncoat who had deceived their High Initiate's sister. Karuth wanted *someone* besides herself and Tarod to know that Strann was as true as the rising sun.

But it was impossible. She dared not trust even Shaill, who, when all was said and done, had cast her lot with Ailind and Tirand. The secret must remain a secret, and she must face her ordeal.

She said nothing, but she pressed Shaill's hand in an answering response, conveying that she was ready, and they began to walk toward the double doors of the dining hall.

12

A dazzle of light, color, music, and warmth greeted Karuth and Shaill as the hall doors opened to admit them. They walked in arm in arm, and in a queasy daze Karuth heard their names being announced above the strains of a slow, formal air.

She saw Ygorla immediately. The usurper was seated on a great chair at the far end of the hall, the chair set upon a dais that lifted her slightly above the heads of the crowd. In the soft brilliance of candlelight and torchlight she was a vision of sheer loveliness. Her black hair, set with a web of tiny diamonds and sapphires, gleamed the color of a star-filled sky, and her pale, flawless skin had a delicate flush that made it look like fine porcelain. The gold-and-sapphire-blue gown reflected the light in shimmering panels, and at her ears, waist, arms, and fingers more jewels glittered.

And on its golden chain at her neck, drawing the eye like a moth to a flame, the stolen soul-gem of Tarod's brother glowed with a deep, cold, and utterly compelling radiance of its own.

Shaill had stopped and was staring at the jewel. Karuth, too, was motionless, but her gaze lay elsewhere. For on a crimson cushion at Ygorla's feet, dressed in brilliant motley and tied to his mistress by a jeweled collar and a slim jeweled chain, which she held negligently in one hand, was Strann.

Karuth felt something catch in the back of her throat, blocking the air that she tried to force into her lungs. Alert to the sudden change in her, Shaill saw now

173

what she had seen, and her fingers tightened on Karuth's arm.

"Have courage, my dear! Don't give him the satisfaction of seeing your distress!"

Karuth bit her tongue as she had had to do before, and suddenly felt the threat of panic assail her. She couldn't go through with this. It was too much to ask of her, too much to expect. What if Strann caught her eye? Or if she should be forced to stand face-to-face with that evil creature who flaunted her power over him as she dangled him like a dog on the end of her leash? It was too much. She'd speak out, she wouldn't be able to control herself but would say something that would put Strann's life in peril—

"Karuth."

The voice startled her and she turned with a nervous jump. Coming toward her, dressed in dark, sober green and looking far older than his years, was Calvi. He bowed with deep respect to the Matriarch, then held out a hand to Karuth.

"Physician-Adept Karuth, will you honor me by permitting me to lead you into the hall?" he asked in a voice that carried clearly.

Karuth looked into his blue eyes, realized what he was doing and why, and felt a rush of gratitude toward him. By setting an immediate and formal claim on her, he was deliberately and publicly elevating her. The High Margrave and whomever he chose to partner were accorded the highest status at any formal function, and by tradition Calvi should have offered his hand instead to the Matriarch. But tonight he had thrown tradition aside, and by this gesture he meant to show the entire company his regard for Karuth and his contempt for anyone who might seek to belittle her.

Karuth's desperately faltering confidence suddenly steadied, and she laid her arm over his in the established manner. "Thank you, High Margrave," she replied. "I am honored."

As they moved off into the throng, Shaill caught a glimpse of the green cloak of a seventh-rank adept and, narrowing her eyes to peer between two artificially and nervously smiling women, saw Tirand a few yards away with a group of the Circle's senior councillors. Tirand had also noticed Calvi's gesture, and the Matriarch felt a momentary regret that it had not been he who had come to Karuth's rescue. To be escorted by the High Margrave would do much to bolster Karuth's courage, and Shaill admired Calvi for such a thoughtful and adult act. But to be escorted by her own brother, and thereby given the much-needed chance to heal the rift, might have been far better still. It was such a pity that Tirand hadn't found the courage to make that all-important first move.

She realized then that others were entering the hall behind her and that she was still standing in the way of the doors. She started to move aside, but was intercepted by a tall, dark figure, who materialized from the press of people.

"Lady Matriarch." Tarod bowed courteously over her hand in a manner that had gone out of fashion nearly a century ago. "My compliments. You are the essence of nobility, and a sharp lesson in contrasts to many others here tonight."

Despite the fact that she couldn't say she liked the Chaos lord, Shaill couldn't suppress a small smile at the nature of his compliment, which appealed to her. "You're too kind, my lord." He himself, she noticed, had made no concessions to the occasion but was wearing his habitual unadorned black. He'd probably have chosen the same clothes to go riding, hunting, or digging ore in the mines of Empty Province, she thought, and that careless—or perhaps deliberate—rebuff to etiquette raised him further in her estimation.

"Are you unescorted?" Tarod asked.

Shaill nodded toward Calvi, who was now firmly steering Karuth toward a group of his friends. "By the usual protocols I'd be escorted by the High Margrave tonight. However, I'm glad to say that Calvi decided to come to Karuth's rescue and has taken her under his wing."

Tarod watched the couple for a few moments.

"That's a very thoughtful deed," he said. "The High Margrave is generous—and kindly—beyond his years."

"He is." Shaill hesitated, then decided to damn caution. The events of the last few days had brought more than one disenchantment, and she suddenly saw no reason why she shouldn't be frank, even with the being who, in theory, she was supposed to have set herself against. "It's unfortunate," she added with more than a hint of acid in her voice, "that certain others don't share your wiser perception."

She saw the quick interest in Tarod's green eyes and knew that he understood her meaning. So he, too, had noticed Ailind's attitude toward Calvi? Interesting. And what, she wondered, did he make of it?

She was trying to find a way to phrase that question with a modicum of delicacy, when Tarod changed the subject. "The creature on her throne is beginning to look restless. I imagine it won't be long before she summons a few choice candidates before the imperial presence."

He spoke lightly enough, but the intrinsic contempt was clear to Shaill. Her expression darkened. "I hope to all the gods—pardon me, my lord—that I shan't be one of them. After what she has done to my friends in Southern Chaun and elsewhere . . ." She shook her head.

"Yes." Tarod's eyes grew suddenly introverted. "Yes . . . I should have spoken to you before, to express my sorrow at their deaths. But somehow no words seem adequate, even now."

Shaill perceived that there was genuine grief beneath that statement. She was surprised and touched, and a little awkwardly she said, "And I should have thanked you, for . . . for what you did for them. . . ."

He held up a hand quickly, forestalling anything more. "Please, Matriarch. I think we'd be wise to draw a curtain over that episode, even though neither of us may be able to forget it." A new and strange light began to glow in his eyes, turning them as hard as the emeralds their color resembled, and with a brief shock Shaill saw something of his true nature in his look. "The usurper will have a very great deal to answer for when she finally falls into our hands."

The Matriarch repressed a shudder at the dire images her imagination conjured and ventured the question that had been in her mind since she entered the hall: "That jewel at her throat. Is it . . . ?" She didn't quite have the courage to finish.

Tarod nodded. "It is." The long fingers of his left hand flexed. "It would give me such pleasure to take that white throat and close my hand around it and . . ." A black aura flickered around his frame, then vanished as swiftly as it had materialized. He looked down at the Matriarch and smiled a cold yet somehow conspiratorial smile. "In time, lady Shaill, in time. But for now we must make a pretense of enjoying ourselves and wait like spiders for the fly to blunder too close to our web." He extended an arm. "Will you grace me with your company for a while?"

She hadn't expected that, and it brought a confused flush to her cheeks. But then she thought, Why not? If nothing more, it would give Ailind cause for speculation, and she was fast coming to realize that she didn't have quite the respect for the lord of Order that her catechisms ordained.

She bowed to him in the manner of the Sisterhood, adding a flourish that she knew from the history records was as archaic as his own earlier gesture to her. "I will be glad to, lord Tarod."

Strann was surreptitiously watching Karuth, and it hurt. He didn't need the deliberate stage whispers that had reached him, as adept after adept passed by the usurper's seat and paid their compliments, to tell him that in the eyes of the entire Circle he was now viewed as something lower than excrement. And the fact that Ygorla had also heard the unsubtle insults to him and was hugely amused by them made the sting all the more painful.

Karuth had caught his eye once. On the High Margrave's arm, with a glass of some dark wine in her free hand, she'd looked back, and he had seen the helpless anguish in her eyes and, in his turn, tried silently to convey something of his own feelings. Whether or not he'd succeeded he didn't know, and he was even starting to fear, irrationally, that she might have been poisoned by the tide of sympathy washing around her and was losing hold of her faith in him. Strann prayed with all his heart that it wasn't so and that somehow, before the night was over, he might find a way to give her the reassurance they both craved.

For now, though, with nothing to do other than make the occasional fawning gesture toward Ygorla, he tried not to watch the hall constantly for the distinctive color of Karuth's dress but to turn his attention to the mission with which Tarod had charged him. As yet there was nothing worthwhile to report. Ygorla had progressed through the predictable gamut of delight at the homage being paid to her, to restlessness, and now to a level of boredom that, if not quickly diverted, would soon become dangerous. A few minutes ago Strann had ingratiatingly suggested that she might be pleased to allow the dancing to begin, and to his relief she had agreed and had sent word for the musicians in the gallery to prepare for the first set. Now she was engrossed in trying to decide which of the many men in the hall she would choose to partner first. Strann suspected that she was torn between Ailind and the High Initiate as her prime victim, although he'd seen her eye light more than once on the High Margrave. For the young man's sake Strann hoped he would not be her choice, and he was relieved when, after some minutes of thought, Ygorla snapped her fingers to bring a minion hurrying to her side and announced that she would dance with Tirand Lin.

Tirand came, reluctantly but stoically, as the dance set was announced. He bowed so stiffly that in a different mood Ygorla would have taken insult, and as she rose from her chair to accept his outstretched hand, he looked once, briefly, at Strann.

Strann recoiled from the gaze as though from a

snake, but the momentary exchange hadn't escaped Ygorla's notice, and she laughed.

"Why, rat, why don't you ask the High Initiate's sister if she would like to step this measure with you?" she said.

Strann steeled himself. "Ah, sweet lady," he replied in the most wistful tone he could muster, "it would be but a poor substitute for my heart's desire! No, I must languish here and dream my hopeless dreams. . . ."

Tirand said something under his breath. Ygorla didn't hear it, but Strann did. He watched the High Initiate lead her away, and there was murder in his heart.

"It nearly kills me to admit it, but she's beautiful. Very beautiful."

Calvi and Karuth were dancing together, in a square completed by Sister Alyssi and a young and frightened second-rank adept. Karuth was trying to concentrate on the steps, but Calvi's words made her shiver. And she hadn't failed to notice how often his gaze had strayed to Ygorla as she led the dance with Tirand.

"Beautiful, yes." She managed, with difficulty, to keep her voice even. "And it's one of her greatest dangers."

"Don't think I don't know it! I only hope, for Tirand's sake, that she doesn't decide to keep him at her side for much longer. Look at his face. If he had a blade now, I think he'd try to kill her." Calvi's eyes glittered. "As would I. Sweet gods, as would I!"

Karuth's fingers tightened their grip on his. "Don't, Calvi. Don't even think it, it's too dangerous!"

He relaxed a fraction. "I know." He forced himself to look at the Matriarch, two squares away. "Shaill dancing with the Chaos lord. Now that *does* surprise me."

Karuth detected the tense inflection and said, "You shouldn't judge lord Tarod so harshly, Calvi. He's not entirely what he seems."

"Isn't he?" The challenge was so swift that it caught

her off guard. "After what I saw of him in the Marble Hall, I beg to differ." He missed a step suddenly as his thoughts overtook him, and it was a few seconds before he found the rhythm again. His expression, Karuth saw, had become peculiarly closed, and he said suddenly, "In fact, I'm rapidly coming to believe that the gods—any and all of the gods—have a good deal less regard for us mere mortals than it suits them to pretend. And I'm ready to include lord Ailind in that sweeping statement."

Karuth looked at him in surprise, then remembered the small incident on the night before their visit to Hannik, when Ailind had so publicly disparaged Calvi. Strann had said afterward that it was almost as though the lord of Order were setting out deliberately to alienate him, and though at the time she hadn't taken that remark seriously, Karuth wondered now if perhaps, unbeknownst to her, there had been other incidents that might add weight to Strann's speculation. But what reason could Ailind possibly have for wishing to estrange Calvi from Order's cause? The idea seemed nonsensical.

She was about to probe further when she realized to her annoyance that the dance was coming to an end. The long lines of couples bowed to each other, and there was a polite ripple of applause. Glancing obliquely along the rows, Karuth saw that Ygorla had engaged Tirand in sprightly but one-sided conversation; then suddenly, as though sensing her scrutiny, the usurper's head came up and their eyes met. Ygorla smiled—not a pleasant smile —spoke to Tirand again, then led him down the hall.

"Oh, gods," Calvi said under his breath, "they're coming toward us."

Karuth stood her ground as Ygorla and her brother approached. Tirand looked haggard, but Ygorla's face was a study in feigned cordiality.

"My dear Karuth!" She smiled archly, and her eyes were filled with mockery and challenge. "We have met before, I think, but all too briefly, and I seem to recall that you were not at your most charming. Still, I like to think we can overlook that little incident." She looked directly at Calvi, a dazzling look that made the young

man blink. "And who," she added in a purring tone, "are
you?"

Calvi stiffened and bowed curtly. "I am Calvi Alacar." Reflexive habit almost prompted him to add "at
your service," but he stopped himself in time, and his
mouth snapped shut.

"Ah! The little brother of the late, lamented Blis."
Ygorla laughed sweetly. "You're a good deal more handsome than your brother was, aren't you, Calvi? Quite the
young blade, even if your clothes are a little drab for my
tastes. Still, there's always room for an improving influence. . . ." She turned again to Karuth. "I've been dancing with your brother, my dear, but I find him intolerably
boring, so you may have him for a while and I shall try
out your partner." She gave Tirand a lively shove that
nearly sent him cannoning into Karuth and moved to
Calvi's side, taking a possessive hold on his arm. "I'm
sure that you'll be extremely well matched." Then she
turned on her heel and raised her voice. "Well? Do you
intend to keep me waiting all night? I wish to dance!
Begin!"

She towed Calvi away to lead the new dance. Tirand
didn't move but stood rigid and wooden at Karuth's side,
and, thinking that he was waiting only for a chance to
excuse himself, she turned and made to walk away. But
he caught her hand.

"Karuth. Dance with me. For appearance' sake if
nothing else."

She hesitated, then relented and tried to put as
cheerful a face on it as possible as they moved together
into the lines of couples. Tirand, though, knew her too
well to be taken in, and as the music struck up, he said in
a hard, fervent undertone, "I'll pay her back for that
insult to you. One way or another."

Karuth could have reminded him that he and she
had exchanged many worse insults in the recent past, but
held her tongue. In his own awkward way Tirand was
trying to be conciliatory, and to spurn his efforts would
be churlish. Besides, she could no longer feel hostile toward him. She, too, had learned the lesson of Hannik,

181

that personal grievances had no relevance when there was a common and far crueller enemy to be faced.

Yet despite the tacit thaw, it seemed impossible for either of them to find anything more to say. They completed the dance in stilted silence, then when no one came to claim Karuth, Tirand asked stiffly if she would take the third set with him. She agreed a little distractedly, noticing that Ygorla hadn't gone in search of a new partner but was still monopolizing Calvi. The music began again, and Tirand, who had also seen them, said, "I saw Calvi escorting you earlier. I thought it was very . . . adult of him."

"I appreciated the gesture." Karuth continued to watch Ygorla and the High Margrave together. They made a handsome pairing. Disturbingly handsome . . .

Tirand cleared his throat. "I feel I should have . . . that is . . . Karuth, I wanted to say that I . . ." Suddenly he stopped dancing and they faced each other. His hazel eyes were filled with sympathy, and the old resentment, though still just detectable, was stale and almost dead. "I'm sorry," he said. "Whatever quarrels we may have had in the past, you're still my sister and you don't deserve this. I just wanted to say it."

They were holding up the line and attracting attention to themselves. Quickly Karuth took her brother's hand.

"Let's sit the dance out, Tirand." His words had warmed her suddenly and unexpectedly, and when she smiled at him, there were faint echoes in her smile of the old, close friendship that they had once enjoyed. "I'd like a glass of wine—come and take one with me."

They moved clear of the dancers and, still hand in hand, headed toward one of the tables laden with food and drink that lined the hall. Before they reached it, however, a voice rang out above the strains of the dance.

"What's this, what's this? Are you bored with your tedious little brother already, dear Karuth?"

Unprepared for this interruption, the musicians scraped to an uncertain halt, and heads turned as Ygorla, with Calvi behind her, swept through the crowd toward

Karuth and Tirand. In the instant before humiliation and
fury made her turn her head away, Karuth saw that
Calvi looked dazed.

Ygorla wagged a mock-admonishing finger. "You
are not enjoying the dance, Karuth. I shan't tolerate this
—I will find you a new partner to step out with, and we'll
dispatch your brother to fetch us all some more wine."
She looked slyly, sidelong, at Tirand. "Did you hear me,
High Initiate? You're little use as a gallant, so maybe
you're better suited to a servant's role. Fetch wine, and
you may wait with it by my chair until the dance is
over."

Tirand's face had turned crimson with rage, and the
veins in his neck stood out as he struggled to control
himself. Only the memory of Ailind's adamant orders
held back the tide of his temper, and he bowed.

"As you wish, lady." His voice was barely recognizable.

Ygorla smirked as he walked away. "And now, my
dear," she said to Karuth, "for *you*. I believe I have just
the partner to suit you on this happy evening." And she
snapped her fingers back toward the dais at the end of the
hall. "Rat! Straighten your whiskers and clean your
paws. I have a little task for you!"

Karuth's mind and body froze. Horrified, unable to
believe that even this monstrous woman could have such
a twisted sense of humor, she could neither move nor
speak but could only stare, blank-eyed, as Strann rose
from his cushion on the dais, hesitated, then came slowly
toward them. Others had now seen the nature of Ygorla's
evil-minded joke, and there were gasps, murmurs of protest. But a look from the usurper silenced them, and then
Strann and Karuth were standing face-to-face.

"Karuth seems to have an unfortunate habit of losing her partners, rat, so you must come to her rescue."
Ygorla picked up the jeweled chain that trailed from
Strann's collar and smiled malevolently at Karuth.
"Maybe if you keep a hold on his leash, he won't run
away from you this time!" And the hall rang with her
laughter before she shouted out, "Music! Music!"

There was nothing anyone dared do. The dance began again. Couples started to move once more in their travesty of enjoyment. Strann and Karuth continued to stare at each other. Then, unable to contain her emotion, Karuth rushed forward, her arms held out. "Strann—" Her voice broke as she cried his name.

"No!" He caught her upper arms, thrusting her back from him to keep her forcibly at arm's length, and with a shock she saw that his expression was cold and disdainful. Then from the corner of his mouth he hissed, *"She's watching us. Dance—make a show of it."*

She didn't know if she could, for she was trembling uncontrollably, but he pulled her into the midst of the line, and instinctively her feet seemed to take over. The couples next to them pointedly moved farther away, glaring at Strann with loathing. He ignored them and spoke again in the urgent stage whisper.

"Knowing her, I suspect she'll give us less than a minute together before she decides to have some more fun, so we must speak quickly."

Karuth swallowed something that seemed to be trying to choke her. "Does she . . . does she know of . . . of your feelings . . . ?"

"No. She thinks I dallied with you to pass the time waiting for her, and it's vital that she should continue to think so. Karuth, listen. Whatever I may say, whatever I may do—no matter what it is, or how it looks in public— you mustn't believe it! Promise me you won't. *Promise* me!"

The hand that held hers closed so tightly on her fingers that the grip sent a shooting, aching pain down her arm. Her throat contracted, and she felt the muscles in her jaw begin to quiver. In a desperate attempt to regain her self-control she bit hard on the insides of her cheeks. "Yes," she whispered back. "I promise, I *promise.* Oh, Strann—"

"Love, there's no time!" Strann's glance flicked quickly sideways. "Listen. You must get the High Margrave away from her. I can't explain why, I haven't any evidence, but she's fascinated by him, and I'm convinced there's great danger in that. It's an instinct, nothing more, but something she said earlier—"

The words snapped off suddenly, and with a jolt Karuth saw Ygorla and Calvi moving toward them.

"Oh, gods . . ." There was so much more that needed to be said, but it was too late. Strann's prediction had been right; they had had their minute, and now Ygorla was bent on further mischief.

As she reached them, Strann turned from Karuth and made a deep, flourishing bow. Pleased, Ygorla bestowed an answering smile on him, then picked up the dangling chain that Karuth hadn't been able to bring herself to touch.

"Come, rat. Leave your pretty plaything—*I* want you now." Sickened, Karuth watched as Strann made a knee to the usurper and kissed her hand—and she was doubly shocked when Calvi giggled.

Ygorla looked coquettishly at the High Margrave. "You see, Calvi? I told you I'd trained him well. Later perhaps I'll show you some of the other tricks he can do. He's quite entertaining in his way." She paused, then a vulpine smile curved her lips. "Or perhaps Karuth might be better qualified to instruct you in the rat's little ways. Eh, Karuth? From what I hear, you've enjoyed a caper or two together during his time at the castle." And she laughed lewdly.

Karuth's face turned dead-white, and she thought she was going to be sick. This monster in human guise, this demoness—she couldn't take any more. She *couldn't.*

Ygorla saw the furious emotions that she struggled to contain, and her laughter became shriller. "Oh, my dear, do I distress you? How disappointing. I would have thought you enough of a grown woman not to be upset by my little jests."

Though the musicians were still manfully playing on, none of the couples on the floor could pretend any longer to ignore the confrontation. Dancing had ceased, and people were watching and listening with a mixture of embarrassment and trepidation. Ygorla loved an audience, and she was determined to make the most of this and to complete Karuth's humiliation. She smiled again. "Or are you piqued, dear Karuth, because my little rat's paws no longer patter across your bedcover at nights?" Calvi giggled again like a drunkard, drawing appalled looks from those nearest to them, and Ygorla jingled Strann's chain, adding carelessly, "If your need is so great, my dear, I might lend him to you for an hour or two. On the condition, of course, that you ask me—or perhaps better still, *beg* me—with the proper deference."

Karuth knew she was going to break. She felt the helpless rush of towering fury and knew that she had no power left in her to fight its onslaught. She was going to launch herself at this woman, hurl herself like a rabid cat, like a dervish, and tear her shining hair out by the handful, and rip the skin from her beautiful face, and claw her sapphire eyes to bloody globules, and—

"I think you'll find that the lady Karuth wants nothing from *you,* madam."

Karuth jolted as though someone had physically struck her, and swung around to see Tarod standing behind her.

Ygorla's eyes blazed with indignation and a tinge of disconcertion. "Where did—" and she bit the words back quickly. Tarod laid a hand on Karuth's shoulder, and as his fingers made contact, she felt an inner strength—or perhaps strength from outside her—quench the inferno of her fury and calm her.

Coldly, Tarod smiled at the usurper. "You will excuse us, madam. I have a prior claim on Karuth's time, and no desire to waste it."

Ygorla had quickly recovered her composure and treated him to a raking glare. "I find you impertinent, Tarod of Chaos. That is not a wise stance to adopt with me." Very pointedly, though with ostensible casualness, she touched one hand to the glowing sapphire at her throat.

Tarod's gaze lingered on the stone for a few seconds. "Oh, I don't think so, my lady," he replied softly but with a lethal edge. "I don't believe even one such as you would sacrifice everything for the sake of a moment's peevishness. Or have I credited you with more intelligence than you actually possess?"

Ygorla's cheeks flamed, and her hand closed tightly around the sapphire. "You are taking a very great risk!" she hissed.

"Of course. It's my nature to do so. And now"—still watching her with baneful intensity, Tarod raised Karuth's left hand to his lips and kissed it—"we will seek out more congenial company and will leave you and this groveling piece of offal to your paltry pleasures." He cast an uncompromisingly savage glance at Strann, a look that promised something far worse than death. "You name your pets aptly." And, shielding Karuth in a fold of his green cloak, he led her away.

There was total and ominous silence in the wake of the Chaos lord's departure. Ygorla seemed to be transfixed: she stood motionless, staring after the two receding figures, and even Strann couldn't begin to judge what thoughts lay behind her jewel-hard eyes. His own heart was thumping fearsomely, but over and above his fear he felt an overwhelming surge of gratitude to Tarod for that last piece of subterfuge. With the deadly look and the searing words, the Chaos lord had cast Strann firmly in the role of Ygorla's faithful cohort, and that, Strann knew, might well have saved his life.

Suddenly the silence was broken by a snort of laughter from Calvi. Astonished, Ygorla turned on her heel. *"What?"* Her voice was a dangerous bark.

Calvi laughed again. He was drunk, Strann saw, but there was more to his state of mind than that, and alarm bells began to ring anew in the bard's mind.

"He—" Calvi reached out and laid a hand on Ygorla's sleeve, a gesture no living soul in his right mind should have dared to make at that moment. "He was so *afraid* of you! And yet he thinks—he thinks—" He dissolved into helpless mirth.

Ygorla stared at him. Then, slowly, her own mouth began to twitch in response. "Oh, yes," she said. "Oh, *yes*! Such posturing, such a show, and all for the sake of that drab woman's pride! Or is there more to it than that, eh?" Turning, she nudged Strann in the ribs. "You'd be the one to know, rat. Now that you've thrown her aside, perhaps she's gone running to Tarod and offered him her charms as a means of drowning her sorrows?"

Strann made a tremendous effort and managed to match her prurient expression with a leer of his own. "Sweet lady, she must be more desperate than even I thought her, to nibble at such a lure!"

Ygorla flung back her hand and laughed uproariously. "Indeed, rat, she must! Well, now." In her disconcertingly mercurial way she abruptly sobered and looked at the sea of nervous faces all around her. "What is this, a celebration or a wake? Tell the scum in the gallery to play more music! I will dance until dawn—and you, Calvi, will step out with me!" She dropped Strann's chain, dismissing him with a careless gesture, and held out both hands to the High Margrave.

Strann watched as Calvi, smiling doltishly, caught her fingers in his, and a cold, clammy sensation slithered across the inner recesses of his mind. He'd tried to warn Karuth in the brief minute they'd had together, but it was too late. Ygorla had chosen her victim, and the High Margrave had had no more chance against her than a butterfly against a hurricane. He was bewitched. From this night onward he would be soft clay in her hands.

They whirled away into the new dance that was striking up, and Strann slunk back to his appointed place on the cushion before the usurper's chair. He felt drear, dismal, and wearied to the bone, and the light and color and movement swirling around him as the festivities began once more had suddenly turned from a charade to a carnival of nightmare. He looked for Tarod and Karuth but couldn't see them in the throng; and anyway, he reminded himself, seeing them would do him little good unless he could speak to them without Ygorla knowing. For tonight, at least, that would be impossible.

Strann hung his head as a feeling close to despair swept over him. There was something deeply evil in the wind, he knew it as surely as he'd ever known anything, and he was powerless to prevent its advance. But as to its nature . . . that was beyond a mere jongleur's ability to know, or even to guess. That, Strann thought, suppressing a chill shiver, was a matter for the gods.

13

"I don't know how to thank you." Karuth stared down at her clasped hands, the knuckles white with tension. "If you hadn't intervened when you did, I—I don't know what would have happened."

Tarod knew very well what would have happened, but he didn't consider it necessary to add to her chagrin by saying so. Within a few minutes of the debacle with Ygorla he'd escorted her from the hall, aware that even with his protection she couldn't have held out for much longer. Now they sat together in her room with a jug of wine between them and the fire, newly rekindled, taking away the chill of the night.

Karuth couldn't quite come to terms with this private and oddly intimate encounter, and her feelings were further complicated by the way in which Tarod had come to her rescue. He had set out, it seemed, to imply deliberately that there was more to the relationship between them than anyone else yet realized, and though she knew that it had been nothing more than a ploy, she still found herself disconcerted. Looking at him now, sitting in a chair on the opposite side of the hearth and idly twirling a long-stemmed wine cup in one hand, she had to suppress a shudder whose nature she couldn't entirely understand. It would be very easy, she thought, for a mortal woman to imagine herself in love with a Chaos lord, or at least deeply infatuated. Tarod's melding of remote yet almost omniscient detachment with a startlingly human compassion made a heady blend, and the fact that he was also a god added spice to that already hazardous brew. As they left the hall together, Karuth had seen others watching them, and their looks of shock and dismay had given her a sharp, unanticipated frisson that was almost pleasurable. Perhaps, she thought, it was simply a reaction to the pity that had been showered on her in the wake of Strann's apparent perfidy, a desire to regain some measure of pride and to turn the public face of defeat into one of triumph. But even in her bleakest moments Karuth didn't believe she was that petty. She knew herself better than that—or at least until now she had believed so.

Tarod's soft laughter broke the train of her thoughts then, and she looked up at him. He was smiling at her, and there was more than a hint of intrigue in the smile.

"You've nothing to fear from me, Karuth," he said. "And, if I may presume to say so, nothing to fear from yourself. Strann's claim is safe enough."

She flushed, feeling shamed and foolish. "If I'd known you could read my thoughts—" she began defensively.

"I can't, as I've told you more than once before. But anyone with a modicum of intelligence could read your face at this moment and add a few choice observations of their own. Don't let it trouble you, Karuth. I take your view of me as a compliment—and besides, our combined wiles stood us in good stead."

"Good stead . . . ?" She echoed the words, baffled.

"Oh, yes. The fact that you came close to losing control and marring Ygorla's prized beauty allowed me to put her to the test. A minor test, I'll grant, but still useful because it told me that she's not so foolish or reckless as to jeopardize herself over a point of principle."

Karuth made a pained moue. "She'd have to be exceptionally unintelligent to do that, my lord."

"True, but it was always a possibility. And then of course there's the fact that we were able to make Strann's position in her esteem a little more secure."

"Yes." She recalled what he'd done, and why. "I thank you for that."

"It's in Chaos's interest as much as yours, I assure you." But the look he gave her seemed to belie the entire truth of the careless claim. There was silence for some while. Then Tarod asked, "Did Strann have anything to tell you?"

The change of tack brought Karuth firmly back to earth, and she frowned. "Yes. Yes, he did. It was about Calvi—"

"Ah." Tarod's tone altered. "What did he say?"

"That it was vital he should be lured away from the usurper's influence." Then she recalled the state Calvi had been in, the way he'd laughed at her predicament as though he'd drunk himself almost insensible, and yet—

She met Tarod's gaze, and her own eyes were suddenly stark. "Strann didn't have the chance to explain what he meant. But the warning was too late, wasn't it? Whatever he suspected had already happened."

It was the confirmation Tarod had sought. "Yes," he said. "It was too late." He sighed exasperatedly. "I should have foreseen something like this. Calvi was all too likely a target, especially in the wake of Ailind's crass stupidity toward him a few nights ago."

Like the Matriarch earlier in the evening, Karuth was surprised to realize that that incident hadn't escaped his notice either. That triggered another thought, and she said, "My lord, Strann made an odd remark to me about that matter. He said—and he wasn't either willing or able to elaborate—that it was almost as if Ailind had set out deliberately to alienate Calvi."

"Did he, now?" Tarod's eyes narrowed sharply. "Why, I wonder, should he think that?"

She couldn't answer, and the Chaos lord said, "This may bear further investigation. I'll see what I can unearth."

"If I can help in any way—"

"As yet, no." Then the darkly thoughtful look vanished, and his expression softened as he rose to his feet. "For now I think what you need above all else is a sound night's sleep, so I'll leave you to your bed. Oh, and don't fear that Ygorla might seek to put more mischief in your path. I'll ensure that she can do no such thing."

Karuth smiled gratefully, but it was an effort. "I

appreciate your kindness, my lord. But it's Strann's safety I fear for, not mine."

"Strann's more than capable of looking after himself, as he proved tonight. He's too useful a foil to the usurper's conceit for her to harm him." Seeing that his reassurance hadn't entirely convinced her, Tarod reached out and touched her cheek lightly, smoothing back a tendril of dark hair from her face. "Try not to be too afraid, Karuth." And, bending, he kissed her brow.

She stayed very still for a long time after he had gone, her eyes focused on nothing, her thoughts in turmoil. Then at last she rose, crossed to the window, and closed the inner shutters. She rarely did such a thing, preferring not to banish light and air entirely from her room even at this time of year. But strains of music from the dining hall were still floating up on the sharp, frosty breeze. She wanted to shut them out. Tonight, she wanted to shut out the entire world and be truly alone.

Ygorla didn't quite carry out her promise or threat to dance until dawn, but it was well into the small hours when, to the immense relief of the assembly, she finally announced that she had had enough of frivolity and intended to retire. And when she swept, laughing and smiling, from the hall and well satisfied with her evening's achievements, Calvi Alacar went with her.

Tirand, who had finally escaped her malicious attentions and taken refuge with the Matriarch and a group of higher adepts, saw the departing pair, and his hand clenched so hard on the stem of his wineglass that he almost snapped it. Uttering a sharp, ugly oath, he left his startled companions and started toward the doors, meaning to intercept the usurper. Before he could approach her, however, he found Ailind barring his path.

"No, Tirand." The lord of Order's expression was cooly unruffled. "Let them go."

"But my lord, we can't allow her to do this! Calvi

needs help. He must be got away, before her influence poisons him!"

Ailind shrugged indifferently. "I suspect it's a little late for that. If the High Margrave is so foolish as to allow himself to be captivated by such a creature, then I fear there's nothing we can do to prevent it."

Appalled, Tirand stared at him. "But—" he began again.

Ailind's eyes flickered with a faintly dangerous light. "You have heard my order, High Initiate. Kindly obey it."

As Tirand backed slowly away, not daring to argue any further, the lord of Order turned to watch Ygorla again. The double doors were opening for her; behind her, pulled along on his jeweled chain, went the sniveling turncoat Strann, a cockerel prancing on a dungheap; and on her arm, his eyes focused with a peculiar, unswerving rapture on the usurper's face, Calvi walked like a man in the throes of a blissful dream.

Very deliberately, very privately, Ailind smiled.

The inner door of Ygorla's apartments slammed shut in Strann's face, and he sank down to the floor of the anteroom, his back against the wall and his eyes tightly shut.

Fool he was, *fool!* He should have seen this, should have been more urgent and explicit in his warning to Karuth. As it was, he hadn't even had time to explain the half of what was in his mind before that evil bitch had pulled them apart as carelessly and maliciously as she'd thrown them together. Now, although he didn't believe for one moment that she'd summon him into her presence again tonight, he still didn't dare leave his post. Giggling like a schoolgirl, and with Calvi bemusedly hanging on her arm, she had ordered him to stay here like an obedient rat until she should call for him again, and the two of them had disappeared into her bedchamber. Strann knew only too well the price of disobeying her, and she was likely as not to send some grotesque elemental to check that he'd not flouted her command.

He didn't know whether to weep, laugh, or scream. Of all the men in the castle she might have picked on to become her paramour, Calvi Alacar had been the least likely and yet now, with the benefit of hindsight, most glaringly obvious choice. To ensnare the brother of the man she had savagely murdered would appeal both to Ygorla's perverted sense of humor and to her colossal ego, and the fact that she had achieved it so easily would be a sobering demonstration to the Circle of her power.

High-pitched laughter floated from the far side of the door, muffled by the thick wall, and Strann tried not to imagine what manner of web Ygorla might be spinning around her hapless victim. He wondered whether Calvi would still be sane by the time dawn broke, or even if he'd live to see the dawn at all. If the mood took her, Ygorla would think nothing of having her pleasures and then killing him as carelessly as she'd killed so many others, and by the same act deliver a fearsome challenge to those who stood against her. Yet, pausing to consider, Strann didn't think it would come to that. Ygorla, he suspected strongly, would find far more entertainment in keeping the High Margrave alive but hopelessly under her spell. And though it made no logical sense, Strann had an equally strong intuition that the usurper wouldn't be the only one to be pleased by that situation.

Tarod had left the hall early, with Karuth. Neither of them yet knew the outcome of Ygorla's latest game, and they hadn't witnessed Tirand Lin's brief confrontation with Ailind as the usurper was making her exit. Strann had. Following on the end of Ygorla's leash, he hadn't passed close enough to hear what the High Initiate had to say to his mentor, but he had seen Tirand summarily dismissed and seen Ailind's private smile, which had looked to him like a smile of satisfaction. Something was afoot, Strann knew it, and he *had* to find a way to get word of it to the Chaos lord.

There was silence now from the inner chamber. Trying to reassure himself that that wasn't necessarily ominous, Strann got carefully to his feet and tiptoed to the outer door. Praying that the latch and hinges wouldn't squeak—they didn't—he eased the door open a crack and looked out into the passage. No one in sight. Just a single torch burning in its sconce a few feet away. How long would it take him to reach the north spire? He didn't dare go to Karuth's room, for if he did, the temptation to stay would be more than he could hope to overcome and that could bring disaster on all their heads. The spire it would have to be; it was a dangerous risk, but there seemed to be no other choice.

He was looking back over his shoulder and trying to force himself to make the decision to go, when the gray cat appeared. It greeted him with a quick, urgent *"prrrt"* that made him start, and he looked down to see it standing by his feet and gazing up at him with intense concentration.

The cat . . . of course! He'd teased Karuth about it, calling the creature her personal familiar, but now the joke took on an altogether new aspect. Could he impart what he wanted to say, and would it understand and take the message to Tarod? Strann was no telepath, but it seemed to him that it was the cats themselves, rather than their human contacts, who dictated the success or otherwise of any communication.

Casting another swift, cautious glance through the open door behind him, he crouched down and held out his fingers for the cat to sniff. *"Go to Tarod,"* he whispered, at the same time trying to conjure and project a mental picture of the Chaos lord's face and the north spire. The cat purred—Strann hoped fervently that this was its way of saying that it understood—and he gave it his message, a series of images that he hoped would convey his meaning while still being simple enough for the little animal to grasp and remember. At last he could do no more, and, feeling mentally drained, he stroked the cat's small, hard head.

"I can only pray now that you comprehend me," he told it softly. "Go, now. Find Tarod."

The cat's tail twitched. Then, silent as a phantom, it

turned and streaked away. Strann stood watching until it
vanished around the corner, then withdrew into the room
and closed the door very softly behind him.

* * *

"The cat's message was quite clear," Tarod said. "The
usurper has ensnared the High Margrave—and Strann is
convinced that Ailind is pleased by the development."

In the unlit spire room, where two worlds had for a
few moments merged, Yandros's dark, silhouetted image
shifted slightly as he made a restless movement with one
hand. "It fits with the pattern we were beginning to suspect, Tarod. Ailind's public treatment of Calvi has already indicated that Order doesn't apparently care
whether or not he remains loyal to them—"

Tarod interrupted. "Strann seems to think that it's
more than carelessness. He believes it could well be a
deliberate ploy."

"To disaffect the High Margrave?" Yandros was surprised. "Now, why in all the many realms of creation
should Aeoris want to bring such a thing about? Calvi's
always been one of his staunchest allies"—he didn't trouble to hide his disdain at that—"and I'd have thought our
friends would be eager to see he remains so. This doesn't
make sense."

"No, but I still think it could be true, Yandros.
Strann's shrewd, and a good deal more intuitive than he
likes to pretend. If he smells something in the wind, I'm
inclined to heed what his nose tells him."

Though he was unwilling to admit it even to his
brother, Yandros felt uneasy. He and Tarod had been
certain for a good while now that something was afoot in
the realm of Order, but this first clue, if indeed it was a
clue and not an entirely false trail, disconcerted him, for
it was in direct contradiction to the kind of strategy that
he would have anticipated from Aeoris.

Leaving further thought on the subject in abeyance
for the moment, he said, "What of our brother's soul-
gem? Have you seen it?"

Tarod nodded somberly. "I have. She wore it to-night, blatantly displayed on a chain at her neck so that the entire company could see it." He paused. "I've also divined the link between her and the stone. She's created a safeguard that ensures that if anything should befall her, the stone will instantly be shattered, and even we wouldn't have the power to break the link in time." His eyes narrowed to slits. "We might scorn her subtler intelligence, but we can't fault her cunning."

"She's issued no direct challenge, though?" Yandros asked.

"No. For the time being it seems to suit her crude disposition simply to flaunt her supremacy at any and every opportunity."

"I hope you haven't risen to her bait."

Tarod smiled thinly, remembering his brief and acerbic exchange with the usurper in the hall. "Not in any way that might put the soul-stone in jeopardy."

"Be sure that you don't. Whatever the temptation, be sure of it. And what of Narid-na-Gost?"

Tarod looked speculatively through the window to where the castle's south spire was silhouetted against dim starlight. "No one has set eyes on him yet. The Circle doesn't even know he's here. He's found himself a hole to crawl into and he seems content to let his daughter soil her hands on his behalf."

"Is he, too, linked to the stone?"

"I believe he is, but I can't be sure. It isn't something I'd care to put to the test."

Yandros's shoulders hunched moodily. "Quite. Well, frustrating though it is, it seems we must continue to wait and watch. Let me know when you have further word from Strann."

Tarod nodded and made ready to dissolve the link between their worlds. Just before he did so, however, Yandros smiled with a brief resurgence of his customary dark humor.

"One last thing, Tarod. Don't let Karuth Piadar foster *too* many notions about your motives. Remember

what happened the last time you developed an affection
for a mortal woman!"

Tarod laughed softly. "I'll remember."

———————————————⟩ ⟨————————————

Even as Tarod and Yandros completed their discussion
and went their separate ways, Ailind, in his chamber in
the east wing, had made contact with Aeoris.

"The trap has sprung exactly according to plan,"
Ailind told his great brother. "The High Margrave is
already besotted by the usurper, and I'd surmise that it
won't be long before he's completely in her sway. Add
that to the fact that he's already disaffected with us, and
the recipe is almost complete."

Aeoris smiled cannily. "Indeed it is. This is excellent
news, Ailind."

"Calvi will of course find himself in conflict with the
Circle now," Ailind said, "and that should heap more
fuel on the fires of his resentment toward Order. Our next
move, I think, must be to play further on that and turn it
to our advantage."

"I foresee no difficulties there," Aeoris told him.
"The High Margrave is fundamentally weak, so it'll be a
simple matter to influence his unconscious mind. The
next stage of our strategy should be easy enough." He
paused. "Have you investigated the matter of the elementals, as I instructed?"

"Yes, brother, I have. As I reported to you, the
usurper has power over them, but she constantly abuses
that power. She seems to take a delight in tormenting
them, or in using them for some trivial purpose and then
destroying them." Ailind raised his pale brows expressively. "They're willing to cooperate with us, very willing
in fact. They see our plan as a means of striking back at
her, and that's what they desire above all else."

Aeoris's expression grew a shade cynical. "Assuming, of course, that the elementals can be made to understand and respect the need for utter secrecy."

"I've seen to it that they do."

"In that case it seems that we're ready to make our next move. I am very pleased, Ailind. *Very* pleased. Now, what of Chaos? Have they made any move?"

Ailind shook his head. "None. It's my belief that they're at a complete stalemate and likely to remain so." He laughed. "After all, what *can* Yandros do that won't imperil his brother's life?"

"Quite." Aeoris smiled again. "Very well. It seems that thus far everything has progressed as smoothly as we could have hoped. You may begin your work with the elementals tonight, and report to me again when there's more to tell. I shall await the next developments with great interest."

The golden light spilling through from the realm of Order faded from the room as Aeoris vanished. For several seconds Ailind stood motionless, his eyes focused on the place where his brother had been, but his mind elsewhere. Then his lip curled faintly, almost cynically, and he raised one hand in a beckoning gesture. Another light, smaller and paler and colder than Aeoris's aura, manifested above his head, and within the light a dimly visible, unhuman form shifted.

"Child of air and water." Ailind looked up at the light and spoke softly but sternly. "Do you and your kindred understand the commission I entrust to you? And do you understand that no trace of what you do tonight must be known to another living entity?"

A thin, sighing voice, like a faraway sea surge or the murmur of a faint breeze, answered him. *"We understand, lord."*

Ailind nodded, satisfied. "Then let us consider the dreams that we shall send to our quarry tonight. . . ."

Ygorla woke shortly after dawn. Despite her indolent self-indulgence she'd never lost the early-rising habit developed during her Southern Chaun childhood, and once her eyes had opened, her avid interest in what the new day might have to offer drove out any further desire for sleep.

At her side, hair a pale cloud among the rumpled pillows and bedcoverings, Calvi Alacar slept on. For the past few minutes he'd been moving restlessly, his eyelids fluttering and, once, a small sigh escaping him. But whatever private dreams had troubled him were gone now, and his recumbent form was peaceful again. She looked at him and smiled a lazily satisfied smile as she thought back on the events of the ball and its aftermath. The High Margrave had proved to be something of a revelation. She'd originally intended only to dangle him like bait on her hook for a while, bewitching him to the point where he was completely under her control, for the sheer pleasure of horrifying the Circle, who thought him so steadfast an ally. Achieving that had been simple: Calvi's personality was unassuming enough to make him easy prey. But if his character was weak, she'd discovered later that his body most certainly wasn't. Though Ygorla was no virgin, Calvi was the first *human* man she'd ever taken to her bed, and the novel experience had delighted her. He had a great deal to recommend him, she thought; youth, good looks, virile vitality—and above all the fact that, thanks to her sorcery, he was now her mental and physical slave.

She yawned and stretched luxuriously, enjoying the sensations that assailed her. There was no need to rise yet. In a while she would demand breakfast for them both, and then she could decide how she might find further advantage in this new and gratifying situation. Rolling over, she reached out to shake Calvi by the shoulder and wake him—

Then froze as she saw Narid-na-Gost squatting at the foot of the bed and leering suggestively at her.

Ygorla's face twisted. *"Father!"* Outrage and fury crackled from her in a palpable aura. "How *dare* you spy on me!"

Calvi mumbled and began to stir. Hastily Ygorla made a pass over his face with one hand, and he sank instantly back into an unnatural sleep from which nothing would wake him until and unless she commanded it. Then she turned to the foot of the bed again. Her father was still crouching there, still grinning, and her mouth set in a ferociously ugly line. "Get out of this room! Get *out*!"

The demon cackled lewdly. "What's the matter, daughter? I've watched you at your carnal pleasures often enough in the past. Why so modest all of a sudden? Are you afraid to let your new paramour see the nature of your origins?"

In a fit of temper Ygorla snatched up a pillow and hurled it at him. He swayed aside, plucked the pillow out of the air as it flew by, and breathed on it. It disintegrated in a brief but spectacular gout of flame, and the demon turned hot crimson eyes on his daughter.

"Your childish games don't impress me!" The show of prurience had dropped away in an instant, and his voice was savage. "You know full well that I haven't the slightest interest in how you choose to squander your time or who you squander it with! And you also know full well why I'm here. This has gone on long enough, Ygorla. I am tired of waiting!"

There was a sharp, tense silence. Ygorla sat unmoving in the bed, her expression thoughtful as she glared back at her sire from under half-hooded eyelids. Then, with great delicacy and precision, she said, *"You* are tired of waiting. I see. And since when has *your* will been paramount, Father?"

Narid-na-Gost hesitated as something in her tone warned him that this was not to be simply another of their frequent wrangles. She sounded too calm, too reasonable, as though she had expected this and had prepared herself for it. And as though she had something in mind that he had overlooked.

He said sharply, "I don't forget the terms of our pact, daughter." A faint but clear emphasis on the word *daughter* would, he hoped, provide a timely reminder of her debt to him. "But it's time now for you to fulfil your part of the bargain we made. It's time to stop toying with these humans and make your demands, so that I in my turn can make mine!"

"You're too impatient, Father. I've told you before: When I'm ready, and *only* when I'm ready, I will make my move. Until I do, I'm afraid that you must learn to curb your haste."

"I have curbed it for long enough!" the demon retorted angrily. "You seem to forget, child, that you owe all you are and all you've achieved to me! *My* powers have brought you this far. I elevated you from nothing, and you'd do well to remember that I could as easily throw you down to become nothing again!"

Ygorla smiled. "Oh, but I don't think you could," she said sweetly. With a deliberate gesture she took the chain of the soul-stone between her thumb and forefinger and, lifting the gem away from her naked breast, spun it gently so that it glittered in the early-morning light.

Something turned cold inside Narid-na-Gost, and when he spoke, his voice betrayed it. "You *dare* to threaten me . . . ?"

She smiled, and there was implacable, arrogant confidence in her eyes. "I don't *threaten* you, dear Father, I simply make a statement of fact. This jewel is the key to everything; to my power in the mortal realm and to the power you wish to wield in the realm of Chaos. You might have stolen it, but *I* possess it now, and the safeguard that prevents Yandros and his brothers from trying to recover it is *my* safeguard."

"That enchantment protects us both!" Narid-na-Gost snarled. "You haven't the power to change it!"

She made a coquettish moue. "Perhaps you're right; but then again, perhaps you're wrong. Would you care to put it to the test?"

The feeling of cold trepidation that had gripped the demon suddenly crystallized into dreadful understanding. His gaze and hers were locked, and though neither gave their feelings away, they both knew the truth. Narid-na-Gost was trapped. He dared not pick up the gauntlet that Ygorla had thrown down with such apparent caprice; for if he did, he might discover too late that he had made a terrible miscalculation. With a certainty that set his mind reeling, he realized that he had underestimated his daughter. Underestimated her will, underestimated her ambition—and above all underestimated the sheer human deviousness by which she'd inveigled him into granting her far more power than was wise.

A few days ago, just before their departure from Summer Isle, Narid-na-Gost had asked himself how long it would be before Ygorla realized that the scales had tilted between them and that he had lost his old supremacy over her. Now the answer confronted him as clearly as if she'd screamed it in his face. She knew. She had learned all he could teach her, taken all he could give to her, and then she had strengthened her skills and her knowledge still further by adding the human dimension that Narid-na-Gost could never attain. She was out of his reach now, beyond his control. And his greatest mistake had been in allowing her to take charge of the Chaos stone.

He said, his voice with an edge like splintered glass, "You still need me, Ygorla. Without me you might rule in this world, but the Chaos realm is another matter."

Did she still believe that? Impossible to tell from her enigmatic smile, her coolly calculating eyes, and even when she shrugged her bare shoulders in apparent acknowledgment, the demon still felt the foreboding chill of uncertainty. Until this moment he had never thought to question his assumption that to reign as Empress of the mortal world would be enough to satisfy her craving for dominion. Now, though, he began to wonder if that had been yet another mistake.

Ygorla smiled then, a small, cruel, and charmless smile, as though she knew his thoughts. "I think," she said, and the Chaos stone flashed deep blue as she twirled it gently again, "that there must be some changes between us, dearest Father. I think that we must come to a new and more appropriate understanding."

The demon's eyes narrowed to slits. "Understanding?"

"Yes." The word was sibilant in the quiet room, like

a snake's hiss. "It's quite simple. One of us, and one alone, holds the power here, which is to say, the power to bend both the Circle and the lords of Chaos to our will. *I* am that one. So *I* will decide when our move is to be made, while *you*"—and the pretense of sweetness in her voice vanished suddenly—"will not *dare* to interfere with my decision!"

Silence fell. They watched each other, he cornered, she haughtily confident. Narid-na-Gost thought of all the precautions he might and should have taken from the very beginning when she was an unfledged child and raw clay in his hands, but it was too late to regret their absence now. It was seven years too late. He had no choice but to concede to her and to withdraw from the argument with what dignity he could still muster.

With a smooth, reptilian movement he climbed off the bed. A faint, dark aura pulsed around him; his expression was bitter and remote.

"You disappoint me, daughter," he said. "I thought you had learned wisdom. Clearly I was wrong. Very well. I shall leave you to your games and return to the spire until you decide that you have need of me." He paused, and for the first time since their alliance had begun, his eyes showed undisguised hatred. "And whatever it pleases you to believe now, you *will* have need of me, Ygorla. Amid all your arrogance and your vanity, don't ever be so unwise as to forget that!"

14

There were few diners in the hall for breakfast that morning, and of the sparse number who did take their places at the restored tables, none seemed to have an appetite. Food was picked at in an atmosphere of brooding silence, and most plates were pushed away with their contents virtually untouched.

There was only one topic of conversation at the tables: the overriding concern, shared by all the adepts, about the fate of the High Margrave. Calvi hadn't been seen since he had left the hall last night on Ygorla's arm, and speculation was rife as to what might have become of him. The Circle had already witnessed the depths of Ygorla's cruelty and contempt for life, and no one doubted that, if it should suit her purpose or her mood, she'd have no hesitation in adding Calvi to the long list of her victims. Though they didn't voice their thoughts aloud, a few of the most pessimistic adepts were convinced that the High Margrave was already dead.

As yet, though, no one had dared to make any inquiries or investigations. Tarod and Ailind might have been able to help, but neither god had been seen since the ball was in full swing. The High Initiate was present in the hall, sitting with the Matriarch at a table near the hearth, but his face wore a bleak and forbidding look that deterred anyone who thought to approach him.

And so the shocked silence that descended on the hall had all the more impact when, as the last dishes were being cleared away, Calvi walked in.

Heads turned, expressions froze. For one moment there was a rush of palpable relief, but it changed abruptly to apprehension as people took in the High Margrave's appearance and, more significantly, his demeanor. Calvi looked as fresh as though he'd just woken from a long, sound, and sober sleep. His skin and hair were newly washed, and he was wearing opulent clothes far removed from his usual style. And the extraordinary, proud smile on his face, and the strange and remote hauteur in his blue eyes as he scanned the room, told the assembled company that something was very, very wrong.

"Well, this is a sorry gathering!" Calvi's voice sounded normal enough, but there was a new confidence underlying his light tone that wasn't altogether pleasant. "Nursing some thick heads, eh?" He laughed—a stilted, artificial laugh—and strode down the central aisle toward a servant who had been clearing one of the tables but now stood arrested, staring at him.

"You! The Empress and I will breakfast in half an hour from now. We want bread and meat, cake and sweetmeats, and two flagons of Prospect wine. See that it isn't late." Then, as eyes widened at his peremptory and quite uncharacteristic discourtesy, Calvi turned and saw the High Initiate and the Matriarch at their table.

"Tirand—Shaill." He bowed with a hint of what could have been interpreted as mockery. "Good morning to you both."

Tirand only stared at him, but Shaill, her eyes troubled, rose to her feet. "Calvi . . . we've been worried about you."

"Worried?" Calvi laughed again, and again the laughter had a peculiar, brittle edge. He sauntered toward the table, took Shaill's hand, and kissed it with an elegant flourish. "And why, dear Matriarch, should you be worried?"

Shaill looked into his eyes, saw what was there, and felt as though something inside her had shriveled. Calvi had the look of a man drugged. His pupils were dilated, the whites of his eyes overbrilliant . . . and there was something else there, something Shaill couldn't name but that struck cold fear into her, for it reeked of corruption.

So she had succeeded, the Matriarch thought bitterly. In one night she had taken the human being who had more cause to loathe her than any other, and she had twisted his mind completely to her will. Calvi had become not only the lover of his brother's murderess but also her slave.

She said aloud, her voice a little unsteady, "When you left the hall last night, with . . . with . . ."

"With the Empress?" Calvi's eyes narrowed slightly as though challenging her to refer to Ygorla by any less complimentary name.

"Yes. With the . . . Empress, we thought—we feared—"

"That she would prove too much for a youth of my tender years?" Another laugh, and Shaill winced inwardly. "Far from it, my dear Shaill, far from it! I assure you—and you may repeat this to your insipid friend Ailind for his edification—that I am *not* the weakling that this entire damned castle seems to think me!"

Shaill recoiled as his tone became suddenly petulant and ugly, and beside her Tirand started to rise as though to protest. Quickly and emphatically the Matriarch trod on the High Initiate's foot, warning him to hold both his tongue and his temper. They had nothing to gain from quarreling with Calvi; indeed it might be a dangerous thing to do if he should carry the tale back to Ygorla. Tirand subsided as he understood her silent message, and Calvi, his good humor instantly restored, made an airy gesture.

"I really haven't the time to stand making small talk," he said, not unpleasantly but in a tone that suggested both Shaill and Tirand were beneath notice. "My lady awaits me, and she is impatient. Good day to you both."

They didn't speak for some seconds as the young man walked away. Then Tirand broke the silence with an explosive oath.

"Damn him for a boorish and insolent puppy! Who does he think he is, that he *dares* to take that tone to you?"

Shaill was still watching Calvi, who by now had nearly reached the door, and her voice was ominous as she replied, "I don't think he knows who he is. Not any more."

Her words brought the High Initiate up short as he realized exactly what she was implying, and she added, "Did you look into his eyes, Tirand?"

"No . . ."

"I did. Whatever it was that I saw looking back at me was not Calvi Alacar."

Tirand was appalled. "You think it was some demonic creation?"

"No, no, that wasn't what I meant. That isn't some simulacrum conjured up as an evil joke. It's Calvi himself, I'm sure of it. But not the Calvi we've always known. He's bewitched. I saw the signs. Whatever that bitch did to him at the ball last night, she's magnified it tenfold now. He's her creature, mind and body, and probably soul into the bargain."

A crash at the far end of the hall startled them as Tirand was about to reply. They looked up and saw a servant sprawling on the floor amid a litter of dropped plates and cups. Calvi stood two paces away, staring at the mess. He was grinning like a deviant child, and the shocked faces of the adepts nearest to the scene told the entire story without any need for explanation. It had been a momentary whim, a petty and spiteful piece of mischief without excuse or rational motive, and as he saw the reactions of his small audience, Calvi laughed loudly, then turned and swaggered out of the hall.

Some of the adepts were already going to the unfortunate servant's aid, and Shaill, who had also started toward them, subsided again as she saw that they had no need of an extra pair of hands. She looked at Tirand.

"Oh, gods," she said softly. "What are we to do?"

Tirand's mouth was a hard, tight line. "I must speak to lord Ailind."

The Matriarch hesitated, then: "Tirand . . . to be frank, do you honestly believe that lord Ailind either can or will do anything to help us?"

The High Initiate's face grew wary. "What do you mean?"

She sighed. "Didn't you ask for his help last night? And didn't he refuse it?"

"I . . . there was nothing he could do."

"But you asked him." Not a question this time but a statement; Shaill had witnessed Tirand's urgent approach to the lord of Order and, like Strann, she'd guessed what had prompted it, even though she'd not been close enough to overhear their exchange.

"I did ask him, yes." It was clear that Tirand didn't like admitting the truth, but he was too honest a man to deny it. "But clearly the circumstances have now changed."

Shaill couldn't quite see the logic of that statement but let it pass. "I think we'd best waste no time," she said. "And if lord Ailind can't act, we must find a way to take matters into our own hands."

Abruptly Tirand got up from the table. "You're right of course." His tone surprised her, for it implied that she'd touched a very raw nerve. "I'll speak to him again now. No"—as she, too, made to rise—"it's all right. Probably better that I see him alone. I'll seek you out a little later and tell you what he has to say."

The Matriarch watched him leave. Privately she was inclined to think that he'd get little more comfort from Ailind than he'd received last night. And though she didn't like the idea of being disloyal to Tirand, she also thought that if her surmise was right, it might be high time to consider looking elsewhere for guidance.

Strann had pretended to be asleep when he heard the door of Ygorla's bedchamber opening. From his heap of cushions on the floor of the outer room, where it amused the usurper to have him lie each night, he kept his breathing light and even and watched through half-open eyes and a carefully placed lock of his hair as Calvi emerged.

He didn't need to see the High Margrave clearly or

catch the words of the brief conversation that passed between him and Ygorla to know that the sorceress had done her work thoroughly and well. The sickly and adoring tone of Calvi's voice, counterpointed by Ygorla's affectedly girlish giggles, told him all he needed to know, and the knowledge turned his stomach. Then the inner door closed again, and Strann shut his eyes quickly as Calvi sauntered across the room, passing close by. He sensed the young man pausing to stare down at him and felt a peculiar, intuitive shudder as his mind picked up the hint of an unpleasant aura. Then Calvi was gone, and moments later Ygorla's voice rang shrilly from the bedchamber.

"*Rat!* Come here!"

Hastily smoothing his hair and adjusting the hated jeweled collar, Strann went to answer her summons. She was sprawled indolently on the bed, dressed only in a thin shift, and she smiled provocatively at him as he entered the room.

"Ah, so you *were* awake. I thought as much."

Strann flushed, realizing he'd made a tactical mistake. But Ygorla misinterpreted the sudden coloring of his cheeks, and a smile spread across her face.

"Why are you up and pattering from your rat hole so early? Are you *jealous,* is that it? You really mustn't be. Calvi is much younger than you, after all, and so much more handsome. And we can't have you entertaining ideas above your station, can we?"

Strann turned his head away and made a good show of seeming downcast. "Lady, a man cannot help having his dreams, however wild and impossible they may be," he said in a sorrowful voice.

She was pleased with his answer and laughed. "Well, dear rat, the best *you* can hope for—and it should be more than enough—is to please me in the small ways that befit your talents. I have a task for you. You should find it entertaining, for it will put that devious, dissembling and tricky little mind of yours to good use."

Though his expression remained neutral, Strann felt a stirring of interest. Ygorla had implied that she was

about to take him into her confidence, which was precisely what Tarod had hoped she would do. He said, "My
Empress, I am yours to command."

"So you are. Well, listen. And sit down. I don't like
it when you loom over me like that. There, on the floor."

He settled, cross-legged and attentive, and she
propped herself up on one elbow, looking at him keenly.

"I know the ways of rats, Strann the Storymaker. I
know that for all their seeming coyness and innocence
they're as curious as cats and as cunning as foxes. And I
have no doubt at all that you know a good deal more
about what is afoot here than you've been willing to admit."

Strann's hands, which had been fidgeting in his lap,
were suddenly very still. Ygorla saw and nodded. "Yes,
you know *far* more than you dare say. How many days
did you spend in the castle, rat, before I arrived? How
many people did you talk to, how many conversations
did you overhear? Don't try to pretend to me that the
presence of a lord of Chaos and a lord of Order within
these walls didn't set your whiskers twitching. Did you
wriggle your way into their confidence, or did you simply
lurk in dark corners with your ears pricked and learn
what you wanted to learn that way?"

Sweating, Strann started to say, "Majesty, I did
only—"

"You did only what suited your purpose, and I don't
doubt that you did it very well." Suddenly she sat up and
leaned forward. One hand cupped around the Chaos
stone at her neck and she held it out to him like a challenge. "Answer me, rat, and answer me truthfully if you
value that carefully repaired hand of yours. Do you know
what this is?"

He had a few seconds, no more, to decide what to
say, and his mind worked as fast as it had ever done in
his life. If he lied, she might sense it, and then he'd lose
far more than the chance to inveigle his way into her
trust. But if he told the truth, she might just as easily tear
him apart for daring to probe into matters that were none

of his concern. Strann hesitated—then decided to risk the truth, or a fair approximation.

He looked up at her and allowed a modicum of guile to creep into his expression, together with a faintly conspiratorial smile. "Lady," he said, "I believe I do."

He didn't need to elaborate. She'd known all along that he was party to a good deal more than she'd ever told him, and the question had been a test of his honesty. Strann felt deeply relieved that he'd chosen the right answer—and doubly thankful that Ygorla had her own erroneous belief as to where and how he had got his information.

"Then," she said sweetly, "if you know what I have in my possession, perhaps you also have an idea of what I intend to do with it?"

Cautiously, Strann ventured, "I . . . wouldn't claim any *knowledge*, Majesty. I have heard rumors, but . . ."

"Ah, rumors. And what conclusions do these rumors lead your wily brain to deduce?"

A long pause. Then Strann said softly, "That although you have the mortal realm in your grasp, lady, there may be . . ." He licked his lips, watching her intently. ". . . There may be, shall we say . . . greater heights to which you wish to ascend."

Ygorla returned his gaze for a moment, her eyes as bright as the great sapphire on its chain and their color far harder. "Yes, rat," she said at last, "you *are* a clever rat, as I suspected. I believe that you're going to be very useful to me in the days to come." She climbed from the bed and walked slowly, negligently to a table where a flagon of her favorite wine stood. "So the lords of Chaos have admitted their dilemma to the Circle, have they?"

"Their dilemma, madam?"

She swung around. "Don't dissemble with me. If you know what this jewel is, then you know perfectly well what I mean."

Strann bowed his head. "I'm not party to the gods' discussions, Majesty. But—"

"But you know how to eavesdrop, and your little friend Karuth was doubtless naive enough to tell you everything you couldn't learn by more furtive means. After all, she seems to have Tarod's ear." Ygorla cackled. "Or possibly a good deal more than his ear, from what we saw last night, eh?"

Fortunately Strann knew both Karuth and Tarod too well to take that bait, and he also laughed. "As I said at the time, Majesty, I believe she would have to be in the depths of despair to turn her face in *that* direction!"

"So you flatter yourself that you've truly broken her heart, do you?" She gave another cackle, and he knew that his calculatedly insulting reference to Tarod had met with her approval. "But that's neither here nor there at present, though it may prove useful later." She made a careless pass in the air, and a ghostly, seven-fingered hand materialized and poured wine from the flagon into a cup before lifting the cup for her to take. She swallowed a good-sized mouthful, said, *"Aaah,"* with relish, waved the elemental into oblivion, then turned on her heel again to look at Strann.

"Answer me a question. In all your probing and prying, has anyone ever spoken to you of a being named Narid-na-Gost?"

Strann hadn't expected that, and it caught him completely unawares. By a stroke of luck, however, Ygorla mistook the cause of his confusion. "No? Ah, then perhaps Chaos has its own reasons for keeping that little secret. But I want you to remember the name, rat. You see, Narid-na-Gost is what I might perhaps term a one-time ally of mine, whose loyalty—and usefulness—is now being called into question."

She turned to face the window as she spoke and so didn't see the astonishment that Strann wasn't quite swift enough to hide. Narid-na-Gost, her own demon sire, no longer her ally? This was dramatic news indeed!

"There was a time," Ygorla said disdainfully, "when I had reason to be grateful to this creature. However"—a petulant edge crept into her voice—"I now suspect that he is less than entirely trustworthy, and that his schemings might interfere with my plans. I wish to find out whether my suspicions are correct."

His pulse overrapid, avid to know more, Strann asked deferentially, "How may I be of assistance to you, my Empress?"

"By using the talents that have already stood you in good stead here, and spying on him." She looked shrewdly at him over her shoulder. "I shall use you as my messenger, to carry word between myself and my fa— and this creature. I want you to worm your way into his confidence and report back to me anything you may discover."

It was an undreamed-of chance, Strann thought, and he pushed down the momentary unpleasant shudder that the thought of treating with a demon aroused in him.

"And the messages I shall carry, Majesty." He smiled and touched one finger to the side of his nose in the age-old gesture of connivance. "Might I assume that they will be . . . calculated to unveil any treachery that might be lurking in this Narid-na-Gost's thoughts?"

Ygorla smiled broadly. "Again, you prove yourself a clever rat. Yes, that is exactly what you may assume, and I'll make full use of your bard's skills to help me compose those messages so that they find their mark. Now." The wine cup was empty. She tossed it aside and clasped her hands together before her face. "My delightful new lover will be returning to my side at any moment, so I'll dismiss you lest he should also become jealous." Taken in by the miserable expression Strann feigned, she laughed lightly, made a mock-coquettish pout at him, and held out a hand. "Go away and play on Karuth Piadar's manzon and write a song for me that extols the virility of Calvi Alacar. I'll summon you again later in the day, and we shall see what's to be done."

"Your will, Majesty, is my delight but also my lonely sorrow," Strann said, making a knee and kissing her outstretched fingers.

Her mind was already distracted. She was growing

bored with him and not really listening. "Yes, yes, I'm sure it is." She patted his head. "Now, go away."

As Strann backed humbly out of the room, she turned her attention to the window again and gazed at the castle's south spire. Strann, she thought, would make an excellent go-between, for the fool was besotted enough to be trustworthy while at the same time conscious of his proper place and sufficiently cowed to obey her instructions in every detail. It would be very interesting indeed to see what manner of intelligence he brought back from his visits to her father in his eyrie. And if what he learned confirmed what she already suspected, then the time might well be ripe for a change to her plans. Narid-na-Gost was proving to be both a nuisance and a hindrance. Until now she had had to swallow her dissatisfaction and put up with his complaints and caveats for the sake of the greater scheme. Since last night's ball, though, the possibility of a new arrangement had occurred to her. As yet the notion was embryonic, but the more she thought about it, the more it appealed to her, for it offered her the potential to rid herself of her sire's hampering influence and at the same time grasp power of an order that would make sovereignty of this mortal world seem a paltry bauble by comparison.

She fingered the Chaos stone on its chain around her neck, caressing its smooth facets with the avaricious delight of a miser counting gold coins. Her father had proved himself a weak fool when he fell prey to her cajolings and allowed her to take sole possession of the gem. Now, if she should choose to do so, she could make some changes to their bargain, and in particular to the arrangements they had made to safeguard them both against any retaliation from Chaos. If she chose . . . *if* she should choose . . . then she had the power to remove a part of that safeguard, the part that protected Narid-na-Gost. It might not be necessary of course, for she believed she could deal with him easily without recourse to drastic measures as yet. But if matters *were* to get out of hand . . . well then, she'd already threatened to do it, and she'd have no compunction in doing it. And her sire would learn the price of crossing her, and it would be a hard lesson.

A small, cold, and satisfied smile played about her lovely face, and with a graceful movement that implied both contempt and utter confidence, she turned her back on the window and the view of the tall south spire.

15

Four more days passed while Ygorla continued to indulge her whims, and still she gave no hint that she was about to issue the challenge for which the Circle and the gods waited. For everyone in the castle it was a nerve-racking interval, and for some individuals in particular it had the proportions of a waking nightmare.

There was now no doubt in anyone's mind that Calvi Alacar was lost. Tirand's second plea to Ailind had met with as little success as the first, and without the god's power to aid them, the adepts were realists enough to acknowledge that they were helpless. Some might have considered an appeal to Tarod, but those who did kept their thoughts to themselves, knowing that Tirand would instantly have vetoed the idea. Reluctantly they were forced to admit that they had only their own resources to fall back on, and they weren't enough.

Calvi, it seemed, knew nothing of the Circle's concern for him, and it was obvious now that if he had known, he would have laughed in their faces. Contrary to expectations, Ygorla hadn't grown bored with him. In fact she was thoroughly enjoying the company of her new lover and plaything and took great delight in parading about the castle with him to flaunt their alliance in the faces of her hosts. This was only an occasional diversion; many of their waking hours, as well as the long winter nights, were spent in the privacy of the usurper's sumptuous bedchamber, where she continued to weave her spells and increase her grip on the young man's mind and body, until her hold was so complete that he had no hope of breaking free.

Nor did Calvi want to break free. Thanks to Ygorla's sorcery he was rapidly discovering a new world of pleasure and power, which until now had been beyond his ability to imagine. Though his nature was fundamentally kindly and decent, he nonetheless had all the ignobler appetites of youth and inexperience, and these, fueled by the resentment that recent events had kindled, were what Ygorla played on. She showed him dark pleasures, the enjoyment to be had from small and needless cruelties, the means to impose his will through arrogance and threats. And when she discovered how deep the seam of resentment ran within him, she taught him the hunger for revenge.

She had quickly found that Calvi's resentments were complex and often illogical but no less intense for that. The chief focus of his anger was Ailind, but his hostility toward the lord of Order was spiced with lesser grudges against anyone who, whether in reality or in his imagination, had slighted him. Slowly, as the enchantment grew stronger and his passion for Ygorla became more intense, he began to speak more freely about his feelings, and they took on an increasingly furious edge that she found it very useful, in the light of her own burgeoning new speculations, to foster. And, though he remembered nothing of them in the mornings, and so said nothing of them to his new lover, Calvi's dreams were heaping coals on the already blazing fire of hatred, contempt, and hunger within him.

In the sight of his peers and former friends who encountered him now, Calvi was degenerating fast. With his vituperative tongue, his eyes glazed either with wine or with the more powerful drug of Ygorla's sorcery, his belligerent posturings, and his petty spites, he had the look of a man who was being slowly but systematically destroyed by the darkest aspects of his own nature. Ygorla was beginning to learn that those dark aspects contained hitherto unplumbed depths. She was beginning to learn that Calvi had a streak of ambition buried deep within his soul that, with a little judicious manipulation, could prove to be a worthy complement to her own.

While Ygorla and Calvi indulged the wildest games that their imaginations could conjure, Strann, too, had been coming to terms with some new and none too pleasant experiences. One of the motives behind Ygorla's decision to use him as a messenger between herself and her father was to deliver a deliberate snub to Narid-na-Gost, a sign that she intended to have no more direct contact with him other than on her terms, and on his first visit to the spire she gave Strann a letter that stated her attitude in no uncertain terms.

That first encounter with the demon was an ordeal that Strann prayed he would never have to face again. After an exhausting climb up the seemingly endless spiral stairs he found Narid-na-Gost in one of the spire's summit rooms, the interior of which he'd turned by sorcery into a scene of relentless crimson. Crimson cushions, crimson rugs, crimson velvet covering every inch of the walls and ceiling; and in the midst of it all the demon himself with his long crimson hair and his twisted body and clawlike hands and feet, and his eyes burning like live coals in his spiteful, unhuman face.

Strann was tested. Narid-na-Gost refused to believe that he hadn't read Ygorla's letter and knew nothing of its contents. And when the threats and the monstrous illusions were finished and he was at last satisfied that his daughter's pet rat had told the truth, the demon had played with him for a while longer before finally letting him go. He conjured ice-cold white serpents that crawled up Strann's legs and wound their coils repulsively around his body. He put out a black tongue that stretched the width of the room, its tip gouting flames that darted at Strann's face. He opened his mouth impossibly wide and vomited huge, venomous toads, which flopped and slithered across the floor before disintegrating at Strann's feet in pools of foul-smelling nacre. But when he saw that the rat, though nauseated, wasn't about to fall to his knees and gibber for an end to the horrors, he lost all interest and dismissed him. As yet, he hadn't opened the letter. And there was no answering message.

Stumbling back down toward the ground, fighting

his rebelling stomach and dreading the thousands of stairs that lay ahead of him before he could breathe cold, clean air once more, Strann knew that he had had a very lucky escape—and he also knew why. For all his threat and blustering, Narid-na-Gost was afraid to cross Ygorla, and that must mean that she had some form of hold over him. Strann couldn't fathom exactly what that hold might be, for from what Yandros had told him at their first encounter on Summer Isle he'd had the impression that Narid-na-Gost was far more powerful than his daughter and had always been the prime mover in the plot against Chaos. Now that view had been turned on its head, and Strann was certain that the soul-stone must be the key to the conundrum. *Did* Narid-na-Gost still control it? Or was the fact that Ygorla now wore the gem in such brazen public display something more than a merely symbolic gesture?

He reached the ground at last, with his head swimming and his stomach churning. Emerging into the bleak daylight, he thought that he'd never been so grateful for the chill bite of winter air in his life, and he stumbled across the empty courtyard to sit for a few minutes on the edge of the central fountain pool while he regained his breath and his wits. His nostrils were filled with an unpleasant scent, the scent of musk and iron that he remembered from Summer Isle and that had pervaded the spire room and now clung to his clothes and hair. He hadn't recognized it in his Summer Isle days, but now he knew precisely what it was: the stench of demons.

The cold of the pool's coping struck up through his clothes into his flesh and he welcomed it, for it went some small way toward cleansing the taint he felt. He remembered the serpents, shuddered violently, and pressed his legs harder against the stonework, then tried to force his mind to stop whirling in confusion and think clearly.

He *must* get word of what had transpired to Tarod. This time, though, the cats would be of no help to him, for the message he had to impart was too complex to trust to their simple senses and his own inadequate ability to communicate with them. He didn't even know if his

last effort had been successful, for there had been no acknowledgment from the Chaos lord, and anyway the
news he'd sent had been public knowledge only a few
hours later. Besides, this message would demand a clear
reply, for he needed guidance now.

He glanced at the north spire, towering on the far
side of the courtyard against the sky's morbid backdrop,
and wondered if Tarod was there. Then the speculation
crumbled as he realized that he couldn't risk trying to
find out. Ygorla expected him back, and for all he knew,
there might be any number of her elemental servants
watching him, invisible or disguised, at this or any other
moment. Direct contact with the Chaos lord was out of
the question. He had to find another means. And certainly he couldn't try to seek out Karuth.

Or could he? The idea came to him slowly, gradually, like an uncertain dawn breaking. It was feasible. Just
feasible . . . and if it worked, then no suspicion could
fall on him, for only he and she of all the living souls in
the castle could possibly know what had taken
place. . . .

Strann stood up. He tried to quash the swift rush of
hope within him, not wanting to tempt fate before the
plan was even half mooted, but he couldn't entirely crush
his eagerness. The one obstacle was Ygorla herself. But
he believed he knew how best to tackle her, and he also
believed that her ego might be unable to resist giving him
permission for what he wanted to do.

Ygorla was delighted by Strann's proposal when he put it
to her later that day. She was already in an ebullient
mood, for Narid-na-Gost's sullen refusal to respond to
her note had been exactly what she had hoped, and the
fact that he had attempted to maltreat her messenger
without actually daring to harm him confirmed her suspicion that he was, indeed, afraid of her. She had given
Strann a jewel—"a mere trifle, and nothing to me"—for
his pains, and his suggestion pleased her still further.

"Public performance of the music you write for me?" She paced across her bedchamber, her face avidly radiant at the prospect. Behind her, on the bed, Calvi sprawled unmoving, with an empty wine flagon lying beside him. Strann thought he was asleep but couldn't be sure. "Yes, rat, I like that notion! A little entertainment, before a selected audience." She laughed, softly at first then with a raucous edge, causing Calvi to stir and mutter a muffled complaint. "I shall order it for tonight, I think, and I shall choose my guest list with the *greatest* care. You will be ready?"

"Naturally, madam. Only—"

"Only what?"

"Well . . ." Strann didn't want to arouse any suspicions in her; he had to make this look very casual. "I might wish that I had a better instrument with which to do you justice, my Empress. Karuth Piadar's manzon is passable enough, I suppose, but it isn't up to my accustomed standard."

She gestured flippantly. "That's easily dealt with. I have elemental servants who can transport your own instrument here from Summer Isle within an hour or less. Nothing less than the best is good enough for my bard. I'll see to it, and the High Initiate's sister may have her own inferior instrument back to do with as she pleases." She flicked him a wicked look. "I *do* hope she won't be mortally offended by your second rejection!"

Quite why Ygorla so enjoyed dwelling on Karuth's reputed heartbreak Strann didn't know, but for once her fondness for gloating was working to his advantage. He joined in her laughter, then returned to his own small corner in the outer chamber to prepare for the evening recital.

When he had left the room, Calvi sat up. He hadn't been sleeping but had been in a languorous semidoze from which it was too much trouble to stir. He'd heard a few snatches of the conversation between Ygorla and Strann, and now, gleefully, Ygorla told him of Strann's idea.

"It might be diverting." Calvi yawned, fumbled for

the wine flagon, found it empty, and dropped it carelessly over the side of the bed. "Damn. I'm thirsty."

"Then you shall have a fresh flagon, or two or three if it pleases you." Ygorla came to join him on the bed and kissed him lasciviously. She liked to indulge him in everything; he was in truth far more of a pet than Strann had ever been. "In a moment you shall have anything you want. But first I want you to tell me which names *you* wish to add to my list of guests for Strann's performance tonight."

"Which names . . . ?" Calvi nibbled at her hair, then at her bare upper arm, breathing in the heady perfume that clung to her skin. "Well, now . . . Ailind of Order, for one. And Tirand Lin."

She laughed softly. "I thought Tirand Lin was your dear and good friend?"

Calvi scowled. "He's no such thing, whatever he might have pretended in the past. I despise him as much as I despise all the others. And he showed his true colors —he supported Ailind against me, and he treated me as though I were an unfledged child and not his rightful superior . . . anyway, I have only *one* friend. My beloved friend, and my sweetest, most beautiful, most powerful Empress. . . ."

She let him kiss her mouth hungrily, returning his ardor with a promise of her own, then whispered in his ear, "And who else will you have me invite, Calvi? Who else?"

"Karuth." His voice was indistinct as his lips tangled in her hair again. In just a few days his long-harbored fondness, even infatuation, for Karuth had twisted into a resentment made the more virulent by her past rejection of him and by her links with the Chaos lord. "Make *her* come, and make her sit at the feet of her old lover." He giggled. "She can bring Tarod with her, and then she'll have two fools to choose from! Make her play for you too. She won't like it, but I will. I'll take great pleasure in seeing her brought down from the saddle of her high horse! Show her how powerful you are, my love. Show her that even the gods can't stand against you!"

His hands started to explore her body, and Ygorla felt an answering fire kindling within herself. They rolled together into the middle of the great bed, and she purred, "Oh, my golden man, you and I are so alike . . . *so* alike. I'm beginning to believe that you are the ally I have been waiting to find for a *very* long time. . . ."

The "invitations" that Ygorla sent out were brief and to the point. Strann the Storymaker was to give a musical recital in the dining hall, and the elementals that carried her message individually to each member of her chosen audience made it quite clear that failure to attend would attract a high forfeit. So at second moonrise Strann's unwilling audience took their places on the chairs set ready for them in a semicircle around the great hearth and waited for the recital to begin.

Strann experienced a new and unpleasant form of stage fright as he waited to make his entrance. He could sense the cold hostility that filled the hall and knew that what he must do would deepen the hatred that the adepts felt for him. His only comfort was the knowledge that Karuth was there, sitting at one end of the first row, with the Matriarch beside her. Tirand, too, was present, but although Ygorla had sent an imperious summons to Tarod and Ailind, neither had deigned to appear.

Ygorla herself was seated on a great double chair of fantastically curlicued precious metals, which a slave force of earth elementals had wrought for her. Calvi lounged at her side, affecting languor and drinking copious quantities of wine, and a solitary stool had been placed before the fire for Strann's use. There was no applause as he took his place, with his own manzon— Ygorla had been as good as her word—clasped in his hands, and he sat down feeling worse than a first-year music student faced with a bored and skeptical panel of Guild masters at a competence test.

He settled the manzon across his knees and made a show of adjusting the tuning. Then, so carelessly that to

uninitiated ears he seemed simply and briefly to be exer-
cising his fingers, he played an arpeggio. And, watching
through half-hooded eyes, he saw Karuth tense as though
an invisible hand had gripped her spine.

For, in the Hand-Speech unique to the Guild of
Master Musicians, Strann had played the code which
said, *Urgent—this news must be carried to the one we both
serve.*

It was such a simple strategy, yet foolproof, for of all
the castle's inhabitants Karuth was the only one who
understood the complex and almost infinitely flexible language of the Guild's most skilled members. Strann had
worked through all the afternoon and early evening to
weave the message he wanted to convey into the songs he
would play and sing tonight in ostensible praise of the
usurper. Ygorla knew nothing of it. Even Tarod and
Ailind, had they been present, wouldn't have recognized
the patterns that Strann's fingers now conjured from the
instrument on his lap. Only Karuth understood, and
knew why he had subjected himself to this shaming and
cruel ordeal.

Strann played. It wasn't a virtuoso performance, but
he didn't care. Ygorla wouldn't know the difference and
there was little point in trying to salvage any of his bard's
innate pride in the face of such a hostile audience. For
something over a hour he went through the motions of
extolling the usurper's beauty, power, and wisdom, songs
he'd composed at her behest on Summer Isle but now
subtly altered to convey the information he needed to
deliver. Ygorla demanded applause, and applause was
coldly and obediently given, but it was a sham, and when
at last the travesty was over, Strann received none of the
accolades he might have expected in happier days but
had only the souring experience of seeing his listeners rise
from their seats the moment they were released, turn
their backs on him, and walk from the hall. But it didn't
matter. His pride could stomach it, for he had done what
he had set out to do. One last glimpse of Karuth, of the
warmth and gratitude in her eyes before the Matriarch
led her away, had confirmed it.

Outside the hall Karuth forced herself not to look back through the double doors at the trio by the hearth: Strann carefully returning his manzon to its case while Ygorla, preening, made ready to depart with Calvi. Karuth was surrounded by people; it was vital that she should find a way to excuse herself, get free of them, and find Tarod quickly. But the Matriarch's arm was linked with hers, and Shaill seemed to have no intention of releasing her—a well-meant gesture and intended to lend her strength and comfort, but at this moment grossly inappropriate.

Shaill was talking to her, expressing anger at the usurper's odious vanity, and sympathy that Karuth should have been faced with such an ordeal. Karuth made vague responses but didn't really listen; her mind was ablaze with the news Strann had imparted to her, and she wondered frantically where Tarod was. He'd said to her, hadn't he, that she need only speak his name for him to hear and answer her? She couldn't say it aloud, not here and now—but would a silent call suffice?

Concentrating her mind as best she could amid the distractions that tried to command her attention, she thought, *Lord Tarod, I need your help! Please, hear me and answer!*

She sensed no response. Shaill was still talking, and now, Karuth saw with a sinking heart, Tirand was approaching them. She knew immediately from the look on his face that he was about to make another effort at a friendly overture, and though she would have welcomed it at any other time, she couldn't afford to consider either his feelings or her own now.

"Karuth." He took her free hand, his clasp tentative but warm. "Are you busy for an hour? I wonder if I might—"

"Karuth." Another voice silenced Tirand in midsentence and made Karuth start. She turned and saw Tarod standing behind her.

"High Initiate." The Chaos lord bowed slightly to Tirand. "You'll forgive my interruption, but I have a prior appointment with Karuth."

227

Tirand's hand dropped away from Karuth's fingers. He looked at her, saw that she wasn't about to gainsay Tarod, and his expression became tight and pained. He said, "Then I shan't impose on you a moment longer," returned the Chaos lord's bow very curtly, and strode away without another glance at his sister.

Shaill, dismayed, said, "Karuth, I really think you—" but Tarod intervened.

"Lady Matriarch." His smile was cool. "You'll pardon us, I'm sure." And before Shaill could utter another word, he led Karuth away.

The castle's entrance hall was deserted, and Karuth would have stopped there, but Tarod led her out through the main doors and into the courtyard. It was bitterly cold with a promise of more snow, and the steps were icy. She slipped and he caught her arm to steady her.

"I'm afraid we must adopt a little subterfuge," he said in an undertone as his green eyes scanned the courtyard.

She shivered, tried to quell it. "It's empty enough here, my lord."

"Empty of people, yes, but it's not human ears that concern me. One moment . . ." Hard, thin fingers gripped hers, and suddenly she yelped aloud in alarm as the scene around them seemed to invert. There came a violent sensation of falling and yet hurtling upward together, and suddenly she found herself in an unfamiliar room, in gloomy darkness, surrounded by the looming shadows of what looked like old lumber.

"I'm sorry to have startled you." Tarod was no more than a silhouette against the narrow embrasure of a window, but she heard the faint humor in his voice. Then a sphere of soft, silver light sprang into being, hovering just above the surface of a small table. The darkness lifted, and Karuth looked around at what she realized now must be one of the unused chambers at the top of the north spire.

She took in the jumble of abandoned furniture piled high around the walls and said, "This is hardly suitable accommodation for you, my lord."

"Oh, it serves me well enough. And it has one great advantage: The usurper's elemental slaves don't dare approach this spire, so we needn't fear any attempts to pry into our business." He laughed. "If any of her spies saw me spirit you away, they'll draw the obvious conclusion and think no more of it."

Karuth felt her cheeks coloring, but made no comment.

"Sit down," Tarod said. "Here, by the table—there's a chair that won't collapse under your weight, and the sphere gives warmth as well as light."

Bemused by the rough conditions that seemed to content him, she sat down gingerly on the chair he indicated, and he perched casually on the edge of the table. "Now. Tell me why you need to speak with me so urgently."

Karuth told him about Strann's subterfuge and the message he had imparted to her through Hand-Speech. Every detail was there; Strann's appointment as mediator between Ygorla and Narid-na-Gost, his encounter in the south spire and his conviction that relations between the usurper and her demon father were rapidly growing fraught. Tarod listened in silence, and when Karuth finished speaking, he steepled his fingers and stared at them.

"Interesting . . . very interesting. A pity Strann doesn't know what was in the letter she wrote, but I can hardly blame him for not daring to read it. Still, even without that information this is very valuable news indeed." He stood up, paced across the room, then sat down again on a battered couch. "So she wants Strann to feed her sire a certain amount of disinformation, does she? In that case I think we might look for a way to add our own spice to the recipes she concocts and shake Narid-na-Gost's confidence a little further. We have one problem, though: how to let Strann know what we want of him."

"I think," Karuth said cautiously, "that he's already considered that, my lord. Earlier today my manzon was returned to me"—she firmly pushed away the ugly memory of the thing that had brought it—"and I gather that

229

Strann has persuaded the usurper to have his own instrument brought here from Summer Isle." She smiled, a quick, humorless quirk. "I suspect we may find that she's inveigled into demanding further recitals before too long."

"With additional musicians to augment Strann's talents? I see." Tarod returned her smile drily. "Very intelligent of him. But doesn't this Hand-Speech, as you call it, impose a limit on the complexity of the messages that can be passed between you?"

Karuth was surprised and a little gratified to find that there was a subject on which she was qualified to instruct him rather than vice versa. "Hand-Speech has very few limitations, my lord. Over the centuries since it was invented it's become almost as complex and sophisticated as the spoken word."

"A language in its own right, yet recognizable as such only to the initiated few. That could prove to be a very valuable tool indeed." Then Tarod's expression altered. "But can you bring yourself to face what this will require of you, Karuth? If the opportunity arises, do you have the stomach for it?"

She knew he implied no slight on her and appreciated the fact that he'd considered her feelings at all. "Oh yes," she said, and looked away from him, not wanting him to see the very private emotions that were suddenly in her eyes. "I can do it, and will gladly. It will at least allow me to feel close to Strann again."

16

Ygorla's challenge was issued at last, and when it came, it took the Circle by surprise. On the fifth morning after the ball a flying flock of the most grotesque elementals that the usurper's skill and imagination could conjure was dispatched from her apartments to carry word to all and sundry that the Empress of Mortal Dominions commanded the Council of Adepts, and all others who considered themselves in any way concerned with statesmanship in the mortal world, to convene in the council hall at sunset. The fact that her messengers dared to approach Tarod and Ailind as well as their human quarry was a measure of Ygorla's growing contempt for the two gods, and though she received no reply from either of them, she believed they would know full well what her summons implied, and would attend.

Her decision to make a public show of her demands had caused another violent quarrel with her sire. Strann had made several more visits to the south spire and was now entrusted with carrying verbal rather than written messages, so he witnessed this clash, the most vituperative yet, at first hand. Narid-na-Gost wanted no dramatic announcement to all and sundry. His intention had been simply to confront Tarod alone and tell him the terms on which his brother's soul-stone could be safeguarded. There was no need, he said furiously to Strann, for this arrogant exhibition. To set out to humiliate the Chaos lords before a large audience, as Ygorla seemed to be doing, might easily provoke them to retaliate. With the final triumph almost within their grasp, that was a blind and stupid action to take for the sake of her personal vanity. Strann dutifully relayed this message to Ygorla, who instantly dispatched him back to the spire to tell her sire that he'd be well advised not to question her decisions but to look to his own part of their bargain if he valued his ambitions. The meeting would take place at sunset, as she had decreed, and she cared nothing for whether or not he chose to attend.

Narid-na-Gost replied to this with a stream of savage invective that nonetheless confirmed what Strann had suspected: He would give way because there was no other choice open to him. Strann was rapidly discovering a great deal about the nature of the deteriorating relationship between Ygorla and her father, and he was certain now that she did indeed have some form of hold over the demon. In the last day or so their arguments had become so bitter that both seemed to have forgotten that Strann himself was anything more than a cipher, on a level with Ygorla's artificially created slaves. Engrossed in their war of words, they simply used him as a go-between without giving a moment's thought to discretion. And Strann had begun to weave his own thread into their tapestry. . . .

Unaware that the manipulative powers of her pet rat were being turned neatly back on herself, Ygorla had instigated a nightly repetition of the first recital and had demanded that other castle musicians should take part. Karuth, of course, was among those commanded to play, and Strann had been greatly impressed by her acting ability when she took her place, to a defiant storm of sympathetic applause from the coerced audience, and bestowed on him a look of proud and caustic disdain that he could almost have believed was genuine.

But the messages that passed between them as they both wove the Hand-Speech into the music they played were a very different matter. Tarod had devised a subtle series of clues, hints, snippets of misleading information for Strann to work into the messages he carried between Ygorla and her father, to deepen the discord between them and foster a new level of uncertainty and mistrust. His prime target, Strann quickly realized, was Narid-na-Gost. The Chaos lords were well aware that the demon was the weaker element of the two, and Tarod was playing on Narid-na-Gost's growing feelings of vulnerability to cultivate in his mind the conviction that his daughter intended to betray him.

The strategy was beginning to work. Strann saw the signs and reported them back through the Hand-Speech each evening. Narid-na-Gost was more than worried now; he was frightened. Frightened that the child of his creation and nurturing had grown into a chimera that not only could he no longer control but that now threatened to turn on and devour him. He was beginning to fear that he might be caught in a trap between the avenging fury of Chaos and the treachery of his own daughter and that the teeth of the trap were about to snap shut and crush him.

Strann didn't know what Tarod eventually intended his strategy to achieve, but he thought it wiser not to concern himself with speculation. His task was to sow the seeds; how and in what form they would germinate was the gods' business, not his. On the day that Ygorla summoned the meeting of the Circle, he carried one last message to Narid-na-Gost. It was a clear challenge. In words that she had insisted he must repeat verbatim she had dared her father to show his face in the council hall or, as she phrased it, "prove yourself the coward that I already know you to be and acknowledge that I have the sole right to speak for us both." Strann didn't repeat the message quite as faithfully as she had ordered him to do but changed the word *right* to *power,* adding a small embellishment of his own to the effect that, should the demon choose to ignore the gauntlet she had thrown down, Ygorla would from now on assume total supremacy without further reference to him in any way . . . and hinting that that was her real desire.

Narid-na-Gost heard this in ice-cold silence, his crimson eyes alight with an unholy fury. When Strann finished and made his customary obeisance—something that, he'd quickly discovered, seemed to stand him in good stead in this creature's presence—there was silence in the spire room for some moments before the demon spoke.

"You will tell my daughter"—there was savage malignancy in the last word—"that I will have no part in her petty and childish games. She may choose to risk all in a flummery parade of self-aggrandizement; I do not. And you will repeat these precise words to her: *The jewel may be your safeguard, but the safeguard is not the key. And the key still lies in my hands, and mine alone.*"

Strann repeated the words as he had been bidden, until the demon was satisfied that there would be no mistake. He began then to bow his way out of the spire room, but as he reached the door, Narid-na-Gost suddenly called him back.

"Rat." He used the name now as carelessly as Ygorla did. "One last matter."

"Sir?" Strann paused and made another bow.

Narid-na-Gost's long, reptilian tongue flicked across his peculiarly white and unnaturally sharp teeth. "I wish to know how my daughter responds to my message. You will return here, and you will tell me. And if you are a wise rat, you'll say nothing of this to her. Do I make my meaning clear?"

"Sir," Strann said, "I am but the Empress's servant—"

"Her servant, yes, but not entirely a fool for all that. Not fool enough to wish to suffer the consequences of betraying my confidence, isn't that so?" He smiled malevolently as he spoke, and a dart of white flame sizzled from his mouth to skim past Strann's face. Strann felt the searing burn of venom and slapped a hand to his cheek. Narid-na-Gost laughed softly.

"Make your pledge of trustworthiness, little man, and I shall negate the poison that at this moment is eating into your skin. Falter, and by sunset you'll be howling for release from its agony."

"My lord." Strann's voice grated; pain was starting to shoot through his face muscles, and it felt like red-hot knives cutting into his flesh. "You have my pledge! I promise it, I *promise* it!"

"Good enough." The demon smiled again. "I think you know, now, the price of disobedience." The agony flared once more and vanished. Strann felt cold sweat break out on his face and torso. "Go, then, and return with whatever intelligence you can glean."

Strann made a further obeisance. "Sir, I will do whatever you ask of me!" And he fled.

He repeated Narid-na-Gost's words as he had been bidden. Ygorla listened with her head tilted to one side like a bird eyeing prey, and when Strann finished, her eyes grew hard as flint, and she laughed with shrill but hearty contempt.

"Oh, so he thinks he can *coerce* me, does he? 'The safeguard is not the key . . .' Dear, dear; how *very* foolish he is!" Then, remembering abruptly that Strann was still in the room, she glanced at him and waved a careless hand. "You are dismissed, rat. Go away and amuse yourself. I shan't want you again until this evening."

She was preoccupied now. Strann knew he could return to the spire without running the risk of being watched by one of her elementals. For once the report he made to Narid-na-Gost would need no embellishment, for he had a shrewd idea of the conclusions the demon would draw from his daughter's silence. He left the room and took great care not to let Ygorla see the slight smile on his face.

———————⟫ ⟪———————

By sunset snow was falling again, and the castle was shrouded in deep, gloomy silence. The crowd that filled the council hall seemed to have caught the mood of the bitter weather, for not a word was spoken as they waited for the usurper to make her entrance.

The high table on the dais where the High Initiate and the most senior councillors customarily sat was still in its usual place, but only three chairs were set behind it now. Three chairs and one cushion, which Karuth recognized immediately as the one on which Strann had squatted at Ygorla's feet on the night of the ball. So she intended to bring him. Doubtless she thought that the presence of so lowly a creature as her pet rat would add further piquancy to the humiliation she meant to inflict on Tarod, and at that thought Karuth looked back over her shoulder, wondering where the Chaos lord might be. Ailind had already arrived and was sitting at the front of the hall beside Tirand, but there was no sign yet of his counterpart. Uneasily Karuth settled back on her chair, trying to stop her hands from fidgeting restlessly in her lap.

Tarod had been in an ominous mood when she'd last seen him this afternoon. Strann, under the pretext of presenting a new piece of music, had managed to arrange a brief and deeply resented rehearsal earlier in the day, and, attended by two shadowy horrors who were present to curb any trouble Ygorla's pet rat might otherwise have had from his coopted musicians, he had passed on details of the latest skirmish between Ygorla and her father. Relaying his message to the Chaos lord, Karuth had found Tarod unwilling even to show his reaction, let alone discuss it with her as he sometimes did. He had dismissed her almost curtly, and there was no reply to convey back to Strann. Some new development was in the wind, she felt, and she feared that it didn't augur well.

Her restive thoughts were interrupted as she heard the sound of the chamber doors opening. Even before she could turn around again, the eldritch notes of an unearthly fanfare rang out through the hall, then the wall torches dipped violently for a moment as a chill, unnatural wind swept over the assembly—and Ygorla appeared.

She was magnificent. Clad from head to foot in black and silver, she swept down the hall's central aisle, and her breathtaking figure was haloed by the shimmering witchlights of a hundred or more tiny elementals that whirled and danced in fantastic patterns around her. A great heart-shaped collar of silver filigree thread framed her proudly exquisite face, and the Chaos stone blazed like an earthbound star on her breast. Calvi walked a pace behind her and a little to one side; he, too, was dressed in black and silver and his face wore a disdainful and triumphant smile. Behind them, holding the long, sweeping train of Ygorla's gown and staring ahead with a face as blank as a mime mask, came Strann.

The entire assembly turned to see the spectacle. A hissing rush of exhaled breath susurrated through the chamber—and took on an edge of suppressed outrage as the adepts saw that on her head the usurper was wearing a glittering, extravagant crown of pure silver set with a myriad jewels, which formed the Seven-Rayed Star of Chaos. The noise died away as Ygorla mounted the steps of the dais. Then as she approached the high table, a voice with no visible source boomed through the hall: *"Rise! All must rise, and make obeisance to their rightful liege Ygorla, Daughter of Chaos and Empress of Mortal Dominions!"*

There was a stirring as fury deepened, but a few adepts were intimidated into obeying the haughty command before they could stop themselves. Others, unsure, looked to the High Initiate for guidance. Karuth saw Ailind make a small, private signal with one hand; then, though with clear reluctance, Tirand rose slowly to his feet.

The usurper walked with elegant deliberation around to the far side of the table. Strann scurried to pull out the central chair of the three, and Calvi draped himself casually in one of the others. Ygorla turned to survey the scene and smiled as she saw that the entire assembly was now standing. Only Ailind hadn't moved but was watching her with laconic interest. She ignored him and waved one hand in a negligent gesture.

The disembodied voice boomed out again: *"The Empress graciously permits her subjects to be seated in her presence."*

The crowd sat, silent now. Ygorla settled in the central chair and looked around her. Her manner was reminiscent of an eagle surveying its potential prey from a great height, and tension began to build stiflingly in the hall as everyone waited for her to speak. Karuth thought, *So, her demon sire hasn't chosen to show his face after all.* What had kept Narid-na-Gost away? she wondered. Fear of Ygorla, as Strann had surmised? Or fear of something else . . . ?

Suddenly Ygorla's voice snapped out. "I see one face is missing from this gathering. Where is Tarod of Chaos?"

Silence greeted her question. Ailind, Karuth saw, was smiling faintly—but Ygorla was not amused.

"I will have an answer!" Her vivid eyes raked the hall again, then she glared at the doors as though silently commanding them to swing open again and admit the errant Tarod. "I demand—"

"Curb your petulance, child. And don't expect me to play this game by your rules."

The voice seemed to speak from nowhere. Then the Chaos lord stepped out from a sharp-edged wing of shadow behind the table.

Karuth's teeth clamped down involuntarily and painfully on her lower lip as shock went through her—for Tarod had thrown off the masquerade of mortality. His face was a savage sculpture, every bone etched beneath his flesh, unhumanly gaunt, unhumanly perfect. His long black hair, like dense, roiling smoke now, rippled and shimmered over his shoulders. And his thin lips smiled down at the usurper with all the knowledge and all the contempt of a being whose life had spanned eternity and to whom the passage of mortal existence was no more than the flick of an eye. An aura flickered grimly around him, an aura of black light, an impossible radiance; and the emerald eyes that Karuth had once unwisely thought so human were shatteringly, arctically lethal. And on Tarod's left hand, the huge, clear gem of a ring flashed out the seven blinding rays of a star. Chaos—*true* Chaos, and not its mere reflection—had stepped into the mortal world.

Karuth didn't know how or when it had happened, but she found herself on her knees on the floor, gripping the back of the chair in front of her. All through the hall other adepts were reacting as the shockwave of Tarod's manifestation spread in a buffeting psychic onslaught. Tirand was on his feet, the Matriarch too. Voices were babbling—Karuth heard more than one involuntary cry of *"Yandros!"*—and for several seconds it seemed that the assembly must collapse into hysteria and anarchy. But then Tarod spoke. His voice was calm, restrained, quite without ceremony, yet every ear in the hall heard him clearly. He said simply, *"Peace."*

In a single moment the panic abated and the crowd was still. People blinked, startled to find their minds suddenly at ease, and chairs scraped as, abashed and a little bewildered, they slowly sat down again. Karuth's knees hurt where sudden and violent contact with the stone floor had bruised them, and her heart was palpitating, but she, too, was gripped and calmed by Tarod's small display of power, and she fumbled her way back to her chair, grateful to find that she could breathe again.

Ygorla was on her feet and stood rigid, staring at the Chaos lord. Her face was dead-white, her rouged mouth a crimson slash by contrast and suddenly ugly, and her jaw worked convulsively as she struggled to spit out the rage pent up within her. Behind the table Strann crouched on his cushion, trying to make himself as small and unobtrusive as possible. Calvi had shrunk into his chair like a cornered animal, and his face looked sick.

Tarod raised his left hand to brush aside a strand of his wild hair, and the image of the seven-rayed star flashed once more from the ring on his finger.

"I believe you have business with me. State it."

"You . . ." Ygorla found her voice at last, in a thin, choked-off screech of fury. "You dare to challenge me, you *dare* to make this pitiful display—" Fumbling, she snatched at the Chaos stone and brandished it before her. *"You know what this is! You know what I can do!"*

Again Tarod smiled his terrible, malignant smile. "Of course. But will you? Or has your sire failed to tell you of the many forms that Chaos's reprisals can take?" He lowered his hand again, and the black aura pulsed with ghastly energy. "He should have warned you that we know how to deal with our own."

A woman adept seated beside Karuth shuddered violently as some small resonance of Tarod's meaning skimmed through the more receptive human minds in the hall, and Karuth herself turned her head away, suddenly and deeply afraid. She had a glimmering of the nature of the gamble Tarod was taking, for she knew how dangerous it could be to place any reliance on the usurper's wisdom. If her control should snap in the face of this challenge, Ygorla might easily make the dire mistake of allowing herself to be goaded into destroying the Chaos stone. If that should happen, she would die within an instant—or perhaps, with Tarod's hand in control, within the next thousand years. But a god would die with her, and Equilibrium would be in ruins. It mustn't come to that, Karuth thought desperately. It *mustn't* come to that!

But it seemed she had underestimated Ygorla. Already the usurper was regaining her self-control and although she didn't quite have the temerity to meet Tarod's glacial gaze, the porcelain color had returned to her cheeks, and the slightest hint of a smile was beginning to play about her lips.

"I think," she said at last, "that even you, Tarod of Chaos, aren't so naïve as to think me *quite* such a fool. We shall sit, and you shall hear what I have to say."

She seated herself once more, pointing to the third, unoccupied seat. Tarod ignored her imperious gesture, and immediately the incorporeal voice rang sharply through the hall.

"All must sit in the Empress's presence! All must sit at the Empress's command!"

Tarod glanced at a place somewhere among the rafters of the high-ceilinged chamber, and a baleful light glittered momentarily in his eyes. The petulant voice cut off instantly, leaving a vacuum that suggested the speaker had not merely been silenced but had ceased to exist.

"Your maladroit posturings bore me," the Chaos lord told Ygorla. "Say what you have to say and don't waste any more of my time."

Ygorla's confidence had slipped a little at his careless removal of her servant, but she rallied quickly.

"Then sit or stand, as you please," she retorted. "And you shall hear my terms."

Tarod smiled sparsely at her use of the singular term. *"Your* terms. So your sire still leaves minions to soil their hands on his behalf, does he?" He laughed. It was a laugh Karuth hoped she would never hear again. "Very well. What are *your* terms?"

This was the moment Ygorla had been waiting for, and despite Tarod's dangerous mood she was determined to make the most of it. She snapped her fingers, and two air elementals materialized, carrying a scroll of parchment between them. They flew to the table while Ygorla smiled and Tarod watched impassively, and laid the scroll before the usurper. Reflexively, as had become her spiteful and shallow habit, Ygorla raised a hand to annihilate the messengers, then saw Tarod's look and changed her mind, instead dismissing them with a wave. As they vanished, she unrolled the document, making a great show of breaking the seal and scanning the flowing, flowery script—not her own—that covered it. At last she spoke.

"I, Ygorla, Daughter of Chaos and Empress of Mortal Dominions, speak thus and command all present to listen and take heed!" It was the language of ceremony, and under her influence it took on a near-farcical overtone of melodrama. But there was nothing farcical about the words Ygorla uttered as, at long last, she issued her ultimate challenge.

The single fulcrum on which the ambitions of the usurper and her demon sire rested was the knowledge that no matter what the cost, no matter what the risk, Yandros of Chaos would not let his brother die. Now, with the calm sweetness of implacable confidence, Ygorla laid down the terms on which his life might be saved. Those terms, she told Tarod, were quite simple. She herself wanted nothing less than complete control of the mortal realm—and her father wanted control of Chaos. So, they proposed a pact, by which Narid-na-Gost should return in triumph to the Chaos realm, where he would be elevated to take Yandros's place as its greatest lord, with

Yandros and his brothers as his lieutenants. Such a thing could be done, for Yandros had the power to exalt any being he chose to his realm's highest ranks. A new age would then begin, she said, a true age of Chaos in which the follies of the past would be wiped out. With a mighty and uncompromising overlord who scorned the weakling tenets that Yandros chose to embrace, and with an earthly Empress to impose that overlord's will in this world, then mortals and gods alike would learn again to fear the titanic, invincible power that was Chaos's true heritage and ultimate destiny. Equilibrium, Ygorla said, her voice rising and ringing through the hall, would be shattered. The strength and influence of Order would be smashed, and its lords banished from the world. Chaos, and Chaos alone, would reign supreme.

The adepts in the council hall listened to the usurper's speech in stunned silence. Since Chaos's predicament had been made public, they had all known what the essence of Ygorla's challenge must inevitably be. But to hear it spoken aloud, to witness the throwing down of the final gauntlet, brought the reality of it home to them in a new way. Many eyes turned surreptitiously and nervously to Ailind, but the lord of Order didn't react to the speech in any way. He simply sat impassive, his expression closed and enigmatic.

Nor had Tarod yet shown any overt response to Ygorla's gleeful diatribe, though to Karuth's hectic imagination it seemed that the black aura glowing around his frame had intensified, honing the planes and angles of his face to a fearsome sculpture. Even when the usurper fell silent at last and turned her challenging blue stare on him, triumph radiating from her, he neither moved nor spoke, only held her gaze.

"Well, my lord?" Patience wasn't in Ygorla's character. She wanted his answer and she wanted it immediately, and her tone was viciously mocking. "What have you to say to me?"

As though an intangible wind had blown through the hall, Tarod's black hair and cloak stirred. Then he smiled a cold, proud, disdainful smile.

"Child," he said, and his voice sent a chill through Karuth, "your pretensions are nothing if not grandiose."

"Pretensions?" Ygorla repeated, almost purring now. "I assure you, Tarod of Chaos, these are no mere pretensions. These are *terms*. Indeed, they are the *only* terms by which you can hope to save the life of your brother and restore him from limbo. He must, of course, be content with a lower status, for I know as well as you do that there can be no more than seven lords of Chaos. But at least he will live. And that, I think, is what Yandros wants above all else."

She was so certain of herself, so assured of victory. Tarod's thin lips curled in a wintry smile. "To think that you can predict Yandros's desires is a very dangerous assumption, Ygorla."

"Oh no, Tarod. For once, I don't believe it is." She was grinning now, laughter bubbling in her throat. "You see, I think Yandros is intelligent enough to understand the consequences of a refusal."

The black aura flickered anew. "One consequence would be your destruction," Tarod reminded her softly.

"I know. But in destroying me you would also destroy your brother, and there would be no new lord of Chaos to take his place." The laughter broke out now, a vindictive and intemperate bark. "The laws of this universe may not permit the existence of more than seven Chaos lords—but they do permit the existence of less. Think of that, noble god! Not seven great masters to rule your realm, but only six." Slowly, calculatedly, she pivoted on her heel until she was looking down from the dais, directly into the eyes of Ailind. Enunciating her words with the greatest deliberation, she added, "What, I wonder, would become of your precious Equilibrium then?"

Her meaning was horribly clear. Six lords of Chaos, but seven lords of Order. The balance would be thrown out of true, and Chaos, weakened by the loss of one of its overlords, would suddenly become exposed and vulnerable to attack. And Ygorla knew, just as Tarod and every adept in the hall also knew, that Aeoris of Order wouldn't neglect such an opportunity to strike a deadly blow against his ancient enemy.

Her heart feeling as though it had constricted to a tight and leaden ball under her ribs, Karuth looked at Ailind and saw that at last the mask of indifference had slipped from his face and a clear emotion was showing through the shield he had created about himself.

Quietly and with the satisfaction of a purpose achieved, Ailind of Order was smiling.

The confrontation ended minutes later. In what might have been a deliberate snub to Tarod's earlier treatment of her elemental servant, Ygorla conjured a repetition of the eldritch fanfare that had announced her arrival in the hall and swept out amid full panoply with Calvi on her arm and Strann hurrying behind them. She had achieved all she had looked for, all she had desired, for Tarod would now put the terms of her pact before his great brother Yandros, and soon she would have Yandros's reply. Ygorla had no doubt in her mind what that reply would be. The Chaos lords were trapped, and she had triumphed.

Before making her grand exit, she had had one final announcement to impart to the assembly—and that, or so she took pleasure in believing, had shocked them more deeply even than her ultimatum to the Chaos lord. From this night on, she told them, a new title would be instigated and proclaimed throughout the world: the title of Emperor-Designate and Noble Consort to the Empress of Mortal Dominions. And the holder of that title was the one-time pretender to the throne of the High Margrave, who now repudiated the validity of his former claim: her own beloved Calvi Alacar.

Her listeners were horrified. She knew it and she exulted in their helpless fury as she swept out of the hall. As the doors closed behind her, uproar broke out. The adepts were on their feet, talking, shouting, arguing, protesting, each voice clamoring to be heard above the rest as they gave vent to their anger and bitterness. Many looked for Ailind, seeking his advice and help, but Ailind was suddenly nowhere to be seen. Some might then have turned in appeal to Tarod, but before they could gather the courage to approach him, he suddenly stepped down from the dais and strode toward the doors. The black aura flared like a nova around him. People shrank out of his path, and those who glimpsed his face as he swept past felt the sharp, twin stabs of awe and fear. Only Karuth went after him, fighting her way through the press of people and trying to reach the clear aisle before it closed in his wake. She saw his left hand make a violent gesture, saw the doors hurtle open in response, smashing back against the wall, and her nerve quailed. But she pressed on and at last reached the corridor outside.

He was walking away toward the castle's main doors, and she broke into a run, trying to catch up and calling out to him. "Lord Tarod!"

He stopped, turned in a single, fluent movement. The black aura vanished when he saw who had hailed him, but his green eyes were murderous as he glared back at her in the corridor's torchlight.

"What is it?" He'd never addressed her in such a baleful tone before, and for the second time the enormity of the gulf between them came shockingly home to Karuth. Breathless, she slid to a halt several feet from him, suddenly afraid to approach too closely.

"Lord Tarod, I—" Then she stopped as she realized that she didn't know what to say. She'd wanted to talk to him, ask questions, offer her help; but she saw now that the impulse was nothing but futile and witless vanity on her part. The last thing Tarod either wanted or needed at this moment was to be plagued with someone else's questions and opinions, and if she believed that the help, however well intentioned, that one insignificant mortal might offer would be of any value to him, then she was a deluded fool.

She hung her head, staring down at the floor. "Forgive me," she whispered. "I—it was nothing, nothing of any importance."

Tarod continued to stare down at her for a few seconds more. Then he turned again, sharply, hair and cloak rippling like a malevolent black wave, and walked away without another word, leaving her alone and feeling thoroughly small and worthless.

17

There were six people in the library: three student adepts, their tutor and two secular teachers. Tarod's sudden appearance in the doorway startled them all to their feet. They knew who he was, though none of them had encountered him directly before now, and their expressions froze in a mixture of awe and consternation.

The Chaos lord's relentless stare raked the vaulted chamber, then he uttered one clipped word.

"Leave."

They didn't hesitate. Abandoning books, notes, discussions, they hastened from the room and away up the spiral stairs. As the door shut behind the last departing figure, Tarod glanced at the wall torches, which instantly went out, then crossed to the small door that led to the Marble Hall. This matter was too serious and too urgent for his normal means of contact with Yandros to suffice. For this he must return to Chaos in person.

The hall's silver door swung noiselessly open for him as he approached it, and he walked through it into the familiar, dim panorama of shifting pastel mists. He ignored the seven great statues save for a brief, cynical glance at the carved figure of Aeoris, and approached the black mosaic in the floor that marked the location of the Chaos Gate. He sensed that no one had entered the hall since his own last visit; the protective link he had established to warn him of any attempt to tamper with the Gate had remained undisturbed, and it seemed that so far Ygorla and her sire lacked either the will or the courage to make any investigations of their own.

Tarod stepped into the black circle. The bond be-

tween the Gate and its creators was a constant that
needed no ritual, no formality. He simply exerted his
will, and the pastel mists shivered briefly as his tall figure
vanished from the mortal world.

When he entered the Chaos realm, someone was
waiting for him. There was a shimmer of white-gold hair;
then small, pale-skinned hands reached out, amber eyes
gazed warmly into his, and a wide, generous mouth
smiled.

"Cyllan . . ." Tarod's black mood melted as he saw
his consort, who had taken the form she'd had as a mortal woman a century ago, the form she knew he loved
best of all. They embraced tightly, and a single pure,
clear note quivered in the air for a moment before fading.

"Yandros told me you were returning." She took his
hand, and they walked away from the strange, metallic-
leafed tree that was the Chaos Gate's present manifestation in this world. Beneath their feet a black sward rus-
tled, the grass turning to silver where it was trodden.

"Only for a short while." He smiled an apology.
"I've urgent news for Yandros and I need to confer with
him more privately than is possible from the castle."

Cyllan looked up at him, her eyes candid. "Something has happened, hasn't it?"

Tarod's smile grew a little harder. "Something has,
love, yes. Though it's only what we'd been expecting and
awaiting." He stared ahead to where tall, green-black
trees arched to form an avenue over the sward. There was
a presence in the avenue and he nodded toward it, ac-
knowledging something that only his senses could detect.
"Yandros is waiting for me. As soon as our business is
done, I'll return to you."

His lips touched hers in the gentle, devoted way she
had known and cherished for so long; another old legacy
of her human origins. Then, dark and quiet as a shadow,
he moved away into the trees.

The unstable and constantly changing scenery of the
Chaos realm often reflected the moods of its highest
lords, and as Tarod approached his great brother, heavy
black clouds began to boil across the heavens, shutting off

the searing bar of light slanting from the distant horizon
and plunging the avenue into darkness. Then lightning
forked with noiseless violence across the sky, briefly illuminating Yandros's gaunt figure. His face was stark, his
eyes jet black and deadly.

"Tarod." They clasped hands with grave but heart-
felt affection, though Tarod felt suppressed anger roiling
in his brother. "Tell me all that happened."

The avenue of trees melted into the walls of a vast,
petrified and vaulted tunnel. Streams of water that blazed
with a blood-red light of their own began to flow down
the walls and formed racing torrents on either side of
them. A far-off sound like the rush of a distant tide whispered among the fantastic rock formations. They walked
through the echoing, empty spaces, and Tarod gave the
grim account of his confrontation with Ygorla and the
pact she had proposed. Yandros listened to the entire
story without speaking, then when Tarod finished, he
stopped and stared hard into the middle distance. In the
streams' gory radiance his gaunt face was hellish.

"She proposes this—she demands this—" He turned
his gaze toward the ceiling far above them, and a huge
concussion shook the entire tunnel as countless tons of
rock exploded skyward. A hundred demented voices
screamed in mad response—screams of rage, of agony, of
other emotions that no mortal mind could have compre-
hended. High above, beyond the broken, jagged silhouettes of the walls' remains, six vast prisms of light hung
over the scene, slowly turning on their axes and pulsing
in perfect sequence and perfect symmetry. Six, where before there had been seven . . .

Yandros laughed. Even Tarod had never heard
laughter of such bitterness, such black and humorless
self-condemnation; and suddenly the shattered walls vanished and they stood on an endless plain of pure ice without a single feature to break its monotony. The prisms,
alone in an otherwise blank sky, poured down a brilliance
as cold and corrosive as acid, and myriad rainbow reflec-
tions shifted restlessly beneath the ice's surface.

"The usurper demands," Yandros said, so softly that

his voice was barely audible, "and we are powerless to oppose her, Tarod. We are *powerless!*"

Tarod didn't reply. There was nothing he could say.

"I've never believed," Yandros continued after a few moments, "that we are invincible. Unlike Aeoris a century ago, I have never made that mistake." He started to prowl across the ice. "Indeed, I *prided* myself on having the wisdom to acknowledge the existence of pitfalls that even gods can fall foul of." Halting, he turned and looked back at Tarod, his eyes flashing a dozen different colors now. "Some of the more pious mortals hold that pride is an undesirable quality and should be eradicated lest it lead to a fall. They have some tedious proverb about it, I believe . . . what do they call the concept?"

"Hubris," Tarod said.

"Hubris." Yandros repeated it, then his thin lips curled in a cynical smile without a trace of amusement. "It's as good a word as any other to describe an arrogant fool, I suppose."

Tarod shook his dark head. "How could you have known, Yandros? How could any of us have anticipated—"

"Don't try to soothe me with platitudes!" The sky cracked in half, shattering the six prisms into a mad frenzy of smashed images, and the ice plain flashed out of existence, leaving them both in a void of total darkness. A fireball seared across the black space between them. Then Yandros spoke again.

"Forgive me, Tarod. I intended no slight against you." A sigh broke the stillness. "For both our sakes, let's find more congenial surroundings."

Knowing his brother's frame of mind, Tarod exerted his will briefly on the substance of Chaos, and they stood together in the turret of a gray stone tower that overlooked a shifting landscape five miles below. Yandros glanced around the circular chamber and laughed with a final, though faintly resentful surrender of his rage.

"You read me too accurately. A sober and innocuous scene to engender a sober and innocuous mood. Ah, well, I suppose it'll serve our purpose as well as anything else." He moved across the floor, and pastel mist reminiscent of the Marble Hall's haze stirred around his feet. "I could move into the mortal realm and take it and all who dwell in it apart; and I would if by doing so I'd achieve my desire. But what would be the use, Tarod? We're faced with a stark choice: We capitulate to the usurper, or our brother dies." He stopped pacing and turned, his eyes burning with pain. "I can't sanction that loss. Not under any circumstances."

"But—" Tarod started to say.

"But at the same time I can't countenance the idea of Narid-na-Gost taking my own place as highest lord of this realm—isn't that what you were about to say? You're right, I can't. It's untenable, *unthinkable*." Thunder boomed dismally outside the turret's narrow embrasure of a window, and something echoed it with a cracked laugh. Yandros's expression grew savage.

"I'm not about to make a noble speech on the benefits of Equilibrium. Its sole function, as it was from the beginning, has been as a source of amusement for us and a marginally preferable alternative to the tedium of ruling our human subjects without any murmur of dissent. But all the same, the thought of returning to the old ways . . ." He shook his head, bizarre lights gleaming in his gold hair. "We never were entirely content to rule unopposed, were we? And when the corrupt human dimension is added to the equation, it becomes repulsive and despicable. Greed, arrogance, petty vindictiveness— all the qualities, for want of a better word, that we despise for their hollow absurdity. That's what Chaos would become, Tarod. That's what it would become under the rule of Narid-na-Gost and his self-aggrandizing daughter: a *mockery*."

"You said, 'would,' " Tarod reminded him gently. "Not 'will'—'would.' " He paused. "Do you have something in mind, Yandros?"

Yandros looked back at him, his eyes tormented. "In truth, my brother, I don't know. One possibility has occurred to me, but it's not something I wish to discuss yet, even with you. I need to consider it further." He started to pace again. "We have time. That's one advantage at least. If the usurper receives no answer from us, then even she won't be so stupid as to jeopardize everything for the sake of a little patience. She'll wait. But Aeoris may not."

Tarod was intrigued. "Aeoris? What have you learned about his machinations?"

Yandros hunched his shoulders. "Nothing concrete. But we both know there's something afoot in the realm of Order and that it isn't simply a manifestation of their delight at our predicament. After all, they'd gain nothing if we were to capitulate to the usurper, for they must know as well as we do that if Narid-na-Gost were to come to power here, his first act would be to launch an attack on their stronghold, and with his daughter enthroned as Empress of the mortal world, their combined power would put Order to rout. So, we can safely assume that Aeoris still shares our desire to see them broken and their souls consigned to the Seven Hells. The only difference in that common aim is that Aeoris would also like to see our brother destroyed in the process, so that Equilibrium can be upset and he can claim his old ascendancy again." His eyes turned silver. "That is what we must prevent, Tarod. That is what we must prevent, no matter what it costs us!"

Tarod nodded grave agreement. "I still can't shake off my suspicion that there's more behind Ailind's treatment of Calvi Alacar than meets the eye," he said.

"No, neither can I. The sudden turning against him, with the result that he's effectively been driven into the usurper's arms . . . it's a little too convenient for my liking. But I can still see no possible rhyme or reason behind such a strategy, and nothing I've gleaned from Order's realm holds any clues. I think we must await developments and hope that Strann may manage to provide us with more information."

"He's already provided one valuable snippet, and that relates to our dealings with Narid-na-Gost himself," Tarod said. "Obviously he's been the prime mover in this from the beginning, and in one sense—because he stands

252

to gain the greater power—he still is. But according to Strann's messages, the tension between him and his daughter is increasing. She's making all the running now, and he no longer trusts her. Add to that the fact that she has possession of the soul-stone, and Narid-na-Gost is faced with several potential problems."

Yandros looked at him keenly. "He's starting to lose his nerve?"

"Strann thinks so. Or at least that he might if the rift between them isn't healed."

"Interesting . . . interesting." Yandros began to pace again. "And of course Strann is doing all he can to ensure that doesn't happen."

"Any chain is only as strong as its weakest link."

"Indeed. I wouldn't have considered Narid-na-Gost to be the weaker of the two, but now that I think about it, I suppose it's logical in a way. He is, after all, only what we made him." He fell silent for a few moments, pondering, then stopped and turned to face Tarod once more. "There may be potential in this; I don't know. Although of course, even if Narid-na-Gost were to be removed from the arena, that would still leave us with the problem of Ygorla herself to solve, and while she holds the soul-stone, she's effectively invulnerable."

"At least her ambitions don't extend in quite the same direction as her sire's," Tarod said.

Yandros's expression changed, and he gave his brother an odd look. "Don't they?"

He was taken aback. "But she's mortal—"

"*Half* mortal," Yandros reminded him, and smiled drily. "And there's a precedent, isn't there, for mortals to hold rank in the realm of Chaos? Don't think for a moment that the usurper doesn't know that. I'm not saying that she *will* start to entertain such ideas. I'm merely pointing out that she *could,* and that it's a possibility we'd be advised to bear in mind."

From beyond the window, far, far below their vantage point, an eldritch choir began to sing in strange and coldly beautiful harmony. Yandros turned his head, listening for a few moments, then he sighed, and the choir and the landscape outside faded into a gray void.

"There's little more we can say for now. Strann's done well so far. Instruct him to carry on as before, and we'll see what further doubts can be insinuated into Narid-na-Gost's head. As for our own endeavors, watch and wait must be our motto, and above all we must avoid being forced into giving the usurper any answer to her ultimatum before we're ready." Suddenly he smiled with a small but distinct spark of the dark humor that was so much a part of his nature. "I'm sorry that you'll have to go back to the mortal world again, but you might as well enjoy your respite while it lasts. I'll call the others together, and we'll celebrate your return, brief though it is."

"I only wish we had more substantial grounds for a celebration."

"So do I. But those grounds will come, in time." Yandros's eyes glinted ferally. "Let's look on this as a rehearsal for that day, shall we?"

Tarod kept Ygorla waiting for two nights and the day between them before he returned to the castle on a dismal, snowy morning with a terse but cogent message from Yandros. The highest Chaos lord would consider the terms of her pact and respond in good time; until then there would be no further communications from his realm.

Ygorla was quite satisfied. She hadn't anticipated an immediate reaction from Chaos, and time was on her side. Yandros could ponder his decision for a year if it pleased him, and she would simply settle down to enjoy the wait. She had no intention of returning to Summer Isle, despite its kinder climate and the palace's greater opulence. The stark grandeur of the Star Peninsula appealed to her sense of the dramatic, and she considered the castle's grim magnificence a more fitting stronghold for the world's Empress. She would stay here, and until

Yandros capitulated, as he surely must, she would continue to amuse herself at the expense of her beleaguered hosts.

Besides, she had another and more immediate matter to preoccupy her at present. After receiving Tarod's curt response, she had dispatched Strann to the south spire to take the news to Narid-na-Gost. The demon didn't know it, but this, in Ygorla's mind, was a final test. In the wake of her verbal challenge to him, and her accusations of cowardice, his failure to appear at the meeting had infuriated her and, finally, goaded her into making the decision she had been considering for some days. Unless Narid-na-Gost's reaction should take some quite unpredicted turn, then the message that Strann dutifully carried would be the last her sire would ever receive from her—save one. And when the time was right, that one, she promised herself gleefully, would deliver the death-blow to his arrogant presumptions.

The demon received Strann and his information in cold silence, then rose from his cushions and moved to the window, staring out over the courtyard with his back to Strann.

"You may convey my indebtedness to my daughter for this news." His voice was icily remote, and his sarcasm as powerful and corrosive as acid. "And you may convey my hope, thin though it is, that she may repent of her crass stupidity, and act on that repentance, before she brings us all to ruin!"

Strann knew better than to venture any comment or opinion, and merely bowed his way out of the demon's presence. He wasted no time in returning to Ygorla with his report, and as he told her what her sire had said, he watched her face, her eyes, her whole demeanor, with covert intensity. Something was in the wind, he knew it as surely as he knew his own name. There had been an aura of excited impatience in the usurper's manner when she'd ordered him to the spire, and now that aura was intensified, and fueled by what appeared to be an extraordinary blend of fury and delight.

When he finished speaking, she said nothing for several seconds. They were in the outer room of her apartments, and she looked quickly about her, her eyes narrowing. He had the distinct impression that she'd suddenly become oblivious of her surroundings and was lost in another dimension of her own devising. Then, abruptly, she snapped her fingers.

"Wait there." She pointed imperiously to Strann's cushion bed in the corner, then swung on her heel and disappeared into her inner, private room. As soon as the door had shut behind her, Strann pressed his ear to the wall. He could hear her talking to Calvi, who was lounging in his usual place on her bed, but the wall's solid stone muffled all but the tone of their voices. Calvi sounded querulous, Ygorla placatory and purring. After a few minutes the sounds subsided, and Strann withdrew hastily to his cushions before the door opened once more.

Ygorla came out, followed by Calvi, who was disheveled and yawning. The young man raked Strann with a look of scorn and dislike and said sullenly, "No, I *don't* want that creature dogging my steps wherever I go. He irritates me, and I shan't tolerate his presence! Send him somewhere else; I don't care where, just so long as he doesn't attach himself to *me*!"

Strann looked away—he'd quickly learned the painful price of any gesture that Calvi might interpret as insouciance—and Ygorla said sweetly, "Of course, dearest one. You needn't trouble yourself about my rat if you don't want to. Only be a sweeting and give me this little time alone to do what needs to be done. I'll send for you just as soon as my work's complete."

"Promise you will."

"Of course I promise." She kissed him lingeringly. "There, now. Enjoy yourself among our subjects, and we'll be together again soon."

Risking a glance through half-lowered lashes, Strann saw Calvi go out into the corridor. Then Ygorla's voice brought him sharply upright.

"As for you, rat . . . well, I must make other provisions, I think. We can't have you running about the castle, twitching your whiskers at all and sundry. Look at me."

Strann's pulse quickened unpleasantly as he slowly and cautiously obeyed. "Madam . . . ?"

Her eyes were twin sapphires, unnaturally bright. He felt the surge of power even as she smiled, even as she raised a careless hand.

Ygorla said, "Sleep." And Strann's consciousness was obliterated even before his body sagged into the cushions' embrace.

Ygorla stared down at his recumbent form for a moment. Then she smiled and, dismissing him from her mind, returned to the inner chamber. She felt a sense of eager anticipation rising within her, as heady as strong wine, and with it a sense of impending freedom that she had never known in all her life. *Freedom*. She savored the word. Freedom, and power. She had made her decision. And when she had taken this one step, nothing would or could stand in the way of her will anymore. *Nothing!*

She snapped her fingers again, and every light in the bedchamber went out, leaving only the mean winter daylight to illuminate the room. Another gesture and the heavy velvet curtains over the window swished shut, granting her total darkness. She wanted no elemental slaves for this, she thought. All that was required was her own power, her own strength, her own supremacy. And no one—not Tarod of Chaos, not Ailind of Order, and above all not her own sire, Narid-na-Gost—would know what she had done. Until the time was right, until the final, triumphant moment came, this would be the greatest secret of all.

She slid her loose robe from her shoulders with sinuous, sensuous grace and let it fall to the floor. Naked, a pale wraith in the darkness, she raised her left hand to the chain at her neck, and her white fingers closed around the Chaos stone. She felt it pulse, like a disembodied heart. She felt the power that linked her and her father inextricably to it. And she smiled as, with meticulous and single-minded care, she began gently to manipulate that power into a new pattern. . . .

Strann could have screamed aloud with sheer relief when he discovered that the recital that evening wasn't to be canceled. He'd been certain that Ygorla would abandon it, and the reason behind his belief made it imperative for him to get a message to Karuth tonight.

Thinking and working with frantic rapidity, Strann composed a new solo piece of music that afternoon. Nothing elaborate, simply an apparent new paean in Ygorla's praise. But in the dining hall that night, before his co-opted audience, he saw Karuth tense like an alerted cat as the first notes flowed from his fingers, and he could only look away from her face as he played on and pray that she'd have the self-control to give nothing away.

His prayers were answered. She collected herself swiftly, and as the recital continued, she gave no further sign that anything out of the ordinary had taken place. But later, when the entertainment was done and he was following Ygorla from the hall like a trained dog on the end of his jeweled leash, Strann saw her rise quickly to her feet, and for one instant their gazes met. He shut his eyes momentarily. She understood. That one glance had confirmed it. Now he could do no more.

Karuth was nervous at the prospect of facing Tarod again after their last encounter. She still felt mortified when she remembered the chilly and almost pitying look he had bestowed on her, silently condemning her petty concerns, and it had delivered a severe blow to her confidence. But the news she now had to impart couldn't be delayed. Embarrassing or not, the encounter had to be braved, and quickly.

She found him through the medium of the gray cat, which came to her only minutes after the recital ended and made it clear that it wanted her to follow. Encouraged by the realization that Tarod must have sent the creature, she accompanied the cat through the maze of corridors and found the Chaos lord in the courtyard. To her relief he made no reference to their last meeting but only looked at her with his disturbingly intent green eyes and made a brief gesture that transported them both to the cluttered room at the top of the north spire.

"What's happened?" He didn't waste words on any preamble and gave her no time to catch her breath after the shock of displacement.

Karuth's doubt and uncertainty were abruptly swept aside; his tone confirmed that he had sensed her urgency, and her bard's training responded in a surge of clarity.

"My lord, Strann thinks that the usurper has broken her sire's link with the Chaos stone." She met his gaze. "He can't be certain, but he has enough evidence to convince him."

Dark fires ignited in Tarod's eyes, and he said softly, "Tell me, Karuth. Tell me everything Strann told you."

She swallowed, and then she began to recite the tale, resorting to the formal style of the Guild, which combined concision with detailed accuracy. Strann had woken from the sleep that Ygorla imposed on him to find the smell of sorcery in his nostrils. From the inner room he'd heard the sound of the usurper's laughter—wild laughter, he said, wild and triumphant. She must have known that the spell she'd cast on him had lapsed, for a minute later she had emerged from her sanctum in a state of excitement and ebullience. She'd hauled him to his feet and whirled him around the antechamber, declaring that the day would soon come when her rat would be privileged to write an epic the like of which the world had never seen. And that epic, she had said, would be in *her* honor and hers alone. Strann knew more than enough about the nature of the quarrels between Ygorla and Narid-na-Gost to draw his own conclusions from that. He'd carried the verbal messages, surreptitiously read some of the letters. He knew how deep the division had become and had put a shrewd interpretation on the veiled threats that Ygorla had delivered more and more frequently to her sire over the past few days. Then this morning her sudden decision to embark on some dark magic, so hard on the heels of the latest vitriolic exchange, had been confirmation enough for Strann.

"He's been half expecting something like this, my lord," Karuth finished uneasily. "He's only sorry that he can't be unequivocally sure of what Ygorla did. But it seems she didn't quite trust him enough to risk his witnessing her spell."

"The fact that she didn't only weighs the evidence in Strann's favor," Tarod said. His expression was thoughtful now, though his eyes were still unquiet. "So, if this is true, it will mean that we now have only one danger to deal with. . . ."

He was musing to himself rather than addressing her, but all the same Karuth ventured to ask, "Can you discover the truth of it, my lord?"

"What?" He seemed momentarily to have forgotten that she was there, but as he turned his head and saw her, his face relaxed a little. "Oh, yes; and I'll do so." He glanced back toward the window, beyond which snow had just begun to fall once more, ethereal against the leaden night sky. "You'd best go now, Karuth. Tell Strann—if you have the chance—that I'm greatly indebted to him for this news."

She rose, then hesitated. "Is there anything more you want him to do, my lord?"

"For the present, no. We'll leave matters to take their own course for the time being. Make sure you say nothing of this to anyone. But if Strann passes on any more information, let me know immediately."

"I shall." She wanted to ask if he in his turn would tell her when he'd confirmed the truth or otherwise of Strann's message, but she couldn't quite muster the courage. Instead she made a formal bow, said, "Good night, my lord," and readied herself for the dizzying, disorientating return to the courtyard.

Tarod continued to watch from the window as she emerged at the foot of the spire and, after a moment's pause to collect her wits, hurried away toward the main doors with her shoulders hunched against the snowfall. Then, without turning, he said quietly and evenly, "Is it true?"

"It's true." Yandros's voice spoke from the gloom behind him, and the figure of the highest Chaos lord shimmered into existence, haloed by a faintly pulsing silver aura. "Strann was right. She's broken Narid-na-Gost's link with the soul-stone and left him effectively unprotected." His thin mouth smiled, making him look vulpine. "A fact that, as yet, he's unaware of."

Tarod returned the smile. "I must admit that I'm surprised by her subtlety. To achieve this without alerting her father—or for that matter alerting me—to her mischief is impressive."

"Oh, certainly. Under other circumstances she might have been a credit to us." Scathing anger colored Yandros's tone. "But now we must ask ourselves what her next move will be."

"You think she has something planned?"

Yandros shrugged. "Nothing immediate, perhaps. She's been content to bide her time until now. But in his present state of mind I doubt if it'll be long before Narid-na-Gost is driven to test his link with the stone. When he discovers what she's done, I think he'll feel he has no choice but to force her hand." His eyes went through several rapid color shifts that finally combined in a disturbing purplish red. "Then, perhaps, we shall see what changes his loyalties have undergone as a result of his daughter's perfidy."

"Should his investigations be . . . prompted?"

"No. I've a reason for not wanting to stir the waters unless I have to. Forgive me, Tarod, but I also have a reason for not wanting to explain that as yet. Leave Narid-na-Gost to come face-to-face with damnation in his own time and in his own way. It'll happen soon enough without our intervention." His golden hair rippled as the aura around him brightened momentarily before his image began to fade. "I only hope that when it does, it won't be a shade *too* soon. . . ."

Calvi hadn't felt like attending the evening recital and had stayed in the apartments he now shared permanently with Ygorla, indulging himself with a tray of sweetmeats and a large flagon of wine. A little bored, though too languid to stir himself to be interested in anything, he passed the hour of his lover's absence sprawled on the great bed thinking idle, pleasurable thoughts. In such a state it was inevitable that he should fall into a doze; and as he dozed, he dreamed.

Only a skilled adept or a natural psychic might have found anything untoward in the faint disturbances that intruded on the bedchamber's stillness as Calvi slept. A slight shifting of the bed-hangings, though there was no draft to stir them. An unexpected hiss from the banked-down fire, accompanied by a small flurry of sparks. The muted and barely audible sound of wine splashing in the flagon as though an unseen hand had stirred or tilted it. Calvi muttered, one hand clenching and opening. Then he laughed aloud in his sleep, a laugh of delight, though not entirely pleasant. The dreams fled. A few minutes later he stirred, opened his eyes, and blinked, half stupefied, in the candlelight. The bed-curtains were still, the fire quiescent. Calvi yawned and poured himself another cup of wine.

Their work completed for the moment, their presence undetected, the elementals faded from the scene. And, alone in his austere quarters in the east wing, Ailind nodded in silent, private satisfaction. . . .

18

Karuth hurried thankfully through the castle's main doorway and out of the snow, pausing to stamp her feet and shake melting flakes from her hair before turning toward the main staircase and her own room. She was halfway up the flight when she met Shaill coming down. The Matriarch's eyes lit keenly at the sight of her, and quickly she drew Karuth aside, into the shadows of the balustrade.

"My dear, I'm glad to have encountered you." She glanced in both directions, ensuring there was no one else in earshot. "There's to be a meeting later tonight, just a very few of us, when the rest of the castle is asleep, and I'd greatly appreciate it if you would attend."

Surprised, Karuth shook off her preoccupations with Strann's message and Tarod's reaction. "A meeting?"

"Yes. It concerns Calvi—that's why the secrecy. Obviously we're anxious that neither he nor the usurper should get to hear of it. We're to gather in the library, at second moonrise. We feel it's a safer rendezvous than anyone's private room; the usurper never ventures there, and if she should get wind of anything, it's the last place she'd think of to look for us. May we count on you to come?"

Karuth was aware that a number of such meetings had taken place recently, small, clandestine gatherings to debate the Circle's troubles and seek answers. However, this was the first time that she had been asked to take part, and the fact that the invitation had been extended now after a long and obvious omission aroused her curiosity. It could imply, she thought, that the Council of

Adepts' attitude toward her loyalty to Chaos might be undergoing a change.

"Yes." She wondered who else was to be present, but decided against asking lest Shaill think she was simply being captious. She'd find out soon enough. "Yes, Shaill, I'll be there."

Second moonrise was late that night, but Karuth had no fear that she might fall asleep and miss her rendezvous. Since the usurper's arrival and her enforced separation from Strann, she had found it hard to sleep for more than an hour or two at a time, and tonight was no exception. She dozed off once or twice as she sat reading in a chair at her fireside, but never for more than a few minutes, and when at last the second moon showed its face above the castle's black wall, she was wide awake and mentally keyed up.

The corridors were dark and deserted, and she was thankful that the snow clouds had passed on into the south, leaving a clear sky that allowed her to find her way through the silent corridors by moonlight. Reaching the courtyard, she checked carefully to be sure that no one was abroad before hastening along the scraped pathway under the stoa to the library door.

The spiral staircase was dimly illuminated by a light from below, and when she entered the library, Karuth found her fellow conspirators already present and waiting for her. There were four of them: Shaill herself; Sister Alyssi, who was one of her seniors and a close confidante; Sen Briaray Olvit—and Tirand. Karuth was surprised to see her brother. She knew how reluctant he had thus far been to take any action over Calvi's bewitchment and she found it hard to believe that Shaill had recruited him to her cause now. As difficult to credit was the idea that he had consented to his sister's invitation, for although their feelings toward each other had warmed lately and the old quarrel had begun to show signs of healing, Karuth still doubted that Tirand was ready to trust her. Then his look of chagrined astonishment told her that he, in his turn, hadn't expected to see her here tonight, and abruptly she realized that this was the Matriarch's doing. Shaill had engineered this encounter for some unfathomable reason of her own, and Karuth turned toward her, her eyes accusing. But Shaill only smiled enigmatically and patted the empty chair beside her own.

"My dear, come and sit down." They were all grouped around one of the library tables, with two lanterns set between them. "We're all present now, so let's begin without any more delay. Alyssi, if you'd be so kind as to lock the door . . . it's probably an unnecessary precaution but you never know." She rubbed her hands together over one of the lanterns, trying to warm them. The library was bitterly cold, and Karuth was thankful that she'd had the foresight to wear her warmest coat.

"Now." The Matriarch nodded her satisfaction as Alyssi returned and retook her seat. "Firstly I must thank you all for leaving your warm beds. I'm sorry to have called this meeting at such an uncivilized hour and in such an uncomfortable setting, but as I'm sure you all appreciate, it's imperative that certain others shouldn't suspect anything untoward." She paused. "And I suppose I'd better be frank with you and add that by 'certain others' I don't just mean the usurper and Calvi."

Sen frowned. "You've lost me, Shaill. Are you saying that there are others in the castle who've fallen under Ygorla's influence?"

"No, I'm not saying that, Sen. I mean, quite simply, that I don't want lord Ailind to know of this discussion."

There was a sharp silence. Everyone but the Matriarch looked at Tirand, expecting him to react. But Tirand didn't react. He only sat, elbows on knees, gazing steadfastly at his own clasped hands.

At last Sen said quietly, "Why, Shaill? Why don't you want lord Ailind to know?"

The Matriarch returned his gaze. "Because I have reluctantly come to the conclusion that, in this matter at least, his interests and ours don't coincide." She nodded in the High Initiate's direction. "I've talked with Tirand about this and explained the reasons for my belief. He doesn't entirely agree with me, but . . . well, Tirand, perhaps it would be better if you were to express it in your own words."

Tirand guessed what the others were thinking and decided to spare them the embarrassment of having to voice it aloud. "I know you're all aware of my loyalty to lord Ailind," he said, "and because of that I don't doubt that you're wondering if Shaill's wise to speak her mind so openly in my presence. So, before I go on, I'll just say that I've given her my promise that not a word of what passes here tonight will go any farther than the confines of this room."

From the sharp flush on Sen's and Karuth's cheeks, and the way in which Alyssi dropped her gaze, he knew his surmise had been right, and he allowed himself a wry smile. "This isn't a suitable time to debate the rights and wrongs of the issue. I'll tell you what I've already told Shaill: that I've now appealed to lord Ailind three times to help Calvi, and each time he's refused."

"Why?" Sen asked.

There was a pause. Then: "He didn't give a reason. Again, I asked him, but . . ." Tirand shrugged, and seemed to have to steel himself before finishing. "He simply said that it isn't for mortals to question the gods' decisions. And . . . I can no longer pretend to be happy with that."

Karuth turned her head away so that the curtain of her hair hid her expression. How many times had she, and doubtless all the others, heard similar words from Ailind's lips? That high-handed attitude had been at the root of her own early clashes with the lord of Order, and more recently it had begun to rankle with an increasing number of adepts, not least Sen. But for Tirand to acknowledge openly that he, too, was beginning to harbor doubts was quite another matter. From the start of this whole ugly affair he had staunchly supported Order's cause and Order's methods almost to the point of pigheadedness. Had Shaill worked some miracle of persuasion on him, or had something else triggered this extraordinary, albeit tentative, change of heart?

She glanced obliquely at her brother, and abruptly the answer came to her. Shaill wasn't behind this, though she might have had a hand in encouraging an already burgeoning feeling. Calvi was the cause. Tirand's loyalties had always run deep, and for years he had felt not only great fondness for Calvi but also a sense of responsibility for him, the more so since the hideous death of Calvi's brother, Blis. Now Calvi was in peril, and for the first time Tirand found his loyalties sharply divided. On the one hand was Ailind, one of the seven gods to whose unquestioning service he had pledged himself; but on the other hand was the harsh reality of a friend in dire need. Forced into a position where he could no longer support one cause without renouncing the other, Tirand's conscience—and his fundamental nature—had forced him to make a clear choice.

He was speaking again now. Karuth was aware that the words didn't come easily to him. Such a drastic change of heart wasn't a light thing to admit, and she was aware that he was still wrangling inwardly with what must seem to him like a betrayal of his pledge to Order. He said, "The simple fact is that I can't accept lord Ailind's insistence that we should leave Calvi to his fate. We *must* try to do something—and if the gods are unwilling to help us, then we must try alone." He leaned back, his expression defensive though also with a hint of relief at having spoken his mind. His eyes met Karuth's. She smiled tentatively and he returned the smile, albeit with a certain wryness.

Sen cleared his throat. "I endorse that sentiment entirely," he said, "and it brings us to the point of this meeting. We know all too well what matter of creature we're up against in any dealings we may have with the usurper. With only our own powers to pit against hers, what can we do to free Calvi from the snare she's tangled around him?" He looked from one to another. "I'll freely admit that I don't know if it's possible. It isn't even as if Calvi's her unwilling prisoner—far from it, in fact."

"That's true, Sen," Tirand put in, "but you're forgetting one thing. Calvi—the *real* Calvi—is no more Ygorla's willing accessory than you or I or anyone else in this room. He's bewitched. If that spell were broken, matters would be very different."

"Yes. Yes, of course." Then Sen frowned. "You know, don't you, that there are rumors flying about that? Some people are starting to say that Calvi's perfectly well aware of what he's doing and that he isn't a victim but a traitor."

Tirand flashed him an angry look. "Yes, I do know. And I've put word out that anyone found spreading those stories will merit severe punishment, whether they're a servant or a seventh-rank adept!"

Sen nodded and hastily returned to the topic at hand. "Well, either way, as I said, we have only our own resources to rely on and no chance of Calvi assisting us." He looked grimly about him. "Which leaves us, I think, with two options to choose from: force or sorcery."

"Sorcery?" Tirand looked appalled. "Against *her*?"

"No, no—even I'm not *that* rash!" Sen said hastily. "I mean against Calvi—a means of breaking the spell she's cast on him and opening his eyes."

"That would effectively amount to the same thing. Attack him, and by implication we attack the usurper too. That's how she'd see it anyway."

Sen shrugged. "But it has to be one or the other. There isn't a third choice."

The Matriarch intervened. "Wait, Sen. Before we pursue this, perhaps I should be honest with Tirand and Karuth and own up to my reason for calling them here tonight." She leaned back in her chair, drew a deep breath, and looked at brother and sister in turn. "I suppose this is as good a moment as any to confess that from the start I've had an ulterior motive. Tirand, Karuth—to put it plainly, my intention tonight is to try to bury the last vestiges of the quarrel between you. I know you've both made tentative moves toward healing the wounds, but neither of you seems able to take the final step. So, I've decided to take it for you, and I've bullied Sen and

Alyssi into coming along to support me and, if necessary, to act as moderators. I'm not ashamed of my tactics, because I feel that we have a common cause that transcends any question of personal animosities or divided allegiances. That cause is Calvi. For his sake, if not for your own or mine, I entreat you both to be formally reconciled and to lend your united and unstinting help in saving our High Margrave."

She finished speaking, and there was a long, uneasy silence. At last Shaill broke it. "Well? Have neither of you anything to say?"

The gazes of brother and sister met across the table. Karuth could feel a flush burning her cheeks. Tirand looked uncertain. Then he bit his lower lip.

"The quarrel between us should never have begun. . . ." he said.

"I didn't seek it." Then Karuth realized that her words could be misinterpreted and added quickly, "That is . . . I'd like to think we could forget our differences." She looked at her brother helplessly. "I can't argue with Shaill's wisdom, and I don't want to. And we were always such good friends in the past."

Shaill reached out and took hold of Karuth's right hand and Tirand's left. "The Circle needs you both now. We *all* need you both. Isn't it time to forgive and forget?"

Sen and Alyssi were staring down at the floor. Tirand hesitated only a bare moment, then said, "I'm willing. If Karuth is."

To her embarrassment and fury, Karuth felt tears welling in her eyes. But she knew that they weren't triggered simply by the prospect of reconciliation. All the other pains and confusions were helplessly tangled in: her separation from Strann, the risks he ran hour by hour, her uncertainties and fears for the future. She blinked rapidly. "Yes," she agreed. "Yes. I'm willing, too. And—" Tirand had made the first gesture, she thought. It was only right that she should add her own contribution. "I apologize to you, Tirand, for my harsh words of the past. They should never have been said or even thought."

The apology was halting, a little stiff, but the relief of having said it was acute. Tirand smiled diffidently. "They're forgotten." He, too, sounded awkward. "And I rescind my own. They were unjust. Very unjust."

With the look of someone whose private theory had been vindicated, Shaill drew their hands together. "There," she said softly. "And yet it's taken an outsider to achieve what you both wanted and could have done a long time ago. Please, now, touch and seal the bargain."

They touched, clasped. Tirand squeezed Karuth's fingers firmly, and she responded, and the Matriarch laid her own clenched fist lightly over theirs. Her gesture made the reconciliation between them formal and binding, and quickly—a little too quickly, Karuth suspected, as though they'd rehearsed for this moment—Sen and Alyssi brought their own fists down on the table to bear witness.

At last the Matriarch sat back, and Tirand and Karuth broke the clasp and withdrew their hands. Karuth didn't quite know whether she wanted to laugh, upbraid Shaill for her sheer presumption, or burst into tears. This was bizarre. The rift healed, the healing formally ratified; yet had anything really changed? It didn't seem so. She felt the same sense of anticlimax she'd felt after passing her various adepts' ranking trials or a Musicians' Guild test, when, expecting great changes within herself, she'd been disappointed to find the world and all within it just the same as before.

Or was that entirely true? There *was* a difference. Not so much a change as a sudden absence of something she'd not even been consciously aware of until now, but that had lurked in the darkest corners of her mind, gnawing silently but persistently at her. She'd never wanted to quarrel with Tirand. She'd never hated him as she had pretended to herself, but with no apparent way to break the deadlock the pretense had been maintained, and it had soured her. Now it was gone, and for the first time since the bitter events of last autumn she felt she had been released from chains that she hadn't even known were binding her.

She looked up, met Tirand's eyes, and guessed that his feelings mirrored hers. She wanted to say something but didn't know what. Then, before she could speak, Shaill preempted her.

"Well! Now that that little matter is resolved to everyone's satisfaction, perhaps we can move on to the business of the night." The change of topic was so abrupt, her words so brisk and prosaic, that Karuth and Tirand blinked in momentary bewilderment, and even Sen and Alyssi looked taken aback. The Matriarch gave them all a dry smile.

"Don't worry, I haven't finished with our newly conciliated friends yet." Now her shrewd gaze focused on brother and sister in turn. "In fact I'm about to put this happy state of affairs to the test by asking Karuth a question. Karuth, Tirand has already told us the results of his appeals to lord Ailind, so we must look elsewhere for Calvi's salvation. What about lord Tarod? Do you think that he might help us where lord Ailind has refused?"

Karuth stared back at her, astounded. She hadn't expected this—and neither had Tirand. The High Initiate was completely nonplussed. He opened his mouth to protest, then suddenly saw the expressions on the faces of Sen and Alyssi. They'd known. In fact, Tirand realized, this must have been part of the Matriarch's plan from the start, perhaps even the sole motive behind this entire scheme. . . .

He shut his mouth, then opened it again. "Shaill—" There was outrage in his tone, but somehow he couldn't find the words he wanted to say.

Shaill took advantage of his helplessness and gave him a pungent smile. "All right, Tirand, I admit it. This is a blatant ploy on my part, and it's what I've been leading up to all along. I know that in the present climate what I've just suggested smacks of heresy, but you should know by now that I'm nothing if not a pragmatist. It's quite simple, my dear. The lords of Order won't help us, so can you give me one good reason why we shouldn't now appeal to the lords of Chaos instead?"

"Because it would be flying in the face of the Circle's pledge of loyalty to Order!"

"A loyalty that even you admit seems a little one-sided," Shaill countered. "Please, Tirand, just for a moment try to step outside your prejudices—and no, don't flare up at me. You *are* prejudiced, of course you are, and I don't mean to denigrate you by saying so. We all have our loyalties and our partialities, and there's nothing at all wrong with that. But they should only go so far. Not far enough to cause a long, bitter, and unnecessary rift between brother and sister"—she raised an expressive eyebrow as she saw her meaning bite home—"and not far enough to blind us to the urgency of our own needs. So I ask you, put your prejudice aside for a moment and think of Calvi. We *must* help him. He's not only our dear friend, he's also our High Margrave. Though I hate to look at matters in such an emotionless light, that outweighs even the more personal considerations. Calvi is the figurehead around which *everything* revolves. If he is lost to us, then the greater part of our hope goes with him. For all our sakes, not just for his, I think we must use any means we can find to free him from the usurper's influence, and that's why I say that if Order has failed us, we must turn to Chaos."

Tirand didn't reply immediately. He was suddenly and terribly torn, for although what Shaill had said went against everything he believed in, everything he stood for, he had to admit that her reasoning was inescapably logical. The gods of Order *had* failed them, and the failure was doubly soured by the fact that Ailind hadn't even been willing to look favorably on their pleas. Would it, he wondered, be such an act of madness or blasphemy to look instead to Tarod of Chaos? Even a day ago the thought that he could have even considered such a possibility would have shocked him to the marrow. But, as Shaill said, it was not only their desire but also their duty to save Calvi from Ygorla. He was their rightful High Margrave, and his security was of paramount concern to the entire world. And that was what made it so hard—

no, he corrected, not hard, *impossible*—to comprehend Ailind's attitude.

Loyalties and partialities, Shaill had said, but they shouldn't go far enough to blind us to the urgency of our own needs. . . . He looked at his sister. "Karuth . . . if I were to agree to approaching . . . lord Tarod . . . do you think he would help us?"

Karuth had watched her brother's silent battle between conscience and necessity, and as he asked the question, she felt that the last barriers between them were crumbling. Yet at the same time her spirits sank, for there was only one answer she could give. Two days ago she might have seen the situation differently, but more recent experience had brought her to a reluctant but inescapable conclusion. Tarod had treated her almost as an equal and certainly as a friend. He had shown her kindness and consideration, he had given her support and confidence when she was at her lowest ebb. But deep down she knew that all the sympathy and generosity went no farther than suited Tarod's purpose. She'd learned the folly of attributing human drives and human emotions to him. The lords of Chaos might appear to show more compassion to their followers than the lords of Order showed to theirs, but when it came to a choice, their own interests were paramount. Fairness and justice didn't enter into the equation. Tarod and his kin weren't men but gods, and in their eyes the fears and hopes of mortals were simply too trivial to be of any account.

Suddenly she understood what had truly motivated Shaill. The Matriarch shared her feelings and her doubts, and without the clouding factor of fierce loyalty to one side or the other to impair her vision, she had foreseen what must inevitably happen when the interests of humans and gods no longer tallied. In this the Circle and their friends were alone. The Matriarch knew it, and she had taken the hazardous gamble that through reconciliation she could open Karuth's and Tirand's eyes to the truth.

Karuth hesitated for another moment. Then, quietly

273

but calmly, she said, "I can't be sure, Tirand. But . . . I don't think that he will."

Tirand gazed back. "Why?"

"Because he wouldn't countenance any move that might jeopardize the safety of his brother's soul-gem."

Shaill's mouth twisted slightly and she spoke up. "I suppose we can hardly blame him for that. After all, there's no reason why he should be any more interested in our concerns than lord Ailind is, if they should happen to clash with his own."

Her words echoed Karuth's private thoughts with painful accuracy, but all the same Karuth instinctively protested, trying to deny it.

"No, Shaill, I don't believe that—"

"But I think you do, in your heart." Shaill's sympathetic tone softened the edge of her words, and she added, "I asked Tirand to be honest with himself a few minutes ago, and now I ask the same of you. We have to face the harsh fact that as far as the gods are concerned, and I mean any and all of the gods, we are very minor players on the stage of this conflict. We are insignificant, our needs and desires have no importance—and to be blunt, if we should interfere in any way with their plans and strategies, I have no doubt we'll discover that we're also expendable." She smiled a strange, bitter little smile. "The gods are good to us in many ways, but it's all too easy to forget the enormous gulf that exists between us and them. Our catechisms tell us that the true natures of Order and Chaos are far beyond our mortal understanding, and I have an uncomfortable suspicion that the reverse may also be true, that the gods in their turn have no concept of what it is to be mortal. In my darkest moments I've begun to ask myself whether we were wise to ask for their help in the first place."

Sen was shocked. "Shaill! Would you rather we'd left ourselves open to the mercy of the usurper? You know what manner of monster she is. You've seen the mayhem she's wreaked throughout the world. . . ."

"I know, Sen, I know, and I'm not saying that would have been a better choice. That wasn't what I meant at all, and I can't properly explain my feeling, other than to say that . . ." She hesitated. "That I fear that we may be in danger of being carried helplessly along on tides we can neither influence nor control, and that those tides could well drown us if we don't take the greatest care."

She looked at them all in turn, waiting for agreement or dissent, but it seemed that for the moment no one else wanted to speak. Karuth, also watching her companions' faces, felt that in the wake of the Matriarch's disquieting words the subject of their discussion had shifted onto a new and more perilous plane. Insignificant and expendable, Shaill had said. Pawns in a game played by other and greater powers. Yet Karuth doubted if in the gods' eyes it amounted even to that. The lords of Chaos and Order were engaged in a battle of wits that could wreak havoc throughout every dimension of the universe—what, then, to them was the fate of one mere human world and its denizens?

She felt suddenly that she had to speak, to make some attempt, however futile, to pull them back from this brink, and perhaps also to quell the sense of helpless terror that was threatening to take a grip on her.

"Shaill." Her voice sounded odd, and she cleared her throat quickly. They all looked at her.

"Shaill, I—I'll speak with lord Tarod, if Tirand agrees to it. I've little hope that his answer will be any more favorable than lord Ailind's, but if Tirand will sanction it, there can be nothing to lose by trying."

"And if Tirand doesn't agree?" the Matriarch said. "What then?"

This, Karuth realized, was another part of Shaill's test. The Matriarch was asking her and Tirand to trust each other, as they had done so readily before their quarrel. *Did* she trust Tirand? Karuth wondered. Surely if she didn't, then all that had happened tonight was a sham.

Tirand was watching her intently. She'd lost the ability to judge his thoughts by the expression on his face, she realized with a small shock. In the old days, that had been something that, like trust, she'd taken for granted, and suddenly she felt a desperate need for that old security, the sense that she could turn again to another human being and not just to a god, whose motives made no allowance for her mortal limitations and concerns.

She looked directly into her brother's eyes.

"If Tirand doesn't agree, then as a Circle adept I will obey the word of my High Initiate, and do nothing."

She didn't imagine the faint, hissing sigh that stirred the library's musty air, but whether it came from the lips of Shaill, Sen, or Tirand she would never know. The Matriarch looked at Tirand.

"Well, High Initiate? The die, I think, is on your side of the board."

Tirand stared down at his hands for several seconds. Then he raised his head.

"I agree. Speak to Tarod of Chaos. I'll sanction it. But if your appeal fails . . ." he shook his head.

Sen spoke up again. "If the appeal to Chaos fails, then we're back to making plans of our own. In fact I think we should do so in any case. I mean no offense, Karuth, but you've already admitted that your chances of success are very remote." Karuth nodded acknowledgment, and the adept continued. "I have the bones of an idea. It's not much to begin with, but we might make something of it."

The Matriarch smiled wryly. "Anything's better than nothing, Sen, and you seem to be the only one among us who has a suggestion of any sort. Tell us."

"Very well." Sen leaned forward, resting his elbows on the table. "It occurs to me that we stand no chance of breaking the bewitchment on Calvi unless we can get him out of the usurper's clutches first. While he's still at her side, we can't affect him. So, I wonder if we can create a diversion to take her from his side and preoccupy her, say for an hour or two, just long enough for us to destroy the geas and bring him back to his right mind."

"It's a possibility." Tirand looked interested though cautious. "But what manner of diversion could we arrange that would bring her running?"

"Well . . ." Sen seemed suddenly reluctant to meet

Karuth's eyes. "She appears to be inordinately fond of her little pet rat, the traitor, Strann." He flinched slightly as he heard Karuth's sharply indrawn breath, but otherwise ignored it. "Perhaps if he were to meet with an unpleasant accident . . . ?"

There was a moment's silence. Then Karuth's voice snapped out with the discordant force of an instrument string breaking.

"No!"

Sen said dully, "Oh, gods . . ." and the Matriarch leaned to catch hold of Karuth's arm.

"My dear, you mustn't allow your feelings to cloud your judgment! Think, I entreat you, before you react. I know that you still have feelings for Strann, but you *must* put them aside once and for all and reconcile yourself to the truth about him!"

Karuth started to say, "It isn't—" but Shaill didn't let her finish. "Karuth, listen to me and take heed. We must give Sen's idea due and full consideration, for it may lead us to a means of saving Calvi. Isn't that more important, *far* more important, than the life of a deceiver who has brought you nothing but misery and harm?" She looked to her colleagues for confirmation. Alyssi nodded vigorously, but neither Sen nor Tirand would meet her gaze.

Karuth sat stony-faced and didn't speak. Shaill patted her hand in a motherly way. "Now, I think that Sen's suggestion should be investigated. It may well be that—"

"Shaill." The High Initiate interrupted her quietly. "I think perhaps it would be a good idea to postpone any further talk until tomorrow."

"But Tirand—"

"No." They all knew the tone, gentle though it was. Tirand was reminding them who held the ultimate authority here. "Under the circumstances I think we should allow Karuth time to consider her feelings and her reactions. It isn't fair to expect her to accept this without a qualm. Besides, the hour's late and we'd be well advised to get some sleep before morning, if we don't want to arouse suspicions."

Shaill hesitated, then gave way. "Yes, I suppose you're right. But time isn't on our side."

"I know. All the same, let's wait until Karuth has spoken to lord Tarod. There's still a chance that Sen's plan won't need to be considered." He rose from his seat, indicating that the meeting was at an end. "Better if we don't all leave together. Sen, you escort Alyssi and the Matriarch back, and Karuth and I will follow in a few minutes. Take this lamp. I'll bring the other and see that we've left no sign of our presence."

A little subdued, they said their good nights, and Karuth watched as Sen's party climbed away up the stairs, their lantern bobbing like a firefly in the darkness. Her heart was pounding as though she had hammers beneath her ribs, and the library seemed suddenly airless and stifling. Tirand, by the door, watched until the lantern was out of sight, then turned, picked up the second lamp, and began to check the vaulted room to ensure that no one had left any telltale clue behind. Karuth stared at him as he moved methodically across the floor and around the table, and her mind whirled. She couldn't do it. She *couldn't*. All this time, unable to trust him, unable to rely on his support . . . The rift might be healed, but could a small ritual gesture *really* wipe out all that had gone before? Was it *enough*?

What would she have done a year ago? The answer was plain: She would have told him the truth, all of it, and never considered for one moment the possibility that he might betray her trust, because that possibility simply hadn't existed. But now . . .

She made a small, involuntary sound of distress, and Tirand stopped and looked back at her. "Karuth?"

Gods, she thought, he knew. She might have lost the old empathy, but he hadn't. She could see it in the sudden intensity of his eyes, the tensing of his face. He wouldn't challenge her directly, but he was aware of her turmoil. She had to decide which way she would gamble. And whatever her decision, the stakes were frighteningly high.

Then she remembered something. One gesture that

would seal a promise beyond any risk of being broken. But to ask it of him . . . would it be an insult, an implication that she still didn't trust him? And would it alienate him and undo what tonight had achieved? Karuth paused another moment and decided that, risk or no, it must be done. It might be her only hope.

She spoke, and her voice sounded like that of a stranger in her own ears. "Tirand . . . if I were to ask you to swear a blood oath with me, what would you say?"

"A blood oath?" The mingling of blood was the most solemn means of sealing a bond, and no one, let alone a high adept of the Circle, would ever break such an oath under any circumstances. Tirand's expression went through several rapid shifts, from surprise to consternation to uncertainty. Then his face stilled and he gazed steadily at her.

"If it's that vital to you, I'll do it."

"It is." She put a hand up to her face. "Oh, it is. It was what Sen said, before you called the meeting to an end. . . . But no one else must know, Tirand. Not Sen, not Shaill, *no* one." Panic gripped her, but she fought it back. She couldn't carry this alone. And by an awful irony, after tonight's events Tirand was the only one she dared confide in.

She stared at the old, uneven table where only a few minutes ago they'd all been sitting. Then she said, quite clearly and calmly, "Tirand, what Sen suggested tonight mustn't be sanctioned. You see, Strann hasn't deceived me. We've been working together, at lord Tarod's behest —and he's no more a traitor than you or I."

19

Tirand stared fixedly at the bright flame of the lantern on the tabletop between himself and his sister. He couldn't bring himself to look up and meet her eyes as he said, "Karuth—I want to believe what you've told me. But I don't know if I can."

Two hours ago she would have flared up at that, thinking he implied that she was a liar. Now, though, she only said, "It's true, Tirand. I haven't been duped."

"Can you be *sure* of that? How do you know that there isn't a double deception at work?"

She smiled a little sadly. "I'm only human. If I had to rely solely on my own judgment, then I couldn't be sure. But Strann couldn't deceive lord Tarod."

Tirand was on the verge of pointing out that if Ailind had misjudged Strann, then Tarod's evaluation could also be flawed. But then he acknowledged that Ailind had recognized the truth of Strann's original story, and his fealty to Chaos. When Strann appeared to change allegiances, the lord of Order simply assumed that, being a craven coward, he had cast in his lot with the safest faction. And that assumption, Tirand reminded himself, still might not be far wrong.

He said aloud, "If I could speak to lord Tarod. . . ." Now at last he did look up at her. "I don't mean to impugn you, Karuth, but to hear it from him . . ."

"Yes, I understand." She made a small gesture implying her own inadequacy. "He once said to me that if I call on him at any time, he'll answer; but I don't like to assume—"

She stopped. Noiselessly the stairs door had swung open, and Tarod, framed in shadows cast by the lantern, stood on the threshold.

They both rose quickly to their feet, Tirand in such disorder that he almost knocked his chair over. Tarod smiled at Karuth, then addressed him directly.

"Good evening, High Initiate. Do I gather that relations between you and your sister have changed somewhat since our last encounter?" He raised a querying eyebrow, and seeing that Tirand was too disconcerted to answer, Karuth said, "My brother and I are—formally reconciled, my lord."

"So the Matriarch has had her way. I thought it wouldn't take her long. She's an eminently determined—and sensible—woman."

Karuth flushed and changed the subject. "My lord, we hoped to speak with you . . ." She floundered, wondering how much she needed to explain. Tarod's sudden and unexpected appearance when the desire to see him had barely formed in her mind had thrown her off balance, and she couldn't imagine how much, or how little, he already knew. Tirand, however, had recovered his composure, and he addressed the Chaos lord directly.

"Sir, Karuth has told me that Strann isn't a traitor to Chaos," he said. "I don't want to doubt her word, but I want to be sure that she's right in her belief."

Tarod looked surprised and, with what might have been a faint flicker of anger, he turned to Karuth. "How much have you told him?"

She stared down at her own feet. "Everything, my lord." Then her head came up again, her expression half appealing, half defiant. "I had to trust someone! There's a plan afoot to use Strann in a scheme to rescue Calvi, and it could mean his death!"

The Chaos lord's eyes burned like cold fire. "And you consider that reason enough to confide his secret to one of Order's most devoted servants?"

"It was reason enough to confide in my brother!" she said pleadingly. "No one else could prohibit the plan from being carried out." She held out her right arm, pushing back the sleeve of her coat to reveal a new, small cut just above the wrist. "We took a blood oath. Tirand won't betray me to lord Ailind."

Tarod turned and raked Tirand with a ferocious glare. "Well, High Initiate?"

Tirand rolled up his own sleeve, exposing a similar cut. "I may be Order's devoted servant, lord Tarod, but I don't take blood oaths lightly—and I don't break them!" he said sharply.

For several seconds the catlike eyes continued to fix him. Tirand held his ground, not looking away, and abruptly Tarod's stance relaxed and the emerald fires lost their fury.

"Very well." He'd sensed enough to satisfy him. For all his faults the High Initiate was strictly honorable, and unless Ailind should get wind of it and force it out of him, the secret was safe enough. "Then you may rest assured, Tirand, that what Karuth has told you is quite true. Strann isn't Ygorla's puppet but mine." The corner of his mouth flicked slightly, but otherwise he ignored Karuth's blanching at his choice of words. "And it wouldn't be in my interests—or yours—if any harm were to befall him through the Circle's interference."

Tirand suspected that he was issuing a thinly veiled threat and looked away. "You must understand our priorities, sir. Calvi is our High Margrave. We *have* to find a way of countering the usurper's influence on him and wresting him from her. She's already made him her consort, and unless we act soon—"

Tarod interrupted. "High Initiate, I'm fully aware of your predicament, and I sympathize with it. But if you think that any ordinary stratagem you might devise would be enough to rescue the High Margrave from Ygorla, you're mistaken. You'd only make matters far worse than they already are and sacrifice the lives of any adepts involved to no good purpose."

"But what other choice do we have?" Tirand looked bitter and angry. "The lords of Order refuse to help us, and Chaos—" He stopped. "Well, I don't know about

Chaos. But I hardly think it likely." He looked helplessly at Karuth, and she spoke up.

"Lord Tarod, *is* there anything you can do to help us to rescue Calvi? And would you be willing, if . . . if . . ." The halting words tailed off.

Tarod gazed down at her. "If I could do so without jeopardizing the safety of my brother's soul-stone? Yes, I would help you. But that isn't possible." He saw that she was about to plead her case further, and continued before she could speak. "No, Karuth. The risks are too great and I won't take them, not for Calvi's sake, not for Strann's, not even for yours."

She made one final, desperate effort. "But if—"

Her voice stopped in midsentence. Tarod hadn't spoken, but his eyes had abruptly taken on a look of cold and dangerous implacability, and it silenced her instantly.

"It's late." One gaunt-fingered hand reached out and came to rest on the door latch. "You'd be advised to get some sleep before dawn breaks." He started to open the door, but Tirand, who hadn't seen what Karuth had seen, said sharply, "Then what *are* we to do, lord Tarod? If neither Order nor Chaos will intervene, what hope is there?"

Tarod looked back at him. "I'm sorry, Tirand," he said. "If I could do anything for Calvi, I would. But it's out of the question while the usurper still threatens Chaos's stability." He paused. "I'd strongly advise you to make no move that might alert Ygorla to your activities or to the fact that Strann isn't quite what he seems. As I said before, it would serve no one if he were to be harmed." Briefly and with his characteristic old-fashioned courtesy he bowed to them in turn. "I wish you both good night."

The door closed behind him. Karuth listened for the sound of footsteps diminishing up the stairs, but there was only silence. At last she turned to look at Tirand.

"Perhaps if I were to approach him again at another time . . ." Her voice wasn't steady.

"No." Tirand shook his head. "There's no point.

Shaill was right, wasn't she? We're just pawns to them, to
all of them." He ventured a thin smile, without humor.
"Maybe we're both learning lessons about our respective
liege lords that neither of us likes."

She didn't answer that, but said quietly, "What
about Sen's plan, Tirand? You can't let it be tried . . .
please, you *can't.*"

Her plea didn't stem from loyalty to Chaos, he
knew, but from something else. The High Initiate sighed
heavily.

"You really love Strann, don't you? It's more than
an infatuation or a passing fancy."

She bit her lip, nodded. "Yes. It's far more than
that."

Tirand didn't understand her feelings, couldn't comprehend them. He hadn't yet discovered what it was like
to love in that way, with body and soul as well as heart
and mind. And that Karuth's love should be given to
Strann, of all men . . . But he knew her well enough to
believe that she must have found depths in her bard that
were hidden from his biased eyes. Above all, he knew
that she was wise enough to judge her own feelings.

He said, "If there's another way, we'll take it. If
not . . . I'll veto Sen's plan. You have my word."

She said nothing, made no move toward him. But
the answering look in her eyes expressed more than any
word or gesture, and brought them closer than they had
been since the days before Ygorla's name had first been
spoken in the castle.

Despite the Matriarch's precautions, tonight's clandestine meeting hadn't gone entirely unnoticed. One pair of
eyes had seen the participants making their way surreptitiously to the library, and when the bobbing light of a
lantern illuminated the first trio emerging from the underground room and hurrying quietly under the stoa to
the main doors, the figure watching from the top of the
south spire took note.

Although he'd never shown himself to the castle dwellers, Narid-na-Gost had taken good care to commit many names and faces to memory, and he knew the identities of all the conspirators. But only three had reappeared. Where, he wondered, were the High Initiate and his sister? Why had they stayed behind? What were they doing—and, far more importantly, what were they *planning* to do?

Narid-na-Gost had his suspicions. He had been waiting for something like this to happen, some move on the part of the castle's innermost coterie, a signal that their period of seemingly helpless inaction was coming to an end. The demon seethed inwardly. This was Ygorla's fault. He had *warned* her, time and time again, against the folly of overconfidence; warned her that these mortals weren't of the same mettle as the weaklings on Summer Isle, and that they wouldn't knuckle under like obedient sheep. But Ygorla no longer listened to anything he had to say. She spurned him; she *scorned* him. And he could no longer control her.

Control. That was the nub of it. The demon rose from his pile of crimson cushions, and his hunched, distorted figure paced restlessly across the spire room. Unanswered questions gnawed at his mind like a predator gnawing the bones of its victim, and his eyes were blood red with anger and frustration. He chewed on one of his clawlike fingernails as he moved lopsidedly back to the window and stared harder into the cold world outside. He had lost control, and he was threatened. He'd known it for some time, but had thought that the threat lay in the effects that Ygorla's blind arrogance would have on Chaos and her apparent willingness to put their schemes at risk for the sake of her childish games. Now he believed that had been a grave mistake. The greatest threat to him came not from Chaos, but from Ygorla herself.

Unable to stay still for more than a few moments at a time, he turned again and returned to his cushions, throwing himself down among their soft luxury and only just resisting an impulse to rip them apart and hurl their shreds about the room. *Calm.* He must stay calm and not let the churning, gnawing, nerve-racking thoughts get the upper hand. But to do that was hard, and growing harder as time went by. What was she planning? That was the vital question. What perfidy was taking shape in his daughter's devious mind, and how could he counter it? Suspicion was piling on suspicion, and the picture was rapidly becoming unpleasant, especially so since she had decided to establish that simpering brat of a High Margrave as her official consort. Why had she done that? What plans did she have for Calvi Alacar?

Another violent movement. Narid-na-Gost kicked the cushions viciously aside and paced across the room once more. Her consort. What were the words she'd used, the words that the rat had reported back to him? "Emperor Designate." *Emperor Designate.* The demon's flesh crawled as he thought of what it might mean. Was *that* what Ygorla secretly plotted to do? Had her ambition now risen to such heights that she thought to usurp his own place in their scheme, and could she be planning to install Calvi Alacar as ruler of this mortal world while she took control of Chaos?

Had Narid-na-Gost been human, he would have broken out into an ice-cold sweat. It made sense; it made terrible, logical sense. Who was the prime mover behind all the quarrels that had led to this present impasse between them? Who had set out, it seemed, deliberately to estrange him, thereby leaving the field clear for her to work her will unhindered by his influence? Oh, she was clever, *clever.* And he'd been a fool not to see the way the wind was blowing until now.

Seven years, he thought savagely, seven years dedicated to teaching her, to nurturing her, to giving her the ability to realize her full power. And now that she'd realized it, she was about to turn on him, laugh at the debt she owed him, and abandon him to ruin. She had the means to do it. She had the Chaos stone—another mark of his stupidity, to have given it into her keeping. She knew the spell by which their lives had both been linked to the fabric of the gem, safeguarding them from any attack by the lords of Chaos, and she knew how to break it.

Then the worst thought of all occurred to him: Perhaps she already *had* broken it. Perhaps even now he no longer had any defense against his former masters and she was waiting only for the right moment to challenge him . . . or even to let Tarod of Chaos know what she had done and weave the destruction of her sire into the bargain she made with Yandros. . . .

A shudder racked Narid-na-Gost, and he hissed like a cornered snake. Behind him one of the cushions burst into flame, ignited by the flash of rage and terror that his mind projected. He snarled, spun around, and doused the fire with a gesture, leaving only a dancing whirl of sparks and a rank smell hanging briefly in the air.

He must test the spell, test his link with the Chaos stone and see if it still held true. Hissing again, he shut his eyes, prepared himself . . . then stopped. Suppose she had set a trap for him? Suppose she had deliberately laid this trail and was only waiting for him to test the link and thus reveal his fear? He wouldn't do it. He wouldn't show weakness and give her the satisfaction of knowing she had alarmed him. Besides, he told himself with renewed ferocity, she hadn't broken the link. She *hadn't*. She wouldn't *dare*.

His eyes snapped open again and he returned to the window. The High Initiate and his sister still hadn't emerged from the library. What were they about? What scheme were they hatching? Before tonight, he knew, they'd barely been on speaking terms. Had that changed, and if so what could it possibly mean? Down there beyond the library itself, Narid-na-Gost knew, lay the Marble Hall, and within the Marble Hall was the Chaos Gate, the doorway to his own ambitions. Was there some connection between the Gate and the adepts' secretive activity? If he could only see through those stone walls, what—

The thought broke off as a faint blur of light appeared at the doorway under the stoa. Narid-na-Gost tensed, craning and rubbing at the misted window and having to resist an impulse to smash the glass. Two figures, one carrying a lantern. Yes; Tirand Lin and Karuth Piadar, and the High Initiate was solicitously holding his sister's arm as they hastened between the pillars toward the steps and the main doors beyond. The demon was unaware of Tarod's visit to the library, but his unhuman senses picked up the fact that there was a new aura about the two hurrying mortals, a tension not of hostility but of collusion, and again he thought of the Marble Hall, to which the High Initiate held the only key. Was *that* it? Had Tirand Lin lost faith and patience with his master Ailind, and was he now turning, through his sister's good offices, to Chaos? And if so, did Ygorla know of it?

Tirand and Karuth ran up the steps and disappeared through the castle's great double doors. For perhaps a minute more Narid-na-Gost continued to watch the courtyard, then he turned from the window and squatted down on his cushions, clenching his hands before his face and staring at them.

The Circle was no longer inactive. He was sure of it now, he had evidence. And he would have taken any wager that Ygorla was far too preoccupied with her own antics to be alert to what was going on under her nose. That was valuable, for it armed him with a weapon he might be able to use against her. And if the worst came to the worst and she should attempt to destroy him—a possibility that Narid-na-Gost was forced to consider—it might also provide him with a means of turning the tables and securing his own life in place of hers. For while he'd never dare to approach Tarod of Chaos and offer him a bargain, the High Initiate was another matter altogether. . . .

For once Calvi woke before Ygorla was stirring. He thought he had been dreaming again, but couldn't recall his dreams and considered the effort of trying to remember too tedious and dull to contemplate. So he lay in a state of drowsy contentment in the half-light of dawn, thinking about what he would demand for breakfast this morning and occasionally turning his head to look with languid pride and satisfaction at the black hair and lovely face of the woman asleep at his side. Last night after her return from the recital, as they bathed in the pleasant afterglow of sated lust, she had told him of some of the plans she was devising for them both. Yandros's capitulation, she had said, was simply a matter of time. The Chaos lord would see eventually that he had no choice but to do as she demanded. Then Calvi's lover, the object of his worship, the light of his life, would not only be undisputed Empress of this world but would also raise her triumphant standard as mistress of Chaos. And he would be at her side.

Calvi smiled a cold and very private smile. They would all dance to a very different tune, he thought, when that day came. No longer would he be Calvi the child, Calvi the inexperienced, unfledged boy, High Margrave in name but in fact treated as little more than a nuisance that must be tolerated for the sake of protocol. He would have power—*real* power and not just the worthless trappings of an ancient title. He'd use it, too. Gods, but he'd use it! Tirand Lin, Shaill Falada, Karuth Piadar, all the others—the list in his head was growing longer by the day—who had scorned him, slighted him, or even crossed him in the smallest way. He would deal with them, and his imagination was already fervidly at work on the prospect. Above all he would relish the humbling of Tarod of Chaos. For on that night in the Marble Hall, when Karuth had defied him and called the Chaos gods into the world, Tarod had been the architect of a bitter humiliation that Calvi would never forget, and Calvi loathed him for it. In truth he'd brought it on himself, and from Tarod's viewpoint it had been nothing more than a minor if necessary rebuke. But nothing would induce Calvi to see the facts in that light. He yearned to pay the black-haired lord back, and Ygorla had promised to grant his desire.

But as he lay beside her in the disordered bed, one hand idly stroking the heavy mass of her hair, he realized that even then, even with Tarod and his own former peers repaid for their arrogance and cast down, one score would still remain to be settled. Abruptly he frowned and sat up, his body tensing involuntarily as his good mood was suddenly clouded by a stab of frustration. Deeply though he hated Tarod, there was one other whom he hated still more—Ailind of Order, together with everything that Ailind stood for. It didn't once occur to him to wonder at the fact that only a few days ago he had been staunchly allied with Order's cause. That was in another life and utterly irrelevant. If he could fulfill one ambition and one alone, Calvi thought, it would be to see Ailind's power broken and his haughty complacency shattered beyond repair. But the lords of Order were beyond even Ygorla's ability to touch . . .

. . . weren't they?

The thought struck so unexpectedly that it shocked him. For several seconds, as the extraordinary idea sank in, he didn't move a muscle but sat staring at the velvet hangings that swathed the bedposts. Then abruptly he slid from the bed and crossed to where a jug of mead and another of wine were set beside two jeweled cups on Ygorla's elaborate dressing table. He filled one of the cups from both jugs—wine and mead made a fearsome cocktail for which he'd recently acquired a great liking— and sank down onto the silk-padded stool, taking several large mouthfuls of the drink in quick succession. His own reflection stared back at him from Ygorla's vast mirror: a young and handsome face but with new hard edges that gave it a cruel look, and shadows of depravity around the blue eyes, which themselves seemed to contain inhumanly cold depths. Behind his own image the glass also showed Ygorla's recumbent form, white-skinned and voluptuous in the bed, with her hair like a tumbling black waterfall, and Calvi felt a surge of haughty pride rise in him as the idea, the wild surmise, began to coalesce in his mind. And the more he thought, and the more mead and wine he drank, and the more he watched his lover's sleeping form in the mirror, the less wild the surmise started to seem. Was she not, after all, invincible? She had conquered an entire world without needing to call on more than a trifling measure of her power. She had trapped the lords of Chaos and had them helpless in her grasp, or as near helpless as made no difference. How could any force in the universe hope to challenge her if she should decide to storm the last remaining bastion and make the *ultimate* conquest . . . the conquest of the realm of Order itself?

Calvi drained his cup and refilled it, his face avid and a strange, greedy light in his eyes. He remembered nothing of his dreams. He was unaware of the elemental forces that had crept to him as he slept and that skillfully yet subtly had manipulated the deeper levels of his unconscious mind. He knew nothing of the titanic power that had motivated those elementals, promising them the chance for revenge on their greatest tormentor if they would relinquish their independent existence for a short while and do the bidding of the gods. But the seeds Ailind and Aeoris had sown in the fertile ground of his imagination were taking root, and his thoughts began to run riot. Ygorla talked of a new age of Chaos—but why stop there? Chaos was only half of the gods' domain. And while Aeoris and his brood still held sway in the realm of Order, Ygorla's supremacy couldn't be complete. But if Order, too, were to be crushed under her heel . . . Calvi laughed a harsh laugh of pleasure at the idea of such a turning of the tables, such a superb and fitting revenge on Ailind and his brothers.

"Calvi?" Ygorla's voice startled him, and he turned to see her awake and sitting up in the bed. Her vivid eyes were sharp and almost suspicious, though her lips smiled as sweetly as ever.

"What are you doing there, golden man?"

Calvi stood up, aware of and pleased by the way her gaze shifted appreciatively across his naked form. Taking his cup, he crossed to the bed, and they indulged in a long, hungry kiss before she held him at arm's length and stared at him again, searchingly.

"You're plotting something, my sweeting. Don't try to deceive me. I know you too well."

"So you do." He turned his head to lick her hand, her wrist, and along her arm to the elbow. "And I am plotting. An idea—a wild, magnificent idea that will fill you with delight. Would you like to know what it is, or should I save it for later?"

Her fingers tangled in his hair. She relaxed her arms enough to allow him to lean forward and kiss her again, nibbling his lower lip as their mouths met.

"I warn you, my dearest, that I don't like to be kept waiting," she murmured in his ear. "If you continue to tease me, then I shall have to *bite* you. So you'd better tell me *everything, now,* don't you think?"

Calvi chuckled softly, nuzzling her hair. Then, coolly and directly, he told her.

She sat back on her heels, staring at him in astonishment. For almost a minute there was complete silence. Then, her eyes narrowed almost to slits, she said in a peculiarly low-pitched voice, "Take control of the realm of Order . . . ?"

"Yes."

Her tongue touched her lower lip. "And why would I want to do that . . . ?"

Calvi smiled wolfishly. "Simply, my love, because it could be yours for the taking." He reached out and caught hold of her hands. "Why should your ambitions end with mastery of Chaos? You're invincible. You know that, you've proved it. So why should you be content to rule Chaos, yet know that there is still one power that opposes you? Your supremacy should be *complete*!"

She regarded him, her mind moving rapidly through this new and as yet unexplored territory. What, she wondered, had put such an idea into his mind? The answer to the question came to her immediately, and she uttered a soft laugh.

"My sweet Calvi, is your hatred for Ailind really so great?"

"Yes!" He was stung by what he took to be a reproof, and suddenly determined to justify himself. "I loathe Ailind of Order just as much as I loathe Tarod of Chaos! He is your enemy, my jewel—he and his brothers, and their miserable master, Aeoris. That alone is enough to make me long to see them trampled, and when I think—"

"And when you think of the way Ailind has dared to treat you since his coming to this world, you want to exact an even greater vengeance." She smiled. "Oh, don't think for one moment that that's a petty motive. It is a *splendid* one, and I admire it!"

In truth she didn't merely admire it, she was deeply impressed. She'd known that under her tutelage Calvi was rapidly casting off the shackles of conventional thought and action that had so hampered him in the past. But *this* . . . even she had never considered such a possibility before. Her mind was racing now, building visions, and abruptly her eyes lost their focus and began to glitter greedily as the visions became clear. To control not only Chaos but Order too, to bring the arrogant Aeoris and his strutting dolt of a brother, Ailind, groveling to their knees before her . . . it would be a greater triumph even than the conquest of Chaos, for, as Calvi had reminded her, the lords of Order were her enemies in a way that Yandros and his kin were not. She might subject Chaos's gods to her rule and manipulate them to her will, but in the realm of Order she could play a very different game indeed.

"It isn't only my hatred of Ailind that drives me." Calvi's grip on her fingers suddenly increased, and his voice became urgent. "Think, my love—think of what might happen if the lords of Order are *not* brought to heel. You are to embark on a new age of Chaos. But when that new age dawns, what will Aeoris and his brothers do? They won't be content to stay quaking in their own realm. They'll muster the full forces of Order against you."

She laughed. "My precious, I see you have the makings of a fine strategist. But I'm ahead of you. Of course that's what Aeoris will do. I've known it from the beginning. But he and his weakling brood can't hope to defeat me. With this world and the world of Chaos under my control, they will be *powerless* against me!"

"They will, yes. But think of what happened in the old days, the days before Equilibrium." Calvi's mouth twisted cynically. "Didn't we both spend enough dreary years being forced to learn our catechisms? The lords of Chaos were banished, but they came back, they challenged Order, and they triumphed. Without control of Order's realm you could banish Aeoris, as he once banished Yandros, in the flick of an eye. But that's all you could do. Yet if you had conquered Order as well as Chaos, you'd never need to be troubled by the possibility of their return, because you could *annihilate* them!"

Ygorla paused, then abruptly realized that, in this at least, his thoughts had run ahead of her own. As a child, hadn't she sat day after day in that hated schoolroom at the Matriarch's cot, listening to Sister Corelm Simik's dry and seemingly endless lectures? Calvi was right. Even if Aeoris and his brother lords were driven far beyond reach of the mortal world, they would use every wile they possessed in an attempt to return, as Yandros had returned a century ago. Their efforts would fail of course— she was scornfully dismissive of any other possibility— but how much better it would be if they could be removed altogether. If she could bring down Aeoris and smash his power once and for all, then the realm of Order would cease even to exist.

Then suddenly a streak of cold realism cut through her mind like a sword blade. She wanted this. She could feel the tingling hunger of new ambition like a ravening animal inside her. But it wasn't possible. She had the means to coerce Chaos to her will, but she had no such power over the lords of Order. Magnificent though the idea was, it couldn't be achieved.

Frustration surged through her, and she snatched her hands from Calvi's grasp, flinging herself off the bed and stalking across the room. Petulantly her voice snapped out.

"It can't be done! *It can't be done!*"

In another dimension, unknown to them both, elemental forces stirred and shifted, and the subtle influence that had shaped Calvi's dreams touched his unwitting mind once more. He drew a sharp, quick breath, and he said, "I think it can."

Ygorla froze. Her back was toward him and her posture rigid. Her hands clenched and unclenched at her sides.

"How?" The single word was sharp with explosive tension. There was a pause. Then:

"By holding them to ransom, just as you hold Chaos. By gaining possession of a lord of Order's soul!"

Preoccupied with her seething frustration, Ygorla had been on the verge of interrupting him and dismissing his arguments, but suddenly what he had said sank in. The soul of one of Aeoris's brothers, or even of Aeoris himself . . . could it be *possible*? Her pulse quickened, and she licked her lips nervously, almost too afraid of disappointment to test the idea.

"I . . ." She stopped, thought again. Did their souls take the same form as the souls of the Chaos lords? She didn't know. But she could surely find out. She could use her elemental slaves. Elementals were outside the gods' jurisdiction and could move freely in their worlds without arousing suspicion. She could send them to the realm of Order on pain of destruction and order them to do what her own sire had done in Chaos: to find where the souls of the high lords were hidden and to bring the information back to her. They could do it, and they wouldn't *dare* betray her.

But even if that was achieved (no, a part of her said; not if, *when*), how could she hope to get her hands on such a stone? The elementals would be of no further use to her. They simply hadn't the power to transport physical objects between dimensions. Ygorla frowned deeply, aware that Calvi was still watching her intently, keyed up and waiting. He believed she could do it and he wanted her to do it, wanted her to make that ultimate statement of her power and supremacy. Ygorla wanted it too. She thought of her cowering, craven father, Narid-na-Gost, and she thought of Ailind with his supercilious, feigned disinterest, and she thought of all the contemptible, weakling mortals scurrying like rats in a run as they chased their own tails in their efforts to outwit her, and suddenly she realized that she had never wanted anything in her life more than she wanted this. Chaos *and* Order. Absolute power, with no one and nothing to oppose her. Oh, yes, she thought. Oh, *yes.* But how could she gain the stone . . . ?

And then, like light dawning on a dark horizon, Ygorla remembered the Chaos Gate.

20

The elemental started to scream on a high, agonized note.

Mistress, spare me! Spare my life, and I will serve you faithfully for eternity, even as I strive to serve you now! I can do no more—I can do no more!

Ygorla snarled like an angry cat, but for once she stayed her hand. She had tested the creature to the limits of its endurance and she was forced to accept that it was neither lying to her nor stinting in its efforts to do her bidding. The harsh and simple facts were clear: What she demanded was beyond its ability to provide.

"There must be a way. There *must!*" Her hair swung like a tide of black water as she turned on her heel and paced across the room. Reaching the bed, she turned and, almost as an afterthought, waved a hand negligently toward the squirming mass of flame that hovered in the middle of the room. Her voice rapped out sharply, "Begone," and with a shrill, desperate whistle of relief the elemental vanished.

Ygorla threw herself down on the bed, hurling pillows away in a fit of pique. The fire elemental had been her last refuge; she'd already put the creatures of earth, water, and air to trial and they'd been of no more use than a prayer in the face of a Warp storm. Her own power had proved inadequate, and her plans were at an impasse because the one last barrier still refused to crumble.

Suddenly, as often happened, her self-control reasserted itself in a rush of clear-headedness, and she jerked upright. There were tears of rage and frustration on her cheeks. She blotted them with a strand of her hair, then sat hugging herself and staring at the empty fireplace, her expression darkly furious. She couldn't let matters rest here. So close to her goal, she couldn't be bested now!

Matters had moved on with startling speed in the day and night since Calvi had first put the notion of invading the realm of Order into Ygorla's head. Fired with hungry enthusiasm for her burgeoning scheme, she had harnessed the elemental forces to her aid and, in a fearsome ritual, had ordered them to enter Aeoris's kingdom and bring back all that they could glean about the nature and whereabouts of the lords of Order's souls. What she had learned had stunned her. Her surmise had been right. Like their cousins of Chaos, the souls of Aeoris and his brothers did indeed take the form of gems, seven diamonds within whose perfect facets pulsed the life essences of Order's own gods. And the elementals had told her the news that she longed above all else to hear—that in their complacency, in their conceit and their assurance of their own invulnerability, Aeoris and his brothers had taken no precautions whatever to guard their soul-gems. After all, what denizen of other realms could threaten Order's stronghold? What power could challenge their security? Order had no demons. The beings created by Aeoris knew their role and their place in his scheme of things, and to challenge the will of their creator was a concept unknown to them. This wasn't Chaos, with its unpredictability, its perversity, its wild and mercurial ways. Nothing disturbed Order's peace. Nothing, to the minds of its overlords, ever could. The gem that Ygorla craved to possess was ready and ripe for the plucking.

Which made her present predicament all the worse. She could visualize her objective; she could *see* it in her mind's eye, glimmering and glittering, with nothing to challenge and nothing to hinder the grasp of her hand. Two steps into Order's realm and she could take the stone as easily as a southern farmer might pick a ripe peach from a tree in his orchard. Neither Ailind nor Aeoris would know what she'd done until it was too late for them to intervene. As the child of a Chaos demon she was beyond their ability to overlook, yet as the daughter of a human mother she could enter their realm without let or hindrance and return triumphant to the mortal world with the prize in her grasp. It was *perfect.*

But for this one final obstacle . . .

She had begun her assault shortly after dawn, stirring Calvi from his slumbers and cajoling, bribing, and finally bullying him to find some means of entertaining himself elsewhere in the castle until evening. She didn't want him involved in this. He had no experience of even the lowest sorcery and might unwittingly make some mistake that would wreck her efforts. Nor had she told him what she intended to do. That, she planned, would come later, when she greeted him in the throes of success and triumphantly revealed her entire plan to him in all its glory. Then she would announce that the last barrier had shattered before her power, that she had taken possession of the Chaos Gate, walked through it into Order's realm to claim a new prize, and now was ready to enter its portal again to become mistress of Chaos and Order together.

The plan was perfect. But it had started to go wrong the moment she summoned her first surge of magical power.

Ygorla wasn't subtle by nature. Not for her any surreptitious ambush to take control of the Gate without another soul the wiser. She scorned such tactics as both dull and feeble. She wanted to attack, directly and flamboyantly. What did it matter if her actions brought Tarod of Chaos running? What could he do to prevent her without jeopardizing his brother's soul, a risk that he would never, *never* take? And the blind fool Ailind, even if he was aware of her work, would think only that she had at last lost patience and was challenging Chaos to give its long-awaited answer. Ailind would sit in his solitary room and smile self-assuredly as he awaited the outcome, oblivious of the truth.

She felt the power rising within her, a dizzying, sensual, and devastating knowledge of self. She could do *anything*! *Nothing* could stand in her way! Black and silver flames shot ceilingward from the floor of her bedchamber, phantom fire that gave off searing, sweltering heat yet didn't burn anything it touched. Voices shrieked inside Ygorla's head; she punched her arms upward, fists clenched, and in her head she shrieked silently with them, like a madwoman, like a creature possessed. The floor seemed to hump up beneath her feet as though vast forces were pushing the castle skyward, then her mind surged out of the room and down into the bones of the great building's foundations, through the library, along the strangely symmetrical passage with its eternal, dim-gray illumination. The silver door, the door of the Marble Hall, seemed to shatter before her, and she was *there* among the pillars and the shifting pastel mists, laughing in mockery and defiance at the seven colossi stern and silent on their plinths, laughing in the carved faces of those who had the temerity to call themselves gods.

She found the Chaos Gate. It drew her as surely as a river was drawn to the sea, and her consciousness homed in on the unadorned black circle in the floor at the Marble Hall's heart. Giddy with excitement, she gathered her power anew, focused her will on the gateway, and screamed the command in her mind.

Open! Open before Ygorla, Empress of Mortal Dominions and Mistress of Chaos! I command you, yield to me, and open!!

In the north spire Tarod's head turned sharply, and his green eyes were suddenly introverted and still. In the dining hall, where his presence had stifled all conversation among the diners, Ailind of Order's expression remained calmly enigmatic. In the gaudy room at the top of the south spire, Narid-na-Gost felt a momentary shudder of something untoward, but Ygorla had taken good care to shield herself from his attentions, and he couldn't summon the courage to investigate.

And in the Marble Hall a quiet but immense force inverted Ygorla's blast of power and flung it indifferently back in her face.

She reeled, staggered, collided painfully with one of the bedposts, and finally righted herself. Her blue eyes were ablaze, and her mind seethed. They had dared to defy her; they had *dared*! The Gate was protected against sorcerous attack! Spittle flecked her lower lip and her chin. She wiped it away with a savage gesture and, breathing hard, returned to the center of the room. She would try again. And if the Gate resisted her a second time, she would *blast* Tarod of Chaos; she would turn on him and take him *apart*—

No, she thought as reason struggled back to the surface from the depths where fury had all but drowned it. No; not that. She wasn't such a fool as to risk putting Chaos in a position where they had nothing to lose. She would try again, but if she failed, then she'd find another way. The elementals, who could go where others were unable to follow, would serve her once more, and they would succeed.

She tried again, and again there was the huge, disinterested shrug of power that flung her back, and the Chaos Gate remained unsullied. Very well, Ygorla said to herself. Very *well*. She allowed herself a few minutes for her pounding heartbeat to slow and her breathing to regain its normal rhythm. Then she took up her stance once again in the center of the room. No black flames this time, no screaming voices. She raised one hand, focused her eyes into another dimension, and her expression grew cruel as she smiled a terrible smile.

"Come, little slaves." Her voice was deadly honey. "Little creatures of earth and air, fire and water. Come to me, if you would live to see another dawn!"

Tarod turned on his heel and said sharply, "Yandros! Yandros, I need to speak with you!"

The spire room darkened as though night had descended. The darkness warped momentarily, then the tall, gaunt figure of his brother stood beside a clutter of jumbled furniture, one hand resting lightly on the broken top of an old table.

Yandros wasn't alone. Tarod's eyes widened in surprise as he saw the second figure, and he said, "Cyllan—"

"I asked her to accompany me." Yandros's face was deadly serious. "Don't ask why now. This isn't the time for it. Will the Gate hold?"

"Yes. The usurper can try any tactic she pleases, but she won't break the barrier. It isn't that that concerns me, Yandros."

"I know, I know." The greatest Chaos lord made a restless gesture that indicated his comprehension. "It's her reasons for launching this attack."

"I can't believe that she's trying to mount an assault on our realm. It makes no sense."

"I agree. So we must look for another motive. Her father?"

"It's possible. Now that she's broken his link with the soul-stone, she may be using this as some form of challenge to him, to force him into facing the reality of his position. But somehow I don't think that's at the root of it."

"No . . . no, there's something else, I *feel* it." Yandros's eyes changed from gold to crimson to a dull, hard bronze. "Do nothing, Tarod. Make no move. Don't even let her know that you're aware of her activities. There's a motive lurking within this that we haven't uncovered yet, and until we know what it is, it could be a grave mistake to react."

"And Narid-na-Gost?" Tarod asked tensely.

Yandros's lip curled cynically. "He's not in any position to trouble us at the moment. Be alert for any move he might make, but that's all." He paused. "You're *sure* that the Gate's safe?"

"Only the Speaking of the Way could counter the barrier I created. Neither the usurper nor her sire even know of the spell's existence."

"Very well. Then keep watch. I have an urgent matter to attend to here; if you need me, I'll answer, but there may be a delay."

Tarod didn't ask what the urgent matter was. This wasn't a time for questions. He nodded to his brother, then looked at Cyllan, who had stood silent by Yandros's side throughout their exchange.

"I hope this will soon be over, love."

"So do I." Her voice caught oddly. "Tarod . . . so do I."

Their hands touched; a brief contact, no more, but he sensed her turmoil. There was something afoot in Chaos; she knew it too, but there was no time and no chance to say any more. Yandros's eyes, purple now, focused on Tarod's face.

"Good luck, my brother. Good hunting."

And Tarod was alone in the spire room.

So now in her bedchamber Ygorla sat seething, and thinking hard and fast. Her own powers had achieved nothing, the elementals had achieved nothing. Reluctantly, furiously, frustratedly, she was obliged to face the unpalatable fact that the Chaos Gate was beyond her ability to control.

The lack of any response from Tarod to her increasingly frantic efforts to force the Gate to yield to her will and open confirmed the thing she had suspected from the start: that the Chaos lord had placed some form of protective geas on it. For a few turbulent minutes she considered storming to the north spire and demanding that the Gate be opened, but common sense prevailed. To use the soul-stone as a safeguard against Chaos's wrath was one thing, but to wield it in an attempt to force them to do her bidding was another and, she suspected, would produce only a stalemate. No, she must work this out for herself and find her own way of solving the conundrum.

It was well past midday now. Snow had been falling since early morning, and the outside world was newly whitened, in stark contrast to the sky's grubby and already darkening gray. She had promised Calvi that her work would be finished by sunset. But what more could she do?

Then, quite suddenly, she thought of her father skulking in his spire hideaway.

She sat bolt upright, the sullen anger of her expres-

sion giving way to a new, eager light. Of course, of *course*!
She was a blockhead not to have thought of it before
now! The Chaos Gate was the axis around which her
sire's entire ambition revolved. He *must* know how to
break down the shield that Tarod had created. Ygorla
smiled unpleasantly. Nothing, of course, would induce
Narid-na-Gost to help her of his own free will. But she
had a hold over him that he wasn't yet aware of. Perhaps,
she thought, it was time to enlighten him, and to offer
him a bargain that he might be very unwise to refuse. . . .

Twenty minutes later Ygorla rose from a table lit-
tered with writing materials and stalked into the anteroom outside her bedchamber. Strann lay where she had
left him early this morning, facedown on his cushions,
unconscious. She stared down at him for a few moments,
checking that the sleeping-geas she'd cast on him was still
effective and that he wasn't feigning. Then, satisfied, she
dismissed the spell with a single thought and completed
the rude awakening by dealing him a sharp blow with the
toe of her shoe. Strann jolted, swore, then opened his
eyes, saw her gazing down at him, and hastily scrambled
to his feet, mumbling abject apologies.

Ygorla ignored his lapse. "Shake off your drowsi-
ness, rat. I have an errand for you."

He looked dazedly about him. "What . . . what
hour is it?"

"It's the middle of the afternoon, and you've slept
like a good rat for hours, so you've no excuse to be a
sluggard now." She was holding a small silk pouch in one
hand, and she thrust it at him. "This contains a letter.
Take it to Narid-na-Gost immediately, await his answer,
and bring it back to me. Don't dawdle, and don't *dare* to
delay for any reason, or I'll remove more than your hand
this time."

Strann's mind was struggling into coherence as the
last effects of the sorcerous sleep faded. Midafternoon?
Gods, she'd put him out for almost the entire day! What
had she been doing? What devious intrigue was she plotting now?

"Well?" She folded her arms. "I've given you your instruction. Do you have any reason to wait around, or have your legs failed you?"

"Majesty," Strann bowed. He felt as if the pouch was burning his hand.

She watched while the door shut behind him and listened as his running steps faded in the direction of the stairs. Then she returned to the inner room and settled herself to wait.

The letter he'd been entrusted to carry seemed to scorch Strann's fingers all the way to the main doors. For the first time he was oblivious of the scathing looks from people he passed in the corridors or on the stairs. He was too preoccupied even to be consciously aware of his surroundings, for the letter and its contents utterly dominated his thoughts.

What had Ygorla been *doing* during the hours while he'd slept? She was so sure of his loyalty that she wouldn't have troubled to hide her activities from him without a very good reason, but this was the second time in a matter of days that she'd done so. Though he hadn't yet been able to get confirmation from Tarod via Karuth, Strann was sure in his own mind of what she'd done on the first occasion. This, though . . .

The memory of her expression as she'd handed him the pouch still nagged at him. She was excited, and he'd have wagered his manzon that what he saw in her face reflected only a fraction of her feelings. Her eyes were unnaturally bright, unnaturally blue, with a glint of fanaticism and of something else. Triumph. That was it; triumph. As though a moment for which she'd long been waiting had finally arrived. Gods, what had she *done*? There was something afoot, he *knew* it. But how could he find out what it was?

He reached the main doors and hastened out into the courtyard, shivering as snow flurried in his face and the bitter wind bit through his thin silk shirt. Starting at a brisk walk toward the south spire—ice made the going too treacherous to move faster—he fiercely pushed away the inner voice that said persuasively, *There's one way to find out, Strann. All you have to do is read the letter.* He couldn't do that. He didn't have the nerve. For all he knew, one of Ygorla's vile elemental creations was following invisibly in his tracks and watching his every move, and if the usurper once caught him prying where prying was forbidden, he'd end up wishing that she'd fed him to her houndcats on Summer Isle.

But if you don't read the letter, how will you discover what she's planning? It may be of vital importance. . . .

He *couldn't.* It was too dangerous, he mustn't even *think* of it. Strann reached the spire, thrust the door open, and hurried inside, thankful to be sheltered from the snow and wind. The door tapped on its latch behind him, slightly ajar. Enough light was seeping through for him to see quite well. Enough light to read by . . . He shut his eyes and tried resolutely to banish temptation, but instead an image of Karuth came into his mind. What would she have done in his place? Walked the safe path or taken the risk? Strann didn't like it, but he had no doubt of the answer to that question. He slipped his hand into the pouch, felt the parchment inside. She hadn't sealed it. Could that be a trap? No, she never sealed the letters she gave him to carry, for she was too arrogant to imagine that he'd dream of disobeying her. That, surely, meant that he must be safe enough?

Strann swore softly. Now or never. He had to stop dithering and make a decision. Oh, damn it, he'd touched the letter; he was halfway to perdition already. Drawing breath, he pulled the parchment from the pouch, unfolded it, and began to read.

Narid-na-Gost was shaking. Though Strann's rigid posture and seemingly unfocused eyes suggested steadfast disregard, he was watching the demon with intent concentration—and inwardly he was terrified.

A low, ugly snarl rose in Narid-na-Gost's throat. His fist closed around the letter, his clawed fingers clamped, and the parchment vaporized with a sinister, implosive sound that left a sensation of intense heat hanging in the air. Then, slowly, the demon turned.

Strann gazed fixedly at the wall, praying silently to all the gods of Chaos that he wasn't about to become the focus of Narid-na-Gost's rage. For what seemed to him like half a lifetime, he endured the burning crimson stare, feeling that at any moment his straining lungs and thundering heart must give out on him altogether. Then, in a tone so mild that it frightened him more than a roar of fury, Narid-na-Gost said, "Are you aware of the content of this letter, rat?"

Strann's throat worked. "No, my lord."

Silence. Did the demon believe him? Impossible to tell. Narid-na-Gost began to pace. Then he stopped and, with his back to Strann, said, "My daughter expects a written reply. She will not receive one. Tell her—" His voice started to rise; with an effort he brought it under control. Strann could see that he was shaking again. "Tell her that my answer is this: that I damn her, and I spit upon her schemings, and that before I succumb to her blackmail, I'll see her rot in the Seven Hells!"

Strann made a good shift of looking baffled and carefully repeated the words until the demon was satisfied that he'd memorized them accurately. He was dismissed unscathed, and as his footsteps clattered away down the spire stairs, Narid-na-Gost moved slowly to the center of the room. He stared at the piled cushions where he customarily lounged. One moment, he thought. One moment, and he would be sure. This time he couldn't deceive himself into ignoring the challenge. He *had* to test the link.

His red eyes closed, and a sound like a snake's hiss broke the silence. A peculiar aura, flickering with dark, murky colors, manifested briefly around the demon's distorted figure, and a smell of musk and hot metal pervaded the room suddenly as he called on his innate powers.

It took only moments. Abruptly the aura vanished, the smell faded, and Narid-na-Gost's eyes flicked open once more. His face was still, utterly without expression, but at the core of his being, in the deepest pit of his psyche, a furnace was igniting, a furnace of fury, hatred, and bitter despair. It had come full circle at last, and there was no more pretense. She had turned on him, severed the last ties between them, and now she was preparing to storm the gates of Chaos and win its highest crown for herself, leaving him to stand alone and unprotected to face the rage of the gods. And he could do nothing whatever to prevent it from happening.

Slowly, very slowly, Narid-na-Gost tilted his head back. His mouth opened, stretched, wider and impossibly wider, lips drawing back from white, savage fangs like a hound baying to the rising moons. From deep down within him, rising like the ominous, advancing howl of a Warp, came a sound that rang shatteringly through the isolated spire room. A primal, unhuman cry of misery and remorse and, above all, of implacable and unequivocal terror.

21

"I feel such a fool." Tirand grinned wryly up at Karuth, trying to hold his arm steady as she'd instructed, despite the awkward angle. "It wouldn't have been so bad if there'd been no one else in the courtyard, but as it was, at least a dozen other people had the entertainment of seeing their High Initiate's dignity thrown to the four winds."

Karuth suppressed an answering smile at the thought. "It could have happened to anyone," she said. "Ice under fresh snow makes a treacherous combination, and I don't doubt that you were in a hurry as usual. Keep still now." One hand held his wrist, the other gently manipulated his fingers, and Tirand winced.

"Anything broken?"

"No, no. Just a wrench. I'll put a herbal salve on it to help reduce the inflammation and a binding to give some support. Provided you favor your other arm, you'll be right again in a few days."

"Lucky for me that I'm right-handed." He watched as she crossed to the infirmary store-cupboard and fetched the salve, then his gaze moved past her to the window. An hour still to sunset, and already many of the castle's windows were lit. And it was still snowing, a steady, depressing fall that showed no sign of abating. Every winter it was the same, Tirand thought. He enjoyed the snow to begin with, enjoyed the clean, white silence of the transformed world, but it soon began to pall, and by the time the winter Quarter-Day was past, he was longing for spring.

Although what this coming spring might bring was something he could hardly bear to consider. . . .

Karuth came back with the salve and a long strip of bandaging. As she sat down beside him and began to apply the soothing lotion, Tirand gave silent thanks, and not for the first time, for Shaill and her stubborn determination to see him and his sister reconciled. He hadn't understood how great the pressure of their estrangement had been until that pressure was suddenly absent, and the ease with which they'd both slipped back into the old, familiar relationship of happier days had been a tremendous relief to him, beleaguered as he was by so many other troubles. He realized now how much he had missed both her moral support and, on a more practical level, the value of her keen intelligence and judgment, and over the past two days he'd tried, on several occasions, to find the right words to express his feelings. Each time he tried, though, either his tongue failed him or some unwelcome interruption put an end to his efforts, and now as she began expertly to tie the bandage around his wrist, he thought to try again. But before he could speak, Karuth suddenly looked up.

"What's that?"

"What's what?" He was irrationally irritated and spoke more sharply than he'd intended to, but she didn't seem to notice. Her head was turned toward the window.

"A sound, a scratching sound. . . . It's coming from outside."

Tirand looked and saw a shadow at the window, blurred by the glass and by the falling snow. Karuth had seen it, too, and she started toward it, but he intercepted her.

"No, let me." Since Ygorla's coming, there had been all too many horrors glimpsed in and about the castle, and instinctively the High Initiate's right hand went to the knife he wore in a sheath on his belt as he approached the window and wrestled it open.

A blast of icy air rushed in, throwing a flurry of snow into his face. With a vehement yowl, as though

310

protesting at the miserable weather, the gray cat jumped over the sill and down onto the infirmary floor.

Karuth said, "What—" but the cat interrupted her with another long-drawn-out cry, almost a howl, and rose up on its hind legs, pawing at her skirt.

Tirand shut the window. "It must be half frozen! What's it doing outside on a day like this?"

Karuth tried to coax the cat toward the fire, but the little creature would have none of it. It looked from one to the other of the two humans, and for a moment it felt confusion, for the message with which it had been entrusted was clear. *Friend,* it had said, *find one of our friends;* and the human with the curling hair and the deep voice wasn't one of the two friends it knew. But the other was, and surely, the cat reasoned, if she was in the company of the deep-voiced one, then he must be a friend too? It couldn't wait until he was gone; this mission was too urgent.

It yowled again, and its brilliant eyes fixed in frantic appeal on Karuth's face as it focused its concentration and tried to convey its message. Karuth's own eyes widened, and she dropped to her knees, suddenly alert.

"Little one, what is it? I can't see clearly!"

The cat repeated its telepathic effort, and images formed hazily in her mind. The library. The first moon hanging alone in the sky above the castle walls. *Urgent, urgent. Tell no one.* And Strann's face . . .

"It's a message from Strann." She stood up, turning quickly to face her brother.

"I know." Tirand was staring at the cat. "The library, between first and second moonrise. I picked up the images too." He was astounded by the strength of the creature's mind, for he was no more of a natural telepath than Karuth.

"Something's wrong." Karuth twisted her hands together nervously. "Strann means to get away from the usurper, to meet me in person—"

"Can he do that?"

She shook her head. "I don't know. He's never been able to before; the dangers have always been too great.

This time, though, he's going to try. There must be something vitally and desperately urgent afoot for him to run such a risk." Suddenly her fists clenched. "I must tell lord Tarod!"

"No, Karuth, wait." Tirand caught her arm as she started toward the door. "I don't think you should."

She stared at him, suspicion suddenly hardening her eyes. "Why not?"

"Don't mistake me. This has nothing to do with loyalties or biases. But Strann said, 'Tell no one'—that was conveyed very clearly. And he sent the cat to *you,* not to Tarod. I'm not saying there's any significance in that, but Strann could have a reason for not wanting Tarod to know."

"I can't imagine what that reason could be."

"Neither can I. But it might be wiser not to take the risk."

She smiled humorlessly. *"You* know about the message."

Tirand shrugged. "Sheer accident, and it can't be changed now. As it is, I think we should say nothing, as Strann asks. And I'll come with you to the rendezvous."

"Oh no, Tirand. Oh no, that wouldn't be wise!"

"I disagree. I don't want to dramatize matters, but it would be foolhardy in the extreme for you to go alone. If something *should* go wrong with Strann's plans . . ." he saw her expression and decided it might be better to leave the rest unsaid.

She hesitated. He was right. Unpalatable though it was, the possibility that something might go amiss had to be considered. On the question of Tarod, too, she couldn't argue with him. If need be, she could call on the Chaos lord for help quickly enough, and it would be safer to follow Strann's instructions to the letter.

Nonetheless it still didn't feel right, and she said uncertainly, "I don't know . . . if you and Strann come face-to-face—"

"With your backing I think I can persuade him to trust me. I've no reason to quarrel with him. After all, we're fighting on the same side now, aren't we?"

"Yes . . . yes, that's true. . . ." She paused again, but only for a moment. "Very well. I'll say nothing to lord Tarod, and we'll go together. And . . . thank you, Tirand."

Tirand nodded. "We can't be sure when Strann will arrive, so I suggest we meet in my study an hour after first moonrise." He smiled a little diffidently. "Clandestine gatherings in the library are getting to be something of a habit!"

Karuth returned the smile. "Let's hope this is the last," she said with feeling.

Like a man awaiting imminent execution, Strann was torn between grimly counting the minutes away and praying for a miracle. The gray cat hadn't returned, so he had no way of knowing whether his message had been delivered or, if it had, who had received it. On a personal level he hoped with all his heart that the creature had gone to Karuth. But his practical self knew that Tarod would be a more powerful ally to have by his side tonight. If, that was, he managed to keep the appointment at all. . . .

He had thought at first that it would be simple. He'd formulated his plan on the way back from the spire, convinced that he would be able to wheedle Ygorla into permitting him to give another recital tonight, even if she wasn't willing to attend the event in person. But for once he'd been wrong. Blank-faced and repeating the words without a trace of vocal expression, he'd delivered Naridna Gost's answer to his daughter's message—and for the first time since the terrible days on Summer Isle he had witnessed one of Ygorla's grand rages. The air in the room had turned black—impossible, Strann knew, but it *had*—and in the midst of it Ygorla stood screaming in fury, wreathed by a blazing silver aura while whiplashes of crimson lightning smashed between the walls in a mad tumult. Cowering in terror, Strann had seen her turn on him and raise her arms high above her head. Fire erupted at her fingertips, the floor warped and shook beneath his tottering feet, and she had shrieked at him to get out, get out, out, *out,* before she incinerated him to a pile of ashes. Strann fled blindly to the antechamber, where he hid under a table with a blanket over his head until after perhaps ten minutes the appalling sounds from the adjoining room ceased and there were no more unholy blasts of light flickering under the door and the stench of burning had finally faded. Then he crawled out from his shelter—and found Ygorla standing in the doorway, staring at him.

Her face was perfectly composed, cold, and disdainful. She said, "The Emperor-Designate will be returning shortly. If *that*"—a careless gesture indicated the room behind her—"isn't cleared before his arrival, there will be deaths. Start work." And she stalked past him to the farther door, where she looked out into the passage and screamed petulantly for servants.

The bedchamber was wrecked. Of the splendid bed only a charred and shapeless hulk remained. Other furniture was smashed to matchwood, and the luxurious rugs had been reduced to an ankle-deep carpet of ash. The walls were criss-crossed with great black streaks that had gouged into the stone beneath the tattered remnants of the wall hangings, and the leading and panes of the window appeared to have fused together into one solid, semiopaque gray mass. Strann and the five castle servants who had come running at Ygorla's summons set to the work of clearing the mess in grim silence. For half an hour or so Ygorla stood in the doorway watching their efforts, but suddenly she grew tired of the game, dismissed them all with a ferocious word, and slammed the door on their hastily departing backs. Five minutes later, when she yelled for her rat, the bedchamber was exactly as it had been before the destructive orgy, and as he entered the room, Strann blinked in astonishment.

Ygorla, who was sitting on the bed, grinned acidly at him. "Surprised, rat? You've underestimated me. That is *never* a wise thing to do."

She was, he realized, in a very dangerous mood, and

the persuasive speech he'd carefully rehearsed on his way back from the spire died on his lips. This was not the moment for cajoling, not even for a mild and tactful suggestion. He stayed silent, head bowed, and she said, "My consort and I shall dine here tonight. I want you close at hand in case I should have any need of you. Sit on your cushions, don't make a sound, and don't *dare* fall asleep. Do you understand?"

"Yes, Majesty." Strann didn't embellish his reply with the usual obsequious compliments; her temper was too uncertain. But as he bowed his way out—she had, it seemed, summoned him for no other reason than to give him that one instruction—his mind and his pulse were racing. What was he to do? He knew full well why she wanted him at a moment's call: Her brain was working feverishly on her next move in the deadly game she played with Narid-na-Gost, and before the night was out, she might want to use him as a messenger once more. To risk sneaking away and incurring her fury if she were to discover his absence would be sheer madness. But Strann *had* to get the news that was burning in his mind to Karuth or Tarod. It couldn't wait, it couldn't be delayed for even one night, for he knew now exactly what Ygorla was planning to do.

Her letter to her father, which Strann read swiftly and secretively at the foot of the spire, had been straightforward and blunt. Narid-na-Gost, she said, was no longer protected by the Chaos stone. She had broken his link with it, and she wished him well of his fate at the hands of Tarod and Yandros when they discovered the truth. There was, however, one way in which her father could save himself. She would restore the link, and thus his protection, if he gave her the means to open the Chaos Gate. She knew, the letter said, that he had the secret. Yield it, and he would be safe. Refuse, and his destruction would be simply a matter of time.

To Strann the meaning in Ygorla's message was clear. She had finished with this world. She had made her final preparations and she intended to launch an attack on the Chaos realm itself. When and how that attack would take place he had no idea, but he knew Ygorla well enough to be certain that her sire's furious rejection of the bargain she offered him wouldn't hold her back for long. Tarod and his brother lords *had* to be warned!

Strann had spent half the afternoon in a whirl of feverish and increasingly frantic mental activity. From the beginning he'd forced himself to accept the fact that any hopes of talking Ygorla into a recital were out of the question. She'd never countenance anything so trivial now, and if he had the audacity to suggest it, he'd probably be treated to another display of her temper, at very best. Yet the cats, which were his only other means of communicating with the world beyond the usurper's apartments, couldn't possibly carry such a complex and detailed message, not even to Tarod, who understood them better than any human could.

There was, Strann decided, only one choice open to him. He must take the enormous gamble of taking the news to his allies in person. A meeting, in some out-of-the-way location and late enough to minimize the chance of disturbance without arousing suspicion, seemed the safest option, so he set his mind to sending out a telepathic call, which he hoped would attract the gray cat— always the most reliable—to him. He was aware that his plan would founder here and now if the cat either didn't hear or chose not to respond, but to his great relief his plea was shortly answered by a soft, furtive mew beyond the outer door. Ygorla was by this time closeted in her bedchamber with Calvi and seemingly determined on distracting herself. Now and then their laughter reached Strann's ears through the wall, and a little earlier a party of nervous kitchen servants had filed to the apartments bearing great quantities of food and drink. Strann took the chance that he wouldn't be interrupted and slipped out to give his message to the waiting cat, stressing the urgency of the mission and telling the creature to find either Tarod or Karuth. Then, tense and alert as a prowling cat himself, he returned to his corner in the antechamber and sat down to face the ordeal of a long wait. Moonrise, he thought, had never seemed so far away.

Calvi was sleepless and bored, and but for pleasant memories of the past few hours he would also have been sulking. He lay amid a tumble of cushions and rugs, stretched at full length before the fire, which burned warmly and unnaturally in the grate without ever needing replenishment, staring into the flames and trying to think of some new amusement with which to divert himself.

He'd wanted to go down to the dining hall this evening, wanted the gratification of watching servants and adepts alike bowing before him and hearing his new title of Emperor on their lips. But Ygorla had vetoed the idea, and when he tried to argue, she had simply dismissed his desires with a careless wave and told him that she had a good reason for wanting to stay in their apartment. Calvi wouldn't have minded that so much if she'd been willing to tell him what the reason was, but she refused, only smiling secretively and saying that he'd find out in good time.

But despite that annoyance the evening had been delightful enough. Ygorla knew exactly how to seduce Calvi out of his sulks, and once she decided to forget Narid-na-Gost for a few hours and concentrate instead on pleasure, her own restless and snappish mood soon faded. So, they gorged themselves on sweetmeats, they saturated their appetite for wine and stronger spirits, and then they indulged themselves in a lustful orgy that finally left them both languidly and narcissistically sated. When Ygorla fell asleep, Calvi had intended to do likewise. But the effects of overeating, combined with the fact that he'd drunk far more than was usual even for him, conspired to keep him awake, and at last he'd given up his efforts and looked for something to while away the time until sleep claimed him. But nothing took his interest. Before Ygorla's influence changed his life, he had been an avid reader; now he despised books as fit only for musty-minded old fools. He didn't know any games that didn't demand an opponent to play against, and anyway, unless he could gamble for high stakes—such as someone else's life—games were insufferably boring. Ygorla's elemental servants might have provided some amusement, but he could neither conjure nor control them. The damned snow was still falling outside, so he couldn't even divert himself by planning a day's riding or hunting. When he was Emperor in fact and not just in name, Calvi thought, it would be different. He could order whatever entertainments he chose, at any time of the day or night, and his minions would jump to obey his whim.

Jump to obey . . . suddenly he smiled as it occurred to him that he'd overlooked something or, rather, someone. Entertainment was to be found only in the next room, where Ygorla's pet rat slept.

Once, Calvi had liked and admired Strann the Storymaker. But that was long ago, before his eyes had been opened. Now he despised the creature—he wouldn't dignify him with the term *man*—and wished that Ygorla would simply dispose of him, preferably in a way that would cause Strann the maximum of pain and terror. He never troubled to analyze the reasons for his change of heart and certainly would have had no time for the idea that jealousy over Karuth lay at the root of it. But the fact that Ygorla seemed to harbor a fondness for her pet irked him, and he often indulged in fond fancies of how *he* would treat the creature, were he to be Strann's master in the Empress's stead.

Well, it might be amusing to test some of those fancies now. Nothing that would displease Ygorla of course, but to inflict a little discomfiture on Strann would while an enjoyable hour away. Calvi lurched to his feet, reached for his wine cup, and tried to refill it from a handy flask. The flask proved to be empty. With a snort of disgust he dropped both it and the cup and strolled to the door. A last glance back toward the bed: Ygorla slept on. Smiling, Calvi slipped through the door into the outer room.

"Rat!" His voice was a rasping whisper. He moved toward Strann's bed, dim in the light of a single candle,

and kicked at the piled cushions. "Wake up, you misbe-
gotten scum!"

There was no response, no stirring, no groaning protest from among the cushions, and slowly it dawned on
Calvi that Strann wasn't there. He blinked, swaying on
his feet. Not *there*? But she'd ordered the creature to
stay. She'd said so. So where was he?

Calvi hiccupped, wiped his mouth with the back of
one hand, and resisted an urge to giggle. The rat, the
good little precious little rat, had disobeyed his mistress!
What *would* Ygorla say when she heard? What would she
do to punish her pet? Calvi had some ideas of his own
about that, and he felt a warm glow of pleasure at the
thought. Just to be sure, though, just to be sure . . .

Stumbling in the gloom, he made his way to the
door, opened it, and looked out. The contrast between
the warmth of Ygorla's rooms and the cold of the corridor was so acute that it shocked him abruptly back to a
degree of sobriety—and he was in time to see, by the light
of the single torch left burning in its wall sconce through
the night, a familiar figure moving with slow, furtive care
toward the turning that led to the main staircase.

Calvi withdrew quickly, shaking his head as the
drunken miasms drained from him. He hadn't been mistaken. That shadowed shape tiptoeing along the corridor
was Strann, he was certain of it. So where, by all that was
unholy, was he going at this hour and in such stealthy
silence? He must wake Ygorla and tell her—

No. No, he wouldn't wake her; not yet, anyway.
How much more amusing it would be to take matters
into his own hands and follow the rat for himself, to
discover what he was up to. Then he could return to
Ygorla and have a story to tell her. She'd be delighted
with his cunning, and he would have the satisfaction of
seeing Strann suffer for his transgression.

Calvi darted back into the bedchamber and snatched
up the first clothes he could find. Coat and boots, too—
Strann's mysterious excursion might not be confined to
the castle interior. He was quite sober now, inspired and
elated by the prospect of intrigue, and he hastened back

to the corridor, pulling on his boots with an ungraceful hopping movement as he went. By the time he emerged from the apartments, Strann had vanished, but Calvi knew which direction he'd taken, and quietly, swiftly, he ran to the passage turning. Still no sign of a fleeting figure in the gloom, but he hurried on to the main stairs, and at the top of the flight he was rewarded by a glimpse of a man-shaped shadow crossing the floor of the hall below and hurrying toward the main doors. Some innate hunting instinct prompted Calvi to wait until his quarry had eased the doors open enough to slip through and disappear into the courtyard, then he skimmed down the stairs in pursuit.

By the time he emerged onto the courtyard steps in Strann's wake, Strann had reached the shelter of the stoa. He carried no lantern, but the blank reflection of snow on the heavy cloud cover threw enough light down into the courtyard for Calvi to make out his dim figure and realize that he was heading toward the library.

The library . . . now, what could the rat want down there at this hour? Calvi scanned the castle's towering walls. All the good people of this forsaken place seemed to be asleep, for no lights shone in any of the windows. Well, well. Secret assignations at midnight? He'd see. He'd find out.

The bitter cold had driven out the last of the drink's effects, and his mind felt as sharp as the icicles that hung from the portico above his head. Strann had reached the library door now. In the silence of falling snow Calvi heard the small sound of unoiled hinges creaking. He smiled, went down the steps, and picked his way carefully across the slippery flagstones to where a path had been cleared under the pillared walkway, then broke into a run. Strann had left the door open—a foolish oversight but it served Calvi's purpose admirably. He eased himself through and began to move with great care down the spiral stairs. He could hear Strann ahead of him; convinced of his safety now, the rat was no longer troubling to go quietly. And there was light filtering up from below. Someone else was already there. . . .

Calvi froze against the wall as a sharp-edged block of brilliance beamed abruptly out and illuminated the rough stonework at the bottom of the stairs. Strann had opened the library door. Calvi waited until he had vanished into the room, then crept closer, his heart crawling under his ribs in suppressed excitement. He reached the last step, stopped, held his breath . . . and heard the voices begin to speak. . . .

22

"Karuth!" She was lit by the glow of two torches burning in their brackets, and in all his life Strann thought he had never seen a sight that moved him more. "Karuth, oh, Karuth—" He ran forward, almost tripping over his own feet in his eagerness to reach her, and his arms locked around her in a desperate embrace that all but crushed the breath from her lungs.

Then he saw Tirand.

"Yandros!" He sprang back, shock bleaching the color from his face, and collided painfully with the edge of a table. "What—"

"Strann, listen!" Karuth caught hold of him again, and he felt her suppressed passion through the tension in her grip. "It's all right, it isn't a trap! Tirand knows, and he's no longer against us. He and I are reconciled and I've told him everything. He's with us, Strann, he's our ally!"

Strann's hazel eyes fixed wildly on Tirand's face, and Tirand looked swiftly away. The High Initiate could have wished himself anywhere but here at this moment, for he'd seen the power of the emotions that had flowed between his sister and her lover in the instant of their reunion, and he was enough of a man of the world to realize that their love for each other was deeply and unshakably real. And something within him envied them both.

"Strann." He took refuge behind stiff formality. "What Karuth says is absolutely true. There probably isn't time to explain it all now, but . . . things have changed. I'm not your enemy. I know now that you've been working on Chaos's behalf from the beginning, and I'm here to help you both if I can." At last he found the self-possession to meet Strann's gaze. "Lord Ailind knows nothing about this, and he won't learn of it from me."

Strann was still dubious. Since the day of his arrival at the castle—and before that, if he was to be strictly honest with himself—the High Initiate had been an antagonist and not a friend. He knew that the original antipathy had stemmed only from Tirand's protective love for his sister, and he also knew that whatever she might pretend to the contrary, Karuth had bitterly regretted their divided loyalties. But Tirand was and had always been Order's staunchest supporter, Ailind's puppet. To claim, now, that that was no longer the case . . . could he trust such an assertion? Or was this some new trick on Order's part?

Karuth guessed what he was thinking, and she said urgently, "Strann, I promise you there's nothing to fear! Tirand and I took a blood oath—"

"A blood oath?" He knew as well as anyone what that meant, and a little of his fearful tension ebbed.

"Yes. Oh, love, it's all right, it's all *right*! Trust me, please!" She pulled him to her fiercely, and he buried his fingers in her hair. Tirand cleared his throat, embarrassed.

"If you'd rather I left—"

"No." Strann looked up at him, and the ghost of a smile played about his face. "No, High Initiate. If Karuth tells me a thing is so, then it's so as far as I'm concerned." He paused. "Besides, the thought that there's someone else in this castle who no longer views me as a worm fit only for crushing beneath their heel is . . . well, it's . . ." He shrugged. "I call myself a bard, but I can't express how thankful I am."

Tirand stared at the floor. "I admire what you've done, Strann. To gamble on keeping the usurper's trust while working against her . . . I'll be truthful and say I didn't think you had such courage in you. I'm . . . glad to be proved wrong."

Karuth turned quickly to the table behind them. "I brought some bread and meat and a small flask of wine." Her gaze searched his face. "Are you hungry, Strann? Does that bitch starve you?"

He was touched by her concern but shook his head. "No, my love. I could have food enough to choke me if I wanted it. Though I wouldn't turn down a mouthful of something to keep out the cold."

His half-humorous confession seemed to break the last of the ice, and with a snort of laughter Tirand sat down, pulling Karuth's flask toward him. "I'll endorse that!" He offered the flask to Karuth, then, when she refused, passed it to Strann. Strann took it and smiled. "I think, High Initiate, that this is the first time we've toasted each other's good health and safety. Long may both continue."

They drank, one after the other. Beyond the door, which Strann had neglected to latch behind him, Calvi held his breath as he listened. And when the flask was set down and Strann began to tell the tale of Ygorla's letter and Narid-na-Gost's furious response, what Calvi heard made his skin crawl with cold rage.

Strann's account of recent events, and the conclusions he'd drawn from them, was terse but cogent. There was no doubt in his mind, he said, that Ygorla's determination to gain control of the Chaos Gate could mean only one thing: She was no longer prepared to wait for Yandros to respond to her ultimatum but intended to launch a direct attack on his realm. Clearly she'd been unable to probe the Gate's secrets alone, so now she was attempting to blackmail her sire into performing the rite that would open it.

Tirand considered this news thoughtfully. "You've encountered the demon, Strann, which is more than anyone else here has done. Do you think he'll capitulate to her demands?"

"For the moment, High Initiate, I don't think he will," Strann replied. "He's no fool. He must be well aware that if he makes a bargain with her, she's unlikely to keep her part of it but will betray him anyway. On the other hand, though, he'll also know that it's only a matter of time before lord Yandros finds out that he's no longer protected by the Chaos stone." He met Tirand's gaze frankly. "When that happens, I hope I don't have to witness the results."

"Quite." Tirand's answering smile was bleak. "So you think that Narid-na-Gost will try to play for time?"

"As far as he's able, yes. But Ygorla's growing impatient. If he doesn't give in to her demands soon, she'll look for another route to her goal." He glanced at Karuth. "The ritual you used to open the Gate—could she use it, too, if she knew of it?"

Karuth nodded. "Anyone could. Lord Tarod closed the Gate again, and he'd know if any attempt was made to use it, but it isn't sealed against the Speaking of the Way."

"We must fervently hope that she doesn't discover the ritual's existence," Tirand said grimly. "Strann, listen. I think we should alert Ta—lord Tarod to this."

Strann's gaze slid sidelong to him and there was a faint resurgence of suspicion in his eyes. "I'm surprised that he doesn't already know, High Initiate."

Karuth's cheeks colored. "We thought—"

Tirand interrupted. "No, Karuth, let's be honest about it. I was the one who thought it better to say nothing to him. The message exhorted us to tell no one, and I argued that 'no one' might include lord Tarod." He shrugged. "My mistake."

The High Initiate, Strann thought, must have a very different relationship with his gods than he and Karuth had with theirs. But he didn't comment on that, only said, "He must be told. We have a little time to play with, but I suspect it'll be a matter of hours rather than days before Ygorla's patience runs out."

"Very well." Tirand rose to his feet, then paused. "I . . . ah . . ." His face colored, and he stared at the floor. "If you would like a little time together, I . . ."

Strann looked up quickly. "I daren't stay away for too long. But . . ."

As the bard's voice tailed off, Tirand fumbled with

something in his belt pouch. He took out a small silver object and, without looking directly at her, pressed it into Karuth's hand.

"It'll be safer for you both there," he said. "Less chance of being overlooked. I'll wait for you in my study, Karuth, and when you return, we'll find lord Tarod."

Karuth's fist closed over the object he had given her. She knew what it was, and she knew, too, that by this gesture Tirand had tacitly brought down the last remaining barriers of disapproval and given her and Strann his blessing. It was the key to the Marble Hall.

Gratitude overflowing in her eyes, she started to thank him, but he waved her into silence.

"There's no time for that now. I'll see you later. Strann." He met the other man's eyes, bowed slightly. "Good luck."

"Thank you, Tirand," Strann said gravely.

The High Initiate smiled slightly at this first use of his given name, then turned and left the library.

As Tirand emerged into the courtyard once more, he didn't see the slight, solitary figure that darted through the main doors in the moment when he paused to turn up his coat collar against the driving snow. Nor, when he reached the end of the stoa, did he notice the single set of footprints, confused among those he and Karuth had left earlier yet not quite covered, which led up the steps ahead of him. By the time he was inside the castle and shaking snow from his boots and hair, Calvi was gone from both sight and earshot, and the High Initiate walked toward his study. With luck the fire would still be alight, if only just, and his steward would have seen to it that there was fresh fuel set by the hearth ready for the morning. He'd mull a jug of wine, Tirand thought, for when Karuth returned. They'd probably both need it.

Trying not to dwell on the subject of Karuth and Strann and his own as yet confused feelings, he opened the study door and went in.

"High Initiate." Ailind's strange eyes were hard and golden in the candlelight that suffused the room. The lord

326

of Order was sitting in Tirand's chair. He smiled, and the smile had a chilly edge.

"Come in, High Initiate, and sit down. I wish to talk to you."

———————⟩ ⟨———————

"Ygorla! Ygorla, wake *up*!"

There was no ceremony and no delicacy about Calvi's efforts as he shook Ygorla by the shoulders with all his strength. She came to abruptly, with a cry of outrage, and as her eyes snapped open, he saw the flash of furious power that came instinctively to her and jumped back in alarm. But then her gaze focused, she recognized him, and the impulse died.

"*Calvi!* What do you mean by this, what hour is it?"

He caught hold of her hands, his own eyes wild with excitement. "Ygorla, listen! I've been out in the castle. I've made a discovery! There's a plot against you—and your precious pet rat is a traitor!"

Her body froze in midmovement. She didn't speak, but a dark aura began to shine ominously around her. Rapidly, garbling the words, Calvi told her all that had happened, from his initial discovery that Strann had left his post to the urgent talk he had overheard in the library.

"Strann's been working with that whore Karuth Piadar and her lord and master all along!" he said breathlessly. "And now Tirand's involved, too, and the three of them mean to enlist Tarod's help to stop you from gaining control of the Chaos Gate!"

Ygorla's eyes glittered like hard gems, and her face was twisted and ugly. "Who else?" she demanded hoarsely. "Who else is with them in this treachery?"

"I don't know." Calvi shook his head. "No other names were spoken. There may be no one else involved. But Ygorla, listen! The letter that Strann read—what does it mean, what was it about? I know you've been planning something, but you haven't told me what it is, and I don't understand! Why is the Chaos Gate so important?"

She didn't answer him for a few moments. Her expression was set now, her eyes narrowed to slits, and he thought that she hadn't absorbed his question. But then she turned to look at him.

"The Chaos Gate," she hissed, "is the last and most powerful key!" Suddenly she spun from the bed, snatching her fur cloak and casting it around herself as she paced across the room, her movements as tense and potentially explosive as those of a cornered cat. "It is the key to mastery of Chaos; it is the key to mastery of Order. Once I control the Gate, I control *everything*! *But I don't yet control it!*"

Then, in a few terse, sharp words she told Calvi what she had done during the past two days. The elementals sent to spy for her in the realm of Order, and their discovery that the souls of Order's lords were more carelessly guarded even than the Chaos stone had been. The knowledge that, through the Gate, she could enter Aeoris's stronghold and snatch the prize that would grant her the power to crush Order under her heel. And lastly the one thing that still eluded her—the power to force the Gate to yield to her will and open.

"If I could breach that barrier just for one *moment*," she said savagely, hurling one arm outward in a wild gesture, "then I would take control, and nothing could stand in my way! But at every turn I am *thwarted*!"

From where he still knelt on the bed Calvi stared at her. "By all the Seven Hells, Ygorla, why didn't you *tell* me?"

She spun on her heel, rage in her eyes. "Tell you? What would have been the point of that? What could *you* have done?"

"I could have told you where to find your missing key!"

There was a long pause. Then, in a dangerously low-pitched voice, Ygorla said, *"What?"*

He sprang down from the bed and came toward her. "Karuth Piadar knows the Gate's secrets. She performed the ritual that opened it and allowed the Chaos lords to enter this world."

Ygorla's rapid breathing rasped in the quiet room. "Are you sure of this?"

Calvi's lips twisted with bitter memory. "I was there when she did it! I stood beside her, as close as I am to you now. She forced me to witness the ceremony."

Ygorla had never been particularly interested in the events of Calvi's life before her influence had changed him. To her his past was irrelevant. But if she had known this, if she had *known* . . .

Slowly a new, cold light began to dawn in her mind. The first hint of a smile tugged at the edges of her mouth, and it was a smile of huge amusement and utter cruelty. Oh, yes; it was *perfect*. She could almost believe that fate had decreed it should happen in this way and no other. . . .

"Calvi." Suddenly her voice was pure sweetness. "You said that Strann and Karuth stayed behind when the High Initiate left the library?"

"Yes." Calvi looked cynical. "He offered to . . . how did he put it? . . . give them a little time together."

"Very noble of him. Then it's likely that they're still there." She grinned. "I think we shall pay them a visit, my sweeting. A little surprise to complete their happiness."

Calvi understood. He returned her grin, showing his teeth. Then, softly and with an unpleasant timbre, he began to laugh.

From his chair in the perfectly proportioned great hall at the heart of his realm, Aeoris, highest lord of Order, contemplated the nature of threads.

There were many different threads in the events currently taking place in the mortal world, and the pattern they had been forming was almost perfected. Patience, care, and tenacity had paid dividends as Aeoris had anticipated, and now the diverse strands of fortuity, coincidence, and careful manipulation were about to converge at last. From the many threads would come one plait, integrated and complete. Such symmetry appealed to Aeoris's coolly meticulous mind, and his stern mouth was smiling as he raised his head to regard the small, raised plinths that stood before each of the seven thrones and the artifacts that lay upon them.

Aeoris had taken great care that these new additions weren't allowed to mar the pure and exact perspectives of this sanctified place. Short-lived though their function would be, aesthetic considerations were, as always, paramount, and the results of his work pleased him. One brief moment was all it would take. And the moment was almost here.

Golden, pupilless eyes gazed into the facets of the jewels on their plinths, and the jewels picked up the light of those eyes and reflected it back in dazzling rainbows. Aeoris smiled again, and his image faded from the hall.

Though he'd thought he had no eyes and no mind for anything but Karuth, the Marble Hall stunned Strann into awed silence. Only the Circle's higher adepts were permitted to enter the hall without the High Initiate's express consent, and the sheer scale of the great chamber, its ceiling and walls invisible in the distance and defying all spatial reason, took his breath away. Holding tightly to his hand, Karuth led him among the forest of columns until they stood before the seven great colossi, the images of the gods of Chaos and Order, towering dim and eerie in the pastel mists.

"Yandr . . ." Strann hastily swallowed the oath before it could fully form. Words failed him, and an awful sense of his own insignificance crawled up from somewhere deep within him and gripped him with steel talons.

Karuth smiled, understanding, as she remembered her own reaction to the statues when she'd first seen them nearly thirty years ago. At the feet of the seventh and last colossus they stopped, and Strann shivered as he looked up at the two carved faces high above him. Both were disconcertingly familiar, and he said, his voice no more than a whisper, "To look at these . . . and then to think how often I've stood face-to-face with the very gods they depict . . ."

Her fingers gripped his more tightly. "I know. Sometimes it's hard to reconcile." Then the effort of maintaining a pretense of normality became too much for her, and she swung around to face him. "Oh, Strann . . . I've missed you so much! And I've been so *afraid* for you!"

He held her tightly, their hair tangling as they kissed. "We've only got a few minutes, love. I daren't stay longer in case Ygorla should find me gone."

Karuth nodded, fighting to regain her composure. "Soon, I hope—I *pray*—this will be over. When it is, I . . ." She swallowed. "There'll be so much to say."

"And so much lost time to make up for." He smiled. "I know it hasn't been long since we were parted, but it feels like a lifetime to me." Then his hazel eyes grew very serious. "I love you, Karuth. You've never doubted that, have you? Whatever I may have been forced to pretend, you've never doubted?"

"No." She didn't quite know whether to cry or laugh. "Never, Strann, never."

And from behind them, in the direction of the silver door, a coolly mocking voice said, "So there is a heart under that drab exterior after all, my dear? How *very* touching!"

They jolted as though they'd been physically struck, and Karuth's fingers dug involuntarily and painfully into the flesh of Strann's arms.

Ygorla had entered the hall with Calvi in complete silence and, as she had hoped, had taken them completely unawares. She stood less than ten paces away, a small, dark and deadly figure in the shifting mist, and she smiled. Strann had seen that smile before, and he looked quickly away.

"What's this, rat? Not pleased to see me?" Ygorla took one step forward. Behind her, Calvi had struck a careless pose, and his eyes were arrogantly self-satisfied.

"Or has my unexpected arrival spoiled your cozy little reunion?"

Strann knew in his gut that the cause was lost, but instinctively he made a desperate effort to save the situation.

"Sweet Majesty!" Pushing Karuth quickly from him, he gave the usurper his habitual sweeping bow. "Your presence is—"

"Be quiet!" The words cracked out harshly, raising shouting echoes in the hall. An ominous aura began to shine darkly around Ygorla's frame, and her voice grew lethal. "Don't dare to speak, traitor. Don't dare to speak, or to move one muscle, or to even *think* of looking at the creature by your side. For if you do, then before you can draw breath again, you will be *ash.*"

Karuth flared angrily. "How dare you—"

"And *you!*" Ygorla made a careless gesture with one hand, and Karuth was thrown back against the feet of the statue. The usurper stared at her with hard, almost crazed eyes. "I will have a use for you in good time. Until then, keep a still tongue if you wish your lover's body to remain intact."

Karuth sprawled against the cold stone. She looked back at Ygorla but she didn't speak again.

With an indolent grace that suggested she was relishing this moment, Ygorla turned to face Strann once more. Strann had covered his face with his hands and stood rigid, silently cursing what he saw as his own careless, reckless stupidity. He had led Karuth into this danger. He had taken too great a gamble—and but for a miracle within the next few minutes, he had killed them both.

"So, rat." In her chillingly mercurial way Ygorla switched from savagery to cloying sweetness. "All along your paws have pattered to the tune of another master while pretending to be an obedient little rodent. You have deceived me. I am *very* disappointed, rat. And I believe I shall have to punish you most severely." So fast that the movement caught even Calvi off guard, she brought one arm up and then sharply down. There was a sound like lightning cracking between clouds, and a white-hot rope spat from her fingers at Strann's unprepared body. Strann screamed shrilly as the rope's coils whirled around his neck and tightened into a burning noose, and Karuth, unable to stop herself, leaped to her feet.

"No! You evil, murdering *serpent*—"

"Back!" The blazing rope ripped from Strann's throat and seared the air inches before Karuth's face, sending her reeling. As she fell to the mosaic floor, the rope winked out of existence, and Ygorla laughed shrilly.

"Come, then, brave Karuth! Get up, and go to your precious mannikin! Run to his side and embrace him—if you can!"

Karuth scrabbled to her feet, goaded by panic and fury. She stumbled toward Strann, her arms outstretched—

And a wall of black flames sprang up around him, trapping him in a tight, searing circle.

"Come, Karuth!" Ygorla goaded gleefully. "Touch him! Surely a high adept like you isn't afraid of my little fire?"

Lungs heaving, teeth clenched, and hatred in her heart, Karuth reached out toward the flames. But she couldn't touch them. They burned not with heat but with cold; terrible, impossible cold that, if she once made contact with it, would petrify her flesh and turn it in an instant to brittle, crumbling dust.

"Strann . . ." Her voice cracked. "Don't move. Whatever you do, *don't touch the fire!"*

"Ah. A spark of wisdom at last." Ygorla clasped her hands together in a theatrical gesture. "I think the time has come for us to make our little bargain."

Karuth looked wildly at her. *"Bargain?* I'd no more bargain with you than with a Warp!"

"But I think you will." The usurper smiled sweetly. "That is, if you love your mannikin as greatly as your behavior seems to suggest. You see, he is the merchandise over which you and I shall be haggling."

The color drained from Karuth's face, and Ygorla laughed again. "Oh, yes. My dear and loyal Calvi was right, wasn't he? You *do* love the little rat, from his twitching nose to the tip of his tail!"

"Calvi—?" Not comprehending, Karuth looked quickly at the young man who still stood in his careless attitude behind the usurper. The muscles around her mouth began to tremble. "*You* betrayed us? But how could you have . . ."

Her voice trailed off as Calvi's eyes met hers. The depth of spiteful resentment in his look shocked her to the marrow. "You should take greater care where you and your brother hold your secret assignations, Karuth Piadar," he said maliciously. "You didn't even have the wit to close the library door. Very foolish of you. Still, your loss is our gain, I assure you." He smiled. "I'll enjoy seeing you all suffer for your stupidity."

For several seconds they continued to gaze at each other. Then, her voice shaking, Karuth said bitterly, "Is that truly what you've become, Calvi? A creature without sense and without compassion? Has she corrupted you so far that there's nothing but a shell left?" She saw the vindictiveness in his eyes and drew a racking breath. "You disgust me. You're no longer fit to call yourself human!" And silently in her mind she sent out a fervent appeal. *Lord Tarod! If you can hear me, if you can intervene, please help us now!*

Calvi uttered a short, acidic laugh. "Your insults don't move me." He turned to Ygorla, gesturing laconically toward Karuth. "Tell her, my love. Tell her what we want, and make her do it! I'm tired of wasting time over them."

The usurper smiled and patted his hand. "Then we'll waste no more, sweeting. So, Karuth—our bargain. It's quite straightforward. I understand that you know the ritual that will open the Chaos Gate. The Speaking of the Way, isn't that what it's called?"

Karuth froze. "Who told—" Then she saw Calvi's triumphant expression and knew the answer.

Ygorla continued. "My dear, I believe that, thanks to our mutual pet there in his fire cage, you are already aware of my intention; and as my beloved consort overheard every word of your little conspiracy, we might do without any tiresome protestations of ignorance." One perfect eyebrow lifted slightly. "You know the rite; I wish it to be performed. So it will suit us all very well if you perform it for me. For you see, if you don't, I shall feel obliged to teach Strann a few small lessons." Her expression shifted suddenly from sweetness to the lethal look of a predator that knew its prey was trapped and cornered beyond hope. "The choice is simple, dear Karuth. Obey me—or Strann will suffer the torments that only I know how to inflict."

The circle of flames agitated violently, and Strann cried out, "Karuth, no! Don't listen to her, don't give in to what she wants! She won't do it!" .

Ygorla studied her fingernails. "I'll begin with his eyes, I think. I know of a being that makes its home in the Seven Hells. A tiny creature, but it has a taste for the . . . shall we say, more *succulent* morsels of the human body."

Karuth turned away. What she said was inaudible.

"Karuth, you mustn't even *think* about it!" Strann shouted. "It would be betraying lord Tarod and lord Yandros! She'll kill us both anyway, whatever happens, and this'll only make everything a hundred times worse!"

Karuth couldn't bring herself to look through the shimmering black fire wall. Only one thing was clear in her mind: She would do anything that might save Strann's life. But would it? *Would* it?

With an effort she forced herself to face Ygorla again. The usurper was smiling again, and the sweetness had returned. Karuth's stomach turned over within her.

"If I agree—"

"Karuth!"

She ignored Strann's renewed protest. "—If I agree, what guarantee do I have that you won't kill him anyway?"

Ygorla shrugged. "None that you would believe, my dear. But I see no reason not to keep my part of the bargain. After all, I might find a further use for you both at some time in the future."

She'd get nothing more, Karuth realized. Slender though the thread of hope was, she had to trust in it. Her silent appeal to Tarod, which she'd frantically repeated, had been useless. The Marble Hall had proved *too* safe, *too* shielded from the world outside, and the Chaos lord was unable to hear her plea.

"Karuth!" Strann called out to her again. "Karuth, I forbid it! I forbid it!"

At last she did look toward him. Beyond the translucent flames he looked like a ghost, his figure dim and insubstantial. Karuth smiled, and in the smile was all the love she felt for him.

Then she said quietly to Ygorla. "You say I have a choice. You're wrong. There's *no* choice, not for me. I'll do what you demand."

23

In his eyrie, Narid-na-Gost paced. To the window; to the door; back to the window. He couldn't remain still for more than a single moment, for each time he halted, it began again; the nagging, the trepidation, the fearful certainty—and the indecision.

From his vantage point high at the spire's summit he had seen it all. The High Initiate and his sister, together once again, hurrying toward another rendezvous in the underground library. Then half an hour later Strann, the rat, hastening in their wake—and behind Strann, furtive as a rat himself, the distinctive fair hair of the arrogant pup who was now installed as Ygorla's consort. Uneasy, and intently curious, the demon had watched the library door until first Calvi—at a run—and then Tirand Lin had returned and made their way back to the castle's main wing.

Narid-na-Gost could make no sense of it, but his bones told him that this latest flurry of activity wouldn't end in yet another hiatus. Then, only minutes after the High Initiate's reemergence, two new figures had appeared in the courtyard.

At first the demon tried to tell himself that he was wrong. But he knew that his eyes didn't lie—and he knew, too, as he watched his daughter sweep across the snow with her fur cloak sparkling on her shoulders and Calvi hanging on her arm, that the moment he had been dreading had finally arrived.

Suddenly the tiny figures far below him had halted. Narid-na-Gost saw Ygorla turn, saw her look up toward the window where he crouched staring. And with his

unhuman sight, which made nothing of the distance and
the falling snow that would have defeated mortal vision,
he saw her smile a smile of utter triumph before she
raised one hand and saluted a mocking farewell.

That sardonic gesture had finally confirmed the demon's deepest terrors. How she had done it he didn't
know and didn't care; the situation was too critical now
for the whys and wherefores to matter anymore. But she
had done it, of that he was certain. She had found a way
to open the Chaos Gate.

So he paced. Window, door, window, door. The
spire room had been reduced to a wreckage of ripped and
tattered scarlet, all the opulent furnishings destroyed in a
moment of wild and uncontrolled panic. It had been, as
Narid-na-Gost now grimly acknowledged, a futile gesture, and in the calm that followed the mental storm he
tried to force himself to a decision. He knew that there
was only one choice left open to him, one hope—and a
slender hope at that—of saving his own skin. He had to
abandon everything, all his plans and ambitions, and go
to Tarod in the north spire to throw himself on the Chaos
lord's mercy and offer to help him overthrow Ygorla. But
to take that step, knowing that there was every chance
Tarod would destroy him—or worse—before he could
even tell his tale . . . Narid-na-Gost didn't know if he
could do it. A savage irony in the wake of all Ygorla's
past taunts, but he didn't know if he had the courage.

Reaching the window yet again, he paused suddenly.
There was no sign of any further activity around the library door, but there *was* a glimmer of light in the otherwise darkened castle, and it shone from the window of
the High Initiate's study. The demon inhaled with a
sharp hiss. Might that be the answer? Tarod might
slaughter him in the flicker of an eye. Tirand Lin,
though, was another matter. If he could persuade the
High Initiate to hear his story, if he could persuade him
to intercede with the gods—

The resolve that Narid-na-Gost had been striving to
find came to him in a rush of relief. There was no time to
waste. He focused on the glass of the window, and the

light in his crimson eyes grew momentarily molten. Soundlessly the window disintegrated, and the bitter night air rushed in, bringing a flurry of snow. Ignoring the icy flakes that stung his face, the demon sprang up onto the sill and stepped out. One glance down at the courtyard a dizzying distance below, and he began to move, smoothly and quickly with a hunched, crablike motion, down the black stone wall of the spire.

"You seem restless, High Initiate. Is anything troubling you?"

The question brought Tirand abruptly back to earth, and he felt chill perspiration break out over his face. He'd been thinking of Karuth, wondering how long she'd be, hoping she wouldn't return before he could get rid of his unwanted visitor, and as he looked up at Ailind, he felt a terrible conviction that guilt and deceit were written clearly on his face. He mumbled a quick assurance that nothing was wrong and that he was simply tired, and the lord of Order smiled in a way that made him quail afresh.

"These are tiring days. Still, I've no doubt that you find some solace in a wine as good as this vintage." He raised the flagon that stood on the table before him. "Another cup?"

"No—no, thank you, my lord." Tirand squirmed inwardly as he watched Ailind refill his own cup. What was the god trying to do? He seemed to have no real reason for seeking Tirand out at this hour, except to make idle small talk and share a drink or two—both quite out of character, for Ailind had always despised the one and had neither need of nor desire for the other. Tirand knew there must be a deeper motive, and he feared that Ailind had somehow discovered the truth about Shaill's secret conclave and what had resulted from it. If that was so, then why couldn't he drop this cold-blooded charade and let the inevitable storm break?

Ailind raised the cup to his lips and drank, taking time to roll the wine appreciatively around his tongue.

"A particularly good year in Southern Chaun," he said reflectively. "I wonder what the coming summer will—" He broke off, his eyes focusing with sudden intensity on the door. Startled, Tirand looked around and saw the latch slowly lifting.

Karuth . . . Alarmed, he started to his feet, but Ailind forestalled him with a swift gesture. "Wait, High Initiate."

Heart pounding, Tirand subsided. The latch stopped moving, and for one hopeful moment he thought that Karuth had sensed Ailind's presence and withdrawn. But then there was a faint rattle, a click, and the door swung open.

What confronted him brought Tirand out of his chair with a shocked oath on his lips. Like the rest of the castle dwellers, he'd never set eyes on Narid-na-Gost, and when he first saw the demon's hunched, white-skinned figure in the doorway, the clawed hands and feet, the matted tangle of crimson hair, his immediate reaction was that this was another of Ygorla's monstrous creations. Instinctively he raised his hand in a protective gesture, intending to curse and banish the warped thing, but before he could speak, Narid-na-Gost forestalled him.

"High Initiate!" The voice was hoarse and unhuman, but there was a fearsome intelligence behind it. "I am Narid-na-Gost, sire of the usurper—and I must speak with you urgently!"

Stunned, Tirand stared at the demon. *"You* are Narid-na-Gost . . . ?"

The demon grimaced sourly "If my name, at least, is known to the Circle, that may save us some time. And time is vital. I—"

"Oh, we all know your name, my friend. Some of us know it *very* well."

Narid-na-Gost hissed in shock. Ailind had been hidden from his sight by the half-open door, but now the lord of Order rose and crossed the room to stand before him. His eyes were venomous, his smile cruel.

"What, I wonder, has finally prompted the worm to

emerge from its hole?" Ailind asked. "Could it be that it finds itself in some straits?"

The demon hissed again, and fire flickered on his tongue. "I don't fear you, Order! You can do nothing to me!"

"True." Ailind studied his own fingernails. "But there are others who can—and will."

"No!" With a boldness and decisiveness that surprised the god, Narid-na-Gost slammed the door at his back and stood, legs braced, glaring at his adversary. "My business is with Tirand Lin, not with Order or Chaos or any of their damned overlords!"

Ailind's eyes flared dangerously. "You take risks, demon! One word to my cousin of Chaos—"

Narid-na-Gost spat a tongue of flame. Inimical to Ailind, it failed to touch him; but the carpet at his feet sizzled briefly, and before he could react, the demon swung to face Tirand.

"High Initiate, hear me out!" His voice was aggressive, but Tirand thought he detected a pleading note. "If you love your sister—"

"Worm, be silent!" Ailind snapped. But Tirand said sharply, "No, my lord, I want to hear him!"

"A liar and deceiver, a demon of Chaos?" Ailind retorted contemptuously. "Tirand, I order you—"

"No." Never before had Tirand used such a tone to the god. But Narid-na-Gost had alerted him, goaded him beyond the bounds of his instinctive obedience. *If you love your sister . . .* and though he wasn't consciously aware of it, Tirand sensed on some deeper level that Ailind didn't want him to know what Narid-na-Gost had come to tell him.

For a second or two his gaze and Ailind's clashed. Then, with a careless but angry movement of one hand, the god gave way. "Hear him, then, as you wish. You won't gain anything by it. It's too late."

Too late? His heart lurching, pressure in his chest, Tirand looked at the demon. "What's this to do with Karuth? Tell me!"

The crimson eyes flicked cannily in Ailind's direction, and Narid-na-Gost told him what he had seen, from Calvi's secretive trailing of Strann to the moment when Ygorla, sweeping across the courtyard, had waved her sardonic farewell to him in his eyrie.

"Even now my daughter is attempting to break through the Chaos Gate," he finished. "And your sister is in the Marble Hall with her. She is in danger, High Initiate. Great danger. I will help you to save her, but you *must* intercede for me with Chaos!"

Tirand was stunned. His first reaction was that the demon must be lying, but that was immediately followed by a rush of logic that chilled his blood. If, as Karuth had told him, Narid-na-Gost had been abandoned by Ygorla and was no longer protected by the stolen Chaos stone, then his one hope of salvation lay in turning against his daughter and helping Chaos to defeat her. He wouldn't have dared approach Tarod directly; he had to have a human go-between. And if he knew that Tirand and Karuth had been reconciled, it was natural that he should have come here.

An image slammed into his mind: Karuth and Strann, together in the Marble Hall. Calvi must have overheard all that was said during their earlier meeting and had reported the truth to Ygorla about her pet rat's trickery—

"*Gods!*" Forgetting propriety, he spat the oath out. "I must help them!"

"Call on Tarod, High Initiate!" Narid-na-Gost urged. "Call on him and ask his aid! Tell him I'm your ally. Tell him that I'm helping you!"

"Yes . . . yes, I . . ." Confusion suddenly followed clarity as panic threatened to get hold of Tirand, and he turned in appeal to Ailind. "My lord, there must be something *you* can do! If the usurper finds Karuth—" Then his voice tailed off as he saw the lord of Order's expression.

Ailind stared back at the High Initiate with cool indifference. "There's no need to work yourself into a ferment, Tirand. I assure you that all is proceeding exactly as planned, and there's no need for concern."

Tirand's jaw worked in disbelief. "But—"

"High Initiate"—impatience tinged the god's voice —"the matter is quite simple. The usurper will indeed open the Chaos Gate, but that's precisely what we want her to do. I regret the necessity of involving Karuth, but you may take comfort from the fact that she is playing a vital part in aiding Order's—and your—cause."

Disbelief began to turn to outrage in Tirand's mind. "You mean that you—you *knew* this was happening? And you've let Karuth walk into a trap?"

The god looked genuinely surprised. "The trap is set to snare Ygorla, not your sister. Our plan has been prepared for a long time. We lacked only a means of showing the usurper how to open the Gate without alerting her to our involvement, and now Karuth will provide that for us when the usurper forces her to perform the ritual." He smiled pityingly. "I understand your feelings. Karuth is still your sister, even if she is a traitor, and it's only natural that you should feel sympathy for her. But you'll agree that one human life can hardly be permitted to stand in the way of our cause."

Standing tense and motionless, staring at him, Tirand realized for the first time how little Ailind really understood about the nature of mortals. In one moment all the incidents, from the greatest to the most trivial, that in recent days had sawed like a knife blade at his loyalty, at his sense of duty and, most of all, at his conscience, came back to him.

He said, his voice catching and rasping in his throat, *"What have you done?"*

Ailind made a dismissive gesture. "Really, Tirand, this childishness—"

Tirand exploded. "Damn you, *answer me!*"

The god's eyes flared with fury. "You *dare* to address me in such a way?"

The last barriers of habit and fear that had held Tirand back collapsed. At this instant Karuth could be dying, and this being, this *creature,* cared nothing for her fate and expected him simply to bend the knee and accept the inevitable. He would not. *He would not!*

He hurled one wild glance at Narid-na-Gost, who was hunched by the door and quivering with impatient agitation. Then, before Ailind could stop him, Tirand summoned all the psychic energy he could muster and yelled at the top of his voice,

"Tarod! Lord Tarod—help me!"

There was a moment's suffocating stillness as the echoes of his voice rang through the study. Then Ailind's eyes turned molten. He started forward—

From the direction of the hearth came a short, emphatic noise, as of a door slamming, and Tarod's dark figure stood between them.

Tirand stumbled back as shock sent a stab of heat and cold through him. The Chaos lord's emerald eyes raked him, raked Ailind, then lit on Narid-na-Gost.

"You—" The word sounded like a death sentence. Narid-na-Gost's nerve snapped. He uttered a cry of terror and vanished, leaving only a metallic stench. Tarod raised a hand as though to blast the spot where he had stood, but Tirand intervened.

"My lord!" He grasped the Chaos god's sleeve. "Karuth's in danger—the usurper's found out about Strann; she's in the Marble Hall now and she means to open the Chaos Gate; and Karuth and Strann are there, and Karuth knows the ritual—Order is behind this, they planned it—"

He was babbling, his mind too turbulent for coherence, but Tarod grasped the gist of his frantic words. Suddenly a great many things began to fall into place in the Chaos lord's mind. He turned on his heel—and was confronted by Ailind's coldly smiling face.

"It's too late to intervene, Chaos. You can't change what's already taken place, and within a matter of minutes we will have both the usurper and your brother's soul!"

Tarod's eyes lit with rage. *"You can do nothing to the gem!"*

"You forget the laws that govern us all. Under one circumstance our power over you is paramount; for if any artifact or being of Chaos should enter our realm, we

344

may control and, if we so wish, destroy it." The lord of Order laughed softly. "The usurper, however, is ignorant of this simple fact. So it was easy for us to sow certain seeds in her mind, through the useful if unwitting offices of the High Margrave—who is a *very* impressionable young man—and to lead her to believe that she might steal from us what she has already stolen from you. At this moment Ygorla is preparing to use the Chaos Gate to enter our realm, certain that by doing so she will gain dominion over three worlds instead of merely two. She'll discover her mistake soon enough, but by then she'll have delivered the soul-stone into our hands. Then, my friend, we shall see some long overdue changes!"

Tirand stared at him as suddenly the entire picture became clear and all the seeming anomalies in Order's behavior were explained: Ailind's alienation of Calvi and refusal to help free him from the usurper's bewitchment; his unwillingness to confide his strategy to the Circle; his insistence that the castle dwellers should make a pretense of capitulating to Ygorla and take care not to goad her to action, so that Order's plan should have time to bear fruit. To the gods, Ygorla was nothing more than a means to an end. What they wanted, and had wanted all along, was to see the Chaos stone destroyed and with it the balance of Equilibrium. It all made sense—and Tirand's one bitterly overwhelming feeling was that Ailind had cold-bloodedly used him and preyed on his loyalties to gain his own ends. Tirand had believed in the justice of Order's cause, believed that the world would be a better place without the influence of Chaos. But Ailind's cold indifference to the plights of Karuth and Calvi gave the lie to that belief.

He said, his voice unsteady, "Shaill was right. You care nothing for us. You use us, and then when we've achieved your purpose for you, you cast us aside!"

Ailind made a sardonic moue. "And would you expect anything more from Chaos, High Initiate? Are you so naive as to think that there's any difference between us?"

As Tirand opened his mouth to argue, Tarod's hand

clamped on his arm. "Tirand, we're wasting time. If Karuth and Strann are to be helped—"

"It's too late for that, Chaos!" Ailind interrupted.

"I don't think so. But you hope, don't you, to distract the High Initiate long enough to *make* it too late." Ailind's momentarily unguarded expression told the Chaos lord that he'd found the mark, and he turned quickly to Tirand.

"I'm going to the Marble Hall. Come with me or not as you wish, but choose now."

Strain and misery racked Tirand's face as he looked up. "I'll come."

Tarod didn't give Ailind time to argue or intervene. Tirand saw what looked like a black vortex rushing toward him. Then the hand still holding his arm increased its grip in a sudden flash of pain, and sound and vision were blotted out as the study vanished.

24

"I stand before you in this place and I walk toward you on this way." Karuth's voice was close to breaking. She was shivering as though with the ague, and the words of the ritual were barely audible as she spoke them. "The way is long but the way is old, and the way is the way of power. I am chosen and I . . ." She glanced sidelong at Ygorla, who was smiling with gleeful anticipation, then at the flickering fire cage beyond her. ". . . and I am willing. With the feet that are my flesh I tread between dimensions, and I shall speak the way."

Oh gods, she thought, *it's beginning.* She could feel a faint, pulsing vibration through the floor's marble mosaic, and she thought—though it might have been imagination—that the colors of the mist were growing denser, darker, and throbbing in time to the silent beat. She didn't dare look at the black circle a few paces from where she stood, too afraid that she'd see it changing, opening into the vortex that heralded the Chaos Gate's manifestation. She'd prayed that the ritual might not work, that without the fierce commitment that had fired her the first time she performed it, the power that controlled the Gate would refuse to respond, but the hope was a vain one. It was coming. She could feel it; she was certain.

She struggled on, her throat closing so that she had to force the words out. "As it was in the days before me, it shall be again. Hear me—hear me, and let the seal be broken!" Now the final declaration, the command that would break the barriers. Karuth cast a look of helpless regret in Strann's direction, torment in her eyes, then drew a deep breath.

"I speak the way. And the way is open."

This time she was ready for the sound-beyond-sound that crashed through her mind like a tidal wave breaking. She glimpsed Calvi reeling back, saw Ygorla's mouth open in astonishment. Then the huge concussion was gone, the mists still, the Marble Hall silent. Her body feeling like a leaden shell in which consciousness was a prisoner, Karuth turned to look at the black circle.

What looked like a dark stream of fog was rushing upward from the circle, forming a hazy column that flowed toward the hall's invisible ceiling. Pinpoints of light danced in it like ripples in a current; and at the heart of the darkness, ghostly as yet but growing clearer and more solid with every moment, was the outline of a huge, black gate.

Karuth heard a sound behind her, a gasp, sharply truncated. Then suddenly there was a blur of movement as the usurper rushed forward.

"Calvi! Calvi, I have it, I have control of it!" Ygorla's voice rose in a shriek as she snatched at Karuth, pushing and pummeling her aside. "Get out of my way, get *back*!" A ferocious shove sent Karuth sprawling, her head cracking agonizingly on the mosaic floor, and light flared around Ygorla, black and purple and shot through with silver striations as she ran to the circle and confronted the spectral image. She flung her arms up and out, and her monstrous aura pulsed with wild energy.

"I am the power and I wield the power! Obey me, I command you—OPEN!"

From the ghostly portal within the dark cloud came a deep sound, as of an ancient key turning—and slowly, relentlessly, the Chaos Gate began to swing back. Beyond was darkness, emptiness, silence, a void and a vacuum waiting to be filled, and Ygorla's intoxicated laughter rang out. Oh, yes, oh *yes*! She had control! The Gate was hers! Still laughing, she focused her will and felt renewed power flood through her. Then she raised one hand, pointed at the Gate, and in her mind uttered a savage decree.

The darkness beyond the Gate shivered once, then shattered. Cool, golden light poured through, dramatically illuminating the usurper's figure and drowning the aura that throbbed around her. Dim and pale within the light, a perfectly symmetrical golden road stretched away before her, the road that would lead her into Order's realm and stronghold.

Ygorla looked back, just once. Sick and giddy from the blow to her skull, Karuth had only a momentary glimpse of her face, but it was enough to make her recoil. The usurper's eyes were alight with hellish joy, her mouth stretched wide, teeth bared in a snarling grimace that combined pride, triumph, and greed into a kind of mad ecstasy. She looked utterly deranged. Then her mad gaze focused on Calvi.

"Kill her, my sweeting," she said. "She's of no use to us anymore."

Like a serpent sloughing away the skin it had outgrown, she cast off the fur cloak, flinging it behind her, and, with a whirl of black hair and shimmering blue gown, stepped into the circle and entered the Chaos Gate. The golden light flared into intolerable brilliance, blinding Karuth. In the moment before she turned her head away with a cry of shock she saw Ygorla silhouetted in radiance, heard her laughter ringing back as though across a thousand miles—

Movement alerted her, and she jerked her head up in time to see Calvi walking toward her. There was an ugly deliberation about his movements, an unhurried sense of purpose. Coolly, carelessly, his right hand played on the hilt of a wicked-bladed knife.

Karuth hunkered into a defensive crouch. She had no weapon, nothing with which to defend herself. And when she looked at the face of her one-time friend, she knew that reason would avail her nothing. Calvi's Empress had given an order; Calvi would obey. And the deed would give him nothing but pleasure. . . .

Two paces from her he stopped, smiled. The smile

made bile rise in Karuth's throat. He didn't even look human anymore.

Calvi took another pace and started to raise the knife. She knew she had only one chance and that almost infinitesimally small. She had no skill, no training. All she had was the fierce will to survive, and that might not be enough. The knife came up—and Karuth sprang to her feet, at the same instant clenching her left fist and launching a punch at Calvi's smiling face. Desperation and instinct made her put her entire weight behind the blow; taken unawares, Calvi tried to jerk his head away, but he wasn't quick enough, and her knuckles drove into his right cheekbone. Calvi gave a rattling gasp of pain, dropped the knife, and fell, lying stunned and unmoving as momentum sent Karuth staggering across the floor. She stood swaying on her feet, breathless and almost as shocked by her success as he had been. He'd forgotten that she was left-handed. He'd expected any attack to come from the right . . . oh, gods, she felt *sick*. Her knuckles pulsed with pain; her whole hand felt dislocated. She wanted to sit down, fall as Calvi had fallen—

She started violently as from across the Marble Hall a frantic but familiar voice yelled her name.

They had arrived together, Tirand, Tarod, and Ailind, and Karuth blinked dazedly as she saw their three figures looming through the mist. Tirand had already seen her and, ignoring Tarod's sharp warning, the High Initiate rushed forward.

"Karuth! Gods, you're safe, you're *safe*!" He caught hold of her arms, trying to steady her, hug her, and look at her all at once. Tarod strode after him. He paused long enough to take in the fact that Karuth was unhurt, then swung on his heel and made a swift gesture toward the fire cage that still imprisoned Strann. The black flames imploded and vanished, and, staggering like a drunkard, Strann stumbled forward to measure his length at the Chaos lord's feet. Tarod heard him swearing forcefully between racking breaths, realized that his wits were still intact, and quickly reached down to haul him upright.

"Strann, where is she? *Where is she?*"

Strann's teeth chattered with reaction. "She—it's too late, my lord! She's—gone through the Gate—"

What Tarod hissed in reply was eclipsed by Ailind's soft but carrying laughter. They both looked up and saw the lord of Order standing a few paces away, gazing at the disarray before him with detached amusement.

"As the rat says, Chaos, it's too late. The trap has sprung, and at this precise moment the usurper is delivering both herself and your brother's soul-stone into Aeoris's safekeeping."

Strann stared at Ailind in total bewilderment. "But she—" He turned to Tarod again. "I thought she meant—"

"To attack the realm of Chaos?" Ailind finished the question for him. "Oh no, rat. She wants more than that. *Far* more. And she has been led to believe—quite erroneously—that she can have it."

Still Strann didn't comprehend, but someone else did. They'd overlooked Calvi, who still lay in the shadow of one of the colossi. Calvi was dazed by Karuth's blow, which had left his entire face feeling as though it were on fire, but he was far from unconscious. He'd heard Ailind's words, and through the haze of disorientation and nausea he grasped at their meaning. *The trap has sprung. . . .* No, he thought giddily, it couldn't be, it *couldn't* be. He had to stop her, had to warn her—

With a convulsive jerk he scrabbled to his feet, twisted about, and started toward the Chaos Gate, still pulsing within the black circle.

"Ygorla!" His voice was hysterical, midway between a scream of fear and a moan of pain. *"Ygorla, come back! It's a trap—come back, come back!"*

"Calvi, don't!" Instinct and old loyalties made Tirand shout the warning. Beyond the Gate the golden light shining from Order's realm began to turn an evil shade of green, and as Calvi reached the circle, Tarod's voice roared out, "High Margrave, NO—"

"Calvi!" Tirand launched himself forward as intuition and terror for Calvi took simultaneous hold of him. He'd gone three paces when Tarod intercepted him, spin-

ning him around and hurling him forcibly back. Tirand started to shout a protest—then the shout became a yell of horrified shock as an explosion of blinding white light blasted outward from the Chaos Gate. Tarod's tall form shielded the High Initiate from the worst of it, but Karuth, and Strann, who had started after Tirand, saw Calvi's running shape outlined suddenly in silver fire and heard his scream of terror and agony as the blast of power hit him full on. He was snatched off his feet, twisting in a crazy tangle of limbs, and then with a shattering boom that shook the Marble Hall from end to end the Chaos Gate slammed shut, hurling him from its portal and flinging his broken body across the floor.

The echoes of the Chaos Gate's closing died slowly away, and not one of the five figures in the hall moved. Tirand, Karuth, and Strann were all frozen, staring in disbelief at Calvi's corpse. Tarod had turned his head aside, his face a bleak mask. Ailind . . . Ailind gazed down at the young High Margrave, no longer smiling but apparently quite emotionless.

Then, feebly but unmistakably, Calvi's fingers moved.

"Calvi . . . ?" Karuth's voice was a fearful whisper. *He wasn't dead.* . . . "Oh, gods!" She forgot all that had happened in recent days, forgot the fact that only minutes ago he'd been intent on killing her. Nothing mattered to her now other than the fact that, once, he had been her dear friend.

"Calvi?" She ran to where he lay and knelt down beside him. At first sight he seemed unmarked, unharmed. But as her hand made contact with him, she felt a deathly chill on his skin and sensed an awful emptiness beneath the mask of his face. She knew then that what she touched was nothing more than a thin, fragile shell, that the flesh and the bone and the soul of the human being beneath had been burned away by the Chaos Gate's power and could not be restored. He wasn't dead yet, but he was dying. And when his eyelids fluttered and weakly opened, she saw that same knowledge in his eyes.

"Calvi . . ." She whispered his name again and

held his hand, desolately and hopelessly aware that she could do nothing more to comfort him now. Strann had moved quietly to stand beside her. He crouched down, and she felt his arm go about her shoulders in a tentative effort to console her in her turn. Tirand, too, was close by. She could hear him murmuring, over and again, his voice breaking. *"I tried to stop him . . . gods, I tried. . . ."*

Calvi's eyes couldn't focus, but his filmy gaze was moving from one to another of the grieving trio grouped around him. Trying not to acknowledge the hollow emptiness she saw behind that gaze, Karuth realized that his look was one of mild and almost childlike puzzlement. He wanted to smile at her but didn't have the strength. And he didn't seem to know who she was.

"Calvi, it's all right. Nothing's wrong. There's nothing wrong, nothing at all. You're safe now." She was hardly aware of what she was saying, and it didn't matter. Words were enough, any words, if only they were kind.

His lips parted, quivered. "Is it . . . morning?"

Tirand made a choked sound and turned away, and Strann said softly, "Yes, Calvi, it's almost morning."

This time he found the strength for the smile to come. "We're going hunting today. Blis and I. In the park."

Karuth looked at Strann, her face agonized. "He's forgotten everything. He thinks he's back on Summer Isle, in the days before—"

"Hush." Strann touched a finger to his lips. "Let him think it. What use would it be to disillusion him now?"

As though the bard had known the moment, or as though his words had conjured it, Calvi breathed out in a gentle sigh. And when Karuth turned back, his blue eyes had closed and his body was utterly quiet and still.

Very slowly Karuth rose to her feet. She felt nothing. The emotion would come later, but for now there was only a detached sense of sorrow at the waste of such a young life. Strann took her hand and squeezed it; she didn't respond. Her gaze was on Ailind, and Ailind looked back at her.

"You could have prevented it." It was a flat statement; no accusation, simply an avowal of fact.

Ailind's expression didn't alter. "I regret the death of the High Margrave," he said. "I had hoped that it might not come to that. But our cause couldn't be jeopardized."

"Your *cause.*" Now the accusation was there, and with it searing contempt. She almost spat his own words back in his face. "You *used* Calvi. But for you and your scheming, he could have been saved!"

"Karuth." A thin but powerful hand came to rest on her shoulder. She looked up and saw Tarod standing beside her. "You'll gain nothing from this. The High Margrave is dead, and his death was an unhappy accident that no one could have foreseen. He was simply reckless enough to try to follow Ygorla through the Chaos Gate, and he was caught in the backlash of power created by the path she forged. It's not relevant. There are more important matters at stake now."

"More important?" She swung around to face him, shocked by his words, then stopped as she saw his eyes. They were just as cold as Ailind's, just as unhuman, just as uninterested in Calvi's plight or her grief. Oh, he'd tried to warn Calvi; yes, he'd done that much. But it had been a reflex, nothing more. Calvi's life hadn't mattered to Chaos any more than it had mattered to Order.

In her mind she suddenly heard the Matriarch's voice and saw her face, grave and unhappy in the lamplit chill of the library. *We are very minor players on the stage of this conflict,* Shaill had said. *We are insignificant; we are expendable. In my darkest moments I've begun to ask myself whether we were wise to ask for the gods' help. . . .*

But then, as Shaill had also said, what choice did they have? What else could they have done?

"Karuth?" Tarod was looking at her, faintly curious, perhaps guessing her thoughts. She shook her head, turned away from him toward Strann, and Ailind said, "She begins to doubt, I think. Perhaps that's just as well, for Chaos will have little to offer her when tonight is over."

Tarod's eyes flared angrily. "You and your brother haven't won this battle yet, Ailind!"

Ailind smiled. "I think we have, cousin." There was a sound from behind them; faint, but it was enough to alert them all. Tarod swung around. The three mortals, seeing his sudden alarm, turned too. And Karuth uttered a startled oath.

The Chaos Gate was still visible within the dark column that flickered above the mosaic circle. And, slowly, for the second time that night, the great black portal was beginning to swing open. . . .

There was light all around her as she stood at the entrance to the gods' own sanctum. Soft light, beautiful and gentle, shone in through the windows of the hall like the afternoon sun pouring in through the colored glass of her palace on Summer Isle. The floor beneath her feet was smooth, unsullied, unpatterned, the walls pure white, the hall's proportions flawless. The air—neither too cool nor too warm—carried a scent of blossoms, and somewhere in the far distance there was birdsong. Everything here was the epitome of calm perfection.

Ygorla was oblivious of the perfection. Her one thought, the one obsession that drove out all else, was a sense of pulsating triumph. She was here—and Aeoris and his bloodless crew, so complacent in their security, knew *nothing*.

The elementals had done their work well. This place was the gods' own hall, they had told her, and lay at the very heart of Order's realm. But the Chaos Gate knew no boundaries. Only will it, the elementals had said, and it shall be. So she had willed it, and in the space of a breath she had stepped into the core of her enemies' stronghold. No guardians to challenge her, no sentinels to raise the alarm, nothing whatever to hinder her. Only the great,

empty chamber, the seven thrones of the lords of Order—
and the prize she had come to claim.

A soft breath escaped her, like the sigh of a lover
contemplating the object of her adoration. But her eyes
glittered with another kind of hunger as she whispered,
"Oh, you fools."

They were there. The fruits were on the tree, ready
and ripe. Seven elegant plinths, clean lined and without
adornment, set before the seven thrones. And in the exact
center of each plinth a huge, multifaceted diamond shone
clear and brilliant. Ygorla gazed at each jewel in turn.
Then her avid gaze returned to the central plinth, and the
largest gem of all. Oh, yes. Oh, *yes.* This was the one. She
could see flecks of gold glistening within its depths, the
rainbow colors of the light that it shed, as though a star
were burning at its heart. This was—could only be—the
soul-stone of Aeoris himself!

Her feet made no sound as she ran the length of the
hall, but her shadow darted with her, stark against the
clean whiteness of walls and pillars. Ygorla stopped before the plinth, and laughter bubbled up within her. Her
right hand closed over the great sapphire of the Chaos
stone, still hanging on its chain at her breast. And her left
hand reached out and plucked the gold-flecked diamond
from its place.

It pulsed in her hand, like a heart torn from a living
body. Her lips curled into a devastating smile of triumph—

And from behind her, softly, gently, slender fingers
touched her shoulder.

"Ygorla." Aeoris's voice was mellifluous, calm, almost—but not quite—benign. "Welcome to my hall."

Ygorla whirled, and her vivid blue eyes widened as
she stared into the stern face of Order's greatest lord. The
silent clash lasted only a moment before confidence swept
her shock aside, and she laughed shrilly.

"So *you* are Aeoris! By all that's unholy, this *is* an
unexpected bonus!"

The god smiled enigmatically. "And for me."

"Oh, I doubt that." Her knuckles whitened as she

gripped the great diamond more tightly. "You've arrived just one moment too late, lord Aeoris. Too late to prevent me from taking something from you that I believe you hold dear!"

Though Aeoris's eyes had no pupil, no iris, but were simply orbs of golden light, she thought that his gaze shifted briefly to her hand. "No, my child," he said carelessly. "You're mistaken. *Quite* mistaken."

Something clutched at Ygorla's gut, and her look grew savage. "Don't try to dissemble with me, godling! I know what this is—*I know what I hold!*"

"Do you?"

The complacency with which he asked the question sent a stab of suspicion through her. It *was* his soul-stone, she *knew* it was. She wasn't mistaken; the elementals couldn't have been wrong. . . .

Her heart began to pound painfully. "I *know* what this is! And I could destroy it now!" Aeoris only continued to smile, and her voice rose to a grating screech in which fear was suddenly taking a hand. "I could crush it, and you would *die*—"

Aeoris laughed softly. "I'm afraid that isn't true, Ygorla. Do you think we're as foolish as our cousins in the Chaos realm? I assure you, we're not. That pretty thing you hold is just a bauble, a worthless toy to tempt a child's greedy hand."

She stared at him in growing horror as confusion swamped her. Then, as though mocking her own favorite gesture, Aeoris snapped his fingers. The jewel in Ygorla's fist turned to sparkling dust that spilled through her fingers and showered to the floor.

"AHH!" She screamed and sprang back, colliding with the plinth and almost losing her balance as she ricocheted away from it. Aeoris watched dispassionately as she strove to collect herself, and his voice was like a knife driving between her ribs into her heart.

"You should learn that those whom you torment can't be trusted forever, Ygorla. Didn't you think that the elementals might have been awaiting the chance to mislead you and to deliver you into my hands?"

"They can't—they didn't—" Her teeth ground together as she battled to get herself under control once more. They'd lied, they'd duped her—but she wasn't done yet! She had power, more power than anyone knew. She'd have revenge; she'd show this creature what she truly was!

"Damn your arrogance!" she shrieked. *"You can do nothing to me, I am Chaos, and I will destroy you! I will DESTROY YOU!!"* She summoned every last dreg of her power, seized on it, focused it into a single, shattering bolt of pure energy, and hurled the bolt directly at the lord of Order's smiling face.

"Oh, you misguided child." The hall formed delicate echoes from the god's voice and cast them back like a soft choir. "Do you truly understand so little?"

Ygorla put her hand to her mouth and bit hard into her own flesh. Above the hand her eyes were insane. "You can't—I have power, I have POWER—"

Aeoris shook his head. "Not here. Chaos is nothing here, and all your sorcery and all your skills are useless. Didn't you realize that, Ygorla? When Chaos enters the realm of Order, its power is shattered. And you are of Chaos, my child." He stretched out a hand toward her. "Don't think of trying again; it's futile. You're mine now, and I'll deal with you as I please."

She couldn't move. On one level everything within her screamed and railed against this moment as triumph turned to downfall and ruin. But on another level she understood that she couldn't fight him. It was over, it was ended—and she was helpless.

Aeoris's hand closed around the chain that held the Chaos stone. There was a sound, small but emphatic, as the links snapped. And Ygorla's prize, the soul of Yandros's brother, dropped into the lord of Order's palm.

If Aeoris had been capable of feeling pity for such a creature, he might have pitied Ygorla then. She fell to her knees, her hands covering her face, not in an attitude of supplication or pleading, for she was too proud for that even now and she knew anyway that it would have achieved nothing. She was looking destruction in the face, and she had despaired.

"Well, Daughter of Chaos." Aeoris was implacable, unmoved. "What shall I do with you now?"

"Kill me." Her voice was harsh, though muffled. "Damn you, don't waste any more time than you must. *Do it!*"

Even now, Aeoris reflected, she wasn't truly afraid of him, and in a way he almost found that amusing. But he wasn't interested in her fate. Her end, he had already decided, was for others to accomplish. A small gift to an ancient adversary. . . .

He said, "No, Ygorla, I won't kill you."

She looked up, hopeful yet at the same time suspecting some new game. Aeoris smiled again.

"Why should I care a whit for your fate? You may return, unscathed, on the road by which you came. I believe that there's someone waiting for you on the other side of the Gate."

For a moment she didn't comprehend. Then understanding dawned.

"Oh, no. . . ." Her voice quavered. "No, not that—not that, *not that! Oh no, no, NO, PLEASE—*"

25

They heard her screaming before they saw her. Howling, yelling, babbling incoherent pleas and exhortations and curses, her voice echoed back through the Chaos Gate, growing louder, drawing closer. There was a blur of movement within the portal, a vivid flicker of blue—and then Ygorla's figure appeared. She was struggling, seemed to be striving to cling to something, but the power that impelled her was far too great to resist, and with a high-pitched shriek she tumbled through the Gate into the mortal world, to lie sprawling on the floor of the Marble Hall.

For several seconds there was silence. They all stared at her—even Karuth, who had returned to kneel beside Calvi's body. Then Tarod, who was closest to the fallen usurper, took two slow, measured steps forward. The sound of his footfalls had an ominous quality, and convulsively Ygorla moved, writhing, shaking hair from her eyes, raising herself on her hands. Her head came up. Tarod stopped, and they looked into each other's eyes. The Chaos lord saw the two broken ends of the chain swinging about her neck where Aeoris had plucked the soul-stone from her, and his mind was swamped by a wave of blinding and infernal rage. He couldn't control it, didn't try; all he knew was that the usurper had been delivered into his hands, but that the moment had come too late.

He drew breath with a sound that made his human audience shudder, and the Marble Hall's drifting mist turned a livid and bruised blue-purple. Tarod was oblivious of it, oblivious of everything but the creature on the

360

floor before him, and all pretense of humanity dropped from him like a mask shattering. His wild black hair became smoke, his face turned bone white and savage, his eyes burned like emerald stars in his skull. Darkness roiled around him, and as he raised his left hand, a searing white light sprang to life above his heart and formed into the shape of a seven-rayed star, the emblem of Chaos. The star began to pulse in a steady, relentless rhythm, and Tarod smiled. . . .

"Back, quickly!" Strann darted to Karuth's side and pulled her to her feet before she could protest. Tirand, too, was retreating hastily, his gaze fixed in mesmerized horror on Tarod, and even Ailind had withdrawn a pace or two, shocked by the aura of unfettered violence that blazed about the Chaos lord's figure. And Ygorla . . .

What Ygorla saw as her blue eyes locked with Tarod's unearthly glare the humans who witnessed her end would never know. But her face contorted into a look that defied sanity, and intelligence fled from her as the Chaos lord's power engulfed all reason, all hope, leaving only primal, animal terror. Then, behind her bulging eyes an appalling silver light flared. Fire—supernatural fire, igniting in her skull and beginning to burn. Ygorla made a hideous, inarticulate noise, shock and agony driving her voice higher and higher. She began to writhe like a snake in a trap; spittle mingled with blood flecked her lips. Then she opened her mouth, and the silver flames were in her throat, consuming her from within, burning flesh and bone and muscle and sinew. Her limbs thrashed and the fire burst through her skin, licking at her gown, her hair, hissing and crackling as her frenzied shrieks, bubbling now as her throat and tongue melted, tore through the Marble Hall. Mercilessly Tarod watched her for perhaps a minute, then he stretched out his hand once more and spoke one word in an alien and unimaginably ancient tongue. The remains of Ygorla's beautiful face turned black, and her squirming body seemed to erupt into a mass of crawling silver striations. A wave of darkness poured from the pulsing star at the Chaos lord's heart. It flowed over her, around her, became a spinning column, utterly black—

There was a small, almost pitiful sound, as if far away some tiny creature had barely found the strength to whimper. The dark, whirling column faded, faded, was gone. And the jetsam of the thing that had been Ygorla, Daughter of Chaos and Empress of Mortal Dominions, had vanished from the world.

Tarod lowered his hand. By the light of the seven-rayed star his face was haggard, and for perhaps a minute he stood unmoving. Then, as though something beyond the reach of lesser perceptions had alerted him, he looked up, looked directly at the Chaos Gate. Chill air streamed from the portal, flinging his hair back in a black wave, and Tarod said in a voice filled with bitter loathing, *"You!"*

Within the Gate's shimmering frame Aeoris of Order smiled serenely back at him.

Karuth, Strann, and Tirand were huddled together at the feet of the seventh colossus, and as the great lord of Order materialized, Karuth heard her brother utter a grotesque sound, quickly choked off. The High Initiate was shaking uncontrollably as instinct and training urged him to fall to his knees before this being, the highest of his gods. But he couldn't do it. Instilled loyalty was curdled by other and more powerful emotions, and he turned away, covering his face with his hands.

Aeoris didn't spare so much as a glance for the three terrified humans. He seemed neither to know nor to care that they were present as he looked at his adversary from Chaos.

"Ah, Tarod." His voice was exquisite. The darkness that gripped the Marble Hall began to lessen. "We meet, I think, under happier circumstances than at our last encounter."

Tarod's lip curled, but he didn't speak, and Aeoris's eerie golden eyes seemed to focus on the place where Ygorla had met her death. "Did her demise give you some small satisfaction? It seems to have given little to your ungrateful mortal friends."

Tarod glanced toward Karuth, Strann, and Tirand. For a moment as their shocked, sick faces stared back at him, he felt contempt, but the feeling quickly muted into something closer to sympathy. His fury was under control now, giving way to a sense of bleak inevitability that almost mirrored their human emotions. What they had seen had stripped away the last of their illusions about the gods they worshipped. They felt helpless, alone, bereft. And at this moment Tarod had a greater affinity with their plight than they could ever know.

Aeoris was well aware of the direction his thoughts were taking. The lord of Order extended a hand. "Is there a question you're reluctant to ask, Tarod? Let me answer it and relieve your apprehension. Yes—I have your brother's soul." His fist uncurled, displaying the great sapphire on his palm. In the uneasy glow that shone within the Chaos Gate its brilliance was dimmed to a shadow, and Tarod's eyes narrowed in pain as he forced himself to turn and gaze at it.

"We offer Chaos a choice," Aeoris went on. "You may leave this world, abandon your claim to any influence here, and accept the exile to which we condemned you once before. But this time you won't return, for if you do . . ." He fingered the stone lightly, not needing to say more, and his mouth curved in a disdainful smile. "Or you may witness the destruction of this jewel, and with it the destruction of your demon brother. You know I have the power to do that. While the jewel is in my realm, it is and will remain vulnerable. And if seven become six, as they must, Chaos will no longer have the strength to match us. So you see, whichever way you choose to turn, we've defeated you." The smile took on an edge of cool triumph. "Consider your answer. I shall return to hear it."

A sweet, musical sound filled the Hall, and Aeoris's image vanished.

For a long time Tarod didn't move but stood facing the Gate, his head bowed. The dark aura still surrounded him, though the light of the star at his heart had gone out. Ailind, who from the moment Ygorla had been hurled back into the mortal world had taken no part in proceedings, still watched from a distance. But Karuth shook off Strann's warning hand, ignored Tirand's hissed caution, and moved slowly toward the Chaos god.

Six paces from him she stopped. "My lord . . . ?"

Tarod's head turned, and for a moment an echo of the deadly fire showed in his eyes before subsiding into an impersonal stare. "What is it?" he asked.

"If we can . . ." She hesitated, started again. "If there is anything we can do . . ."

"Do?" His tone was acid, but then, again, he seemed to relent. "No, Karuth. There's nothing."

She hung her head. "I feel responsible, my lord. If I hadn't given way to her . . . But it was . . ."

He knew what she was trying to say, and sighed. "I don't condemn you for the decision you made." He shrugged, a peculiarly and disconcertingly human nuance after all that had gone before. "The usurper would have found the secret one way or another, and you couldn't have known how she intended to use the Gate." His eyes grew introverted. "None of us knew that. With one exception." Over his shoulder he gave Ailind a look that expressed such hatred that Karuth felt a shiver rack her.

Ailind returned the look impassively. "You're wasting time, Chaos. My brother awaits his answer, and procrastination won't change the inevitable." There was a distinct undercurrent of glee in his voice. Karuth had never heard such a note before, and it gave her an ugly presentiment of what she, and anyone else who had pledged their support to Chaos, might look forward to if the gods of Order had their way.

Tarod, though, was unmoved by Ailind's gloating. He'd exorcised his rage in destroying Ygorla, and only the bleakness was left now. He felt beyond the reach even of anger. And in one sense Ailind was right. The moment couldn't be deferred forever, and the choice had to be made. But he couldn't make it. He didn't have the sanction, and he wouldn't have wanted to take such a responsibility. He turned to Karuth.

"Go back to Strann and your brother, Karuth. This

isn't over yet." He glanced once more at Ailind, then at the two men waiting silent and uneasy beside the statue. "If you wish to, you may leave now."

"I'd rather stay, my lord. And I think Strann and Tirand feel as I do. If we have your permission . . ."

"As you please. It makes no difference." He watched her walk slowly back to rejoin her companions, then abruptly shook off his thoughts and faced the Chaos Gate again. His aura pulsed suddenly with renewed energy and, starkly yet in a way that carried icily through the hall, he spoke one word, one name.

"Yandros."

Beyond the Chaos Gate dim colors loomed like the spectral herald of a Warp storm, and against their gloomy backdrop a figure appeared. Narrow, feline eyes that constantly changed color regarded the scene before them for a few moments, then Yandros, Tarod's brother and overlord, stepped through into the mortal realm.

Karuth saw Tirand's eyes widen in surprise, though he made no sound, and Strann, seeing it too, suppressed a wry smile. Mercurial as ever, Yandros had chosen to disparage any show of his true nature and had adopted the same unassuming aspect in which he'd first made himself known to Strann on Summer Isle. Only those extraordinary eyes, and the unnaturally bright gold of his long hair, gave the lie to the image he presented. But despite his appearance Strann knew instinctively that he was in a very dangerous mood.

There was no formal greeting between the two lords. Tarod simply said, "We have lost, Yandros."

"Yes." Yandros's voice was quiet, but there was a molten quality beneath the calm. "I know, Tarod. There's nothing more to be done." He raised his gaze to take in Ailind, who stood smiling a short way off. His eyes turned scarlet. "Call your cowardly brother, creature of Order. Let's have this over with."

Strann alone saw Tarod's quick frisson of surprise at such an apparently easy surrender. And he also saw the slight motion of Yandros's hand that signaled his fellow lord to silence. Strann started to turn to Karuth, but then thought it wiser, at least for the moment, to say nothing. He returned his attention to the scene, doubly watchful now.

Ailind walked toward the Chaos Gate and, reaching it, bowed low.

"My brother Aeoris!" His voice rang out in a way that contrasted sharply with the Chaos lord's disparagement of any ceremony. "We await your presence!"

Again there was the rush of cold air as the sullen colors beyond the Gate gave way to a brighter, clearer light. Then Aeoris stood within the portal, the Chaos stone displayed in his hand.

The two ancient and inimical enemies gazed at one another, and Aeoris broke the silence first.

"Well, Chaos? You know my ultimatum. Which will you choose—exile, or your brother's destruction?"

Suddenly, shockingly, Yandros laughed. It was the most savage and malignant sound that his mortal listeners had ever heard, and as it died away, he answered Aeoris with scorching contempt.

"A century of Equilibrium, and you haven't changed one whit! Still the same bombast and arrogance, and now you have the gall to think you can compel *me*? I scorn your demands, Aeoris, for you're a liar and a dissembler, and you always have been!"

Aeoris's expression darkened. "Don't try my patience, Yandros. I've waited long enough. Make your choice, or I'll make it for you!"

"Will you?" The Chaos lord's eyes glittered balefully. "I doubt that. You won't destroy my brother's soulstone." His lip twisted in a sneer. "You haven't the courage. And before I bend the knee to you, I'll see us both in the Seven Hells!"

Aeoris contemplated Yandros's vicious words for a few moments, seeming to weigh them in his mind. Then he said, quite calmly, "Very well. If you refuse to see reason, then you leave me no choice." His mouth pursed in a mock show of regret. "You're a greater fool even than I thought."

For one wild, giddying moment Karuth was certain

that the lord of Order wouldn't do it. It was a pretense, a
bluff. It *couldn't* be happening, it wasn't *possible* . . .

Aeoris's hand closed over the Chaos stone. Disbelief
flowered across Tarod's face. He cried out, started forward—

And a thousand glittering sapphire shards fell from
Aeoris's fingers.

For the space of a heartbeat there was total stillness.
Then, with no warning, the Marble Hall was rocked by a
colossal blast of power. As Karuth staggered back, clap-
ping her hands to her ears and shouting an inchoate protest, a spear of blue lightning flashed between the pillars
and hit one of the seven statues with a titanic *crack*. The
statue split, rocked precariously—and one of its twin
faces shattered into fragments that hurtled down in an
avalanche to the floor.

Tarod flung back his head and uttered a cry of horror and grief and despair, his voice searing through the
din of crashing masonry. Ailind rushed forward, his face
exultant, while the three humans could only cower
against the base of the seventh colossus as debris rained
around them and hurled up a cloud of choking, blinding
dust. Aeoris was laughing triumphantly, holding up his
empty hand . . . and only Yandros, alone of them all,
did nothing. The Chaos lord stood motionless, one hand
covering his eyes, and he looked isolated and suddenly
vulnerable.

The echoes of the huge concussion, and of the statue's destruction, rolled away and finally receded into
nothing. Dust settled. A boulder-sized fragment rocked
once or twice with a faint grinding noise and then was
still. From the Gate Aeoris's milky golden eyes gazed on
Yandros's still figure.

"Your brother is dead, Yandros." He folded both
hands across his breast and stepped serenely from the
portal into the silent hall. Light like the mellow sunlight
of high summer glowed around him and seemed to suf-
fuse his plain white garments. His golden cloak brushed
the mosaic floor with a faint susurrus. He walked with
unhurried deliberation to where Yandros stood and

stopped two paces from him. "You must give us best now. Equilibrium is finished. The balance has tilted in our favor, and it can never swing back again, for we are still seven but you and your kin number only six."

Very, very slowly Yandros raised his head. Only Aeoris and Strann saw his face, for Tarod and Ailind were behind him and Karuth had turned away, pressing her cheek against her brother's shoulder and immobilized by shock and misery. What Strann saw made him suck a convulsive breath between his teeth. Yandros's eyes were filled with grief, and mingling with the grief was a loathing beyond comprehension. An unholy lust for vengeance burned in his look like molten steel in a furnace—but his lips were smiling. An old smile, old beyond measure, ruthlessly sure, lethally wise.

"You're wrong, old friend." The Chaos lord's voice was like a knife in Strann's brain. "We are seven." He pointed toward the Chaos Gate at Aeoris's back.

The Gate's image warped. From its heart came a violent blaze of green-gold radiance, and a newcomer appeared in the portal. Strann bit back an involuntary oath as he saw the slim, almost boyish figure, the near-white hair, the strange amber eyes, the overgenerous mouth. She wore a starkly simple gown almost as white as her hair, and the cloak that fell from her shoulders was a perfect match with the emerald of Tarod's eyes.

Strann clawed at Karuth, incoherent, trying to make her look, make her *see*. But it was Tarod's voice that roused her. Stunned, rigid, the black-haired lord said incredulously, *"Cyllan . . ."*

She stepped from the Gate. A seven-rayed star pulsed at her breast, dark topaz shot through with the hues of blood. Her eyes burned as she turned to regard Aeoris, and her expression was one of withering disgust. Ignoring the lord of Order's shock, Yandros bowed to her in a manner that conveyed a salute between equals. Then he looked at his brother.

"It was the only way, Tarod. And your consort will be a gracious and worthy addition to our ranks."

Suddenly Aeoris's voice barked out. "Yandros!"

Yandros turned to look at him.

"What's the meaning of this?" Aeoris was seething with outrage. "What trickery are you trying to perpetrate?"

"No trickery at all, old friend." Yandros's smile was almost mild. He took Cyllan's hand and led her forward. "Allow me to present to you my sister in spirit, newly elevated by my decree to the thrones of Chaos—the seventh of our number."

Aeoris's face turned dead-white. "You're trying to flout the laws that govern us all! One of your lords is dead, and his place can't be filled by another—the laws are *irrevocable!*"

"Indeed they are." Yandros agreed icily. "But though a dead god can't be supplanted, you and I both have the sanction to cast down a living fellow lord and choose another to take his place. That, my good master of Order, is what I have done." He turned his back on his adversary and looked to where Tarod and Cyllan stood side by side. His smile was sad, but underlying the sadness was pride in them both.

"I would have done anything within my power to save our brother's life," he said quietly to Tarod. "But I knew that if matters went against us, that might prove impossible at the last. So I planned a contingency. I hoped that I wouldn't have to use it, but when this creature"—he gestured contemptuously over his shoulder in Aeoris's direction—"snared the usurper and then delivered his ultimatum, I . . ." He shrugged, feigning a carelessness that deceived no one. "I had no other choice. I ritually cast out our brother before Aeoris could destroy his soul, and I elevated Cyllan to the place that had been his." He pivoted on one heel, and his eyes glittered silver as he regarded Aeoris again. "When you destroyed the sapphire, you didn't destroy the soul of a god. You simply killed a being who no longer counted for anything among us."

From a short way off Ailind spoke for the first time. "My brother, is this true?" There was fury and anguish in his voice. "Is it *possible?*"

Aeoris shot him a glare that made his displeasure at the question obvious. "It's true," he said curtly, then looked back at Yandros. Naked loathing showed in his face. "I didn't think you'd make such a sacrifice, Chaos. I thought that even *you* had more loyalty than that!"

"Necessity makes its own demands." Yandros's eyes were arctic. "And I think I know all my brothers well enough to be sure that any one of them would prefer death to an eternity in subjection to you."

Aeoris's eyes flared with molten anger, but before he could speak again, Yandros held up a hand.

"It's over, Aeoris. Accept it." His voice was cold and remote. "You achieved your greatest aim when you murdered my brother, and the price I've had to pay to thwart the rest of your scheme is higher than you'll ever know. You haven't won this battle outright, but then again you haven't lost . . . and neither have we. Go back to your own realm, lord of Order, and be satisfied with what your machinations have brought you. I've nothing more to say to you."

Aeoris paused. Then his stern mouth twisted at one side in a humorless, ironic smile.

"If nothing else, I suppose I must salute your ingenuity, Yandros." His head came up, and he swept the Marble Hall with a haughty glare that finally came to rest with some venom on Tirand. The High Initiate looked quickly away, and Aeoris continued. "For once I agree with you. We have nothing more to say to each other. We shall take our leave, at least for the present. But there will be other times and other means. . . . And there are some mortals who'd do well to consider the fact that their gods have long memories!" Now his gaze raked Yandros again. "We'll encounter each other again before too long, Chaos. I shall await that day with relish!"

He summoned Ailind to his side with a brusque gesture. Together they moved toward the Chaos Gate and stepped through the portal. Light flickered beyond the Gate, like distant summer lightning, then a sweet, ringing sound almost too high for human ears filled the Marble Hall briefly and the two lords of Order were gone.

Silence fell. Yandros, Tarod, and Cyllan stood together, still watching the Gate. Yandros was smiling, though the smile was poignant and sorrowful. Tarod's hand rested lightly on Cyllan's shoulder; his eyes smoldered. And a short way from them, forgotten and forlorn and already part of a past that seemed to be receding into the hazy phantasms of nightmare, the body of Calvi Alacar, firstly High Margrave and then Emperor-Designate but now nothing more than a lifeless shell, lay still and quiet among the debris of the shattered statue.

Karuth felt a hand clasp and grip hers, and as though in a dream, she turned her head. Strann was beside her, and Tirand beyond him. Their eyes were haunted, their faces bloodless. They looked as though they had lived five cruel lifetimes in the space of a mere hour, and though the thought was hideously incongruous, Karuth felt thankful that she had no mirror to show her her own face.

Suddenly Strann put his free hand to his mouth as tension, like an overtuned string in his gut, snapped. He looked at Karuth, and the look conveyed everything that he didn't know if he'd ever be able to say: his love and his fear, the horrors and uncertainties of the past months . . . and, overriding all else, a sense of stunned and incredulous relief.

"Oh, gods . . ." His irreverent whisper seemed to fill the Marble Hall. "I think I want to sit down."

26

Strann gazed out of the window at the first hints of dawn that were lightening the sky, and thought, *Tonight the greatest of the gods walked among us. Maybe one day in the future I'll be able to convince myself that all this did happen as I recall it. Or maybe I'll never truly believe it.*

What had happened after Aeoris's and Ailind's departure had brought him back to earth with such a crash that when he looked back on it, he almost wanted to laugh, though the laughter would have been uncomfortably close to hysteria. Everything had seemed so *normal.* The High Initiate's study, warmly lamplit and with the fire in the grate still burning. Tirand had poured wine into a crock, added spices, and set it at the hearth to warm through, and the gods of Chaos had drunk the mulled brew with the High Initiate as though they were as human as any Circle adepts. But Yandros had had a hand in that, Strann knew. He'd done something to all their minds, something that made the horrors they had witnessed fade like smoke on the wind and brought them to a state of calm acceptance. The aftershock might set in later, but they would have at least some respite, and for that Strann was deeply grateful.

There had been, as Yandros said, no need to rouse the castle's sleeping inhabitants. What must be said could be said without other witnesses, and what transpired could be revealed at a more suitable time. Just one small matter remained to be resolved . . . and Strann remembered with a sharp frisson the look in Cyllan's amber eyes as she'd turned to the highest lord and, quietly but emphatically, asked him to put that matter into her hands.

Cyllan . . . mustn't think of her so disrespectfully now, Strann reminded himself. She was no longer simply a remote figure from history, commemorated only in a musical epic. *Lady* Cyllan—like lord Yandros and lord Tarod; one with them, and a god—goddess—of Chaos in her own right. Tonight she'd done a goddess's work. He'd heard the single, devastating scream that had echoed from the south spire, and to divert himself from what his imagination tried to conjure, he'd concentrated on marveling at the fact that that cry didn't wake the dead, let alone the entire castle. There had been no mercy for Narid-na-Gost, not at her hands. Had the demon joined his daughter in the Seven Hells? Strann wondered. Or had they both simply ceased to exist in any form? He didn't know the answer and hoped fervently that he never would. It was the gods' business, and he'd had enough of the gods' business to last him a lifetime.

But when that unpleasantness was over and Cyllan returned to the lamplit study, there had been many things to say. A hot-and-cold flush came over Strann as he remembered how he and Karuth had stood together before Yandros, and the words that the great god had spoken to them.

"Strann the Storymaker." It was so long since anyone had used that old epithet that despite himself Strann had found the courage to look up in surprise. Yandros's unhuman eyes were quiescent, their rainbow colors subdued, and Strann had the feeling that the god was laughing at him, though by no means unkindly. "You're an unlikely champion, but you've proved to be a worthy one. I thank you. And I won't forget your courage and your loyalty."

Strann flushed to the roots of his hair and mumbled a stumbling disavowal, and Yandros's gaze turned to Karuth.

"He doesn't change." A flicker of dark humor caught at the corners of his mouth. "Perhaps you can persuade him to acknowledge a few truths about himself, Karuth—though if you can, you'll have achieved more than Tarod and I could do!"

"My lord . . ." Karuth cast her gaze down, but Strann could see the pleasure that suffused her face. Then Yandros looked up and across the room to where Tirand stood by the hearth. The High Initiate's expression was bleak. He'd barely uttered a word since their return from the Marble Hall, and now, as he returned Yandros's gaze, he couldn't stop himself from flinching.

"Tirand." The unexpected compassion in the Chaos lord's voice surprised Strann and clearly took Tirand completely aback. "Don't stand apart, High Initiate. We owe a debt to you too—though I suspect you might be even less willing than Strann is to shoulder the accolade." The humor in his expression became faintly malevolent. "Is it such a betrayal of your principles to accept Chaos's thanks?"

Tirand's face turned scarlet, and his jaw worked spasmodically before he could make himself reply.

"Lord Yandros, I . . . I . . ." He couldn't finish.

"You acted as your conscience dictated. Where's the discredit in that, Tirand? It's simply fortunate for us that your conscience *did* prove stronger than the training your predecessors had instilled in you."

Whether the goad was deliberate or not, only Yandros would ever know, but Tirand's head came up sharply.

"I've never denied the *principle* of Equilibrium, lord Yandros."

"No, you haven't," Yandros agreed, then laughed softly. "Though I imagine there were times when you were tempted . . . ?"

Memories of past interviews with Ailind in this very room flooded into the High Initiate's mind. "I . . . yes. That's true. But—"

"But at the last he chose to listen to his own mind and heart." Tarod interrupted, rising from the chair he'd taken near the door. "Don't torment him any further, Yandros. They've all been through enough." He turned to the High Initiate. "Yandros and I lost a brother tonight, Tirand, and whatever else may happen, the scar will never truly heal. But you played your part in ensur-

ing that we didn't lose more even than that." He glanced
at Cyllan, who had sat silent beside him since her return
from the south spire. "I've made a few unfavorable comparisons in the past. Yet there is something about him
that reminds me of Keridil."

Cyllan's amber eyes glinted faintly, almost ferally,
Strann thought. "There are differences, but they aren't
necessarily to Tirand's discredit."

The High Initiate had looked swiftly away at that
observation, Strann remembered; and he also remembered that as a child Tirand had known Keridil Toln, his
illustrious forerunner and the architect—albeit reluctant
—of the changes that had brought Chaos back to the
world. Strann had the suspicion that Cyllan was paying
Tirand a compliment that he didn't quite feel able to cope
with.

"So," Yandros said. "What now, High Initiate?"

Tirand looked at him nervously. "Now, my
lord . . . ?"

"Yes. You have some decisions to make, I think."
The Chaos lord couldn't resist another slight touch of
malice. Tirand might have absolved himself in Chaos's
eyes, but Yandros wasn't about to let him think that the
past would be entirely forgotten. "About the Circle's allegiances in general, and yours in particular."

Tirand licked dry lips, reached toward his untouched wine cup, then thought better of it. "Are you
saying, my lord, that . . ." he searched carefully for his
words, ". . . that Equilibrium is . . . over?"

Yandros looked quite surprised. "Oh, no." He
picked up his own cup, twirled it, then laughed shortly.
"I learned a long time ago that life without a measure of
conflict lacks spice and savor, and I've no intention of
wishing such a dull existence on mortals. You're quite
free to direct your loyalty wherever you please, Tirand,
though I think you might find it harder than you imagine
to reinstate yourself in Aeoris's good graces. As he himself said, he has a long memory."

Karuth's head came up quickly. "He can't do anything to harm Tirand?"

"No, no. The pledge I forced on him a hundred years ago, not to intervene in mortal affairs unless called on to do so, still stands, as it does for us." His eyes turned a nacreous green and glinted maliciously. "As it always did."

Tirand hung his head. "I acknowledge my mistake, lord Yandros."

"Indeed you do. And you'll make amends for it when you lead your adepts in a ritual to undo the anathema that you pronounced on us, and restore their free choice." He made a negligent gesture. "It isn't necessary of course. But it will please me to see the formalities observed."

Tirand nodded acquiescence. Yandros's tone had been casual, almost gentle, but the High Initiate was wise enough to take the implied warning.

"We'll rebuild the statue," Karuth said, eager to please the great lord. "We'll call in the world's finest stonemasons to remake the carving. . . ." She hesitated, and her glance slid uncertainly to her left. "That is, if . . . if the lady Cyllan will consent?"

Cyllan looked back at her, and a slow smile lit her face as though the thought hadn't occurred to her until that moment. "I'll consent gladly, Karuth," she said in her husky voice. "And I thank you for the compliment."

Yandros took a mouthful of wine. "It's a good thought, Karuth, but I suspect you'll all have more urgent matters to occupy you for some time to come. The usurper wreaked a great deal of havoc throughout the provinces, and restoration of despoiled lands and lives—not to mention morale—must, I think, be your first priority." He looked at Tirand again. "It won't be an easy task, and many people will be looking to the High Initiate for inspiration and guidance."

Tirand made as though to reply, but then changed his mind and stared down at the floor instead. Karuth asked, "Will you help us, lord Yandros?"

"No, I will not." The Chaos lord saw her eyes widen in chagrin and surprise, and continued before she could speak. "We had one concern and one only when we came to your world, Karuth—to defeat and destroy the usurper. Now that that has been achieved, our involvement is ended." His mouth quirked. "If we were to help you restore what you've lost, then Aeoris would also consider himself justified in taking a hand. Would you want that?"

"No." She looked away. "But others might, and if, as you say, we should each choose our allegiances—"

"Then, my dear Karuth, you would find yourselves caught for the second time between two inimical powers who would both be too preoccupied with their own conflicts to care much for the fate of humans! Allegiances notwithstanding, I'm sure you'll agree that *no* mortal in their right mind would wish that on the world again!" Karuth's cheeks reddened with shame and a sense of foolishness, and Yandros relented. "Your world shouldn't be the gods' battleground, Karuth. We and the lords of Order have other and better ways to perpetuate our eternal war. It's far better for you—and for us—that you should be left to resolve your troubles by your own wits and skills." He smiled suddenly. "Although I trust you won't ever forget that we'll watch your efforts with great interest. And if another Ygorla should ever arise—"

"Gods forbid!" Strann said it before he could stop himself. Tarod laughed, and Yandros turned a shrewd gaze on the bard.

"Strann, you have an extraordinary talent for making an apt point at an inappropriate moment," he said drily. "We don't forbid anything. That's the whole point of Equilibrium, though I'm beginning to despair of mortals ever truly comprehending the idea. So if, as I was saying, another Ygorla should ever try to seize power in this realm, then I hope that the Circle will consider its position a little more carefully before deciding whether Chaos or Order is better equipped to deal with the matter. Don't you agree, Tirand?"

Tirand didn't answer at once, and when he did eventually look up, Strann was alerted instantly to a change in him. There was a new resolve in the High Initiate's eyes, a new certainty, and his mouth had a determined set to it.

Covertly Strann glanced at Karuth, but she seemed not to have noticed.

Tirand said, "I agree, lord Yandros. But if such a time should ever come again, I won't be the one who has to make that decision."

Yandros gave another of his sharp, truncated laughs. "You're an optimist after all, Tirand. I'd never have thought it!"

Tarod leaned forward, his expression suddenly serious. "I don't think that was what the High Initiate meant, Yandros." His catlike emerald gaze shifted to Tirand. "Was it?"

Tirand turned, and their eyes met. Yes, Tirand thought; Tarod would be the first to comprehend. He'd known Keridil Toln so well, known him in the early years of his tenure here, known him through the monumental days of Change and, when those days were over and the new age began, had watched Keridil's struggle to bring himself and his world to terms with Equilibrium. Tarod knew the nature of the burden Keridil had carried. He, of all of them, would understand why Tirand didn't feel equal to the example Keridil had set.

He broke the gaze, looked at Yandros again.

"My lord," he said, and suddenly his voice was stiffly formal, "I feel it only right that I make my intention clear now, before the—the highest of witnesses." He drew breath. "I intend to resign from the office of High Initiate."

Silence came down hard on the room. Karuth's mouth opened, but she was too astounded to speak. Tarod and Cyllan exchanged a very private look, and Strann could only stare at his own feet. At last, very quietly, Yandros spoke.

"Why?"

"Because . . ." Tirand bit his lip. The admission didn't come easily. "Because I consider myself unfit to hold such an office."

Karuth started to protest, but Yandros turned quickly on her.

"Be silent, Karuth!" He sounded angry. "Let your brother speak. Go on, Tirand."

Tirand flushed. "It's quite simple, lord Yandros. I've failed in my duty on two counts. Firstly I tried to go against the tenets of Equilibrium as they were laid down a century ago; and in so doing I broke both my inauguration oath and the trust that Keridil Toln handed down to his successors. Secondly I allowed blind prejudice to cloud my judgment and to close my ears to others' wisdom. That doesn't make for a fit High Initiate, my lord."

Yandros considered this for a few moments, then shook his head. "You take too much on yourself, Tirand. No one can achieve perfection—and no one expects it, even from you."

Tirand's face took on the stubborn look that Karuth knew so well, and in that moment she realized that not even Yandros was going to sway him. His mind was made up.

"I admit that. But even if perfection isn't attainable, the High Initiate above almost all others must strive to be as *near* perfect as he can. He must do his best, at all times."

"Haven't you done your best, as you judged it?"

"I like to think so. But it proves only that my best isn't good enough. I'm not fit to hold my rank, and therefore I intend to step down." His gaze flicked uneasily from one to another of the silent faces around him. "We have difficult times ahead of us, Circle and Sisterhood and Margravates alike. People will need help from us all, and in particular they'll look to the Star Peninsula for guidance and leadership—and for reassurance that the gods are still watching over them." His eyes grew hard, self-mocking. "They can have no true confidence in a man who, through his own willful stupidity, has offended Order and Chaos alike."

Tarod said, "They won't see it in that way, Tirand."

"Perhaps not, my lord. But *I* do, and my conscience won't permit me to take any other course." He looked up quickly and met Yandros's gaze with a frankness that seemed to surprise the Chaos lord. "It'll be hard enough for me to live with the knowledge of my own mistakes and weaknesses. Please don't compound my inadequacy any further by forcing me to stay on."

There was a long pause. Karuth was staring at the fireplace, her face still and desolate. Eventually Yandros ended the hiatus.

"Are you quite sure this is what you want, Tirand?"

Tirand nodded emphatically. "I'm certain, lord Yandros. I'll do anything and everything I can to help in the work of putting our world to rights after Ygorla's depredations. But not as High Initiate." He almost, though not quite, managed a weak laugh. "I'd rather turn my hand to restoring the farmlands or rebuilding shattered homes. I might find I have some undiscovered talents."

Yandros sighed. "It must be as you wish, Tirand. Very well, I accept your decision in this matter . . . though I must admit that I'd never imagined *I* would be the one to hear and acknowledge your declaration." He smiled, suddenly vulpine, at such an irony, then his expression sobered again. "But of course there's the question of who will follow you. You must know that you have the right to name your successor."

"Yes, my lord. I've considered that and I know my mind." Tirand paused, then, quite suddenly and unexpectedly, turned to his sister. "I name Karuth."

She argued with him, intensely, sometimes even violently. She didn't want to be High Initiate, she said. And even if she were willing, what made him think for one moment that she was as fit for the role as he was, let alone fitter? Tirand laughed at that—the first wholehearted laugh, Karuth realized later, that she'd heard him utter in many days—and reminded her, though without rancor, that she'd held a very different view not so long ago. That brought a deep flush to her cheeks as she remembered her bitter words during one of the fiercest of their quarrels, and she abandoned the tack, arguing instead that it was unprecedented for the High Initiate's rank to be held by a woman. Tirand, though, swept that protest aside. What did precedent matter? Tradition wasn't immutable law. And, he added, hadn't Yandros set his own example this very night, by elevating the lady Cyllan to the thrones of Chaos? Tarod had laughed unrestrainedly at that, and his and Yandros's obvious approval had finally broken down the last of Karuth's defenses. Queasy with trepidation, not daring yet even to think about what this meant and what the future would hold, she accepted. And the warm, grateful, and thankful embrace in which Tirand held her when the acceptance was given made Strann look away, suddenly moved.

Before the gods took their leave, they had all had a private word for each of the three humans. What Yandros said to him was something Strann would never reveal to another living soul but would cherish only in his most private thoughts, and when he made his last bow to the great lord, his skin prickling hot and cold, Cyllan moved silently to his side.

"Good-bye, Strann the Storymaker." There was mischief in her eyes, reminding him that once she, too, had known the uncertainties of a wanderer's life when she was nothing more than a human drover-girl. "Perhaps one day you'll write an epic in Chaos's honor, to match *Equilibrium*."

Strann remembered Blis Alacar's wedding celebrations long ago on Summer Isle. So much had sprung from that night: his first meeting with Karuth when they had played the duet called "Silverhair, Goldeneyes" together. . . . He smiled, and made his very best bow to her.

"I could never do you justice, lady Cyllan. No one could."

She had spoken then to Karuth, she and Tarod together. Strann discreetly withdrew, aware that their exchange wasn't for his or anyone else's ears. But he saw Tarod take Karuth's hands and bend to kiss her cheek in a salute that was . . . brotherly? No, not that. But sincere. Then Cyllan, too, kissed her, and murmured something in her ear. Karuth tensed, then smiled a smile of gratitude and understanding. And moments later Strann, Karuth, and Tirand were alone.

Tirand looked at them both. A strange calm seemed to have come over him, and he smiled, tentatively but with warmth.

"It must be nearly dawn," he said quietly. "There'll be a very great deal to do tomorrow, so perhaps we should all sleep while we can. I wish you both good night."

They'd watched him climb the stairs, following only when he was out of sight. In her bedchamber Karuth lit neither lamp nor candle. The curtains were half open and the snow-light was enough to show the room's furnishings in dim silhouette. As they settled together beneath the bedcoverings, Karuth shivering a little at the contrast of cold sheets and Strann's warm body, he said softly, "What did she say?"

In the dark he couldn't see her face, but the tone of her voice gave away her feelings. "She said . . . 'Don't be afraid of the future. However great the darkness, there's always some hope of light.'" She moved against him. "I'll never forget those words. Ever."

Strann didn't know how to answer her, but there was no need, for even as she spoke, her eyes were closing as a weariness that went beyond the exhaustion of body and mind to her very soul overcame her. Within moments she was asleep.

Now he sat, as he had sat through the remaining hours of darkness, waiting by the window for dawn to break and steeling himself to the knowledge of what the morning would bring. For when it came, when she woke, he must tell her that he was going to leave the castle.

Strann didn't want it to be this way, but he had turned it over and over in his mind and knew that there was no other choice. If he truly loved Karuth, then for her sake he must go. To stay here, as her consort or lover or friend or whatever she wanted him to be, would do cruel injustice to them both. Before Ygorla's coming it might have been different, but now the world had branded Strann the Storymaker a traitor, and for a traitor to sit at the High Initiate's side was unthinkable. Karuth would have enough prejudice and uncertainty to overcome without that. Perhaps she could have overcome it; perhaps in her new role she would command enough respect and affection for it not to matter. But, contrary to the pose he'd adopted for most of his life, Strann had his pride, and he could never live with the idea that his soiled reputation had been scrubbed clean only through her. He wanted—*needed*—to redeem himself solely by his own efforts and on his own merits. Then and only then could he return to Karuth, if she still wanted him, and feel that he had truly earned her esteem and her love.

Would she still want him? He didn't know, but the risk must be taken. And though it was small comfort to him now, he had a purpose to fulfill. He intended to go back to his old traveling life, province to province, carrying news, songs, stories, and, above all, helping to impart understanding. Ygorla's murderous reign had shattered people's confidence along with so much else. Many would still believe that the usurper had been in league with Chaos, while others feared that their gods must have abandoned them altogether. Strann would tell the *true* story, the tale of a demon's treachery, of a half-human woman's greedy ambition, and finally of the great conflict between the gods that led to Ygorla's downfall and the death of a Chaos lord. He'd write new ballads too, for where speeches and orations were quickly forgotten, music stayed in its listeners' memories. An elegy for Yandros's dead brother; and a new song to honor Cyllan, though this time as lady of Chaos. No, of course he wouldn't do her justice. He wouldn't do justice to any of the momentous events that had reshaped so many lives. But he could at least try, and in trying hope to win back his sense of worth and with it his old place in the world's affections.

He looked through the window again and saw that a pale but vivid light had touched the summits of the castle spires. Whether or not it was an omen, and whether or not Yandros had had any hand in it, Strann didn't know; but it seemed that the snow-clouds had passed on and the sun was breaking through. Below in the courtyard, untrammeled by footprints at this early hour, the snow blanket sparkled as though someone had scattered a thick layer of gems across it. Then the soft glow of a lamp showed suddenly in a lower-floor window, and the sound of a door shutting echoed in the silence.

Strann turned from the window. By the growing daylight he could see Karuth clearly now. She slept peacefully on, her hair tumbled on the pillow that she clutched tightly against her cheek. He rose and returned to the bed, taking care not to wake her as he slipped under the blankets, and his arms slid around her, drawing her close to him.

He would leave; he would redeem himself. But not yet. Not until spring arrived and the mountain passes were clear. Until then—if she wanted him—he'd stay, and perhaps together they could begin to heal the wounds. And whatever their futures might be, whether the links they'd forge should diverge or hold fast, in his mind and his heart she'd always be his Karuth.

He kissed her gently, his lips finding their way through the curtain of her dark hair to the warm skin beneath, and his voice was soft against her sleeping face.

"My Karuth. Always, love. Always."

Epilogue: Summer Eve

The past few days had been so warm that there was barely the need for a fire in the High Initiate's study, but the logs in the hearth added an extra dimension to the light of lamps and candles as the short northern summer night descended. Karuth sat back in her chair and removed her gold-rimmed eyeglasses before pressing thumb and forefinger to the bridge of her nose to ease tension in her brow. The piled papers on the desk before her swam out of focus, though her distant vision remained keen, and she sighed half in sadness and half in amusement as she wondered yet again what Strann would think of her new accoutrements. She hadn't liked admitting the fact that her close vision needed help, for it was a sign of age —maturity, as Sanquar had tactfully put it—and although there were plenty of adepts younger than herself who made use of the bothersome things, Karuth had enough vanity to dislike the need for them. But Sanquar had insisted, and as Sanquar was now the castle's senior physician, she had bowed to his will.

Anyway she'd read enough for one evening. Reports, dispatches, tithe lists . . . since the passes had opened again after the winter snows, trains had been coming in from every province. The burgeoning summer had increased the traffic threefold, and each new arrival meant more paperwork and more demands on her time. Not that she really minded. She'd always had a talent for administration, however reluctant she might be to admit it, and the increasing signs that the world was returning to some semblance of normality more than made up for the tedium of her work.

385

And today, two messenger birds had come in with letters that were especially welcome.

She picked up one of those letters and fingered it, as though contact with the parchment could in some arcane way bring her physically closer to its author. Dearest Tirand. He wrote so keenly of his work in Han Province, and she was glad that he'd finally allowed the combined efforts of the Matriarch and the Margrave of West High Land to persuade him to step, temporarily, into the role of regent there. It would be a long time before the people of Han recovered from the horrors Ygorla had inflicted on their province, and in particular the hideous murders of the Margrave and his family. Tirand had both their trust and their respect, and until the lengthy formalities of establishing a new Margravate could be completed, he would hold the province together and give them cause for optimism.

Then there was his news of Ilase. . . . Karuth smiled a very private smile. She couldn't recall Ilase's face, but remembered her dimly as a pretty, dark-haired but painfully shy girl to whom Tirand had paid attention at the High Margrave's wedding some years ago. It seemed they'd met again by pure chance at an official function with which Ilase's father was involved, and the embryonic but interrupted romance had blossomed. Tirand didn't so much as hint at it, but Karuth knew her brother well enough to suspect that an announcement of their betrothal would be made before the year's end. Ilase's family were grape growers, winemakers, wealthy and well respected in Han society. That life would suit Tirand very well. Above all it would be a life of peace, as far removed as it was possible to be from the responsibilities of the old days. Tirand had had more than enough of those responsibilities, Karuth knew. They'd talked long and profoundly before his departure, and he'd confessed to her that the changes that the last days of Ygorla's terror had imposed on him went far deeper than he'd initially realized. Despite the events that had finally led him to throw in his lot with Chaos he couldn't give fealty to Yandros, for the old ties that had bound him all his life were still there. Yet how could he continue to worship his own gods of Order when those gods had shown such cynical contempt for their followers and had used them only as pawns in their greater game? He had earned Chaos's gratitude and Order's enmity, Tirand said, and neither was justified. He wanted no more dealings with the gods. He would continue to honor them, as everyone must, but in his heart he had lost faith.

Karuth understood, for her faith, too, had been sorely tested. But as time passed and the sharp edges of memory softened, she was slowly coming to accept one truth: that gods, like mortals, were selfish. She'd expected perfection from her deities, omniscience and omnipotence and, in discovering her mistake, had learned that the gods existed not to serve their followers but to serve themselves. In the past she'd berated herself for investing them—and Tarod in particular—with human qualities. Now, ironically, it seemed that hadn't been so great an error. It was hard to adjust to such a revelation, and Karuth could no longer pay homage to the gods in quite the way her catechisms had taught her. Yet something else had taken the place of blind obedience and unquestioning trust, something that came closer to a sense of fellow-feeling and understanding—and of freedom. Whatever their motives, the gods *had* freed the world from Ygorla's yoke, and for that alone their worshippers would always be grateful. Yet, perhaps unwittingly, they'd granted another freedom, freedom from the tyranny of fear. Their very fallibility had proved to Karuth that there was no need for humanity to be afraid of its gods. And it had shown her the true value of Equilibrium. No matter what the future might hold, there must *always* be a choice for humankind. Anything else was unthinkable. And as High Initiate and appointed avatar of the lords of both Chaos and Order, Karuth would do her duty and give homage to Yandros and Aeoris alike.

Her hand moved then to the second letter, and her somber thoughts were submerged in a smile as she felt the thin roughness of the paper. Thrift was an ingrained habit that Strann would probably never throw off, not even if . . . no. Not if, *when. When* he came back for good. He would. She was as certain of that as she was certain that the sun would rise tomorrow morning, and she was learning to be patient. He was somewhere in the Great Eastern Flatlands now, and his droll account of his recent journeyings had made her laugh aloud. He was winning them around, slowly but surely. Already his new songs had reached a wide audience, and they were serving their purpose well. Strann was doing Yandros's work . . . he among all of them, Karuth thought, had kept *his* faith in the gods. And today's message-scroll had contained the scores of two new pieces—one an elegy to the dead lord of Chaos, the other . . . well, the other was a private matter and would not be played until the day when they could play it together.

Karuth wished that Strann could have been with her tomorrow, to share the summer Quarter-Day celebrations. There was to be a great gathering at the Star Peninsula, as at all the province capitals, to celebrate the midpoint of the year, and though it wouldn't be her first official function as High Initiate, it was the first real test of her popularity. Sen and the Council of Adepts dismissed her qualms as nonsense, and she had even received a message of brotherhood and goodwill from the new High Margrave, the distant cousin of the Alacar family who had succeeded with quiet, sad dignity to the Summer Isle throne after Calvi's death. But despite all their kind assurances, Karuth didn't know if she was ready for such an occasion as this. A day of rejoicing, a great thanksgiving for the world's deliverance from the usurper's ravages. And amid all the laughter and the pleasure, she would feel utterly alone, for all those who were dearest to her, human and unhuman, were gone. Calvi was dead, his soul—she hoped and daily prayed— at rest. Tarod, lord of Chaos, no longer stalked the castle corridors, and the room at the top of the north spire was cold and empty and abandoned. The Matriarch, Shaill, busy at her cot in Southern Chaun, directing her Sisterhood in their work of bringing comfort and succor to the bereaved and bewildered folk of the provinces. Tirand, their old bond newly mended but still with so much left unsaid, gone to Han, working hard, and perhaps happier than he'd ever been before in his life. Others—dead, lost, or simply too involved with the work of restoration, the work that must be done, to find the time to travel north and hold her hand.

And Strann . . .

Strann. Tears spilled suddenly down Karuth's cheeks, but in a way they were tears of release rather than regret. Strann, the reluctant hero, the unlikely constant, the one sound and solid foundation in her life despite all that appearances might suggest. He wouldn't come back this year, but next year might be different. Next year he might have earned the right, in his own eyes, to stand at her side. Then, she thought, then there would be a day of rejoicing that would make the Star Peninsula resound!

She sniffed and impatiently wiped her eyes. What would they think now, Sen and all the other senior adepts, if they could see their High Initiate giving way to such emotional self-indulgence? She'd been overworking, that was the trouble. Shaill would have taken her to task and prescribed a sound night's sleep and a good breakfast. Shaill, to quote one of her favorite remarks, was a great believer in breakfast. Tomorrow there would be the ceremonies, and the singing and dancing, and people from all the strata of society, from Margraves, nobles, and merchants to traders and drovers and hucksters, all arriving to join the Circle in celebrating summer and the growing crops and the new mood of optimism that was sweeping the world. Fool she was, *fool,* to think that for one single moment she would be alone.

The latch of her door clicked. Karuth looked up, blinking, surprised by the unexpected intrusion and expecting to see either Sen or one of her stewards, come to remind her that the hour was late and she needed her sleep. They were all so solicitous. . . .

But what she saw as the door swung quietly open wasn't Sen, or a steward, or any other human presence. The gray cat paused on the threshold, haloed by torchlight from the corridor and hall beyond. And just for a moment, a fleeting, dreamlike, and possibly unreal instant, Karuth thought she saw behind its inscrutable gaze the amber eyes of Cyllan, lady of Chaos, who had known what it was to be born mortal, and who had learned what it was to love and to fear and to be reconciled to both. In her mind a silver voice seemed to speak, words that, as she'd once told Strann, would be with her for as long as she lived: *However great the darkness, there's always hope of light. . . .*

Then the momentary image was gone. Illogically, absurdly, Karuth realized that she didn't know whether or not the cat had a name, but that didn't matter now. It was here; that was what counted. They were *all* here, in spirit if not in flesh.

She leaned forward, holding out her hand, and the gray cat ran to her, springing up onto her lap and settling itself as though it had never known any other home. Its small, hard head pushed lovingly against her hand as she stroked its fur, and contentedly, confidently, drowning the faint crackle of the logs burning in the study hearth, the little creature began to purr.

Enter the magical worlds of
MARGARET WEIS and
TRACY HICKMAN

The Darksword Trilogy:

☐ **Forging the Darksword**
(26894-5 * $4.95/$5.95 in Canada)

☐ **Doom of the Darksword**
(27164-4 * $4.95/$5.95 in Canada)

☐ **Triumph of the Darksword**
(27406-6 * $4.95/$5.95 in Canada)

☐ **Darksword Adventures**
(27600-X * $4.50/$5.50 in Canada)

Rose of the Prophet

☐ **The Will of the Wanderer**
(27638-7 * $4.50/$5.50 in Canada)

☐ **The Paladin of the Night**
(27902-5 * $4.95/$5.95 in Canada)

☐ **The Prophet of Ahkran**
(28143-7 * $4.95/$5.95 in Canada)

The Death Gate Cycle

☐ **Dragon Wing** (28639-0 * $4.95/$5.95 in Canada)
☐ **Elven Star** (29098-3 * $5.50/$6.50 in Canada)
☐ **Fire Sea** (07406-7 * $20.00/$25.00 in Canada)

**Look for all these titles by Margaret Weis and Tracy Hickman wherever
Bantam Spectra Books are sold, or use this page for ordering:**